A Place Called Hope

They made no attempt to kiss, merely stood and trembled, their bodies pressed close, clinging to what both of them had longed for in all the months they had known one another.

At last, gently, he put her from him, not far, his hands still on her, holding her shoulders, for he could not bear to let go. It was as though, now that this moment for which they had both waited was here, they did not know what to do with it.

She spoke first. "I had to come. You see I don't think I can . . . go on without you. If you go away I don't know how I shall manage . . ."

About the author

Audrey Howard was born in Liverpool in 1929. Before she began to write she had a variety of jobs, among them hairdresser, model, shop assistant, cleaner and civil servant. In 1981, while living in Australia, she wrote the first of her bestselling novels. There are now twenty-five – the most recent, *The Seasons Will Pass*, was shortlisted for the Parker Romantic Novel of the Year Award in 2001. She lives in St Anne's on Sea, her childhood home.

A Place Called Hope

Audrey Howard

CORONET BOOKS
Hodder & Stoughton

First published in Great Britain in 2001 by
Hodder and Stoughton
First published in paperback in 2001 by
Hodder and Stoughton
A division of Hodder Headline

A Coronet Paperback

13

ISBN 978-0-340-76929-4

Typeset by Palimpsest Book Production Limited,
Polmont, Stirlingshire
Printed and bound by CPI Group
(UK) Ltd, Croydon, CR0 4YY

Hodder and Stoughton
A division of Hodder Headline
338 Euston Road
London NW1 3BH

A Place
Called Hope

1

It was summer up on the wild moors of Northumberland but as was so often the case, even in this season, it was chilly and overcast and the servants shivered in their thin summer outfits, inclined to stamp their feet and move about until quelled by a disapproving glare from the butler.

The man on the far side of the driveway stared in amazement, evidently wondering what the devil was going on and why the indoor servants were congregated at the front door this late in the afternoon, then he remembered that this was the day the master's wife was to come home. He had just stepped out from the dense strip of woodland to the side of the house where he had been checking on the birds he was hand-rearing for the ritual slaughter which would take place at his master's shoot next month. Since he could hardly continue to saunter across the turning circle in front of the house where the servants were assembled, he stayed where he was, partly hidden by the towering and shapely masses of the luxurious sycamore trees which had been planted generations ago to shelter the fortified manor house of Newton Law. Newton Law stood in an exposed position on a windy hillside above the River Coquet, and the woodland, which curved to the sides and back of the house, kept off the worst of the weather. Among the sycamores had grown oak and hornbeam, beech and holly, and the dog which accompanied him everywhere, a chocolate-coloured labrador, took the opportunity to cock his leg against a handy trunk before lying down at his feet.

The man was tall, standing head and shoulders above the other menservants who were grouped at the top of the steps. He leaned his back against the rough bark of the sycamore, one heel resting on the trunk behind him, one hand deep in the pocket of his corduroy breeches. He had a shotgun broken over his arm. He was young, lean and straight as an arrow. No bulk about him, but a taut whipcord strength which seemed to promise toughness. He wore no cap and his hair was short, brown and curly. His grey, cat-like eyes were set in a clever face, watchful, keen and alert as though he were well accustomed to guarding his back and not only that but looking for danger ahead. His mouth had a humorous twist to it though it made no attempt at a smile now. He had heard rumours among the other servants, who were only too willing to repeat them, vague whispers about his master and his master's wife who was reported to be of a frail and sensitive nature but he had cut them short, those who liked to gossip, seriously offending them, he knew, with what they saw as his aloof refusal to engage in it.

The splendid carriage carrying Lady Blenkinsopp drove up the gravelled driveway towards the house. The coachman, dressed in the immaculate Blenkinsopp livery of dark blue and maroon, reined in the two, coal-black carriage horses to an expert halt in front of the wide, shallow steps at the top of which his master and his master's three spinster daughters stood, aware that should he not give the dedicated service his master demanded he would be dismissed on the spot.

In order of precedence the servants stood in two tidy lines at the side of the open front door, Holmes the butler, Mrs Armitage the housekeeper, Mrs Fowkes the cook who was "professed" in French cooking, two footmen, Nanny Briggs with Master Robert in her arms and a dozen assorted maidservants. They were a sombre group, the maids shivering in plain black cotton dresses, white aprons and caps, the housekeeper dressed the same but much more grandly with her ruched muslin cap and the belt about her waist from which hung the housekeeper's silver chatelaine. The butler was dressed in a black frock coat and white tie, as dignified as an archbishop, but forgetting for a brief moment to keep an eye on his black-coated underlings in his eagerness to get a glimpse of the occupant of the carriage. They all, except the master and his daughters, seemed to hold their breath.

The man watched as the coachman jumped down from his box and with the flourish used by all official door-openers, opened the carriage door and let down the small step, holding out his hand to its occupant, who, it was noticed, at least by the watching man, took a long time in taking it. Sir Robert continued to stand glowering at the top of the steps, making no attempt to go down them to greet his wife, and the man wondered why his employer found it necessary to go to all this trouble, lining up the servants, making all this fuss, standing in the damp chill of a summer afternoon just

as though royalty were about to step down from the
carriage. He himself had never met Lady Blenkinsopp,
having come as gamekeeper to Sir Robert a few weeks
after she had mysteriously gone to visit her cousin in
Liverpool, which in itself was not mysterious but the
length of her stay was, since she had borne Sir Robert
a son in December who was now six months old.

A dainty grey kid boot emerged and placed itself
carefully on the step and a small grey-gloved hand
reached out and took that of the coachman. He smiled
up encouragingly into the carriage and when the
woman finally alighted the watching man saw the reason why. It was not just the courteous smile a servant
gives his mistress but the respectful and unconscious
admiration a man shows a beautiful woman.

She was quite the loveliest young creature the hidden gamekeeper had ever seen. She was dressed in a
gown of silvery grey grosgrain. Her bonnet was the
same colour, just a wisp of silk and white ruched lace,
the whole creation so simple and yet so perfect for
her was it any wonder the servants held their breath
in rapt admiration. It was as though none of them
had seen her before and yet, he had heard, she had
married Sir Robert in the early part of last year. His
own mouth hung foolishly open, he was suddenly
aware, and he shut it hastily as she began to climb
the steps towards her husband. She held up her full
skirt with both hands, her back straight and proud,
like that of a young empress who can think of no
reason why she should be afraid, a sight that did
not seem to please her husband overmuch, for he
was seen to frown. Under her bonnet her hair was
smooth, spun silver mixed with gold and pale streaked

amber. The watching man could not see the colour of
her eyes, just the profile of her face, her straight little
nose, her rosy mouth, her rounded chin, the outline
of her small, childish breasts under the smooth bodice
of her gown.

As she reached the top step a fleeting ray of sunshine
broke through the overcast, accentuating the alarming
contrast between the smiling face of the lovely young
woman and the gloating triumph on the coarsened
features of her elderly husband. He reached out a
fat, hairy hand to take possession of her, to make
his claim for all to see, fastening it on to her upper
arm in what seemed to the watching gamekeeper to
be a brutally fierce grip and it was then that he realised
the purpose of this charade. *She was his*, his employer
was saying. This woman belonged to him to do with as
he liked, and though the company were only servants
there were men among them who would know exactly
what that meant.

He felt the strangest sensation in his stomach and
for an appalled and amazing moment thought he was
about to be sick. His stomach turned over, wobbling
like a jelly not quite set, and he became aware that
what he felt was revulsion. Sir Robert Blenkinsopp
was a man in his fifties. His daughters were all in
their twenties or even older and yet this little silvery
thing who, he was sure, would be in Sir Robert's bed
before the hour was out, was like a child, ethereal and
virginal, and yet, since they had a son, had already
been subjected to the indignities this gross man must
have forced on her. He could not clear his vision of
the horrifying pictures this conjured up: pictures of the
nightly outrage Sir Robert's gross body would inflict

on hers in the marriage bed, and the images made his gorge rise. But then how was he to know what was in this woman's life? She might think a fair exchange had been made. Her innocent loveliness and a son thrown in for good measure, for money and a title. A lot of women did, so what in hell's name was he thinking of, he asked himself, for it was nothing to do with him. Though he doubted she enjoyed his master's embrace, for what woman would, she obviously thought the trade was a fair one. How was he to know what had compelled her to marry him? Sir Robert was an extremely wealthy man, a man with an old name, an ancient baronetcy and he might be presumed to be a good match for any woman. Women could be strong creatures and just because he himself was sickened at the thought of her clasped in Sir Robert's meaty arms and subjected to his sweaty fondling it didn't mean *she* was!

And yet as he watched he saw a faint rippling, too slight to be called a shudder, run down her back as her husband placed a heavy arm across her shoulders and began to draw her inside. She was about to go with him when her gaze fell on the woman who held the child in her arms and at once she threw off her husband's arm and ran to the child.

"Darling . . . oh my darling," he heard her say, her face, which was clearly revealed to him under the brim of her bonnet, filled with a depthless joy. Her skin glowed and her eyes were luminous with a lovely translucency as though behind them a candle flame had been lit.

"Sweetheart . . . my little love . . . how you've grown," she murmured and before the grim-faced woman who had the boy in her arms could object Lady Blenkinsopp reached for him and cradled him close to her own breast. She looked down into his infant face which was rosy with good health but without that smiling interest a child of his age usually shows and then began to shower kisses on his forehead, his cheeks and into that ticklish spot under his chin which will make any child gurgle with delight.

The infant was plainly amazed, staring with eyes wide with wonder but not, those who watched thought, displeased. His face began to crease into a smile and he reached up a fat hand to touch his mother's mouth.

Sir Robert's harsh voice cut through the scene like a hammer striking a stone, sharp and violent and plainly incensed. "That's enough, Amy. Give the child back to his nurse and come into the house. As you see the household is here to welcome you back into the fold, so to speak, and Agnes" – with a vague wave of his beefy hand towards his eldest daughter – "who has a soft heart" – the words spoken as though he considered his daughter to be soft in the head as well as the heart – "thought you might like to have a glimpse of the child despite the fact that you chose to abandon him six months ago. But I am prepared to forget that . . ." which the watching servants could see was not true, the maidservants themselves shuddering at what lay before their mistress in the next few hours. Not for a gold clock would any one of them change places with her. "Now then, return him to Nanny Briggs. You may see him later in the nursery. I believe you owe some time to your husband and daughters," indicating astonishingly the three old maids who were her senior by years.

He was so sure of her he turned, taking a step or two through the wide front door into the equally wide hallway but it seemed she either did not hear him or, if she did, chose to ignore him.

Even from where he stood fifty yards away the gamekeeper felt the blast of Sir Robert's annoyance. It was no more than that at the moment but it was ready to turn into a violence none of the household cared to contemplate. No one had denied Sir Robert Blenkinsopp since he was a toddling child, certainly not his indulgent parents nor the tutors they had employed to give him an education. Had he been sent to school where he would have been treated with the discipline a growing boy needs his character might have been different, though there were those who swore he had been born with a mean streak, a perverse cruelty which impelled him to dominate every living creature that came into his power whether it be animal or human. The grooms had been heard to say, though not in his presence, naturally, that he had spoiled more horses than any other ten men in the county and his first wife, or so they said, had died simply because she could think of no other way to escape him. His daughters were carbon copies of their mother, timid, placating, terrified of his raised voice, and though they would have enormous dowries when, and if, they married not one man had put in a bid for them, since none of them could stomach having Sir Robert Blenkinsopp for a father-in-law.

"Amy, did you hear me?" His voice was harsh and threatening, telling her, and those about her, that she would be sorry if she disobeyed him and those assembled shrank within themselves, praying that Lady

Blenkinsopp would have the sense to hand her son back to his nurse and scuttle after her husband.

But she did neither and the man watching heard his own voice whisper in his throat. *Don't oppose him, m'lady. Do as he says. Be careful or you will pay for it. You have just arrived and only God knows what he will do to you if you cross him in front of the servants. Give the child back and go with him, please . . . please. I have seen the way he treats his animals . . . please . . .*

At last she kissed the child, whispering something in his ear, stroking his plump cheek, taking her time about it while Sir Robert's face became an ugly, mottled purple.

"I'll be up presently, Nanny," they all heard her say as she handed the boy back to his nurse, while Nanny looked at Sir Robert like a rabbit faced with a stoat as though to say she hoped to God he didn't blame her for his wife's behaviour.

"You'll go up when I say you'll go up, madam," Sir Robert thundered, gripping her upper arm with a hard and vicious hand and dragging her away from the servants. "I don't want that lad spoiled by your lackadaisical ways, d'you hear? Nanny follows my orders and has him trained."

"He is not a puppy, Robert, and as his mother I think I know best what . . ."

It was like watching a dainty kitten bristle unwisely up to an ugly and ferocious bulldog which looked as though, shown any more defiance, it would simply tear her to pieces. The gamekeeper thought he had never seen anything quite so brave as Amy Blenkinsopp as she faced up to her husband in those first few moments of her homecoming. God only knew why she had left home so soon after the birth of her child, or why she had remained away all these months. What mother abandons her child, especially to a brute like Sir Robert Blenkinsopp, but having worked for the baronet these past six months he thought he could guess. He himself had had just about enough of the man and was seriously thinking of looking for another post. Good God, the man was an oppressive tyrant, a lecher, a debaucher of women and it was a well-known fact hereabouts that Mrs Armitage had great difficulty in finding and keeping female servants. He had a violent temper and was prone to murderous rages and what this poor little thing was about to suffer didn't bear thinking about.

"Madam, if I hear one more word from you on the subject of my son I shall deny you access to him completely. He has managed well enough without you these past six months and will continue to do so. Now, if you would come inside . . ."

"Robert, I think you should know that I have no intention of giving up my son again." She seemed totally unshaken by her husband's threats and those who watched wanted to put out a hand and draw her carefully away from him, for did she not know what danger she was putting herself in? They remembered well how it had been when she first came as a bride to this house, looking as exquisite as she did now but so terrified she seemed to freeze wherever anyone placed her, afraid of him, of course, and of them all, poor little thing. Within a month he had her trodden underfoot like a broken violet.

"If you say one more word, lady, I shall be forced

to take steps to restrain you. Perhaps lock you in your room until you have come to your senses. Now come inside and allow the servants to resume their duties. You will want to bathe after your journey and to change for dinner, I'm sure. Come, take my arm and allow me to escort you."

"Robert . . ."

"Not another word, my dear." He took her arm with a savagery that nearly lifted her from her feet and the man who watched almost broke his cover, filled with an overwhelming desire to knock his master to the ground, to take his master's wife gently from his grasp, to protect her as any right-minded man would protect a defenceless female from a brute, but how in hell's name could he do that? She was the wife of Sir Robert Blenkinsopp who had a perfect right to treat her as he pleased. She had no rights under the law. She was the property of Sir Robert, as his horses and dogs were his property and should any man interfere with that right he could be prosecuted under the law.

This time she went with him, since it was obvious to them all that with his hand gripping her arm like a steel claw she had no choice.

"Thank you, Holmes," Sir Robert barked over his shoulder to the butler. "Dismiss the servants and send them back to their duties."

"Very good, Sir Robert."

The man in the strip of woodland stood for ten minutes after all signs of Lady Blenkinsopp's "welcome home" had been cleared away. The steps were deserted except for a housemaid who came out presently and began to sweep them vigorously as though to remove all signs of the reception. He watched her for a moment, wondering at the drag of his heart, wondering at the wretchedness he felt; then, as though the incident had made up his mind, since he knew he could not remain here and watch the destruction of the lovely woman who had just arrived home, turned in the direction of his own small cottage, determined to see Sir Robert in the morning and hand in his resignation. By then – dear sweet Jesus, the images in his mind plagued him – she would have suffered the attentions of her husband in their marriage bed and really, he could not bear to stay and see the results of them.

But it seemed Lady Blenkinsopp was not the same person who had fled from her brutal husband six months ago and the moment she was alone in the bedroom she was, that night, to share with him, she left it and calmly walked up the uncarpeted stairs to the nursery floor, bursting in on the astounded Nanny Briggs who was just about to bathe Master Robert, and sweeping him into her arms. Even he was astounded!

"Thank you, Nanny, I will take over," Lady Blenkinsopp was reported to have said. "You may go down to the kitchens for a cup of tea, or whatever you care to do. I presume one of the maids will bring up Robby's tea. Now, have you an apron I could borrow?"

For two or three moments Nanny Briggs was struck dumb. Robby for God's sake, and how would Sir Robert like that? What was the world coming to when a slip of a thing like Lady Benkinsopp could override the orders of her husband, the baronet, a man who was known to like his own way and who could be nasty when thwarted. As indeed could Nanny Briggs. Her face hardened into stone, her mouth a thin line of fury. She was a woman of forty years or so, who had reared many children of the gentry and even the peerage and she, who had been given full rein in that rearing, was not about to allow this dainty little creature to defy not only her husband, but herself.

"Please, Lady Blenkinsopp, let me have the child." Her voice was tart, like that of Nanny chiding a naughty and disobedient child, but Lady Blenkinsopp seemed unaware of the danger she courted. She had calmly reached for the bell to summon whoever it was in the kitchen who saw to the needs of the nursery. She turned to the window, which was heavily barred, and, doing her best to peer between the bars, began to point out to the wide-eyed baby the swallows which dipped in a cloud over the roof, a placidly moving herd of cows in the far meadow, and a man who she presumed to be a gardener walking across the lawn carrying a garden fork. The baby was too intrigued by her smiling face, the movement of her lips even to turn his head to look where she pointed.

"M'lady, I really do think it would be best if you handed Master Robert to me. He has his own routine, as I have, and will be upset if it is disrupted."

"You mean you will, don't you, Nanny?"

It was at this moment that there was a knock on the door, which opened at once, interrupting what promised to be a fight to the death if the look on Nanny Briggs's face was anything to go by. An immaculately dressed maidservant entered, a young woman who was plain and serviceable but had a kind face in which bright blue eyes shone. The sort of young woman who would be of no interest to the lusts of Sir Robert Blenkinsopp.

She was plainly bewildered, having just seen her ladyship marched up the stairs and into her bedroom by Sir Robert and where, one supposed, she was bathing and changing for dinner as commanded. He had not stayed to see this, as they had all expected, shivering with disgust at the thought of it, poor little lady, but had returned to the drawing-room where he was drinking a great quantity of brandy as was his custom.

She bobbed a curtsey. She was not sure whether to address herself to Nanny, who was the ruler up here, or to her mistress who, though she was the wife of the master, was not.

"Aah, there you are," Lady Blenkinsopp was reported to have said pleasantly. "May I know your name?"

"Tansy, m'lady." Tansy's eyes became an even brighter blue and she could hardly wait to get back to the kitchen to inform them of this latest lunacy on the part of their mistress. You could tell by Nanny's face that some sort of argument was taking place. The boy was held in his mother's arms, bemused but ready to chuckle as she kissed him and smiled into his face, and Nanny Briggs glared at the pair of them as though she would dearly love to snatch her charge back and order his mother from the room.

"Very well, Tansy, I am about to bathe Robby and then, perhaps in half an hour, would you bring up whatever it is he has for his tea."

"I can do that, m'lady," Nanny said through clenched teeth. "At this time of day he has bread and milk and I have a pan in which the milk is heated over the fire. So if you would hand him back . . ."

"No, Nanny, I will not hand him back. You make him sound like some parcel that has been delivered to the wrong address. I will keep Tansy here in case I should need anything but I would be glad if you would leave us alone for now."

"Sir Robert will not be pleased, your ladyship. I cannot imagine he—"

"That is between my husband and myself, Nanny, and certainly nothing to do with you."

As Tansy told it later to the open-mouthed circle of servants in the kitchen, if looks could kill Lady Blenkinsopp would have been lying dead at her feet but the nurse left the room quietly enough and they both knew where she was off to.

"An' what happened then, Tansy?" the scullery-maid wanted to know and though Mrs Armitage was aware she should send them all about their business, since gossip was frowned upon, she herself hung on Tansy's words.

"Well, he come stormin' up like a devil from hell with *her* behind him an' honest to God, if I could have jumped out the window I would have done but she just went on bathing the boy, kneeling there on't floor, laughing and tickling bairn and Master Robert laughing back which I've never seen him do with *her*.

" 'What the hell's the meaning o' this, madam?' master said, you know how he does, all snarling and slavering like a madman and with Nanny behind him all smiles, but by God, didn't her ladyship just go on playin' with the little lad."

"Holy Mary Mother O' God," breathed the scullery-maid, a devout Catholic. She even crossed herself. "What 'appened next?"

"Give that child to his nurse, if you please," he roars at top of his voice an' I swear he only just stopped himself from knocking her on her back and grabbing the bairn from the bath. Master Robert was screaming his head off and it was bloody pandemonium but she wasn't 'aving it, no, not for all the tea in China. She wouldn't give in, not her, an' it wasn't until Nanny grabbed bairn an' *he* grabbed her ladyship an' dragged her from the room . . . well, I tell you this, I wouldn't like to be in her shoes when" – Tansy was seen to gulp and was almost in tears – "when he gets her alone in . . . well, upstairs."

They all fell silent, even the menfolk, for though they would have liked to be in Sir Robert's shoes, and no mistake, they were all aware of what he would inflict on that slender little woman who was his wife when he had her behind locked doors tonight.

There were many of the women servants who slept uneasily that night. It was quiet on the upstairs floor where Sir Robert and Lady Blenkinsopp shared a room. There were no screams nor cries of horror, no shrieks for help or roars of thunderous rage, and in his cottage on the far side of the wood the gamekeeper drank a full bottle of his master's whisky in an attempt to shut out the images in which Sir Robert abused his wife in the house on the far side of the trees. It did no good.

He must have slept, for the hammering on his door brought him to a shuddering jolt from his old armchair where he had spent the night.

"You've to come quick, Duffy," a heavily breathing gardener's boy told him, his face bright with excitement. "Master's bin took badly. John-Henry's gone fer't doctor."

"Took badly?" He scratched his tousled head, unable to assimilate this piece of astounding news after what his mind had conjured up throughout the night.

"Aye, found at foot o' stairs this mornin' by Maddy who screamed fit ter raise dead, or so they said."

"Is . . . is he alive?"

"Oh aye, but he's right poorly. Can't move or owt an' they need a 'and ter carry him upstairs."

"Is . . . is her ladyship all right?"

"Oh aye, right as ninepence. Givin' orders and calm as a cucumber though she did 'ave a black eye."

"A black eye?"

"Aye, he give it 'er, so they say, when . . . well, when he took her inter their bedroom last night ter . . ."

The gamekeeper recoiled visibly and the boy stared, inclined to back away from him he looked so menacing, but after a word to the big dog the man banged his front door and began to run towards the house.

2

Lady Blenkinsopp watched dispassionately as the man who was her husband was lifted on to a makeshift stretcher by a man she had never seen before, the two footmen and a groom, for it took four of them to lift him. His body was as lifeless and flaccid as a deflated balloon, but his eyes were alive in his contorted, lopsided face and they glared at her with a hatred, a malevolence which said that just let him get his strength back and by God she'd know about it. She'd regret what she'd done to him for the rest of her life which he'd make sure was the most wretched any woman had ever suffered. As soon as he was on his feet, his suffused eyes told her, she'd best look to herself, for no one else would.

His three daughters fluttered about like moths round a candle and Amy knew that if he had been able he would have told them to bugger off and leave him alone for all the use they were and it was true, for they were more hindrance than help, getting in the way of the men who carried the stretcher and uttering small shrieks of dismay. One of them, she thought it was Agnes, held a fat tabby in her arms, clutching it to her flat chest with thin, straining arms. All three sisters wore plain, no-nonsense house robes in a sensible shade of dark blue.

She could hardly walk upright she was so flayed by pain, though she let none of the servants see it. They could, however, not miss the state of her eye, which Robert had put his fist into last night when she had objected to being sodomised, but the rest of her poor aching and abused body was hidden beneath the modest folds of her high-necked velvet housegown, the one she had thrown on when they had come hammering at her door. She could feel the seed he had pumped into her and the blood from the wounds he had inflicted as he did it slither nastily down the inside of her thigh, but to look at her, apart from her battered face, which seemed to tell the whole story, she might have spent the night in a deep and peaceful sleep. She had even brushed her hair which hung to her waist, thick and curling, like a living curtain of silk, in an attempt to calm herself, and the gamekeeper thought he had never seen a more beautiful or tragic creature. She reminded him of a doe he and his kind had once, long ago, cornered in a coppice. The doe had her fawn with her and though she knew instinctively she had no chance she had tried to defend the baby until some laughing, jeering member of the nobility, who did such things for sport, put a bullet in her.

"Take him to the room at the top of the stairs, Holmes," she said quietly to the butler who was directing operations. "The bed is made up, I believe," to the housekeeper, who nodded. The bed in every bedroom in the house was made up, for Mrs Armitage was a splendidly efficient woman who knew exactly how to run a house such as this where guests often turned up unexpectedly.

Sir Robert flashed his ferociously bloodshot eyes about the crowd of excited servants, glaring at his twittering daughters, and grunted something. Nothing any of them could understand. Saliva ran from the corner of his mouth which twisted grotesquely as he did his best to speak but Lady Blenkinsopp seemed not to notice. She drew her skirt to one side as the men struggled past her with the supine form of her husband, who was sprawled on a hastily removed door from the gardener's shed, then, as they heaved him up the stairs, she followed calmly, picking up her long skirt in order to negotiate the stairs with more ease. Only the gamekeeper as he glanced back at her saw the flicker of agony in her blue-grey eyes and the clenching of her hands in the folds of her velvet skirt. She had a sort of tranquil innocence about her, an air of serenity which sat at odds with what they all hazarded had been done to her last night.

The bedroom to which they took their master was a grand front bedroom, large, spacious with a somewhat faded magnificence about it, kept for only the most privileged of Sir Robert's house guests. Sir Robert was enormously wealthy, but it was known he did not spend his money lavishly, especially on trifles such as renewing carpets and curtains which had been put there by his mother when she came to Newton Law as a bride.

A maid was already busy at the fire, another fiddling with the curtains and Mrs Armitage had drawn back the snow-white cotton sheets and the faded tapestried coverlet to allow the men to lay Sir Robert, still in his nightshirt, beneath them. You could see it in all their eyes, the wondering, the querying glances they exchanged, for what the devil had gone on last night while they all lay in their beds to bring their master to the state he was now in? How had he come to be lying paralysed at the foot of the stairs? What had happened in the bedroom he shared with his wife, apart from the obvious, that is, for that bruise was blooming a lovely plum colour about their mistress's eye? What had he been doing out on the landing and how long had he been lying there at the foot of the stairs? Maddy, who was the under-parlour-maid and had been on her way to clear the grates and light the downstairs fires, left her bed at six and apart from a quick cup of tea provided by Ruth, a kitchen-maid, had gone straight to her work. She'd dropped her housemaid's box with a clatter and her brushes and polishes were still scattered all over the hall floor. She'd never get over the shock, she'd tearfully told Elspeth, who was also a kitchen-maid. Sir Robert lying there with his nightshirt up around his waist showing all his . . . well, Elspeth would know what she meant, and honestly she hadn't known whether to cover him decently or leave him where he was and run screaming for the kitchen. She had chosen the latter and it had been Mr Holmes who had drawn down his master's nightshirt.

Amy watched the flurry of activity around the bed with the detached air of a bystander, holding herself with her head high, her face expressionless, and the gamekeeper, who it was thought had handled his master somewhat roughly, watched her carefully without appearing to do so. He had moved away from the bed, then walked to the window and, glancing out into the garden, announced that the doctor was here.

"Is there anything else we can do for you, m'lady?" he added, moving to stand beside her, his attitude protective though none of them recognised it.

"No, I think not, thank you . . . er . . ."

"Duffy, m'lady. Would you like someone to stay with you while the doctor is here? Just in case Sir Robert needs turning or . . ."

Amy looked directly into the intense face of the man who had spoken to her and even in the fog of confusion which seemed to have drifted round her ever since Robert had fallen down the stairs, recognised the long-vowelled, cultured tone and pronunciation of the privileged classes in his voice. Had she seen him before? She thought not. Who was he? She knew most of the servants, for they had been here when she came as a bride but this one was a stranger. *Was* he a servant? He didn't sound like one. He was tall, lean with a pleasant face and his eyes seemed to be saying something to her. What? She didn't know and at this precise moment was too weary, too injured to care.

"You are . . . ?"

"Gamekeeper, m'lady." But by then the doctor had entered the room, led by the self-important and imposing figure of the butler who frowned when he saw that the gamekeeper was still here and, what's more, was engaging her ladyship in conversation.

"That will be all, Duffy," he said stiffly. "Get back to your duties."

It took Doctor Parsons an hour to pronounce on Sir Robert's health, or lack of it. A stroke, which would account for his tumble down the stairs and his two broken legs. He was paralysed on one side of his body and the other side was not sufficient to support him, and his speech was affected. Now Lady Blenkinsopp was to try not to worry. Though he could not say conclusively that Sir Robert would be as he was now for the rest of his days, these things had rarely been known to improve. But as long as he had plenty of help, nurses and so on, Sir Robert could be made very comfortable. Perhaps eventually sit in his chair by the window . . .

He went on in this vein for several minutes until he realised that Lady Blenkinsopp was barely listening. He was too discreet to ask what Sir Robert was doing wandering about at the head of the stairs in the middle of the night, for Newton Law was not one of those modern houses that had had installed one of the miraculous and up-to-date bathrooms. He was to be kept warm and fed light foods and of course, there was no need for him to tell them, he was not to be moved yet. His legs had been set with a great deal of groaning on the part of Sir Robert, and he, the doctor, would send over a nurse who would see to all Sir Robert's needs. Though he did not say so they were not the sort of needs a lady of delicate breeding should be bothered with nor would be expected to undertake.

He took her hand most kindly, feeling the tremble in them and, recognising the signs of acute shock, led her to a chair in the corner of the room where they could not be overheard by the patient, pulling up another he sat down next to her.

"This is going to be a long job, m'lady, and will need all your strength. Your husband has had a stroke *and* a bad fall. I did warn him some time ago. Now, is there

anything I can do? A man to help the nurse, perhaps.
There are such people trained to . . . and Sir Robert is
a big man."

"Thank you, Doctor, you are most kind."

"Not at all. Now may I suggest you let your maid get
you into a bath and then to bed. There is nothing for
you to do here. One of the menservants can sit with
Sir Robert until I return with the nurse and when I do I
shall tell them not to disturb you." Like all males he was
particularly affected by the almost ethereal loveliness,
the untouched, virginal fragility of Lady Blenkinsopp
and yet who, from the rumours that abounded in a
community such as this one, must have known, now
and in the past, more of sexual abuse than many a
whore. Faced with her soft, almost childish beauty, her
vulnerability, he felt a great need to give her the strong,
male protection she so obviously needed, and him
over fifty and reckoned to be long past such things!

He sighed at the sadness of it. "And that eye of yours
needs attending to," he went on gently. "A fall, you say
. . ." though it was obvious he didn't believe her. "Have
you a lotion?"

"No, but . . ."

"I have something in my bag. Now, let me send for
your maid."

For the simple reason that she could remember no
name among the household servants except that of the
maid who had come to the nursery the day before,
Tansy was sent for.

It caused consternation in the kitchen, for Tansy was
a chambermaid with no experience in the "maiding"
of ladies.

"But what does she want *her* for, Mr Holmes?" Mrs

Armitage wanted to know indignantly. Tansy Moore, plain and wholesome Tansy, had worked at Newton Law for eight years ever since she had come as a girl of twelve from the village of Thropton where her father was blacksmith. As would be expected from his trade he was a big man and had bred big children and Tansy was strong, tall and a good, hard worker. In fact one of Mrs Armitage's best and she was not sure she liked the idea of her being whisked off by her ladyship with the intention, or so it seemed, of caring for the delicate little woman who was their mistress. Mind you, from all accounts she'd stood up to Sir Robert in the nursery and, by the look of her, in their bedroom last night, which had earned her the black eye she sported this morning.

"Don't ask me, Mrs Armitage, but she's been asked for by name. Now get yourself up there, girl, and look sharp," he said to the slack-jawed chambermaid. "I was told to send you up and she wants a bath so you, Tilly, Elspeth and Ruth, take up the hot water—"

"I'd best see to the towels," Mrs Armitage interrupted him, for she was as eager as the other servants to get a good look at the state of her mistress, who had just spent the night in the clutches of a man who was considered by many to be the cruellest man in the county, but Mr Holmes put up a stern hand.

"It's Tansy only, Mrs Armitage. She said so."

"Well, I can't imagine why she picked—"

"It is not for us to question our betters, Mrs Armitage, so if you would arrange it immediately."

"Of course, Mr Holmes."

*　　*　　*

The bath was placed before the enormous fire that blazed in her ladyship's grate and filled with successive buckets of hot and cold water until Tansy deemed it just right for her mistress to climb into. Her mistress sat to the side of the fireplace, dazed and listless, not quite aware of what was happening around her, and it was not until the other maids had gone and Tansy awkwardly indicated that the bath was ready that her mistress came out of her trance.

She stood up, so small and frail she barely came up to Tansy's strapping shoulder, and so obviously hurting Tansy wondered why she had not noticed it before. She looked up at Tansy with one eye, for the other was rapidly closing.

"I can manage now, Tansy, if you would just leave the towels handy."

"Eeh, I don't think so, m'lady. You look all in and is it any wonder," then could have bitten her tongue, for might not Lady Blenkinsopp think she meant what had been done to her in Sir Robert's bed last night? She blushed a painful scarlet, since she herself was still a virgin, though Alfred, one of the grooms, was doing his best to change that state.

"See, won't you take off your night things and let me give you a hand into the bath. I've put in some of them scented bath salts that were on your dressing-table and the water's just right. See, let me help you." Her heart bled for this poor woman who, by the look of her, had spent a night in hell. There wasn't a female in the house who hadn't thought about her last night when that bloody husband of hers had dragged her into this very room and locked the door behind them.

Amy lifted her head and looked up into the kind,

rosy face of the maidservant who had come up to the nursery yesterday and had witnessed her own shaming treatment at Robert's hands. Apart from that she could not say she remembered her from last year but she supposed she must have seen her about the house. The trouble was last year had gone by in a haze of pain and terror and only one face stood clear in her memory.

"Tansy . . ."

"Yes, m'lady?" Tansy smiled encouragingly.

"May I ask you something?"

"Of course, m'lady."

"I need someone . . . someone to help me. I fear I am . . . injured and cannot . . . manage on my own."

"That's what I'm here for, m'lady. Now, take off your robe and . . ."

"Have I your promise that . . . that you will not speak of what you see to anyone . . . when I am unclothed, I mean."

"M'lady?" Tansy was clearly puzzled.

"Your promise if you please, or I must ask you to leave."

She was so polite, so gracious, just as though she and Tansy were of the same class. Well, perhaps not quite like that but she had a sweetness about her, a calmness of manner, a pleasing way of addressing her servants which Tansy knew was the mark of a true lady. She did not speak down to them, or treat them like the inferior beings some of the gentry considered them to be, just as though they had been put on this earth for the sole purpose of waiting on *them*. It had been remarked on last year when the poor little soul had been buffeted from here to there and back again by her husband. But for all that, she seemed now to have a core of strength in her that was lacking last year so perhaps, with their master confined to his bed for a while, she might show them all a thing or two. Tansy did hope so!

"Of course, m'lady," she replied. "I'm not overfond of gossip meself. Me ma used to say 'least said soonest mended' but see, let me undo those buttons and then . . ."

Slowly the maid unpeeled the velvet house robe from her mistress's body which was naked beneath it. It took her a while, since where her ladyship had bled the material had stuck in the wounds. Teeth marks, Tansy would have said, and scratches so deep it looked as though she had been attacked by a wolf. While her mistress stood unmoved, Tansy wept, her face awash with compassionate tears, her hands doing their best to be gentle and all the time she kept repeating, "Oh, my bonny lass . . . Oh, my bonny lass." Surely, her simple soul kept saying to her, no human could have done this, no man that walked on two legs, and all the time Lady Blenkinsopp merely stood and turned when she was told, then was almost lifted by the distraught maid into the soft, warm water of the bath. Tansy sponged her abused body, her eyes seeing but not believing the trickle of blood that still dribbled from between her ladyship's legs, gently crooning to her as one might a cruelly treated child. She even washed her hair, some part of her woman's mind knowing that her mistress would want every part of her cleansed of the beast who had laid his evil hands on her.

When her mistress was in her clean nightgown and seated in the chair before the fire, Tansy rang the bell.

A flush-faced Dulcie, who was a chambermaid and had fought with Maddy for the privilege, came knocking on the door. Tansy told her to strip the bed and make it up with clean bedding, remove the bath and towels and her ladyship would like a pot of tea and perhaps a sliver or two of hot toast and butter. While Tansy was issuing her orders her ladyship had seemed to drowse by the fire, content, it seemed, to leave it all to Tansy who, Dulcie reported, had it all in hand and looked as though she'd been at it all her life! There was not one of them who would not have liked the job of looking after Lady Blenkinsopp but really, if you could have seen that Tansy, there was no question that the right one had been chosen.

She drank her tea and even ate the toast, and when Tansy put her in the bed and seemed ready to kiss her goodnight as she might an exhausted child, she fell at once into a deep and trouble-free sleep. Tansy would stay with her, she had said, and there was nothing to fear now. As Amy's eyes closed, imprinted on her eyelids came the face of a man, a compassionate face with silvery grey eyes. She wondered who he was.

She slept for twenty-four hours and the first smiling face she saw was Tansy's.

"There you are, m'lady," she said, just as though Amy had been off on some junket during the night. "How are you feeling today? You certainly slept well."

"I certainly did, Tansy." She stretched and yawned and then winced as the movement snatched at every bite and bruise on her body. She noticed that Tansy winced in sympathy. She knew she would have to rest for a few days until she was healed but the ordeal she had gone through at Robert's hands didn't seem to have done any permanent damage. The ordeal! Sweet God, what a word to describe what he had done to her in their bed. What a word to describe the degrading acts he had subjected her to and which she must learn to think of dispassionately – if she thought of them at all – since she had expected it. She had been armoured against it by her own resolve to make this life of hers how she chose it to be. On her way back to Newton Law she had gathered the strength she had built up within herself over the past six months and it had protected her through the evil of Sir Robert Blenkinsopp's treatment of her. She knew he had been humiliated by her defiance of him in front of the servants and it was perhaps this that had made him so vilely cruel, but the little fortress she had erected inside her, brick by slow brick, had kept her innermost soul, the part where her husband could not reach, safe and well and ready to go on. She must not dwell on the services he had forced her to perform for his mad, perverted pleasure but look on them as the price she had to pay – and only once – to win herself a decent life. It was over now. Finished. As *he* was and from now on she would be mistress of Newton Law and there was nothing Robert could do to stop her, or so the doctor implied, from bringing up her son, *his* son in any way she wanted. To live the gracious life she envisaged for herself and her child. She had stood at the top of the stairs looking down at him sprawled at the bottom with his nightshirt obscenely up about his waist and it had evoked nothing in her but relief. She had been ready to cower but instead she had watched him fall, then as he lay like an insect pinned to a sheet of mounting paper she had simply walked away back to their room, got into bed and waited. She had been numb, mindless, senseless, but on this bright new day she was no longer any of these things. She was Lady Blenkinsopp whose husband had had a tragic accident. She had a child she meant to love and a house she meant to turn into a proper home for that child and for herself, and she meant to start today.

"Are you hungry, m'lady?" Tansy was saying, hanging over the bed in a way Mrs Armitage would have deplored.

"I am that, Tansy. Order me some more toast, will you, but first I would be glad if you would go up to the nursery and ask Nanny to bring my son to me."

Tansy pulled a face, for as yet she had not learned the refinements of being a lady's maid. She had rarely come into contact with the "front" of the house, since her duties as chambermaid were performed when Sir Robert and his guests were at breakfast, and she showed her feelings readily, but Amy did not mind. It was refreshing to be waited on by someone who was not only kind and strong and loyal, which it seemed Tansy would be, but someone who spoke up naturally, though not rudely, of course, and said what she thought.

"She'll not like that, m'lady."

"Should that concern me, Tansy?" her ladyship asked somewhat haughtily, then she relented and smiled impishly. "And you're right, she won't like it but I think I might enjoy . . . annoying her! Then, after I have played with my son I must go and see my husband."

Tansy pulled another face. "Doctor's been a few times and said not to disturb you, and that there nurse is in charge now. And there's a big brute of a fellow who's to see to Sir Robert's lifting and such and'll sleep in the little dressing-room off. Mind you, that there nurse is a bonny big lass with muscles on her like a prizefighter. She'd need to be, wouldn't she, the job she's got. Now then, m'lady, what are you to wear? I've had a root through your wardrobe and found this here garment," holding up a rich woollen robe of lavender blue. "That . . . that other thing" – meaning the velvet bedrobe – "well, I chucked it into't fire in laundry. I didn't want them lot downstairs getting a look at it."

"Thank you, Tansy. I don't know what I would have done without you. I hope you will consider being my . . . my personal maid. But we'll talk about that when you've brought Robby to see me. He and I have a lot of catching up to do. I might even take him to visit his father. Let him see how well his son and I are getting on. Do you know if a perambulator was ordered after . . . after I left in December? I want to get him out into the sunshine and . . ."

She stopped for breath. Her eye had totally closed up during the night, the lid a deep purple swelling, but the undamaged eye shone a clear blue grey, almost silver in her battered face and Tansy marvelled, for it was obvious that, with the master bedfast changes were to be made at Newton Law, and for the better, it seemed!

3

Tansy was right. Nanny Briggs was not at all pleased to have what she called "hers and baby's routine" disturbed and she'd better go right back to Lady Blenkinsopp and explain this to her, she told Tansy. It was clear she'd never heard anything so preposterous, and though she didn't actually say so Tansy could see she was ready for battle. No, Nanny said crisply, sure that her orders would be obeyed, for hadn't they always, Tansy was to tell her ladyship, that's if her ladyship insisted, which Nanny doubted she would, that she'd bring baby down the minute he was dressed and fed, probably in about an hour.

"She wants him now, Nanny," Tansy said bravely, for if anyone could be called a tartar, Nanny Briggs could. To tell the truth the servants were somewhat afraid of her and had often said to one another, not in her presence, of course, woe betide that poor little beggar as he grew.

"I'm afraid that's not possible, tell Lady Blenkinsopp. Baby would be totally disorientated if I was to take him down at this moment. He is expecting his breakfast and then his bath so please be good enough to convey this message to Lady Blenkinsopp."

"Rightio," Tansy said cheerfully, "but she'll not like it."

She didn't. She sat in her chair by the window looking out on to the wide sloping stretch of lawn and colourful flowerbeds put in by a previous Lady Blenkinsopp, watching as gardeners trundled their wheelbarrows, weeded and hoed and attended to the small pony which pulled the lawnmower. Once, it was said, the formal gardens that surrounded the house had been considered to be as important as the building itself but they had largely been destroyed by the landscaped parklands and vistas of the last century. But what remained was pleasant and she would enjoy walking with her son along the wandering paths and down to the small lake, which was really no more than a pond with ducks and swans on it. There were woods at the sides and to the rear of the house but the view at the front was open and quite magnificent, leading in a series of grass-covered hills to the valley at the bottom where the River Coquet ran, and on the far side of which the land rose again in a great sweep of undulating gorse and heather and bracken. It was criss-crossed by green tracks and old drovers' roads. The River Coquet, which was known as the queen of Northumberland's rivers, and had no comparison for its ever-changing and yet never-ceasing beauty, started its life at the old Roman camp on Dere Street, high in the Cheviot Hills, and one day, when she was strong and her son was older, she would take him up there.

It was a clear day and she could just make out the glint of the river in the valley bottom and to the left and right beyond the woods the vast tract of moorland, all of which belonged to her husband. A pony then, for her son, and a quiet mare for herself though it was a long time, before she married in fact, since she had ridden. She had become pregnant at once and Sir Robert had forbade her even to go near the stables, let alone get up on a horse. As she studied the prospect beyond the gardens she wondered why she had ever thought it bleak and inhospitable, for what lay before her was quite magnificent. Perhaps it was because when she was here last, as the wretched plaything of Sir Robert Blenkinsopp, her senses had been dulled by the bleakness of her own misery.

She had eaten more toast, this time with some special marmalade Cook thought she might like. Her own making, of course, but if her ladyship wanted anything else, bacon or mushrooms, or even a bowl of creamy porridge she'd only to say so. She sent a message back by the housemaid – Morna, what a pretty name – saying Cook was very kind but at the moment she had little appetite. Perhaps tomorrow.

Cook had been gratified by her ladyship's gracious message and all about the kitchen there was a general air of accord, almost a holiday mood, though none of them had ever known one, just as though the return of their mistress had lightened the house like the sun peeping in at a window previously curtained. They felt somewhat guilty what with Sir Robert flat on his back in one of the spare bedrooms but nevertheless the atmosphere was one of good things to come.

"Nanny says she can't disturb Master Robert at the moment, m'lady, but will be down as soon as possible. She's throng at the minute, she says." Tansy spoke with the characteristic rolling "r" of her Northumberland forebears, using many a word Amy was not certain of –

such as "throng" which she knew meant busy – though she got her general meaning. Tansy was doing her best to keep the scornful laughter from her voice, for it was so very evident that Nanny had made a grave mistake in underestimating the strength of their master's wife, the mother of Nanny's charge and she just prayed she would be there when Nanny got her come-uppance.

"Is she indeed! Well, go right back, Tansy, and tell her that if Robby isn't on my lap in the next five minutes she may pack her bags and leave. I will not be disobeyed in my own house."

"Shall I tell her that, m'lady?"

"If you like, Tansy."

"Rightio."

Nanny Briggs scarcely knocked on Lady Blenkinsopp's door as she bristled through it and marched purposefully across the frayed carpet to where her ladyship sat by the open window, Tansy close behind her. She'd stand no nonsense from this slip of a girl, she didn't care who she was, the expression on her face said. Here was baby still in his nightclothes, his breakfast not yet eaten and she was demanding he be brought down to "play" with him, she suspected, which was, in her opinion, not good for him. Strict routine was her god, right down to minutes and seconds and though Sir Robert was indisposed, she had been told, she'd march right in there and inform him that his flibbertigibbet wife was undermining her authority and what was he to do about it?

Nanny had not yet been told of the true seriousness of her master's condition. Indeed none of them had, though rumours had spread through the house.

"Now then, m'lady, we really can't have this, you know. Baby and I have strict order in the nursery or we would be all at sixes and sevens, wouldn't we? A child of his age—"

"A child of his age, indeed of any age, should be with his mother and if you would hand him over I would be obliged."

"But m'lady—"

"And if you should defy my orders again you will find yourself without a job. Now, give me my son." She held out her arms but still Nanny Briggs, who believed she had the full force of this child's father behind her, would not part with the wide-eyed baby who was looking at his mother with somewhat fearful interest. He saw little of any of the servants, only Nanny, and it was weeks since his father had sent for him to look him over, as he called it. A new face was a milestone in his young life and one that apparently needed some digesting.

"I must have a word with Sir Robert first, m'lady. I cannot go against his express wishes."

Amy stood up and though she came barely to Nanny's chin she exuded such cold anger Nanny wilted and without another word put her son in her arms. The baby seemed mesmerised by his mother, watching every expression on her face, but he was quiet for a child of his age, strangely inanimate, and Amy felt her heart lurch with guilt, for it was her desertion of him that had put him in the care of this grim woman Robert had employed. He needed stimulation, laughter, songs, books, colour in the drab nursery where he spent most of his day, toys to amuse him and she meant to provide him with them all.

"You may go,..Nanny. Tansy will go with you and bring down . . . well, whatever he wears during the day. I shall dress him and then we may go into the garden."

"M'lady, Sir Robert will not like it," Nanny blustered. "I'm afraid I shall have to report—"

"Do so, Nanny, if you can get past the doctor. Anyway, I shall be going in to see him myself shortly and I shall tell him of your displeasure."

With a contemptuous gesture she dismissed the nurse then sat down with the baby facing her on her lap. Mother and son studied one another with great intensity. He was a handsome child with none of his father's coarseness but then perhaps Sir Robert had not always been so. His self-indulgent, intemperate and sybaritic lifestyle from his youth was what was marked in his face. The boy had her grey-blue eyes with long, feathery brown eyelashes like her own but his hair was dark, glossy, inclined to wave on his neat head, the colour of all the Blenkinsopps. His cheeks were rounded and, considering his confinement to the nursery, rosy and his skin had a golden tone. His nose was the blob of an infant and his mouth a pouting, rosy bud. He had two diminutive teeth. He stared and stared and when, thinking it might make him laugh as it had once done her cousin's children, she said "Boo" at him, he jumped and looked somewhat nervous.

"Oh, darling, what a lot you have to learn," she told him, bending to kiss his cheek. "I'm sorry if I startled you but before long you'll be playing 'peek-a-boo' and laughing just like Roddy and Ewan used to do."

Roddy and Ewan were the sons of her cousin in whose house she had stayed for the past six months.

"We used to play lots of lovely games and I am going to teach you all of them. I shall make you laugh, for I swear I have never seen a more solemn little scrap. Won't you smile for Mama, please." But Robby Blenkinsopp was not familiar with smiling, at least not yet.

Tansy returned with several little garments which she said Nanny had thought suitable, though it was obvious they were not to her ladyship's taste. They would have to send for the seamstress, she said, pulling her face, and see that her son had clothes more appropriate for a boy like those her cousin's children had worn. These garments were more suited to a baby girl. A dress of white lawn with a white petticoat beneath it and under that what Tansy told her was a "liberty bodice". There was a towelling square which Tansy showed her how to fasten on the lower regions of the big-eyed baby who had put his thumb in his mouth, and for comfort was sucking steadily.

"I bet Nanny wouldn't let him do that," Tansy remarked. "I've seen a pot of mustard up there an' I bet she smears it on his thumb, poor little scrap."

"She'll not do it again, Tansy," Amy said quietly.

When he was dressed, which Amy had performed on the floor for safety's sake, she explained to Tansy, she bent over him and as she did so her hair fell over her face and tickled his cheek. He looked uncertain, then, to her and Tansy's huge delight, he smiled shyly.

"There, did you see that, Tansy? He liked that. Oh my darling, you liked that, didn't you?" She bent over him again and, expecting it this time, Robby gave a slow baby chuckle.

The two women were enraptured and the boy watched carefully to see what else might happen, for he did not want to miss it. Amy sent Tansy down to the kitchen while she continued to play with her son, sending a message to Cook that she thought she might like some of that porridge after all, and a pot of coffee. She was feeling hungry now, she said to tell her. In fact Tansy could make that two bowls of porridge!

"What's happening, Tansy?" In the kitchen they crowded round her, even Mrs Armitage who did her best to pretend she wasn't really listening. Their life was so routinely boring that anything that came to break up its drabness was greeted with great enthusiasm and this was one of those occasions. It seemed Nanny Briggs had sent down for a tray of tea and toast and was reported to be sitting by the fire in the day nursery, jabbing a needle in a bit of sewing with such force, Dulcie, who had taken it up to her, said she looked as though she'd like to be sticking it into some human flesh. Could it be her ladyship? she begged Tansy to tell her.

"Aye, bonny lass, it could," Tansy informed her cheerfully as she set up her mistress's tray. Cook was busy at the range stirring up a big pan of porridge. "She's got bairn with her the day."

"Never!"

"Aye, Nanny didn't care for it neither but there was nothing she could do. Eeh, she's got some spirit in her has her ladyship. She made short work o' that there Nanny, I can tell you," Tansy added admiringly, putting a jug of fresh cream on the tray beside the silver coffee pot and the dainty bone china cup and saucer.

They ate the porridge between them, Amy and her

son, taking turn and turn about, the baby opening his mouth wide for every spoonful and even smacking his lips over it, Amy pointed out to Tansy.

She had him on her hip when she went to enquire politely after her husband. She wore white, a simple gown of muslin, the hem and modest neckline edged with ruffles of lace. There was a narrow silver ribbon about her waist, tied in a bow at the front and another in her hair which fell down her back to her waist. She was quite breathtakingly beautiful except for the damage done to one side of her face, and the man who had done it to her lay on the bed like a felled log. The doctor was with him. Robert had been stripped down to the loose nightshirt he wore, lying on his back, the mountain of his belly straining towards the ceiling, and she shuddered, turning her head away as though she could not bear the sight which seemed to have awoken some memory in her. Both his legs were wrapped about in tight bandages. The nurse had evidently been washing him, and beside the nurse stood a silent, hulking brute of a man ready to turn and lift the patient at the doctor's command.

At the sight of her Robert seemed suddenly to come alive. He had been lying passively, submitting to the doctor's ministrations, his unfocused eyes staring somewhere over his shoulder. One side of his face had slipped so that one eye was lower than the other and out of the corner of his mouth on this side ran a dribble of saliva. His vacant look gave him the expression of not being there, of being unaware of the other occupants of the room, rejecting them as not worth his consideration, withdrawn into some corner of himself where he would stay until he regained his health, which she was sure he was intent on doing. If only to punish her.

It was his eyes that suddenly lived. He could move no part of him beyond a mere twitch of one arm and leg and a slight turning of his head but his eyes were ready to pop right out of their sockets as his rage erupted. His mouth moved and twisted, snarled, really, and spittle flew all over the doctor who stepped back in disgust. The doctor turned.

"Lady Blenkinsopp, you should not be in here just now. We are readying your husband for the day, making him as comfortable as possible." From the bed came the most hideous of sounds, rusty noises mixed with a kind of braying and a squawking which might have been made by an animal. The nurse was doing her best to calm him, shooting glances at the doctor as if asking him would it not be better if her ladyship was removed since it seemed to upset her patient. The baby began to cry. His arms crept round his mother's neck and he burrowed his tearful face beneath her chin.

"Perhaps you had better leave, m'lady," the doctor said soothingly. "My advice is to wait a day or two to visit him," though it was a mystery to him why she should want to do so at all after the "shiner" he had given her the night before last. Of course, some women were willing to put up with such treatment since very often they had no choice but Lady Blenkinsopp did not strike him as that kind. Not now. Last year when he had attended her during her pregnancy and then at the birth of her son she had been a frail little thing, afraid of her own shadow and terrified of her husband but now her attitude was quite different. She was looking towards the bed with what seemed total indifference, even a small smile on her face, but her concern for her child was evident.

"Of course. I'll take Robby away since he seems to be frightened." And who could blame him as the sounds from the bed became even more horrific. "I'm about to take a walk in the garden, should you need me, Doctor," and with that she sauntered from the room without a word to her stricken husband.

He couldn't take his eyes off her. From his hiding place he had seen her come from the side of the house where a door opened on to a small, walled garden in which herbs grew and through which she must have entered. He wasn't really spying on her, he told himself. He had legitimate business in the woodland where his work as gamekeeper took him, checking that the fox that had been seen a few days ago had not taken any of his master's birds. The moment she had appeared he had frozen behind the trunk of a vast oak tree. She had the baby in her arms, holding him on her hip as she strolled down to the lake, pointing out to the child, who seemed totally bemused, two meadow pipits which, as they did in summer, nested in these parts.

"Look, darling," she was saying, "look at the lovely birds, and see," as a swirl of swallows suddenly took flight, darting over their heads and making for the trees. "Those are swallows and down there, on the other side of the river those are cows and after we have had a look at the ducks . . . we should have brought some bread to feed them; but perhaps tomorrow. Shall we go and take a peep at the horses? You'd like that, wouldn't you?"

The child was looking about him in wonder. A couple of gardeners stopped what they were doing and watched her go by, smiling with pleasure, for she and her son were a joy to see.

"Good morning," she called out as they doffed their caps respectfully. "Isn't it a lovely day?" Which it was as far as the weather was concerned but she seemed unduly cheerful for a woman who, so it was whispered, had been assaulted by that brute of a man who was her husband. Fallen down the stairs, he had, though no one knew how and if she'd pushed him they certainly wouldn't blame her. Would you look at her pretty face all smashed up on one side, and how in hell's name had she managed to pry Master Robert from that martinet who was his nurse? Sir Robert would have something to say about that when he found out and probably give her a shiner to match the one she'd already got.

The man watched her progress. She continued talking and laughing as though the child were old enough to understand every word and, not only that, was taking part in the conversation. She'd taken off her cream kid boots and stockings, leaving them beside the path that had led him to her and was pointing her bare toes like a ballet dancer before every step. He wondered if she had any idea how beautiful she was.

It was the dog who alerted her to his presence. A big, brown dog who bounded to her side, dancing and jumping in that idiotic way of a friendly animal, wanting her to bend towards him, nosing her hand and, she swore, smiling cheerfully.

He had no choice but to leave the woodland and run after the labrador. "Dick, behave yourself, you foolish pup, and come to heel," but the dog, still young and silly, took no notice.

Amy turned at the sound of his voice and watched as he came towards her and still the dog nuzzled at her skirt.

"Well trained, I see," she said, laughing, the first time he had seen her do so. Her face lit up and her eyes were chips of sparkling blue diamonds and her rosy lips stretched over her small white teeth. He was enchanted, though the inscrutable expression on his face gave no hint of it.

"I'm sorry, m'lady, I do apologise. He is only young and though that is no excuse he does love a fuss being made of him. I'll take him and shut him in the stable and—"

"No, don't do that. See, he is settling already." They both watched as the animal, scenting something he thought might be of interest, darted off towards the lake, nosing about in a clump of weeds, and the ducks, who had been diving and gliding in perfect peace, suddenly scattered.

The man sighed, then ran after the dog, catching him by the collar and slipping a leash on him. "I'm supposed to be training him to retrieve when the shooting season starts but he's a long way to go yet. Perhaps next year."

As though it were the most natural thing in the world he fell in beside her, sauntering down to the lake where the ducks were still scolding Dick from a safe distance.

"Look, darling, ducks, aren't they clever diving like that?" she said and the child stared, still mesmerised and the gamekeeper wondered if the child had ever been out of that nursery where he had lived with his nanny. He himself had certainly never seen him and had not given it a thought at the time, but the big wondering eyes of the infant, the thumb securely plugged in his mouth seemed to indicate he was somewhat overwhelmed by it all.

They stood for several minutes watching the antics of the ducks then began to meander along the path that surrounded the lake. It led into the woodland following the curve of the lake and when she hoisted the child higher on her hip he pointed to a log which lay at right angles to the path.

"Perhaps you would like to rest, m'lady. The boy is heavy . . ." He almost said "for one so frail" but it was not his place to comment on her ladyship's appearance. "He will be quite safe on the grass."

The baby sat where he was put, as still as a mouse caught unawares by a sizeable cat. He gazed about him in amazement then tentatively put out a plump hand and touched a fallen leaf. With a shy glance at his mother as though to ask if it was allowed, he picked it up and studied it with enormously solemn interest, then put it in his mouth.

They both leaped forward, she and the man, relieving the child of the leaf, laughing as they did so, looking round them for something more suitable for him to chew on.

"He's not used to being . . . to being outdoors," she apologised, wondering as she did so why, since he was a servant, she supposed, though that cultured voice of his proclaimed he was not from round these parts.

"No. I haven't seen him."

"His nanny's a bit of an ogre and . . . well, I cannot

approve of the way she was bringing him up. A child needs . . . more. I'm sorry, I know I should remember but your name has slipped my mind."

"Duffy, m'lady."

"You were there . . . the other night, weren't you, Duffy?"

His face tightened and he looked away from her, not wishing her to see what was in his eyes. It was as though he were shaming her all over again by admitting that he had seen what she had suffered at the hands of her husband. He could not even bear to contemplate what had taken place in the bed she had shared with Sir Robert. No man could, at least any decent man. All over the estate male servants would be wondering and whispering about the events that had taken place and he wanted to . . . well, what could he do to stop it? Nothing. They were not wicked like his master was wicked, but they were men and could not help but speculate. Poor little girl, they would be saying, for that was how she seemed. A child, probably no more than eighteen or nineteen and yet she had known more horror and pain in a year than any woman would in a lifetime. But at the same time she did not seem to be in any way embarrassed, or even affected adversely by her experiences. She might be a dainty slip of a thing who looked as though a bit of a breeze might blow her over, but by God she must be strong. She had abandoned the fallen log and was lying on her stomach, her pretty white gown covered with bits of bark and leaves, her face close to the child's, trying to make him laugh by tickling his nose with a leaf.

She turned her head to look at him as he answered her.

"Yes, m'lady. I was one of those who helped to carry Sir Robert to his bed."

"I thought I had seen you before. I remember . . . you were kind."

"Oh no, m'lady."

"Yes, you were," she said gravely.

There was silence for several minutes, a peaceful silence broken only by the sound of birds in the branches above their heads and the soft noises of what seemed to be pleasure coming from young Master Robert who had made another grab, this time for his mother's curls.

"How is Sir Robert, m'lady?" he asked stiffly. He was squatting on his haunches, his back to a tree, the dog between his legs. His face was totally without expression, as hers was as she answered.

"He . . . has had a stroke, Duffy and I do believe the doctor thinks he will never walk again."

"How . . . sad, m'lady."

"Is it, Duffy?"

"Well, it's not for me to say, m'lady." He bent to peer into her face which was suddenly strained.

"He cannot speak either."

"Really. Then he will be confined to his bed?"

"Yes, so in future you and the other servants will have to deal with me in anything that concerns the house or the estate." And suddenly she began to smile, and then to laugh, the laughter of a child who has surprisingly escaped the schoolroom to which she has been cruelly confined and is now free to romp and play, and Duffy was not sure whether it was because her husband was as good as dead or because her child opened his baby mouth on a huge grin and began to crawl clumsily towards her. He held out his arms to be picked up and the man felt tears prick his eyes at the sheer, unallayed joy that poured from Lady Amy Blenkinsopp and enfolded not only the child but himself in its magic.

4

It was a fortnight later when callers began to arrive. She had received several notes from the local landowners, the gentry who were friends of her husband, to say how sorry they were to hear of his accident and as soon as Sir Robert felt fit enough to see anyone they would visit him. None of them seemed to know any details, only that he was confined to bed but the moment he was able would Lady Blenkinsopp, who they were pleased to welcome home, let them know and they would call immediately.

She wrote back to say that at the moment Sir Robert was not up to receiving callers, but it seemed the gentlemen who had gambled, ridden to hounds with him, walked with him in a line across his moor shooting at anything that flew, at the right season, of course, and who had generally caroused with him, in a discreet sort of way, naturally, since they were gentlemen, were not to be put off. During Race Week they had been accustomed to get up sporting parties, taking a house in Newcastle, driving out to Town Moor for the day's races, though the delectable Lady Blenkinsopp had not been included since she was already pregnant. They had even been known to go as far afield as

Newmarket, Ascot, Sandown, Goodwood, Doncaster and Epsom, living the life of the leisured classes to which they belonged.

They remembered the very pretty but almost speechless little thing Sir Robert had brought home last year; in fact they had envied him his access to such delectable flesh. Now they were convinced that even if Robert was incapacitated he would still be in charge and she would be no obstacle to their demands to visit their old friend. She was timid, retiring, appallingly gauche in company and now all they needed to do was to ride over to Robert's place, unannounced, naturally, and they would soon be reunited with their old friend, overriding any nervous objection she might make. Old Robert would need cheering up. After all, if any one of them had been struck down Robert would have been the first to call, to fetch some sort of sick-bed offering and tell them they would soon be on their feet again.

Amy was in her bedroom, watched by the indulgent Tansy who was as infatuated with Robby Blenkinsopp as his mother, lying on her back on the carpet with her son astride her playing "horseys", one of the games he was beginning increasingly to enjoy. It had taken no more than a few days for the child to realise that this pretty lady was no threat to him, indeed was great fun, which had been hard to recognise at first since it was unknown to him. He had been unsure, tentative in his approach to anything she might offer him such as a ball made out of brightly coloured wool which one of the maids had fashioned for him. She had been horrified when she realised that there was not one object in the nursery that might be regarded as a plaything. Not a

teddy or a golly or a book and this very day she meant
to drive into the small market town of Allenbury and
rectify the omission. Poor little boy, she kept saying to
Tansy, desolate to think of how he might have grown
up if she had not come home. Half-witted probably,
since it seemed for the past few months of his life, ever
since he had begun to look about him, there had been
nothing for him to look at but the four brown walls of
the nursery.

Nanny Briggs had lasted no more than three days,
because, in her own words, she could not sit about
in the nursery doing absolutely nothing while Lady
Blenkinsopp made a nonsense of her upbringing of Sir
Robert's son. It was not right that a child, particularly a
boy child, should share his mother's bedroom, which
he now did, for it seemed Lady Blenkinsopp no longer
trusted her and she could see that he was being ruined.
She glared down at her former charge who sat on the
floor with a glittering dazzle of Lady Blenkinsopp's
jewellery, worth thousands, in his eager fists. Rubies
and diamonds and pearls, necklaces and bracelets
that had belonged to Sir Robert's mother and which,
in the early days of their marriage he had insisted
his wife wore – and nothing else – in the pivacy of
their bedroom, though of course Nanny Briggs had
no knowledge of this. So, if Lady Blenkinsopp would
be good enough to give her a character reference she
would be gratified, for she had the chance of a good
job, with a good family, down south in Yorkshire. It
had taken Amy some serious thought, dismayed at
the idea of some other poor child being treated as
Robby had been, but in the end she had written a
somewhat terse testimonial stating that Nanny Briggs

was of good character, saying nothing about her care of children.

Nanny had taken it, packed her bags and left without a word to anyone, not even Sir Robert whom the doctor absolutely forbade her to "bother". She would have liked to complain bitterly about her treatment at the hands of his wife and ask him if he knew what was happening in his own house but, unable to do so, she had satisfied herself with writing him a long letter from Yorkshire which his wife had opened and read and thrown to the back of the fire.

For the past fortnight Amy had allowed all the refinements of the ladylike behaviour that was expected in the society in which she had been brought up to go to the devil. Since no baby carriage was provided, she ordered one, said to be the same make used by Her Majesty the Queen for her own children, from Hitchings Baby Store in Ludgate Hill and when it came she and Robby, who was growing increasingly heavy, would be able to trundle all over the estate. She had already taken him to the stables and had discovered a small trap in the coach house which could be pulled by a quiet and steady pony. John-Henry, the head groom, had one that would be just right for her, he had told her. Her name was Victoria and she was old now, for she had once pulled Sir Robert's mother about the grounds. He would ask the carpenter to fix a sturdy seat for the boy, who gazed at him from his mother's arms in silent wonder, so that when her ladyship was driving the vehicle Master Robert would be safe as houses.

The servants were astounded by her behaviour, though not displeased, for it was a lovely sight to see mother and son together. She spent all her time with the baby, in the garden when it was fine, in her bedroom when it was not, playing with him by the hour, watching him when he slept, usually accompanied by Tansy who had, as yet, not learned the intricacies of being a lady's maid. She was more companion, nursemaid, the bearer of messages from her ladyship to the kitchen, for they were all vastly interested in the progress of her ladyship and the baby she had deserted six months ago. The gardeners and grooms had reported that he was a fine little chap, a bit solemn but ready to smile when encouraged. The maids longed to see the lad, they told Tansy, if Lady Blenkinsopp would bring him down to the kitchen one day, and Tansy had promised to pass on the message.

Amy knew that soon she must set her house in order. She had toyed with the idea of asking Tansy to be Robby's nursemaid since the child had taken to her, but Tansy was such a lively, cheerful companion she didn't want to lose her. So she must be taught her duties as lady's maid and a good-natured, easy-going, trustworthy nanny must be found for Robby. Now that her husband was so severely incapacitated she meant to take over the running of the estate, with Duffy's help since Duffy seemed to know all there was to know about it. In fact he could have done it himself, for he had once been in charge of just such an estate in Cheshire, he told her in one of their almost daily chats. Sir Robert was well looked after by the silently efficient giant called Platt, and Doctor Parsons's nurse was still in attendance, though the doctor had told her only this morning on his daily visit that there was not a lot for the nurse to do now. In a few weeks Sir Robert would need the splints taken off his legs but in the meanwhile Platt could see to all his requirements and the nurse could be found more urgent work in the doctor's practice.

Her husband's daughters, Agnes, Mary and Jane, were more than happy to sit with him, to read the newspapers to him, ignoring his gibbering and gobbling and maddened, bloodshot eyes as they had never been able to ignore him before his accident. Amy was of the opinion that they were enjoying themselves for the first time in their barren lives, able to do as they pleased without fear of being ranted at. Not that they wanted to do much, being of rather nervous natures and could you blame them. They liked to sew and paint and play the piano, ride carefully round the estate in the little governess cart which had been their mother's, all the things they had been taught well-brought-up young ladies should do, but now they could do these things without their father shouting that it was time they had husbands and what the bloody hell did they think they were doing sitting about his drawing-room, not even ornamental which would have been something in their favour, when they should be giving him grandchildren. Not that that mattered now, he used to say coarsely, since his new wife had obliged him with a son and would, if he had anything to do with it, which he had, give him another dozen before her breeding days were over. It had been an unusual day when he had not reduced at least one of them to tears at some point, or to deep and embarrassed flushes with his coarseness.

Now that he was out of the way, as they silently and thankfully thought of him, Amy and they ate dinner every evening, finding one another's company quite pleasant, though she knew her hoydenish ways with their father's son was a worry to them. Should their father recover, which the doctor had informed them sadly was not likely, would he not punish them all, most particularly his lovely and astonishingly lively wife, for what had gone on while he was laid up?

Amy's first caller was Edward Pearson, a gentleman farmer and one of the so-called "leisured classes" whose grandfather had been so successful in the breeding of the Durham Shorthorn, known for its good meat and heavy milk yield, it had made him a small fortune. Like all the other gentlemen in this part of Northumberland, including Sir Robert Blenkinsopp, he also had his finger in many pies which, like his cattle, brought him in a steadily increasing revenue. Railways, mining, the rents from his tenant farmers and shipbuilding were but a few, enabling him to keep a stable of pedigree hunters and live a life that would have astounded his own great-grandfather who had been a small hill-farmer living on the high pastures where he grazed his stock. He was not the gentleman Sir Robert was, indeed none of the community was, but he was sufficiently wealthy and influential in his position as magistrate in Alnwick to mix with the best in society and he considered himself to be Sir Robert's equal in all but the length of his pedigree.

The knock at the door interrupted Amy's game with Robby. She called out to whoever it was to come in and Clara entered. Clara, under-housemaid below Morna, her face rosy with excitement, announced that there was a visitor to see Sir Robert and should she show him up. Not to her mistress's bedroom, of course, but to the one where Sir Robert was incarcerated, though Clara did not use this word!

Amy grabbed at her son and leaped to her feet, putting the baby on Tansy's lap, smoothing down her rumpled skirts and dragging her hands through her tangled hair.

"Who is it, Clara?" Amy asked, her hand to her breast in some trepidation. She had been expecting this, since she was aware that her husband had many friends in the district, men with whom he drank and gambled and whored, men like himself with more money than they knew what to do with, whose wives were content to sit at home, indeed had no other choice, and let them get on with it. They were all much of an age, most with elderly wives and grown families, spending their days in the winter riding to hounds with the Lawdale Hunt as countrymen do. They hand-reared their game birds and foxes for half the year and then slaughtered them the other half. They played whist, faro, poker and most nights, when the ladies had retired, got so drunk their footmen had to see them to their beds.

Edward Pearson was a big, florid-faced gentleman who leaped to his feet as Amy entered the drawing-room, advancing towards her enthusiastically, for she was certainly one of the best-looking women he had ever set eyes on. She had changed since he had seen her, which would be last autumn when she had cowered and flinched from the slightest word her husband uttered. She had lost her looks somewhat, due to her pregnancy they had all supposed, so that in her role as plain and timid mouse they had taken no notice of her. Even their wives had ignored her, for she had nothing to say on any subject that interested them.

Now she was flushed, one could almost say dishevelled, just as though she had hastily pulled herself together after some glorious romp or other. It could not be with old Robert, that was for sure, and when she smiled charmingly and held out her hand, explaining that she had been playing with her son, though he was surprised since his own wife had never done such a thing in her life, he said he understood. She had a faint discoloration to her face about her eye just as though she had been recently slapped.

"Now then, my dear," he said when they were seated, "what's this I hear about Sir Robert? Your note spoke of an accident but didn't say of what sort. Not a fall from his horse, I hope."

Amy managed to hang her head prettily as though momentarily overcome with distress and for a horrid moment thought that Mr Pearson might be about to lean forward and take her hand in his, which was as large and hairy as Robert's. The image made her shudder but fortunately Mr Pearson did not notice.

"Oh no, Mr Pearson. It happened during the night. Sir Robert, for some reason, got up, perhaps to investigate a noise, I don't know, and in the dark fell down the stairs. I was asleep and he was not found until morning. I'm sorry to say he had an apoplectic stroke and in the fall broke both his legs."

"My dear Lady Blenkinsopp, I am appalled." Edward Pearson reared back in horror, almost spilling his cup of coffee which stood on a small side table. "When does the doctor expect him to . . ."

"Oh, he's not expected to recover, Mr Pearson. He

might live for many years, Doctor Parsons informed me, with the right care, but he will never walk again. One side of his body is totally useless and his speech is badly affected."

"Dear God, we had no idea . . ."

"We?"

"His many friends, Lady Blenkinsopp. Tom Henry and George Linton and a host of others who have told me they are to call on you. They hope to see Sir Robert and tell him . . . as I did . . ."

"You may see him, if you wish, Mr Pearson. I'm sure a visit from an old friend can do him nothing but good. I'll take you up."

Edward Pearson, after the tale of woe Lady Blenkinsopp had just told him, was not awfully sure he wanted to be "taken up" to see his old friend. Like most men he had a horror of illness. He had imagined that old Robert had taken a tumble from Jason, his hunter, and had broken a bone, which they had all done at some time in their lives, but this sounded horrific. Surely he was best left on his own to recover, even a little bit, but no, his wife seemed strangely eager, which quite amazed him, to lead him out of the drawing-room, up the stairs and to the room where his old friend lay.

"Perhaps it might be better if I was to leave, my dear," he protested. "I don't want to put you to any trouble."

"It's no trouble, Mr Pearson." Lady Blenkinsopp smiled serenely, lifting a hand to push back a long curly strand of silver hair which drifted across her face. Edward Pearson watched mesmerised, his mind conjecturing on the possibility as to whether his old friend had had time to take this gorgeous creature to bed before he had his unfortunate accident. Hell's teeth, what a waste . . . what a waste!

"Are you sure Sir Robert is up to visitors, my dear? I should have sent a note to say . . ."

"Not at all, Mr Pearson. A visit from an old friend will do him the world of good. You can tell him all the local news."

"Well, if you're sure."

"Come with me, sir. His man is with him. The doctor employed him to do the heavy lifting, but he is somewhat . . . slow and will be no trouble to you. It was his strength that was needed not his thinking powers."

He followed her slight, swaying figure up the stairs, breathing in the faint but lovely fragrance which seemed to come from her wide skirts. She was in white, a creamy white with short sleeves and a high neck. The bodice fitted smoothly to her small, rounded breasts and round her tiny waist was a wide sash of rose-pink satin. Her hair hung tantalisingly to her buttocks, swinging as she walked and he almost put out a hand to touch it. God, she was lovely. What a waste, what a waste, his brain kept repeating.

Though the window was open there was a stale smell in the bedroom to which she led him. As she ushered him through the door he was reminded of sickrooms everywhere. The one where his own mother had died, and others on his estate, which, as a good Christian landlord, he had visited. A mixture of cleaned-up bodily waste which, no matter what was done, still hung on the air, the foul breath of the man who was ill, and the seldom-washed body of the hulking figure of the man who sat in the corner staring at absolutely nothing.

"Here's someone to see you, Robert," Lady Blenkinsopp announced cheerfully, standing well back from the door and motioning to the visitor that he was to approach the bed. Sir Robert, she explained, as though he were either deaf or a lunatic, could not turn his head and to see who was there the visitor must stand, or sit, close to the bed. The hulk had stood up as they entered and she gestured to him to get a chair for Mr Pearson.

"It was, without a doubt, the worst ten minutes I have ever spent in my entire life," Edward was to tell his wife later, as distressed as she was ever to see him. "You could tell the last thing the poor old bugger wanted was anyone hanging about and babbling on about bloody nothing, apart from the fact that he was the most god-awful mess you ever saw. Dribbling and twisting his face into the most unspeakable shapes, his eyes rolling as he tried to say something and all the while she stood there at the window and watched, and I swear to God she enjoyed every minute of it."

"Oh no, Edward! Not that little bit of a thing who wouldn't say boo to a goose."

"Aye, that was then but you should see her now. You must admit he treated her, and those daughters of his and, come to think about it, his first wife . . . what was her name?"

"Eleanor."

"Aye, well, he had a bad mouth on him at times and I heard a whisper he knocked her about."

"Who, Eleanor?" Annette Pearson was vastly diverted. It always amazed her to hear of any woman letting any man "knock her about" and her Edward knew that if he ever tried it on her he'd be sorry. He had married her for her money, she knew that, and the fact that she was as tall as him and probably a couple of stones heavier, made her a doughty opponent. She'd given him three sons and two daughters so he'd got his money's worth.

"No, this one. That's why she ran away in December last year, they say, and he wasn't overly concerned, since she'd given him the son he wanted. Well, she's back, which is only as it should be, but I reckon she'll give him no more lads, that's for sure."

They came one by one, reluctantly, Amy could see that, all the gentlemen with whom he drank and gambled, obviously informed by Edward Pearson what to expect. George Linton, whose estate ran side by side with Sir Robert's, Thomas Henry who was a banker and had a fine home in Alnwick, James Sharp, the owner of a lead mine over Bishop Auckland way and shares in the Bedlington Iron Works near Morpeth, who sat beside Robert and mumbled their condolences, telling him they would be over to see him again soon as they almost ran from his bedroom, their manner saying it would be the last he would see of them. After his shock and fury at being looked over pityingly by Edward Pearson, which had rendered him almost senseless with frustration, he had simply stared at his old friend, but when the next visitor arrived it was on her, his wife, that his eyes had held. They were steady, hating, red and drooping, the wrinkled, almost lashless lids livid but in them was something that told her she would live to regret this, this being put on show for the benefit of men who had not even been his equals, but were now superior beings since they could walk and talk and ride and make love to their wives.

She would smile, her eyes wide and innocent, her manner meek, acting the part of the sorrowing wife. He would hiss in the back of his throat and the hulk who stood and waited for his orders, to lift him, to turn him, to massage him, to bathe him, to feed him and do all the hateful things that the wreck that was now Sir Robert Blenkinsopp needed doing for him, watched indifferently.

On occasion she even brought his son in to see him, or rather for him to see his son, though she kept the baby well away from the bed. Robby had begun to babble now, to chuckle and reach out for anything that caught his eye and she marvelled at the recuperative powers of a child. He was standing on her knee as she sat by the open window, her hands supporting him beneath his armpits, and with a chuckle he reached for her earrings, pulling at them as he tried to get them into his mouth.

"Look at him, Robert," she would say. "Look how your son has come on since I got rid of that harridan you put in charge of him. Yes, I actually let him sit in my lap which you denied me months ago, d'you remember? He is kissed and cuddled and if he grows up 'soft' – isn't that the word you used when he was born and you found me nursing him? – then at least he knows he is loved, and there's absolutely nothing you can do about it, is there. I love him and he is learning to love me. Your son. *My* son who will be brought up as I think fit. He will be a normal, noisy, affectionate little boy who will learn to give affection as well as receive it. Now, I think you must accept that I am in charge of you, your son, your home, your servants, your estate and I find it . . . rewarding that after all you did to me you are to be punished. I despise you for the degradation and abuse you heaped on me but I don't intend to let it spoil my life. You shall not be a part of my life, you see. I am strong now, Robert. You brutalised me for months which is why I ran away. I felt I would rather die than remain with you but my cousin and her husband slowly rebuilt my health and strength and gave me back something I thought I had lost: my self-esteem, my confidence in myself which is why, when you finally demanded I came home, I believed I could live as your wife again. I was wrong and I will thank God every day of my life for the event that has saved me from that, and from you. You will be shut up here like that character in a novel, the title of which slips my memory but I believe he went mad, the prisoner, I mean."

He would strain to speak, the veins swelling in his forehead, the sinews in his throat standing out like whipcord as he struggled to get even the merest whisper of loathing past his stretched lips. The cruel effort of will, the dominant will that had charged through every obstacle life might have the audacity to put in his way, struggled to get free, strove to get at her, to reach her, even if it was only with words. He was in pain, she could see that, and she watched it impassively remembering the pain she had been subjected to on the night she'd returned to Newton Law. Even yet she bore the marks of his brutality on her body.

She stood up and turned to look out of the window

which had the same view as her own. Mr Weston, who was head gardener, was walking the length of a rose bed which was a magnificent blaze of red and pink and cream. With great care he was dead-heading those that were going over, placing the fading blossoms in a basket. Behind him walked a lad, whose name she thought was Herbie, respectfully watching and listening to the drone of Mr Weston's voice.

Down by the wood a brown shape suddenly shot from beneath the laden summer branches of the trees, scooting across the lawn with its nose to the ground and Mr Weston glanced up from his task, a look of annoyance on his face. If that dratted dog spoiled his lawn he'd have something to say to that gamekeeper who owned the thing, his expression said. Following his dog came the owner himself, strolling in that easy, graceful way of his as though he had all the time in the world. She had noticed he had an unhurried way of moving as though the world were such a pleasant place it was a sin to hurry and perhaps miss something. It slowed you down, she had found when she was with him, made you want to stand and look about you, to sniff the air above a bed of lavender, to watch a breeze move through the shivering branch of a tree. He was not wearing a jacket, for it was a warm sunny day and as soon as she had finished here she would take Robby down there and let him crawl about on the grass. She had a sudden urge to run, to get down there before Duffy disappeared, she didn't know why, only that it seemed imperative she leave this place of hopelessness and misery and get out into the sunshine where men were whole and decent and had kindness in their souls.

The baby lifted his arm and pointed, turning to look into her face and beginning to jabber. The men below him were slowly becoming familiar to him, especially Duffy who had been known to carry him if he met her ladyship on her walks through the woods.

"Yes, darling, it's Duffy and will you look at Dick. Mr Weston will be none too pleased if he digs a hole in his lawn which he seems bent on doing. Oh, dear . . ." and she began to laugh.

Robby Blenkinsopp watched her face, quite mesmerised, and then he began to laugh too and his father glared with eyes that seemed to glow red in the shadow about his bed. They were filled with malevolent hatred.

5

The man on the bed opened his mouth and from it came what sounded like a pig grunting. The man sitting vacantly beside him took no notice, for he was used to such noises. They meant nothing and if they did it was not his business to make any sense of them. He was employed to keep his patient clean, to lift him from side to side to prevent bedsores, to see to his bodily needs, to change his nightgown, to feed him and generally just keep him alive in as much comfort as was possible. The doctor came in once a week to check him, a couple of plain women cleaned the bedroom and changed the bed, scurrying in and out like scared rabbits, and now and again Lady Blenkinsopp came in and sat by the window, studying the man who was her husband. He didn't know why and it was not his place to ask. He was only sullenly aware that it kept him on his toes, so to speak, since he never knew when she was coming. It was never the same time each day or the same day each week and he knew it would be more than his job was worth to be found shirking.

He thrust his hand down his breeches and vigorously scratched the wiry hair in his crotch then lifted the same hand to his mouth and rooted among his rotting teeth until he found a fragment of food from his last meal. He fished it out on the end of his finger, looked it over carefully then popped it back in his mouth.

The man on the bed grunted again and Platt glanced indifferently in his direction, his expression changing to one of oafish astonishment when the man lifted his paralysed hand, which had been lying flaccidly by his side on the bed, waved it in the air in the manner of a magician performing a party trick, then let it flop down again. All the time his eyes were on Platt, sending him some message that Platt could not decipher. It was the first time his charge had moved, except for a restless rolling of his head on the pillow since his accident four months ago.

Platt stood up and moved uncertainly round the bed. Should he fetch someone? his anguished expression seemed to ask, for Platt was no good with decisions. He liked to be told what to do and exactly when to do it; what to expect in the patients he "minded", most from families with money, like this one, who could afford to have a full-time attendant for a sick member who was a bit of a nuisance to the rest of them. They were not concerned with the day-to-day doings of the patient which was why they employed him, but this was different and might he be expected to report it to someone? The man's wife, for instance, or . . . well, someone? Sir Robert had lain like a log for so long, doing nowt, saying nowt, it had quite put the wind up him to see that hand wave in the air.

He moved another step towards the door and Sir Robert Blenkinsopp shook his head almost violently,

his eyes again shooting some message to the bewildered attendant.

"Ah'll fetch someone," Platt mumbled, and again
Sir Robert shook his head. Something unintelligible
gobbled from his mouth, along with the dribble he
could not control, but Platt was not repelled. He'd
seen far worse than this in some of the patients he
had had in his charge and was past caring what they
looked like, or even smelled like. This was a good way
of earning a living. He'd nowt to do all day but sit here
and doze if he wanted to, or stare into space and wait
for the food which turned up with pleasing regularity
and was the best he'd ever eaten. He slept soundly
in a comfortable bed in a small room which led off
this one, the door open, of course, in case his patient
should need him but as the poor old bugger could do
no more than grunt it seemed a waste of time, and so
far he had slept peacefully through every night. He got
a day off once a fortnight when one of the footmen
took over from him and the only thing he missed was
the feel of a woman. Some of the maids here weren't
bad-looking, not that it would bother him if they were
as ugly as Punch's hump as long as they had the right
equipment between their legs, but so far he had been
unlucky. He meant to go into Allenbury on his next
day off and see what was on offer. You could usually
pick up a tart at one of the public houses.

He eyed Sir Robert warily for a moment, undecided
what to do, for it seemed to him, though slow thinking
not short of cunning, that the man was trying to
tell him something, but what the poor sod wanted,
short of standing on his own two legs, he could not
imagine. He looked about him as though searching for

inspiration but all he saw was the solid comfort of the room. A fire crackled and spat in the blackleaded grate and beside it stood a well-polished copper coal scuttle which the housemaid had just refilled and brought up. Sir Robert lay in what was known as a "half-tester" bed with fringed drapes forming a three-sided tent. There were matching curtains at the windows and a flowery carpet which all gave a sense of warmth and luxury. The wardrobe was of mahogany, as was the dressing-table and the marble-topped washstand. A damask-covered sofa with a serpentine back and curving legs stood at the foot of the bed. There was an easy chair by the bed in which he himself lolled and a stool in front of the dressing-table. On either side of the bed were cupboards for chamber pots, one of which he himself used to the disgust of the chambermaid, since she had to empty it along with Sir Robert's "slops", and which matched the ewer and basin on the washstand in a pleasing design of birds and flowers. It was a large room with two bay windows which looked out on to the front of the house and in one of the bays was the chair in which her ladyship sat to scrutinise her husband. As far away from the bed as possible!

Sir Robert made a great effort and lifting his hand again appeared to be trying to point in the direction of the dressing-table. Platt's eyes followed in bewilderment, for there was nothing on the dressing-table top but the paraphernalia of illness which the doctor left for him to deal with. A bottle of something, the contents of which he was to rub each day into the patient's back and various portions of his anatomy that might develop bedsores. Another that contained medicine to soothe Sir Robert's restlessness but which, recently, Sir Robert had steadfastly refused to take and he didn't care, did he, Platt said to himself. If the old codger wanted to twitch and froth and gibber it was nowt to do with him. There could be no complaints from the patient about him, could there, meaning himself, a thought which often made him titter.

Sir Robert seemed to snarl, lifting the corner of his top lip like the picture of an animal Platt had once seen on a poster on the wall of a public house which a passing pedestrian had explained to him was advertising a circus.

"Did yer want summat?" he asked curiously, the first remark he had ever addressed to his patient.

Again Sir Robert's hand lifted and again it appeared to be pointing at the dressing-table and in his eyes was a pinprick of light, and though Platt was not capable of forming such an idea there was a flicker of intelligence in them that said that inside Sir Robert Blenkinsopp's head there was still a working brain.

Platt walked slowly towards the dressing-table, looking back at his master, since for the first time in four months he began to think of him as such. He stopped, then, in a sudden flash of brilliance, or so it seemed to him, he opened the top drawer and peered inside. There were several objects of the sort gentlemen would use, bottles with silver lids, crystal pots for pomade, shaving brushes, a silver ring box and a silver match container and striker. There was a silver clothes-brush and a cologne bottle and a silver-topped glass box used for tie-pins and other accessories, all put safely away when Sir Robert took over occupancy of the room.

He lifted out one container, peering at it in bewilderment, having no idea what its use might be. It was a crystal pot in which pomade was kept. He was just about to unscrew the silver lid and have a sniff at its contents when a renewed grunting from the bed made him turn his head to look at his patient. Sir Robert was again waving his hand in the air, wearily this time as though the effort had exhausted him but there was no mistaking what the movement meant. He was telling Platt to come back to the bedside and bring the handsome object with him. His face was twisted in what seemed to be agony but he persisted and, understanding at last, slowly Platt did as he was told. He held the pot in his great hairy hand. It was for the use of a gentleman not that of a common man and it looked incongruous resting on his hard palm. It was very obviously worth a few bob, or so he imagined, and as the thought squeezed itself into his small brain he looked up and saw what was in his master's face. It was jerking and gobbling but the message was clear in his small, green eyes, one of which winked, the wink a message between two men who could do business.

Platt considered it from every angle then nodded slowly.

"Yer want me ter do summat?" he proclaimed, beginning to smile, as he could see there was a chance to earn a guinea or two here, or perhaps more, for no one but him took the slightest interest in what went on in this room and Sir Robert wasn't going to tell them, was he?

As the notion passed through his brain it also flittered across his vacant face and at once Sir Robert began to snarl and spit, this time like a beast of prey,

and though the man was totally helpless and at anyone's mercy, Platt felt a shiver of fear run through his
enormous frame. If he'd a mind to he could have lifted
his master and flung him quite easily from the window
but it was not his master's physical strength he feared
but the obvious menace in the man's eyes. There was
something nasty there, something he thought might
be called *evil* though it was not a word he had used
before. He was frightened of nothing. From a young
age he had terrorised boys his own size with his
strength, and even bigger lads, for they could sense
in him something that made them back away. Now
he felt the same unease run through him and it was
only by a great effort that he prevented himself from
stepping back from the bed.

Sir Robert actually managed a smile, then he
nodded.

"What?" Platt breathed heavily, leaning forward as
though expecting Sir Robert to tell him. Sir Robert
indicated the object in his hand, raising his eyebrows,
then, with a great effort that had the sweat breaking
out on his forehead he mouthed the word "sell".

"Sell? What d'yer mean?"

Again Sir Robert raised his eyebrows but this time
with a gathering frustration.

It took almost ten minutes before Platt finally got the
message which was that on his next day off he was to
go into Newcastle where he would not be known and
where there would be any number of shops ready to
buy such pretty trinkets without any questions asked.
He could walk to Allenbury and from there get a train
to the city. Platt, who had never in his life been on
a train, felt his stomach drop into the crotch of his

baggy pants but when it was revealed to him who was to benefit from the sale of the trinkets, yes, all of them, he felt the strength return.

"Howay, man, that's fine an' dandy but let me ask yer this. Why?"

Again Sir Robert winked and gabbled and winked and gabbled and at last it began to percolate into Platt's brain what Sir Robert was up to. He had no money about him and no way of getting any, at least at the moment, but if Platt was willing to be his confederate in this, Platt would not go unrewarded. There would be all kinds of services Platt could do for his master but this was the first and it was a gesture of goodwill to let the minder know that if he kept faith with the man who was in his care, Sir Robert would see him right.

Again he raised his hand, this time to his mouth and made a fumbling attempt to hold his lips together.

Platt frowned and Sir Robert turned a dangerous scarlet as though it were all he could do to curb his violent temper and show patience, for it was evident it would be needed. Again he made a gesture of closing and fastening his lips together and Platt smiled in triumph.

"Aye, man, aye. Say nowt, is that it? Keep this between us two, aye. I get yer. Will there be owt else, like?"

Sir Robert was coming very rapidly to the end of his dwindling strength, but making one last effort he put his hand on the coverlet and with two fingers made a creeping movement, like a fat spider manoeuvring itself across the bed, the illusion heightened by the thick mat of hair on the back of the hand and along each finger.

Again Platt scowled, then, as though the game were fast becoming familiar to him, he beamed, showing the green slime and rotted food between his teeth. Sir Robert himself was seen to shudder.

"Yer want ter walk again, wi' me ter help yer, is that it?"

Sir Robert sighed and nodded and his wet lips formed what might have been a smile then he drifted off to sleep, exhausted but satisfied.

She came in later that day and took her accustomed seat by the window which she opened, wafting in some fresh air with a fan she always carried when she visited her husband, then began the kind of one-sided conversation that Platt had got used to, prattling on about the doings of the house, not for Sir Robert's entertainment but to let him know that she was in charge of it. Even *he* understood that!

"If you hear noises, Robert, don't be alarmed. I'm having some alterations done to the house," she said in that casual way she had as though she were holding a conversation with an acquaintance who would not be unduly concerned. "There are repairs needing to be done. Mr Wanless" – who was the estate carpenter – "tells me there is a leak in the roof just over the attic and some work needed on the stables. You have expensive animals in there and they need the best of quarters, or so John-Henry tells me. They are never ridden, of course, except by the grooms and stable lads who give them exercise and I was wondering whether it might be an idea to get rid of some of them."

Sir Robert's eyes shot open. He had been pretending to be asleep as he did very often when she was there, and when she brought his son in who, by now, was scuttling round like a little monkey, breathing heavily as he hauled himself up on to chairs, even attempting the bed which fortunately was too high for him. He was into everything he could reach, fetching out the chamber pot from the cupboard, luckily empty, and squealing with rapture over the smallest thing, a noisy, demanding baby who never stopped talking in his own inimitable way. Sir Robert would pretend he hadn't noticed, refusing to look at his handsome son. It was as though she had turned the boy into a shrieking monster with her slack, lackadaisical ways and his father wanted nothing to do with him, or her. If he could have prevented her visits he would have done so but he couldn't so he shut himself off inside his head which he turned away.

Now he turned to glare at her, mouthing something, the words of which neither she, nor Platt, who sat quietly by the bed, could understand, though their meaning was very clear.

"I can see you're not pleased, Robert, but if I'm to stay here and bring up our son we must have a home that his friends can visit. I don't think you've spent a penny on the place since your mother came here as a bride which must have been sixty years ago. And is there any need for so many animals eating their heads off in the stables? I would say not but that can keep. The house is my main concern at the moment."

He gobbled and glared and almost lifted his arm to wave it threateningly at her but resisted at the last moment and she did not notice. His face was like a turkey cock, scarlet and sweated and she watched him dispassionately. He had put on weight due to his inactivity and love of food, the only pleasure left to him. He had lost what little hair he had during the last four months and the thought came into her mind that he really was the most grotesque creature she had ever seen. Why couldn't he have died in the fall, leaving her a widow? It would have been so much simpler and probably better for him since an active man like him, even at his age, must despair of the life he led. She thought it was perhaps his hatred of her that kept him alive and wondered if it might be more humane if she left him totally alone. She did not come in here to taunt him, though who would blame her if she did, knowing what he was, but to . . . to . . . why did she come in here? she asked herself for the hundredth time. Was it perhaps to let him see what a lovely boy they had, now that he was free of the cruel restraints Nanny Briggs had put on him? He was growing fast in his babyhood, smiling at anyone who gave him a glance and there were many of those, for the servants, when they got a chance, spoiled him lavishly.

"Some of the furnishings are so faded and worn it's a wonder the curtains don't fall off the rails. Of course I shan't get rid of the rosewood furniture or the Satinwood which is quite beautiful if a little old-fashioned, but men are to come in on Monday and start on my bedroom. I thought a delicate shade of the palest green watered silk for the walls, peach velvet curtains and a carpet of the two colours combined with cream. What d'you think?"

Platt looked enquiringly at his master as though expecting an answer but Sir Robert merely opened his mouth wide on a silent howl.

"And the nursery has already been done. You really

should see it. That attic room was quite unsuitable. It seemed that a space for the cot and a bed for the nurse would do for previous Blenkinsopp children with a bit of drugget by the fireplace but I'm afraid I didn't agree. I've had the place made bigger by knocking a wall down – perhaps you would not have heard the noise so far away. I covered the walls with plain white paper and then stuck pictures all over it of animals and birds and flowers, with the figures of the alphabet in bright colours, nursery rhymes and such. I even got Mr Weston to make me up some window boxes with geraniums in them, for they are such a lovely bright colour, don't you agree? And there's carpet fitted from wall to wall. Quite plain but easy on the knees of a crawling child. Robby has dozens of books on shelves that he can reach himself and I almost bought up the toy shop in Allenbury. It really is splendid. It's a pity you can't see it."

When she had gone Platt was presented with his patient having what looked like a fit and for a moment he considered sending for Doctor Parsons but instead forced a large spoonful of the "quietening" medicine down his patient's throat. He went to sleep almost at once and Platt, after closing the window Lady Blenkinsopp had opened, since there was a draught cutting through the usual fug, settled himself in the chair before the fire and dreamed of what he would do with the money Sir Robert had promised him. A woman first and, who knows, with a bit of cash in his pocket he might persuade one of the female servants who were employed in the house to accommodate him in the future. Thrusting his hand into the baggy reaches of his trousers he fondled the bulge that grew there while his eyes became unfocused at the prospect of what lay before him. He groaned convulsively as his hand had the desired effect but though it brought him some relief it was not as good as a woman, was it.

Tansy was the first to notice her mistress was putting on weight. Well, she would, wouldn't she, since she attended to her ladyship in the full capacity of a lady's maid. Lady Blenkinsopp, who had been called on by Mrs Edward Pearson, Mrs Thomas Henry and Mrs George Linton, the wives of three of Sir Robert's good friends – none of whom had visited again – had been surprised and pleased when Mrs Henry, whose father was a baronet, on hearing that Tansy needed some training, had offered to take her into her own home for a fortnight for an extensive course on how to become a lady's maid.

"She can accompany my maid in all her duties and Mary can also show her how to care for your clothes, to make repairs, how to dress your hair" – which was badly in need of attention, the ladies thought, since it hung down her ladyship's back fastened with no more than a bunch of scarlet ribbon – "to see to your jewellery; well, you will know what I mean, for I am sure your previous maids would have known the proper way to go about things. I think a fortnight will give her the rudiments if you can manage without her for so long."

The ladies beamed at one another and at Lady Blenkinsopp who, though she was still somewhat tongue-tied, certainly looked better than the last time they had seen her before the birth of her son. Positively plump she was now. Was she to entertain during the coming winter, they asked her, and could they count on her to join them in their own entertainments which would be many and various? She was polite, smiling but non-committal.

Tansy did not enjoy the experience one little bit and told the other servants they didn't know when they were well off, for Mrs Henry was a stingy old beggar who kept an eye on every ruddy penny her house-keeper spent. Her servants were all on short rations and she expected them to work the clock round for small wages. Why anyone stayed there was a mystery to her and she'd never been so glad to get home in her life. There was none of the friendly chit-chat that went on round the kitchen table at Newton Law and she had lost several pounds in weight the food was so poor. For the servants at any rate, though the family ate well enough and if Maddy would pass her another of Cook's fancies and pour her a second cup of tea while Mrs Armitage was in her parlour, she'd be ever so grateful. Mind, she was glad she'd been. She was a bright girl with a good retentive memory and she had learned what was neccesary to make a start on her new career. The rest she would learn as she went along. There was a new book just published by a Mrs Beeton which was full of handy hints, not just for a lady's maid but for a whole household and her ladyship had promised Tansy she would have one. Tansy was learning to read, with her mistress's help, and her future looked rosy.

That night she had her first chance to show what she had learned when she pinned up her ladyship's hair into a shining coil which glinted silver in the lamplight, and fixed a pink silk rose in its centre.

But when it came to her ladyship's gown, which was of a pink so pale it was almost white, one she had not worn for several weeks, she was flabbergasted when the hooks and eyes would not even meet, let alone fasten.

She did her best. Both she and her mistress were red-faced with the effort but it was no good, the bodice of the gown just would not come together. They stood in front of the long cheval glass mirror and looked at one another, Tansy a foot taller than her ladyship and her ladyship pulled a face, then sighed deeply. And yet it was not a sigh of unhappiness. In fact Tansy would have said just the opposite, for there was a glow about Lady Blenkinsopp, a certain brilliance in her long, blue-grey eyes, a luminous smile about her rosy lips. She was very lovely and when she spoke Tansy wondered why it was she was so transformed.

"I suppose you must know, Tansy," she said, sighing again with what seemed to be great satisfaction.

"What, m'lady?"

"I am with child. I am to have a brother or sister for my Robby." She whirled to face Tansy and Tansy was astounded at the happiness on her face. Of course, all women wanted a child, children, but surely not one conceived in the way this child had been conceived. Tansy would never forget the sight of her ladyship's poor bleeding body on the night Sir Robert tumbled down the stairs, nor the desolation of heart which seemed, for that one night only, to harrow her mistress. She had recovered, basking in the joy of her son and the respect and affection given her by the servants who had all taken to "the poor little thing" as they had originally called her. She was busy all day long, humming sometimes, her baby son beside her, designing this lovely room and the nursery where the little lad bloomed under the kind and cheerful care of the good-natured woman her ladyship had herself chosen. He loved Nanny Morag and when his mother was not available seemed content to stay in her care. There was always one servant or another up there in that bright nursery, on the pretext of performing some task who popped in to see him, and he thrived on it, holding out his arms and shouting his pleasure at all and sundry.

Now there was to be another one and though it was something she would never understand, her mistress seemed delighted about it. Mind you, it would be lovely to have another baby about the place. Just wait until she told the others. But as though reading her mind her mistress took her hand and held it in that lovely way she had.

"Don't tell anyone, will you, Tansy. Not just yet. See what you can do with my gowns to hide it for a while."

"Of course, m'lady, but not for long. Man, you must be a good four months." Now and again Tansy forgot her place and spoke in the way of her class.

"Mmm, probably," her ladyship said, somewhat vaguely, which further mystified her maid, for if there was one conception that could be pinpointed almost to the hour, it was this one.

6

As summer ran into autumn, as the trees under which they played turned from every shade of green to every shade of brown and flame and gold, she and the baby carriage were a familiar sight, trundling along paths brilliantly bordered by Mr Weston's carefully tended chrysanthemums and dahlias which wound about the gardens. They criss-crossed Mr Weston's precious lawn and threaded their haphazard way between the vegetables in the kitchen garden where Mr Purvis and Herbie, one of the gardener's lads, were earthing up the celery to preserve the plants from the coming frosts. Further along against the high wall carrots and potatoes and parsnips were being dug up, using a three-pronged potato fork, by Jimmy and Henry and placed carefully in baskets. They would be taken to pits in the open ground, properly drained, and covered, first with a layer of earth then with a thatching of clean straw then with another layer of soil thick enough to protect them from the severest frosts. Mr Weston was making war on the caterpillars that were invading his cabbages, a yearly task and one that made him curse under his breath and play merry hell with the lads. He removed his cap respectfully when the mistress passed by, waving at the child who had begun to wave back. He had winced when he saw the carriage's wheels cutting into the smooth green patina of the lawn he and his staff had created over the years but then wasn't it a grand sight to see her ladyship so happy and hear the sound of her voice as she talked to the baby and his babbling answers. They laughed, she and her son, no one knew what at but she apparently did, and after all she had suffered at the hands of the master – though this was never voiced out loud, of course – it was time she had a bit of happiness.

There was a wide cobbled yard enclosed by stables and a coach house. Beyond that was the kitchen garden and behind that an orchard which, in springtime, she had been told by Mr Weston, was full of daffodils and narcissi and later the bluebells grew so thickly that the ground beneath the fruit trees was a blue mist. Banked behind the orchard rose the woods. She would stop and talk to them all, ask after this and that plant and show great interest in their work before wending her way to the paddock where the horses had just been put out. She would call to one of the grooms and ask to be told their names and then repeat them to her son. Jason and Prince and Holly, Hercules, Oscar, Bandit and Diamond and the baby would listen and look on wide-eyed.

"That 'un would be canny fer the lad when he's growed, your ladyship," John-Henry told her, pointing out a fat brown cob which sidled alongside a magnificent ebony hunter. "He's sturdy an' placid an' just right fer a youngster. Name of Buttons. He were bought for one of the young ladies the day but none of 'em ever took to it."

"Look, darling, the pony's called Buttons. D'you think you'd like to ride him one day?"

The boy studied the horses, and indeed everything about him with great interest, pointing and babbling, showing off his new teeth to the groom in a wide grin.

Everywhere she went her ladyship proudly showed off the baby and didn't seem to mind who picked him up, and it was said in the kitchen, relayed by Tansy, that she had vowed that her son, after his starved beginning when he had known no human contact except for that nurse of his, would from now on share his life with everyone on the estate. It had become a happy house, a house with love in it, though they all shied away from the room at the top of the stairs where the master lay, and it was all thanks to her. She had become a great favourite in the kitchen where she went regularly with the child who was made much of by the maidservants.

"Can I have a turn?" was the constant cry as he was passed from hand to hand, kissed on his rosy cheeks, called "Hinny" or "Kitling", tickled and chucked under the chin by the besotted staff to make him laugh, for they were enchanted with his slow, baby chuckle and vied with one another to coax it out of him. All the while her ladyship stood and watched, even sat down at the kitchen table to sip a cup of tea, which was a bit informal for Mrs Armitage's liking and she made sure none of them sat down with her, which she could see they would have liked to do, and her ladyship would have made no objection, for it was her nature to be good-hearted. She would eat several of Cook's almond shortcakes and declare them to be delicious so that Cook preened just as though the good Queen up in London had declared a fondness for her baking. When she had drunk her tea and eaten her shortcake she would drift off with the bairn chuckling in her arms and they would sigh with pleasure before getting on with their chores, for she made a small moment of joy in their dull, hardworking day. She showed very little interest in the domestic side of the house, leaving it all to Mrs Armitage, Mrs Fowkes who was the cook, and Mr Holmes the butler, though to be honest Mr Holmes was often to wonder what to do with himself now that there was little or no entertaining at Newton Law. Mind you, now that their father was confined to his room his three daughters had taken up what were described as "good works", showing an interest in Church affairs, visiting the old and sick on their father's estate, and more and more frequently had small tea parties for the minister and the ladies they had become involved with. There were fêtes and bazaars in aid of the needy to be organised at the small church in Allenbury where they were now regular churchgoers, and their lives had been transformed. Holmes did his duty in supervising the serving of tea to their guests but it was nothing like the days when Sir Robert had entertained, being genteel and decorous. Still it was something, Mr Holmes was heard to say to Mrs Armitage.

The servants talked among themselves about this, especially after the wives of their master's friends had been to call on their mistress, for surely this would be the start of the dinner parties, the dances, the sporting parties that Sir Robert had favoured. Not that his daughters had ever moved in their social circle but perhaps now, with a bit of encouragement from her ladyship and the end of the derision they had suffered with their father, they might find themselves a husband apiece.

When it was discovered that her ladyship was to have another child they understood, of course. No lady went about much in society when she was with child and so they settled down and awaited the winter. They didn't know what to make of the coming of the new baby at first. Of course it was grand to think of another infant in the house, company for Master Robby, but none of them, the women at least, could forget that awful night when the master had fallen down the stairs and what, presumably, had gone on before between him and her ladyship. He had dragged her into their bedroom and for a while though they could hear his voice shouting and cursing, there had been no sound from her. Well, whatever had gone on, he had got her pregnant again and could you deny she wasn't happy now with that bairn? She whizzed that baby carriage round and round the oval beds filled with glossy-leaved rhododendrons and hardy juniper bushes, with yellow-leaved euphorbia and red-berried rowan, her skirts dipping, her hair swinging out like a silken curtain of amber in the sunshine, the baby squealing with delight and you couldn't help but smile, could you? They were sometimes alarmed that she went about on her own, except for the bairn, wondering why she didn't take that there Nanny with her, or her own maid, but it seemed that Nanny was to be used only when absolutely necessary and that Lady Blenkinsopp meant to bring up her own child, for now at any rate. Their mistress did not reveal the true reason, even to herself.

Sometimes she disappeared into the stretch of woodland that surrounded the house, dragging the baby carriage through the falling leaves, brushing against the dying bracken along the narrow paths, and the man who daily watched over her, ready to go to her rescue should she get into difficulty, felt the leap of gladness in his heart at the sight of her, wondering why this particular woman, of all the women he had known, should bring this stirring to his blood. There was no answer, or if there was he had not yet found it.

It was always the dog who alerted her to his presence. Dick would gallop up to the perambulator, head on and ready to spring into it if he was allowed and the baby would hang dangerously out and reach for him, screaming with delight.

"Dick," the gamekeeper called, making believe that he just happened to be in this bit of woodland. "Stop making such a damn nuisance of yourself. Lie down, sir, lie down at once."

The dog, busy with licking the baby's hand to their mutual delight, ignored him.

Amy leaned on the handle of the baby carriage, smiling wryly.

"You don't seem to be making much progress with Dick, Duffy. I see he's just as daft and disobedient as ever."

"That's my fault, I'm afraid, m'lady. I'm not as firm with him as I should be. When an animal is your . . . main companion you're inclined to be indulgent. He's a great soft wight and a great lover of human beings." He bent to put an affectionate hand on the animal's head to hide what was in his eyes. It always took a moment or two after they had met for him to get himself in hand.

"I can see that. He certainly seems to make a great deal of Robby, as Robby does of him. It's just a shame he's so big."

Duffy looked thoughtful for a moment then, turning courteously in the direction in which she had been walking, indicated with his hand that they should continue.

It was October and the light beneath the trees had changed with the coming of autumn. It was a fine day, the sun low, and even as they walked a shower of leaves drifted slowly down upon their heads and all about them the hornbeams and beeches had begun to close down for the winter. Falling with the leaves were the beech mast and the three-lobed hornbeam fruit.

Though fine, it was cold and Amy and her son were warmly wrapped. She wore a honey-coloured woollen gown, simple and suitable for morning wear, beneath her rich chocolate-coloured cloak of serviceable wool. The cloak was lined with a fur the colour of barley and had a hood which was flung back and over it hung her glorious hair. She had stout boots of sensible brown on her feet. Her son, swathed in soft rugs, was wrapped about in a woollen outfit which consisted of long leggings with feet in them and a little coat. On his brown curls was perched a bright red bonnet from beneath which his vivid grey eyes peeped and his bright cheeks glowed. On his hands were knitted mittens of the same colour, both sent up from the kitchen as a "bit of a present for the little mite". When Amy had run downstairs to thank them nobody would own up as to who had made them. They were from them all, Cook said somewhat tearfully, and if her ladyship had no objection was it all right if they made some more little garments. They all loved the little lad and were glad to give him something after what . . . well . . . Cook had blown her nose and turned away before she said too much.

"I'll walk with you, if I may," Duffy said now. "I'm checking the nests. I'm supposed to set traps to snare the weasels and foxes and indeed all the predators that are after Sir Robert's game, but since his accident and the fact that none is being shot the birds have proliferated and . . . well, perhaps I shouldn't say it but it seems to me the wildlife . . ."

"Deserve a good feed?" She looked up into his face and grinned infectiously and he grinned back.

"M'lady, I'd get fired if I was to say such a thing. It's my job to rear Sir Robert's game so that he and the other gentlemen can enjoy a day's shooting and if old Mr Fox bags it first, well, this year it doesn't seem to matter. One way or the other they will perish but this year not by the gun."

"No, and from what the doctor says, not next year either. He has confirmed that my husband is not likely to walk again, Duffy."

"I'm sorry to hear that, m'lady." His face was expressionless.

They were walking through a narrow stretch of woodland which had become choked along its path with the vegetation that grew beneath the trees. The floor of the woodland where it was shaded from the sun was covered with earth-carpeting mosses, many of which grew over fallen logs and the cut stumps of trees. The high rainfall and upland mists kept the ground moist and fungi grew, toadstools at this time of the year bringing attractive shapes and colour to the woodland floor.

"Look, there's some Slippery Jack," he said, pointing to the ground round the trunk of a conifer. "It's edible, but that one isn't. It's called the Sickener and is poisonous."

"You must teach Robby, Duffy. I dare say a day will come when he plays up here without me and he must learn all there is to know about such things. About berries and toadstools."

"Don't worry, m'lady. I'll take him out and teach him country ways."

Why should it make her feel comforted? she thought. What was it about this man that made her feel safe, protected? There was no danger to her out here or indeed anywhere now that Robert was fast in his bed and yet this man's strong but gentle presence gave her a feeling of security. She seemed to see him almost every day and indeed had found herself looking out for him. While he was around she had nothing to fear, for herself or her son, she told herself, though why that thought should come into her head was a mystery. She was among her own people who were, she thought, fond of her, as she was of them. There were gardeners and groundsmen about the place, all within calling distance and yet the presence of this quiet man in this quiet woodland gave her a sense of peace and safety.

There was wood sorrel and sweet violet beneath their feet, almost hidden beneath the soggy carpet of fallen leaves, and in the trees squirrels flitted along the branches as they searched busily for winter food for storage. She breathed deeply of the fragrant earth smell, drawing it into her lungs, unaware of the lift and thrust of her breasts as she did so, or of the gamekeeper's reaction to the movement.

Before she knew what he was up to Duffy had reached forward and lifted the child from his baby carriage, swinging him up against his shoulder, striding out ahead of her.

"Look, Robby, can you see them? Squirrels. They're looking for nuts." It took the startled baby a moment or two to spot the little creatures but when he did he was enthralled, turning to his mother to point a plump finger.

"Yes, sweetheart, are they not wonderful?" She paused to stand beside the tall, lean figure of the man, peering up into the trees, her lovely thoat arched and white against the dark trunks.

Duffy looked hastily away. "And there, see, there are two finches," he continued harshly but the child was not quick enough to see them. He resumed walking, the child still in his arms and Amy struggled on behind with the carriage which was far easier to push without her son in it. Duffy went on talking to the boy, then, as though it were part of their conversation, without turning in her direction said, "That thing is far too heavy for you to push along this path and you'll have to turn back when you get to the stream."

If she was surprised to be spoken to so curtly by her husband's gamekeeper she did not show it.

"Yes, I know."

"It might be as well if you remained on the paths in the garden, unless you will allow me to help you."

She was astounded. "But your work . . . ?"

"I have little enough to do now that Sir Robert is . . . incapacitated. It would be no trouble. I know you're fond of the wood and when the boy is walking he will enjoy it."

"He is only ten months old, Duffy."

"I know, but he is an active child and, I apologise if I take liberties, m'lady, but . . ."

"I should be glad of a little help, Duffy, but how will you know when . . ."

"I'm often around and . . . if I'm not here to help will you promise to bring the child's nursemaid to push the carriage?"

It was his way of saying that he knew of her condition and for some reason she could not fathom, though it had not concerned her to be looked at by the other male servants, it did now. She didn't know why, for Duffy was not a man to stare. In fact he barely looked at her. The dog trotted at his side now that the greetings were over and he strode ahead, carefully marking the path where she should go. When they reached the stream he easily lifted the carriage, with Robby in it and placed it on the further side, then leaned back to give her his hand to help her over. She wore no gloves and neither did he. His hand was warm, brown, slender, long-fingered, hard on the palms and she remembered a saying that her own father, a keen horseman, had been fond of quoting. "Horseman's hands," he would say, of a man who spent his days in the saddle and because of it had developed strong hands and thighs, a keen eye for hazards, a graceful balance and a straight but fluid back. Duffy had all of these and yet he was a gamekeeper, which was a job that a working-class man, a common man, was employed in.

Without thinking she said, "Where do you come from, Duffy?" For along with his gentlemanly manners, his easy carriage, his air of pride, was his way of speaking which was definitely not of Northumberland. And it was definitely not that of a working man. He was educated, his choice of words told her that.

"Cheshire, m'lady." His voice was brusque, inviting no further questions. He had picked Robby out of the perambulator again, probably to make it lighter for her to push, she supposed, and was still walking ahead of her.

"Would you like to go some way up on to the moorland, m'lady?" he asked her, stopping for a moment. "You could leave the carriage here while I'll carry the lad. It's not too far and there's a fine view from Weeping Stones. You can see right down to the valley bottom and the river flowing through it and then up to the woods on the far side. It's not too steep and it's well worth the climb."

"Weeping Stones? How did that get its name?"

"They say that the ghost of a weeping girl who lost her lover in some war, no one seems to know which one, haunts the place." He smiled wryly. "Not that I've heard or seen her myself and I go up there quite often."

"Do you, Duffy?" She watched the softness that came suddenly to his face.

"Yes, it's . . . it's a favourite place of mine. Peaceful, isolated."

She had no idea why Duffy should need peace or isolation but, lifting her skirts, which were not really made for tramping the moor in, she followed his straight back, putting her feet where he did and noticing as they climbed the firm muscles in his calf and the lean line of his buttocks which were clearly defined in his tight breeches. She was amazed and ashamed, as though she had been caught assessing the shape of him which, if she was honest, was very pleasing. Hastily she dragged her eyes away and kept them fixed firmly on the heel of his boots. He carried the child with ease, the dog running ahead and nosing the tussocky grass on either side of the rough sheep track, turning now and again to check that his master was close behind him. He himself turned frequently to check on her.

Clouds had come down as they progressed higher up the moor, though there were still racing gaps of sunshine. The clouds were low, the colour of the underbelly of the sheep which were everywhere, dove grey lined with silver, skimmed with a shimmering white and backed in patches by shades of blue. The wind sang in her ears and lifted her hair in a flag about her head and she felt the exhilaration and the sheer joy of being alive fill her from her tingling toes, warm inside her boots, to the whipping exuberance of her hair.

She was gasping for breath when they reached Weeping Stones and he turned solicitously and took her arm, leading her, laughing and puffing, to a nest of grey pitted boulders where he sat her down. Those at the back of her kept the wind at bay and those at the sides were low enough to look over down into the Coquetdale Valley. The baby was placed on the grass where he began to investigate a clump of pink thrift that grew there, jabbering softly to himself as his clumsy fingers attempted to pick the head off one of the stalks.

They sat shoulder to shoulder, saying nothing at first while she got her breath back, at ease with one another as though they were not mistress and servant but old friends who, because of the length of their friendship, had no need to talk. They gazed out at the superb view that was spread like a counterpane beneath them, the greens and greys and bronzes merging with the brilliant slashes of the browning bracken and the blue of scudding shadows. He pointed out the small hill-farms, all of them on her husband's estate, which dotted the landscape. Thin wisps of smoke drifted from chimneys, then were snatched away in the wind and, so small they were no more than dots, men could be seen working minuscule patches of fields. Life was hard in the upper dales and surrounding hills but it bred a rugged independence and a curious gentleness in the hill-farmers, he told her, and one day, when the boy was older, he would take her to meet them and their families. They were her people as much as the house servants were her people and were curious about her. They had all known old Lady Blenkinsopp, for her husband had been a kind and fair landlord and her ladyship had felt herself responsible for the families who worked her husband's land.

He pointed out what were called "cleughs" and "riggs" in these parts but which she would call valleys and ridges. In the old days herdsmen used to bring their cattle up here to the high pastures to graze, he said, and there were still stone-built sheds dotted about, most in a state of disrepair, where they themselves had sheltered. He'd done it himself, he told her, when he had been caught in a storm.

The boy began to crawl about until he met the warm flanks of the dog who panted at his master's feet, whereupon he leaned against him and fell into the swift and almost death-like sleep of the small child. The dog put out his long tongue and licked his face gently then sighed and fell asleep himself.

They smiled at one another, like parents who are convinced their child can only be the most gifted in the world.

Again there was silence until she spoke, saying the words as though the conversation had never been interrupted.

"I've never been to Cheshire."

He looked at her, startled, she thought, and she had time to notice again the cat-like grey of his eyes, the deep sable of the pupils and the incredible length of his thick brown lashes.

"I beg your pardon?"

"You said you came from Cheshire. Won't you tell me about it? It's fairly obvious you come from – excuse me – but from what is known as a *good* family and yet you are working in a job which is . . . is . . ."

"Usually reserved for the lower classes?"

"Yes, I suppose so. But please, don't tell me if you'd rather not. I don't mean to pry. What you are and where you come from is your own business though I'm surprised my husband employed you. It would make him suspicious."

"I work for next to nothing, m'lady, that's why."

"Aah, that would do it."

"Yes." They smiled in unison. As though he had said

too much he sprang up suddenly and so did the dog who started to bark and woke the child who, finding himself in a strange place with unfamiliar noises about him, began to wail. At once Duffy picked him up, holding him high under the armpits. He tossed him in the air a time or two and the tears changed to shrieks of delight and the awkward moment was past.

The baby carriage was where they had left it. Robby was tucked under the warm covers and before they had got through the woodland was fast asleep again, his rosy mouth slightly parted on a small bubble.

There was no one about as they stepped out on to the lawn. He had pushed the baby carriage himself, negotiating the dips and hollows and rutted path in order, she knew, to save her the effort, and if either of them thought it odd that the gamekeeper should push the son of his master by the side of his master's wife, they did not comment on it.

"Thank you, Duffy. It was lovely. Perhaps . . . ?"

"Yes, m'lady." He was tall and she was small and as she looked up into his intent face she could sense the moment was somehow important though she did not know why.

"Perhaps we could do it again before . . ."

"Before?" Though she was certain he knew what she meant. Very soon her pregnancy would keep her closer to the house.

"Soon . . . perhaps we could do it again."

"Of course, m'lady." For a breathless moment he almost put up a hand to cup her cheek, her rosy cheek which was so like her child's, then he turned and with a word to Dick strode across the lawn and disappeared into the woodland on the far side of the wide lawn. She watched him go, unaware that she herself was being watched.

"It's gamekeeper, sir. She's gan off somewhere wi't gamekeeper, like. Bairn's with her in't carriage. Fancy, an' her in't family way."

A sound came from the bed, hoarse and though no words were distinguishable, obscene. The man at the window turned and grimaced as though to show his own surprise at her ladyship's behaviour, for by now he and his master had somehow found a way to communicate with one another and it seemed he knew just what he meant. It was him who had told Sir Robert that his wife was pregnant again. Though it had stunned his master at first, Platt could see he was triumphant when he finally assimilated the news, for if no one else knew what he had done to his wife on the night she returned, he did, and it had perked him up no end to realise that he had got her with child because of it. At the same time it maddened him because he knew it would be the last time he would do so. Still, he had plans, plans that kept him alive as he lay stinking in his bed.

He mumbled something else and Platt ambled over to the bed, for sometimes he needed to see his master's lips to recognise what he was trying to say.

"She's gan inter't house, sir, wi't bairn. What? Well, I'll do me best," as Sir Robert grunted something, lifting both his hands now to emphasise his point with some nasty gesture which Platt seemed to recognise. "D'yer mean now, wi't bairn?"

Sir Robert nodded emphatically, twisting his loose wet lips into what he thought was a smile.

"I thought yer didn't want 'er ter know yer could speak, like." Although it was doubtful anyone but himself would call what Sir Robert did "speaking".

Again Sir Robert mouthed something and with a resigned shrug Platt was about to leave the room when his master violently beckoned him back.

"What now?" he said, somewhat impatiently, but one menacing look from the man in the bed shut him up, for even in the state he lay in Sir Robert was a frightening figure.

Sir Robert babbled and gestured and dribbled and Platt watched and listened intently.

"Right," he said at last. "Just as yer say, sir. Leave it fer now." And as he turned away and sat down in his customary chair he felt a shiver of disgust run through him, for he wouldn't like to be in her ladyship's shoes when this foul beast got hold of her.

7

It was Mrs Armitage who alerted her, in a most apologetic manner, to the state of the household accounts.

"The tradesmen are beginning to . . . well, they know they will be paid in the end, m'lady, and are prepared to wait for a certain length of time, but without the funds I received each month from Sir Robert I have been unable to settle their bills. I am in charge, you see. I have the books here if you would care to peruse them. In them I write an accurate registry of all sums paid for the expenses of the house and balance them against what Sir Robert gives me. Gave me," she corrected herself. She squared her shoulders as though ready to do battle with her mistress should her mistress doubt her word.

Amy, who was resting on the chaise-longue in front of the fire in her brand-new sitting-room, looked quite horrified and she carefully put her son, who was reaching for the earrings that dangled so tantalisingly from his mother's ears, on the floor, where he at once stood up and tried to climb back into her lap.

She turned to her maid who was – in Mrs Armitage's opinion – *lolling* in a chair pulled up to the fireplace, sewing on something of her ladyship's but looking for all the world as though she considered herself to be an equal of her mistress. Her ladyship was really asking for trouble – in Mrs Armitage's opinion – in allowing a servant to take advantage as she did with Tansy. Why, she treated the girl as though she were a friend, or at least a paid companion, and no good would come of it in the end. She was too soft, was her ladyship, too tempered, too indulgent – in her opinion – though the other servants thought the world of her.

"Tansy," she said, "be a dear and take Robby up to Nanny Morag, will you, and then go and have a cup of tea or something in the kitchen. Mrs Armitage and I have some serious talking to do. Really, Mrs Armitage, how can you ever forgive me? Please, won't you sit down, oh, and Tansy," turning to her maid who had scooped Robby, protesting loudly, on to her hip, "will you bring a pot of coffee and two cups."

Mrs Armitage was dumbfounded. She had never in her life sat down with the mistress of the house and she had no intention of doing so now. Really, you'd think Lady Blenkinsopp would know the niceties of polite society having been brought up in it. Her own brother was a baronet somewhere in Lancashire and her mother, on being widowed, had married a viscount.

"Please, m'lady, I would be glad if you would look over the account books and then perhaps, at a later date, arrangements can be made for the household allowance to be resumed. I would be relieved to . . . er, settle the outstanding bills. The tradesmen are inclined to be . . . truculent. If you were to speak to Sir Robert . . ." Though how this was to be achieved in view of his condition which, according to the maids who cleaned his room and changed his bed, was little better than an idiot child, she had no idea. That was her ladyship's responsibility. Sometimes she, and Mr Holmes said the same, wondered what they were to do about their positions. There was absolutely no entertaining done and half the servants, especially the footmen who could not be expected to do nothing but clean the knives and shoes, trim the lamps and see to the master's clothes all day long – since he wore none – could really be got rid of. Would the old days ever come back? they asked one another and the sad answer seemed to be no.

"Very well, Mrs Armitage, leave it with me and I'll see what can be done. I really cannot apologise enough. It has been most remiss of me to neglect this aspect of the housekeeping but ... well, what with one thing and another I seem to ... but don't worry, I'll see to it at once."

"Thank you, m'lady." Mrs Armitage, all black bombazine and outrage, moved majestically towards the door, allowing herself a glance at the lovely, firelit room, sniffing as she considered where the money was to come from to pay for it.

They all knew the gamekeeper was different to them, different in the way he talked, in the way he kept himself to himself, showing no inclination to pass the time of day with anyone, male or female. In his polite but firm refusal to eat in the servants hall with the rest of the outdoor staff, saying he preferred to cook for himself in the tiny gamekeeper's cottage he occupied on the bit of land between the kitchen garden and the orchard. Well, let him, Cook had been heard to say.

Any chap who would rather eat the sort of meals a man alone knocks up rather than the good grub she put on the table was welcome to it. Mind you, whatever he fed himself on he looked well on it, if you liked a fellow a bit on the lean side.

It was said that his cottage was full of books and that he spent his spare time reading far into the night, or at least so Dulcie, the chambermaid, reported, for she had seen a light in his window when all the rest of them were asleep. Dulcie had taken a fancy to Duffy the minute she had clapped eyes on him and you had to agree he was an attractive chap, but he'd shown no preference for her even though she was quite a bonny lass herself.

How did she know he was reading? Tilly had wanted to know, for there was a bit of rivalry between herself and Dulcie since she wouldn't have minded a chance to do some sparking with the gamekeeper herself.

"I were passin' his place on me way to me ma's and when I peeped in and saw the bookcases filled with books, in fact books all over the place, I thought ter meself that that was what he must be doin' so late at night. A bit readin'. What else would he be doin'?"

"Haway, man, you were passin' his place on the way ter yer ma's? Yer ma an' da's farm's t'other way."

"Well, I were gannin' fer a bit walk."

Tilly chortled and had it not been for Cook's sharp intervention they might have become seriously involved in a quarrel. Over what? as she said to them, for the man had no interest in either of them so she'd be obliged if Dulcie would get herself up the stairs and change the master's bed.

"Oh, Cook, must I? I hate gannin' in there. It frightens

me ter death," Dulcie wailed, beginning to wring her hands, and the rest of the maids looked sympathetic, for it'd frighten them to death an' all. But though Dulcie was chambermaid, so was Tilly who had been made up when Tansy became her ladyship's personal maid, and the two girls took it in turns to see to Sir Robert's bedroom.

"Well . . ." Cook said hesitantly, for she would have shared their fear of entering that room had she to do it, the room where not only Sir Robert lay, stinking to high heaven from what she'd heard, gibbering and jabbering and frothing at the mouth, but that hulk of a man sat and leered at them.

"Yer feel as if yer'd no clothes on," Tilly had cried, "the way he looks at yer."

It was enough to put the fear of God in any woman and for the past five months the chambermaids had argued and wept over the task. When their meals were taken up to the two men the maidservant who carried it placed the tray on the floor, knocked on the door and then ran like the dickens for the stairs.

"How about the pair of you gan in together?" she said at last. "That's if Mrs Armitage agrees," for the housekeeper was in charge of the servants and decided what their duties should be. And so it was. Tilly and Dulcie were vastly relieved, though it was still the low point of the day when they entered Sir Robert's room to do the fire and dust and polish and see to the bed. Even Mrs Armitage, they had noticed, didn't go in to check on their work, so unless her ladyship complained they decided the quicker they got up there and out again, no matter how the work was skimped, it wouldn't matter.

Her ladyship now went in to see the master once a week, or at least she went into his room, presumably to make sure that he was being properly looked after, but only for a minute or two and Dulcie, who had been there on one occasion, reported that she hadn't spoken one word to him, nor even looked in his direction and could you blame her. With her in the family way! Everyone knew how a dreadful sight could mark an unborn child for life. They'd heard of appalling birthmarks and other deformities being inflicted on innocent babies, and anyway that man up there was paid to look after him. Sir Robert was hardly capable of holding a conversation with his wife, or indeed with anyone, so Cameron, the brawny Scottish footman, had told them when it was his turn to sit with Sir Robert on the minder's days off.

The discussion about the gamekeeper's books and his predilection for reading them far into the night was further interrupted by a knock at the back door, and when it was opened who should be standing on the doorstep but the man himself.

At once Dulcie and Tilly, who were just about to take their chambermaids' work boxes up to the master's bedroom, collecting clean bed linen on the way from the linen cupboard, stopped in their tracks and began to simper and pat their hair, twitching their aprons and fiddling with their caps. He might not yet have taken any interest in either of them but that didn't mean they had to give up trying, did it?

"Good morning," he said in that lovely voice he had, in that way of speaking he had which was a mark of the gentry and which made him so different to any of them.

"Good morning," Cook answered. It was Mrs Armitage's day off and she and Mr Holmes had gone off together, which was somewhat surprising, but then who were they, their underlings, to question them. "What can we do for you, Duffy?" she asked him, falling under the influence of his slow and easy smile.

"May I step inside, Cook?" he asked her pleasantly. He smiled down at his feet as he lifted first one and then the other. "My boots are clean."

"I can see that, lad. Come in, do. P'raps you'd like a cup of tea. There's one just made." While the women looked over their shoulders at him and smiled the two footmen and Nipper, the boot-boy, the only three males in the room, wondered what all the fuss was about.

"Thank you, Cook, but no. I just wanted a word with her ladyship. Would one of the maids run up and ask her if it's convenient?"

They turned as one and their mouths fell open in astonishment. The outdoor staff didn't have anything to do with their mistress unless it was outside when she stopped and spoke to them should *she* want to! She might send messages through the indoor staff, and they might do the same. Perhaps asking if she wanted a particular horse saddled, or her carriage brought round to the front door, or the gig harnessed the day but they did not ask to see *her*.

"Well, I'm not sure if her ladyship's . . ."

He smiled winningly but there was also something in his manner, something all the landed classes, the gentry, those in a privileged position in life possessed, though why it should seem so in his case was a mystery to her. An air of command that seemed to speak to her who was of the servant class, and before she knew what she was doing she had waved her hand at Morna and told her to scoot upstairs and see if her ladyship could see her husband's game-keeper.

"Thank you, Cook," he said courteously, bending his head in her direction so that she felt quite flustered. "Only I have something for the boy that I want her to see."

At once the awkwardness was dissipated with his words. They all drifted towards him but he waved them back, laughing in a way they had never seen before. He was usually so grave, so quiet, now he seemed almost merry.

"No, ladies, let the little master see first and then I'm sure you'll—"

He was interrupted by a breathless Morna who said that her ladyship had given permission for Duffy to go up at once. She was in the room that adjoined her bedroom and which she had made into a pleasant sitting-room. A door had been knocked through from her bedroom and it had been redecorated throughout in those lovely pastel colours she favoured of peach, cream and the palest green. There were flowers everywhere and Master Robby's toys all over the floor, bowls of pot-pourri which she made herself, lovely pictures on the wall and at night candles galore. It was a treat to go in there.

Morna took him up the wide staircase and past the closed door behind which Sir Robert lay, scurrying in the way that had become a habit with the maidservants. That man who looked after him had been known to open the door suddenly as they were passing, laughing in that nasty way of his when they almost jumped out of their skins.

She knocked on the door, then when a voice within called to come in, flung it open and declared dramatically, as though she were announcing the Lord Mayor of London, "Duffy, the gamekeeper, m'lady." She stood for a moment in the doorway, waiting for something that could be reported back to the kitchen but her ladyship just nodded at her and told her that would be all. Unless Duffy would like refreshments of some sort?

Refreshments! Refreshments for the gamekeeper of all people, just as though he were a gentleman come to call and yet was that not what he was, or what he seemed to be, a gentleman? He certainly wasn't one of *them*, that was for sure, but even so, to offer him refreshments! Wait until she told them in the kitchen.

"No, m'lady, thank you," he told her quietly, standing just inside the doorway and Morna was forced to close the door.

"Come in, Duffy, and sit down," her ladyship told him in that gracious way she had, smiling as though she were genuinely pleased to see him. She was dressed in some loose garment, the sort of thing women wear when they are alone, or with their husbands, he supposed, in a shade that reminded him of apple blossom. It seemed to foam like apple blossom too and for a moment he was lost for words. Her hair had been tied back carelessly with a ribbon which matched the gown and her feet were bare. He couldn't speak. He knew he looked a fool but he couldn't help it. She was so glorious. Despite being fastened back her hair had a tendency to drift into long curling strands, falling about her neck and ears. Her skin was as though it had been polished, warm as clotted cream and from the folds of her gown wafted a fragrance that he could not identify.

He managed to clear his throat enough to speak, though he thought it sounded more like a frog's croak than his own voice. He hadn't been as awkward as this with a woman since his first encounter with an obliging dairy-maid when he was fifteen. Then he had squeaked and fumbled, a boy trying to be a man, and now he felt exactly the same. No, he didn't! Then he had been excited, his young man's body eager to get to grips with her rounded female curves, but this was nothing like that.

He loved this woman and what he felt for her was nothing like that. It was a dull day and a lamp had been lit on a table beside her. The glow put pin-points of light in her great blue-grey eyes and threw the shadows of her long, fine lashes, so like those of a child, on to her cheeks. Her soft, coral mouth was parted and he wanted to lean forward and put his own against it, tenderly, sweetly and with all the love he had for her.

He pushed his hand through his thick, tumbled hair and turned away from her while he did his best to get his confounded senses under control, staring blindly at a little picture on the wall, a sketch really, of a bird in flight, no more than an impression of wings against drifting clouds, but lovely, and unusual. He swung round to face her and did his best to smile.

"What is it, Duffy?" she said. Her eyebrows rose delicately as she asked the question and he watched them, and her soft mouth as she spoke, wondering what the hell he was doing here and how he could leave without making a damn fool of himself.

"What is it?" she asked again. Her voice was low and sounded somewhat tremulous, though he didn't know why. She seemed, unlike him, to be in perfect command of herself, a lady of quality interviewing one of her husband's servants, but even so there was something strange in the way she looked at him.

"M'lady," he managed to get out at last, "I was hoping Master Robby might be here. I have something for him, with your permission, of course."

"For Robby?" She leaned forward and her eyes turned to a depthless, smoky blue. Her loose gown fell open at the neck, just a fraction, but it revealed the rich cream of the top of her breasts and for an awful, wonderful moment he couldn't drag his gaze away. She was pregnant, he knew that, and the thought that it was the beast whose door they had passed on their way here who had made her that way turned his stomach and brought a bitter bile to his mouth. He fought to tear his mind away from the picture, doing his best to smile convincingly and he must have succeeded, for she smiled back, her cheeks as pink as a child's with excitement.

"What is it?" she whispered. In his mesmerised state he was not aware that she was studying him with the same intensity, that she was contemplating the dark grey of his eyes and watching as he blinked, a long, slow, drooping of his thick lashes. About his eyes were faint lines, a small fanning-out from the corners, pale in the sun-darkened skin of his face. He wore a short, gamekeeper's cape with many pockets, and a pair of pale-buff riding breeches which were not the sort usually worn by a man in his position. They fitted smoothly to his lean hips and neat buttocks and strong, muscled thighs, tucked into knee-high, well-polished brown boots. Round his amber-tinted throat was tied a silk scarf and she wondered idly where the breeches and the scarf had come from.

He did his best to maintain a friendly, casual manner although even that was not correct, since a servant is not friendly, nor casual with the woman who is married to the man who employs him.

"This," he said and with the air of a magician withdrew from the pockets of his capacious cape two snuffling bundles of wheaten-coloured fur. They were tiny and for a moment she did not recognise them for what they were, thinking he had perhaps rescued a couple of wild animal pups, perhaps fox cubs, though the colour was not that of a fox, then they began to yelp and she saw that they were indeed pups, but of the canine variety. He kneeled down and placed them gently on her carpet and at once one of them found Robby's fluffy toy and began to worry it, growling ferociously. The other promptly lifted his leg and made water against her chair leg.

"They're Border terriers. One for the boy and one for . . . for . . ." He paused. "They won't grow very big but they're as brave as lions." He rescued the one that had wet her chair leg and hurriedly wiped the leg with his own clean handkerchief. "They'll need house-training, of course," he added hastily.

She was enchanted. At once she kneeled down on the carpet, no more than two feet from where he did the same, her lovely gown spread out about her as she reached for one of the pups, then the other, cradling them to her breast, kissing their faces, squealing as their rough, black tongues found her cheeks. Their bright eyes and black noses, their worrying, sharp little teeth, their frantic wriggling delighted her and she began to laugh.

"Duffy, Duffy, they're adorable. Wherever did you get them? Oh, they're the sweetest things I have ever seen and Robby will adore them. See, ring that bell, will you? It connects directly with the nursery and Morag will bring Robby down. Oh Lord . . . please rescue me, Duffy, before they have me flat on my back."

He leaned forward and deftly lifted the pups from where they had perched beneath her chin, laughing with her now, all tension gone from between them in the shared pleasure of the moment. And when Robby was brought down and Morag was dismissed, since it was obvious she thought the whole thing quite mad, the three of them remained on the floor while the boy crawled after first one inquisitive animal then the other. Bedlam reigned and for several minutes he thought the boy was going to have hysterics but eventually order was regained.

"Hold them gently, Robby," he told him. "No, son, not like that or you'll strangle the poor thing. See, watch what I do," and before long, worn out with the excitement, the boy and the puppies fell asleep in a companionable heap in front of the fire.

They were quiet then, Duffy and Amy, sitting one on either side of the fire, dreaming into the coals, contemplating the boy and the puppies, smiling at one another occasionally, but when Duffy stirred and began to show signs that he must be off about his duties, for he was, after all, no more than a servant, Amy put up a hand to detain him.

"Yes, m'lady?" he questioned, leaning forward solicitously and for a moment she felt a tremor of annoyance go through her. She did wish he would not call her by her title. It did not seem right somehow and yet she knew it was the only way he could address her. He was her only friend in this house. Oh, the servants were kind and Tansy was always ready for "a bit chat", as she put it, but she was not educated, she had not been brought up in Amy Blenkinsopp's world and would not understand its complexities. There was a mystery concerning this man. He was so obviously of the same class as herself and how lovely it would be to have someone to turn to, to talk to, to discuss this problem which Miss Armitage had presented her with. It had come at her like a bolt from the blue, which was ridiculous really, for surely any woman with a grain of sense would realise that a house this size and with so many servants would need a great deal of money for its upkeep. The trouble was, she had no idea how to solve it. Well, she knew she had to seek legal advice, she had said as much to Robert months ago, but how to go about it and . . .

He touched her hand and she felt a great desire to put hers in his.

"M'lady?" he enquired gently.

"It's . . . about money, Duffy."

"Money?" He seemed surprised, for surely there was no shortage of that in this house.

"Yes, Mrs Armitage has been up to see me and tells me that none of the household bills has been paid and the tradesmen are becoming awkward. And who can blame them? Apparently my husband gave her an allowance, a household allowance, but since his illness naturally it has stopped."

"You must see Sir Robert's solicitor, m'lady, and at once. Ask him to call and let him see the condition Sir Robert is in. Get Doctor Parsons in on it. He'll be able to explain to the solicitor the long-term condition of your husband, show him that he is no longer capable of dealing with the expenses of this house. You must ask for . . . well, I'm not sure what it is called, having no experience of the law but it will give you the power to draw on Sir Robert's estate. I'm sure it will be quite simple, m'lady, for no one can expect you to run the house without money. The servants will need paying," failing to tell her that he himself had not been paid for five months.

"Yes, I see that but I have no idea who Sir Robert's solicitor might be."

"Ask Holmes. Butlers always know everything that is going on in a house. Sir Robert's solicitor, or even bank manager, will have called and Holmes will know his name."

Her face cleared and she let out a great sigh, lying back on her chaise-longue and for the first time he noticed the bulge of her belly. It was more pronounced than he had expected it to be. It was November and he judged her to be five months along. Though he loved her and she was carrying another man's child, got on her by the savagery of rape, he found he was not repelled by her fecund body. He wanted nothing more in this world than to look after her, to take on any of the worries she might have, guard her, protect her from the terrors of the world, but he had no right, now, or ever. The gulf between them was unbridgeable and this enchantment must be torn away, for it was trapping him, making him helpless. She was another man's wife, for Christ's sake, carrying his child and he had no right to be here, let alone advising her on how to gain control of her husband's fortune, but she was so lovely . . .

Of its own volition his hand rose, reaching out to tuck a wayward tendril of silver behind her ear and he saw her eyes widen but she did not draw back.

' "Of course, that's the answer," she said somewhat vaguely, her eyes great pools of wonder, then she seemed to pull herself together, as he did, almost giving herself a shake.

"Will you . . . be there when the solicitor comes? I'll feel better with someone . . . I know."

"M'lady," he answered gently. "You know I cannot. How would it look if Lady Blenkinsopp had her husband's gamekeeper involved in such a delicate matter? You know it's not because I don't wish to help you but you must think of . . . of how it would look."

"Of course, I'm being silly . . ." Her head dropped for a moment and again he was struck by her defence-lessness. And yet, despite her fragility, her air of vulnerability, he knew she was a strong woman. She must be to have survived as she had if the tales of humiliation and degradation she had suffered were true.

Then she lifted her head proudly, for she came, not just from a long line of the privileged classes but from the strong stock of her mother's family who had, long ago, been colliers, though her mother, the viscountess, would sooner forget it.

"You're right, Duffy. Thank you, and thank you for the puppies. It was . . . kind of you to remember him."

He bowed his head then lifted it to look into her eyes.

"It was nothing, m'lady, but . . ."

"Yes, Duffy?"

"If ever I can do you . . . and yours a kindness you must promise to . . ."

"I will, Duffy."

A pledge had been made and acknowledged, though neither quite knew what it was.

8

Mr Sinclair, the solicitor, and Mr Bewick, the bank manager, were appalled and distressed, not only by the mumbling wreck on the bed whom they scarcely recognised as their old friend and business associate, Sir Robert Blenkinsopp, but for the lovely woman who was his wife. They had heard, as who had not, of Sir Robert's unfortunate accident but had no idea that it had been so serious. Like Edward Pearson and the others before them they shuffled round the bed, trying not to stare and yet they had to *look* at him, hadn't they? Both were men of property and position, leading figures in their own sphere but the man on the bed had not only wealth but a title to go with it and must be accorded the respect he was due, no matter what his circumstances might be at the moment.

"Sir Robert," Mr Sinclair, who was a stout, well-dressed and obviously affluent solicitor with a thriving business in Allenbury, managed to utter, "I cannot tell you how sorry I am to find you in this state but I'm sure the good doctor here" – nodding in Doctor Parsons' direction – "will soon have you right again. Is that not so, Doctor?"

Doctor Parsons looked grim and said nothing. He

had positioned himself at the head of the bed, just next to the pillow on which Sir Robert's head tossed and turned and where he could see every occupant of the room, including Lady Blenkinsopp who was looking plumper than he had expected. She had returned in June and by his reckoning her child was due at the beginning of March, an easy enough date to arrive at since, from what had been told him, she and her husband had had conjugal relations on that one night only. Still she was already quite cumbersome, probably looking that way in contrast to her normal slenderness. He was not awfully sure he liked her to be the witness of such a gross object as her husband, nor subjected to the atmosphere of the sickroom which was none too fresh, since women in her condition were known to be susceptible to such things. He must have a word with that man of Sir Robert's and instruct him to open the window more often. It might be a cold, damp November day but a bit of fresh air would not go amiss.

The gentlemen evidently agreed with him and one of them had actually taken his handkerchief from his pocket and was holding it to his nose, pretending as he did so to be giving it a thorough blow!

Mr Bewick, the owner of the bank where Sir Robert's sizeable account was deposited, cleared his throat and plunged in to do his bit. Although Sir Robert's friend and gaming companion Mr Thomas Henry was also a banker, it was Sir Robert's habit to let as few people as possible know what he was worth and despite being aware that Thomas resented this he did his business with Mr Bewick's bank in Alnwick.

"We are here to do what we can to facilitate the

releasing of funds to your wife," Mr Bewick began, his voice unctuous. He pulled at the tight collar of his immaculate shirt, for the air in the room seemed to be strangling him and it was perhaps this that compelled the gentlemen to conduct their business at what seemed to the good doctor to be breakneck speed. And after all they were here only to confirm that Sir Robert was not, at this moment, capable of managing his own financial affairs. "Lady Blenkinsopp needs to be able to pay her bills, after all, Sir Robert," he went on, attempting levity, though God knew there was nothing to laugh at in this room.

Sir Robert made some hoarse sound in the back of his throat, guttural and phlegmy, and both men stepped back hastily as saliva sprayed them. Lady Blenkinsopp, who was heavy with child – to this monster, they presumed distastefully – was seen to turn to the window which she opened a crack. The enormous hulk of a man who stood at Sir Robert's bedside showed his rotting teeth in what might have been a smile.

Mr Bewick continued. "Until you are able to conduct your own affairs, Sir Robert, it seems there is no alternative but to pass to her ladyship the necessary monies to run your estate."

Again Sir Robert gargled something. It sounded as though he were strangling. His face had turned from the pallor of illness that comes from being confined indoors to a vivid puce and both men turned to the doctor in alarm, for it seemed to them he was about to have another apoplectic stroke of the sort that had brought him to this state in the first place. His eyes were red with madness, roaming about in their deep sockets, enraged as a bull which is tormented by a plague of wasps but it was not at them his rage was directed, or so it seemed to them, but at the woman who stood quietly by the window. You could see the astonishment in both their faces as they turned to look at her, for it was not her fault that the man was where he was, or was it something else that they knew nothing about? Of course, no man likes to hand over the reins to a woman, even if that woman was his wife and carrying his child but it seemed to them he had no choice. They would, naturally, keep a very strict eye on Lady Blenkinsopp's finances but she was after all a gentlewoman and must have the means to live like one.

The doctor stepped forward and, taking Sir Robert's flaccid hand in his, felt his pulse, glancing at the minder who seemed to know what was required of him. He crossed the room, took a small phial from the dresser and placed a few drops of its contents in a tumbler to which he added water from the jug.

Though it was very evident that Sir Robert was not at all happy about it, the liquid was poured down his throat and slowly he became calm.

"There, old fellow, there, you'll feel better now," the doctor told him kindly, then turned, shrugged, and gave the two gentlemen a knowing look. "Will there be anything else, gentlemen?" he asked them, his manner suggesting that surely they had seen enough.

"Well . . . no, I don't think so," Mr Bewick answered, for what else was there? They could not question their client on whether he wished to hand over to his wife the custody of what was a very large fortune and the doctor had told them that though he thought his patient understood a little of what was said to him, he certainly could make no reasoned decision.

They bowed their heads sorrowfully over the bed, telling their client that they were sure he would be up and about again in no time at all, at which remark Doctor Parsons was heard to snort, and thankfully backed out of the room.

Amy, who had been sipping tiny, shallow breaths the whole time she had been in Robert's room let it out on a shuddering sigh, doing her best to dissipate the smell, and even the taste, of that foul room and the foul man in it, from her soul. That was where it lodged whenever she went in there, in the very centre of her being, and it took her a long time to rid herself of it. Sometimes she was forced to get out into the open air, taking Robby with her, breathing deeply of the smell of the bark on the old sweet chestnut, the pungent layers of the fallen leaves, the scent of the crab-apple and sloe in the hedge at the back of the coach house and listen to the sweet song of the thrush which trilled its heart out in the depth of the wood.

At the beginning of his illness she had gone to his room almost every day and she was ashamed now to think that she had gone there for one reason only and that was to gloat. To get revenge for the cruelty she had known at his hands. He had taken her son from her and without thought for the boy's welfare had placed him with a cold-hearted woman who, if left with him much longer, would have seriously stunted his emotional growth. She had loathed him for his treatment of herself but she would never forgive him for what he had done to his own son in the first few months of his life. She had wanted to let him see how content she now was and how sweet and sunny-natured – *soft* he would have called it – his boy had turned out and how the pair of them were better off without him. He had terrorised her and would have done the same with Robby – look at his daughters – if he had not had the stroke and tumbled down the stairs, and she thanked whoever it was up there who watched over her and Robby, every day of her new life.

She had enjoyed that feeling for many weeks until she realised that she was not only punishing her husband, who deserved it, with her visits but herself who did not. And she had begun to suspect that her visits, the stimulation of hating her and doing his best to answer her back, were doing him good. That he enjoyed it and so, apart from checking that he was being well looked after by the man the doctor had put in charge of him, she no longer visited the room where her husband rotted. That was what he was doing, rotting away and she did not wish to be a spectator.

Now she led the three gentlemen along the wide hallway and into her sitting-room which was bright and cheerful with fire-glow. There was a small table set out with tea things and Morna stood by it ready to pass the cups and plates to the visitors.

For a quarter of an hour they chatted of this and that while they sipped their tea. The two business gentlemen did their best not to look at her too much, though of course Doctor Parsons was well used to the sight of a woman in the last months of pregnancy. But she was such a lovely woman, her soft blue-grey eyes the exact colour of a wood pigeon's feathers, her gaze serene and untroubled. They could see that she was well versed in the way to entertain gentlemen of her own class, keeping the topic of conversation light and of nothing much in particular. She had been brought up as a lady in her mama's home and had all the accomplishments her mama had insisted upon. She could play the piano and sang a little. She could paint and sew on a fine piece of embroidery and she knew the gentlemen thought her charming, which is what she wanted them to think. She hoped they also thought her capable of managing Robert's finances.

Doctor Parsons, who had other patients waiting for him, put his cup and saucer down with a businesslike air and, relieved, so did the other two gentlemen.

"Now then, gentlemen, you have seen my patient and must have formed an opinion on his state of mind. I am not saying, since medical science does not really know, that he will be incapable of deciding his own affairs in the future with regard to his capital, to his investments, which I'm sure will be in good hands, to this estate, and to his income from them all. I have no idea what . . . assets Sir Robert has, and it is not my intention to ask but all I *can* say is that at the moment he cannot tell us what his wishes are, nor do I believe he ever will. He is a prisoner in his own body. He cannot move. His thoughts are inside his head but he cannot convey them to us. He has this house, his wife, a child . . . er, children, and many servants to support and with no way of conveying to us how he wishes to treat them, someone must, and that person can only be his wife, since she is the only one to know what is needed."

"We are talking about a lot of money, Doctor Parsons. A great deal of money," Mr Bewick said, which, put in a light-minded woman's hands might be frittered away on foolish extravagances, though he did not voice this last.

"And if Sir Robert should recover and find . . ."

"That I have spent all his money on French gowns and sable wraps, how would it look if you had given me the power to do so? Is that what you imply, Mr Sinclair?"

"Please, your ladyship." Mr Sinclair, who had meant exactly that, was quite mortified.

"Mr Sinclair, I do not want to get my hands on my husband's money, as you seem to think, so that I might live a high old life such as many of the landed classes do . . ." including my husband, but, like Mr Bewick, she didn't say it, though that's what she meant. "I have a son, Mr Bewick, and another child to come. Would you see them starve?"

Neither gentleman could bring himself to look at her, though the image of her delicate loveliness was painted vividly on their minds. She was dressed in a loose-fitting gown the colour of pale honey, a soft wool edged at the neck and wrists with a fall of cream lace. Her hair had been brushed back until it gleamed in the firelight, fastened on the nape of her neck in a coil tied with a knot of honey-coloured satin. She had on satin slippers in the same shade. Her skin had a rich hue like clotted cream, the sort that was made in Devonshire from where Mr Bewick came and which he remembered from his childhood. How such a beautiful creature could have managed to . . . to . . . mate with the brute who lay upstairs like a felled log, totally helpless, totally disgusting was uppermost in both their minds. The thought of it made them shudder, though they were of an era and class which was not unduly sensitive about such things. Many women, young and lovely women, married men old enough to be their fathers or even grandfathers and it was not thought to be out of the ordinary. A gentleman had often his way to make in the world before he thought of marriage and unless he took as his bride a young, *breeding* woman he might be denied the son that gentlemen needed. Sir Robert had such a son and another child on the way and that was as it should be, but to be struck down just when he had available to him this beautiful young woman must be driving him to the edge of madness. If he was not already there which it had seemed to them he was!

But the doctor was right. This estate needed a steady flow of cash to keep it in the condition in which it should be kept and the upkeep of the house was not inconsiderable. There were servants to be paid and of course Lady Blenkinsopp, being who she was, must have a decent dress allowance. Soon, one supposed, she would be entertaining again and must have the wherewithal to offer the hospitality a lady in her position would be expected to provide and, of course, there would be schooling to be planned for her children. A hundred and one things which must be considered in a legal fashion, so that she might have the means to carry out her duties as the wife of a baronet. And in the unlikely possibility of Sir Robert recovering, which the doctor seemed to think improbable, it must also be made clear that he would then take over from his wife.

They both glanced about the lovely room and in their expressions could be seen the same thought:

that someone with taste and discernment had done something to it and who could it be but her ladyship. Her choice was quietly elegant, soft, mellow, charming, just like herself. Pastel hues on the walls and in the carpet and curtains and yet there were a child's toys about as though the son of Sir Robert and Lady Blenkinsopp had played here recently. Mr Bewick had smilingly removed a rather battered soft rabbit, knitted and stuffed by kind-heated Cook, from the seat in which he had been about to sit, handing it to her ladyship. There were even two small puppies entwined in a basket, both in the sleep that comes to young animals, both human and canine.

"Your son's, I presume," he had said, nodding at the puppies, the moment softening even further the attitude of the two gentlemen who normally would not dream of including a mother and her child in the same breath as business.

"I do hope you will not think me extravagant if I tell you that I have already had some alterations, decorations done to the house," she murmured softly. "I had no idea that . . . that I might be making it awkward for . . . well, that there might be some doubt as to my right to spend my husband's money. I would not, naturally, have done so if I had for a moment thought . . ."

Both gentlemen reared up in their seats, exclaiming as one that she must not trouble herself about such things. She had only to send the bills to them, indeed any future bills she might incur in the upkeep of the house or the estate and they would attend to them between them. With Doctor Parsons' personal guarantee that Sir Robert was not himself, they would both be in a position to see that she had no need to worry about money.

"In fact, I think it might be wise for a document to be executed allowing your ladyship to draw on the account at the bank," Mr Bewick added, smiling benevolently as though it were his own money her ladyship was to be allowed to draw on. "I shall always be glad to see you there, m'lady, whenever you are in town and I'm sure Mr Sinclair will say the same."

Mr Sinclair bowed over her hand, praying she would not stand up and reveal that awkward bulge. Amy, smiling to herself, remained seated as the gentlemen were shown out. It would not do to upset further their already shocked susceptibilities.

Robby was just beginning to walk, falling over and picking himself up at every other step, wandering from one marvel to another in the bleak winter garden, the puppies not helping since they would insist on jumping up at him and when he was down, jumping all over him. His baby carriage was rarely used these days, as there was always someone to pick him up and carry him for her ladyship, a gardener, a groom, for they were all taken up with the little chap.

"Oh, m'lady, d'you think you should?" Nanny Morag had said anxiously when her mistress flung open the nursery door already wrapped up in her fur-lined cloak, stout boots on her feet, and stated her intention of taking her son for a walk. "Won't ye bide indoors on such a day? The lad'll be plodgin' in all the puddles, the wee rattle scawp. It's only just stopped teemin' down wi' rain the day. Why aye, it's not fit to be out in."

"Nanny, it's not raining now and both Robby and

myself have been fastened in all day and need a breath of fresh air in our lungs, don't we, my darling? You'd love to come for a walk with Mama, wouldn't you?" She scooped her son up into her arms, raining small kisses on his rosy cheeks until he squealed with delight while Nanny Morag hovered at her side, ready to beseech her mistress not to lift the lad, not in her condition.

"And I'm sure Nanny will be glad to see the back of Briar and Brackan," which were the names given to the wee devils – Morag's description – who had come to plague the life out of her, "so get him ready, Nanny, will you."

"I'm sure it's comin' on to rain again, your ladyship," Nanny protested but the mistress was having none of it, so with great exhortations to keep her little dear "well lapped up" the nurse handed him over to his mother, watching for them as they staggered from the side door and began to make their way across the sodden lawn. Sure enough, the lad "plodged" in every puddle he came to and not only that but her ladyship did the same, the pair of them screaming with laughter. The lad tried to climb on to one of the stone benches which stood against the shrubbery, then fell off and her ladyship ran to pick him up, *ran*, mind you, like a nimble girl of sixteen, looking not much older, neither, but you had to smile, she said later to Dulcie, when she came to bring up a scuttle of coal for the nursery fire, you couldn't help it. Them puppies were a scream, at least when they were out of her road, she said, splashing in the puddles with the boy, tumbling him down, all four of them larking about and going wild with it just like bairns let out of school and her ladyship was the worst of the lot!

He was where she had hoped he would be, just inside the wood. He had Dick on his leash so that the animal wouldn't bound out and begin to leap over them all, child, woman, puppies in the intensity of the excitement though it was very hard, for Briar and Bracken were still at that trying stage and Dick wasn't much better.

"Oh, let him off now, Duffy," she called out to him. "They've got to get used to each other."

"It's the boy, m'lady. He'll have him flat on his back and keep him pinned there until he's been given a good wash."

"He won't mind, will you, darling." And for a few minutes the man and the woman stood leaning against a tree trunk, their shoulders not quite touching, watching the animals and the boy, their faces smiling indulgently until at last everything settled down and they turned and began to walk through the woodland towards the edge where the moorland began. It was a favourite walk now though the pull up towards Weeping Stones was really getting too much for her. Duffy always picked up the boy and put him on his shoulders, Robby clutching Duffy's dark hair in a tenacious grip. Though nothing was said, for by some unspoken agreement her coming child was never mentioned, as she grew bigger he had begun to take her arm, almost lifting her from her feet as they climbed upwards.

The animals and the child frisked round them as the man and the woman settled themselves in the customary place on the flat rock, their backs leaning on a jutting boulder, looking down into the valley below, breathing in the tangy moorland air. Duffy

was, as usual, hatless and a sliver of sunshine put a
copper tinge in the dark thickness of his hair which,
after Robby's handling, stood out about his head.
She smiled and, without thinking, her hand rose and
touched it, smoothing it down just as she might have
done had it been her son. He did not move, nor even
blink at her touch, nor even acknowledge it but kept
his eyes steadfastly on the view below him as though
the incident had not happened and for a confused
moment she wanted to . . . to ask him if she had
given offence. He was her husband's gamekeeper.
She was her husband's wife and was carrying a child
and might he not be . . . be repelled by the fact? Some
men would, she knew, but then he turned and his eyes
were untroubled and she knew it was all right.

They smiled at one another and turned back to look
at the panorama before them, both of them sighing
at some pleasure that was in them but which they
couldn't name, nor even tried to. As she had several
weeks ago she wondered why she had thought the
landscape bleak, forbidding, even menacing, for it
was quite superb, a vast unfolding of dreaming hills
stretching out for as far as the eye could see in every
colour nature could provide. When she had first seen
it she had been living in a state of terror, degraded
by what her brutal husband did to her nightly and
this had coloured every aspect of her life so that her
eyes were blind and her ears deaf to this calm beauty
about her. Now, with this kind man beside her and her
child safe and well she saw it with fresh eyes and was
at peace with it.

The silence was comfortable though it was not really
quiet, for the boy was squealing and the puppies

yipping their excitement while the big dog chivvied them from here to there and back again until he was satisfied that they were all safe.

"He's appointed himself nursemaid," Duffy said wryly. Then, "Look" – he pointed to where a shape hung in the sky as if on a string, its wings beating rapidly – "see that bird up there? It's a kestrel. It'll be hunting mice or voles."

They watched it together, their hands shading their eyes, then settled back against the boulder. Again there was a gentle silence but for the haunting cry of a curlew higher up the moor in the dying heather and the challenging call of the grouse.

"I saw the gentlemen call this morning," he said formally. "I hope everything has been arranged to your ladyship's satisfaction and that the advice I gave you—"

"Duffy, I really cannot bear the way you speak to me."

Astonished, he turned to her, on his face an expression of appalled concern, for the last thing in the world he wanted to do was to hurt this already wounded woman.

"Dear God, if I have said anything to offend you, or if you think I am speaking out of turn . . . stepping out of my place . . ."

"Your place! What the devil *is* your place, Duffy? Certainly not just that of . . . I don't know what I would do if—" She stopped abruptly and bent her head, and her hair, which had come loose in the rough and tumble with her child, hid her face from him.

"Please, m'lady, won't you . . ."

"Do you know, Duffy, there is not one person in

my world who calls me by my name and I miss it. I want *someone* to say it occasionally." Her voice was so soft he had to bend his head to hear her. "You speak of knowing your place as though you were a servant and yet you know you are more than that."

"I *am* a servant, m'lady. Your husband pays my wages."

"Not for the last five months he hasn't. None of the servants has been paid . . . but that's not what I'm saying. I can no more think of you as an employee of my husband than I can think of . . . my husband as my husband. He is a man who has shown me nothing but cruelty and you are a man who has shown me nothing but kindness. I like to think we . . . are friends so won't you please call me by my name."

She lifted her head and tucked her hair behind her ear, her gaze clear and steady and he felt himself tremble with the longing to pull her into his arms and tell her that she would always be safe with him, safe, protected, loved. That she had nothing to fear . . .

"Say my name, Duffy," she commanded him and he began to laugh.

"You speak to me of friendship and yet you order me like a servant. 'Say my name, Duffy,' with all the imperious hauteur of Lady Blenkinsopp."

"Please, don't tease me. Just promise you will call me by my name when we are alone."

"Very well, then, Amy." His tone was infinitely tender, and she felt her heart lift and even smile!

"Yes," she said, "and I would like to call you by your given name, if I may?"

She was startled when he sat back and stared out

over the valley, his face not cold, far from it, but sad, pensive and for the moment closed up.

"What is it? Have I said something?"

"No, but I would rather keep my name . . . apart from my life here."

"You don't trust me?"

"Dear God, it's not that." Again he was appalled, leaning forward to look into her face, his own filled with dismay.

"Then . . . ?"

"Please, m'lady . . ."

"Amy."

His face softened. "Amy."

"I won't press you since you must have some reason for keeping your identity secret but . . . we are friends."

"Friends." He grinned and held out his hand and she put hers in it, then, releasing it with a certain reluctance, he leaped to his feet and began to collect the animals and the child, lifting the laughing boy up on to his shoulders. Gently he helped Amy to her feet, then, checking that the little expedition was all in order, began to lead them down the track towards the house.

9

It was mid-December, a cold, dismal day, ready to teem down with rain, as Tansy reported, for she'd had it from Cook who'd had it from Mr Weston who was seldom wrong about such things. He had a nose for the weather, had Joshua Weston, especially in these parts, for hadn't he lived here all his life, in fact had never travelled any further than five miles from the cottage in which he was born. The clouds hung down so low they touched the rooftops and the rolling hills of the moorland were totally obliterated. Even though it wasn't yet raining drops of moisture fell from the naked branches of the trees and the woodland floor was so clogged with the dense carpet of summer's leaves it was ankle-deep and difficult to walk in, at least in her condition.

It had been so for several days now and Amy restlessly fretted from room to room, from window to window as though searching for a break in the weather and determined to make the most of it the minute the slightest beam of sunlight broke through. If it had not been for the servants she would probably have ventured out on her own; even just a short walk across the lawn would have been welcome but there was such an outcry from Tansy, from Nanny Morag, and from Duffy when she had last seen him at the beginning of the week that she had let herself be overruled. They didn't say it, naturally, for it was not their place to comment on their mistress's enormously ballooning belly but they were worried just the same about her shortage of breath, her swollen ankles and fingers, her excessive bulk and her increasing weariness, which, they said to one another, was really only to be expected but not *quite* so early in her pregnancy. She no longer darted about in the wake of her son but lumbered far behind him and the puppies so that Nanny Morag, when she did manage to get out, insisted on going with her, arguing with her which took a bit of courage, for her ladyship had changed since she had first crept over the threshold in the wake of her new husband more than eighteen months ago and was now inclined to be haughty if denied her way.

Amy sighed and with a great effort heaved herself to her feet, her hand to her distended belly where the child kicked and wriggled so that the front of her skirt was lively with movement. She calculated in her head the weeks to the birth of the child, for she knew exactly when it had been conceived, wishing it was all over and the baby safely delivered. Not long now by her reckoning but in the meantime, at this, the lowest point in the year's calendar, it was hard to accept that she must stay indoors. She wandered to the window, looking out at the deserted, desolate garden, wondering what the outside servants did with themselves on a day like this and, as if on cue, Mr Weston and his deputy Mr Purvis stomped round the corner of the house, a square of sacking draped across their shoulders against the weather and each with a pair of pruning shears in his hands. She was beginning to learn something about the care of the garden, for she often stopped to speak to one or other of the gardeners, or even the gardening lads, to ask what was going on. The men were gratified by her interest and had carefully explained it all to her. At this time of the year the pruning, digging, pointing and top dressing of the shrubberies took place which was what Mr Weston and Mr Purvis were about. Following them with a wheelbarrow came Henry and Herbie, two of Mr Weston's lads, larking about a bit without Mr Weston's fierce eye on them, chasing one another with the wheelbarrow. Last month she had watched with great interest the planting of tulip bulbs in the cleared beds and already the crowns were coming through the soil. If there was a heavy frost they would have to be covered with a light matting to protect them. It was good to see them, to see the promise of the spring to come when, with her two children, she would be free again.

But in the meanwhile she must find something to occupy her. The trouble was that she had no one to whom she could talk. No one who was knowledgeable about what was going on in the world beyond the confines of the estate and who could discuss it with her. She read *The Times* which was still brought over from Allenbury, since it had been ordered by Robert and no one had thought to cancel it. The concern about the war that had broken out between the northern and southern states of America was reported, though not a great deal seemed to be happening at the moment other than that a Federal ship had boarded the British steamer *Trent* and forcibly taken two rebel commissioners – as those who fought for the south were called – and their secretaries into their custory. Her Majesty's government was furious about it, demanding restitution, and there seemed to be a possibility that war might break out between Britain and America unless the commissioners were given up. Duffy would have known what it was all about but unless she went out into the grounds there was no chance that she could talk to him about it, and who else was there?

Returning to her chair by the fire she picked up a scrap of embroidery but had taken no more than two stitches when she threw it vigorously to the opposite chair. She had been brought up by her mother to sit all day sewing on a scrap of something or other, waiting for callers and she had done so docilely, for she had been a different woman then, believing her mother knew what was best for her and obeying her wishes implicitly. She had not even been a woman but an innocent child who had had her world shattered obscenely by the man her mother had given her to in marriage. The girl who had once placidly done what was expected of her had died on her wedding night and the foolish scrap of embroidery with which women of her class were expected to fill their days exasperated her, but she must find something to occupy her if she was not to run mad. She had already been up to the nursery with the intention of having a romp with Robby but she had been met by Nanny Morag with her finger to her lips as she indicated that the boy was fast in rosy, rumpled sleep in his cot. Even the two puppies, who were growing fast, were twitching on the hearth-rug in a sleep to match Robby's.

"Bring them all down when Robby wakes, Nanny," she whispered. "I'm bored out of my mind with being forced to stay indoors. I've half a mind to wrap myself up and take myself off for a walk. Oh, not far, I promise, and not out of sight of the house," as the nursemaid started to protest. "Oh, very well, I'll stay indoors for now but the minute the weather lifts I'm off so don't try and stop me."

"No, m'lady," Nanny said politely, though a glance out of the window at the rain which had begun to lash down told her that her ladyship had not much chance of a walk today.

Amy wandered back down the stairs, then, on an impulse, went down the next flight into the wide hallway. There was a grand fire crackling in the hearth putting rosy dancing spirals on the walls and ceiling. The walnut longcase clock at the foot of the stairs struck the hour and Clara, who was busy attacking the semicircular table which stood to the right of the fireplace against the wall, gave it an exasperated look. She renewed her endeavour, her arm going backwards and forwards with her duster as she polished, her behind keeping the same rhythm. At the sound of her mistress at her back she swung round and sketched a curtsey, her face rosy with her efforts.

"Good morning, Clara, but what a dreadful day."

"Mornin', yer ladyship, it is an' all."

"I'm looking for something to do," her ladyship murmured as she trailed up the hall towards the kitchen door carrying her huge belly before her and Clara watched her, wishing she could say the same. When she'd finished the polishing there were the inside windows to do, the grates polished along with the fenders and the fire-irons and even though her mistress seldom sat downstairs, the fires in the drawing-room and the breakfast-room to see to. She and Cissie had done the beds and taken the plate to Cameron, the footman, for a good going over with the knives which needed sharpening, but though there were only four adult members of the family in residence, since they did not count Sir Robert who was in a world apart from them, she was always found something to do.

As Amy pushed open the kitchen door and entered the heart of the house, which was always warm and welcoming, she was reminded that the servants, along with the rest of the country, were plunged into the deepest gloom over the sudden death of the Prince Consort, husband to their dear Queen. Almost of their own accord, for she had not insisted on it, they all wore black except for their caps and aprons, even the footman when he discarded his jacket in the butler's pantry, where he was busy with the plate, wearing a black armband.

They did not notice her enter the room and she stood for a moment just inside the door watching the furious activity which always seemed to take place under the stern guidance of Mrs Fowkes, the cook. They were preparing lunch for herself and Sir Robert's daughters who, she presumed, were ensconced in the drawing-room with their sewing, or whatever it was they found to do all day. Now and again they dutifully visited their father but, as this seemed to upset not only them but him, they kept the visits to the minimum. They sometimes climbed the stairs to the nursery to admire their little half-brother and exclaim on how he had grown but they were confirmed spinsters with no interest in children except those they helped in their charity work. They were not unkind, just uninterested.

Cook, brisk and buxom, was vigorously stirring something in a large bowl which she held to her hip, at the same time walking round the table overseeing the activities of her handmaidens. Tansy, whose duties as her ladyship's maid did not keep her fully occupied since, when her ladyship was dressed and ready for the day, she went nowhere, had been put to mixing up a batch of scones, under Cook's supervision, of course, since Cook did not believe in idle hands. Tilly who often helped out in the kitchen was chopping something on a board, Elspeth was loading a tray with cutlery preparatory to taking it into the dining-room to set the table for lunch, and Ruth, her face bright red with the heat and her exertions, was at the open oven door basting a succulent piece of sizzling pork. The other maids, those not occupied in various parts of the house, were busy at some task Cook had set them. The scullery-maid, whose name Amy thought was Phyllis, was on her knees with a bucket and scrubbing brush. The only one doing nothing was the kitchen tabby which was curled in its own tail on the mat before the fire. The tabby belonged to Cook and was a pampered member of the household.

"Phyllis man, ye're in me road so will ye be quick an' finish that dratted floor before I fall over ye an' break me neck an' then where will we be, tell me that?"

"I dinna know, Cook," Phyllis answered. "'Tis this fat. It'd set hard on't floor an's a devil ter get off."

"Well be quick about it, man."

It always amused Amy the way these hardworking, mainly good-natured northeners adressed one another as "man" whether they were speaking to a male or a female!

"Yes, Cook."

They all continued to swirl about the table, busy with their respective chores, the only one to notice her ladyship at the door the little skivvy whose head could just be seen in its enormous mob cap above the edge of the window to the scullery. Her mouth fell open. She looked in a haunted sort of way at Cook as though afraid that something might be asked of *her* who was the only one aware of her ladyship's presence, then turned to stare again in horror at her mistress. Her mouth worked as though she were trying to say something but no sound came from it and if it had would not have been heard above the racket of the kitchen. Her ballooning cap completely covered her hair and had it not been for her ears would have fallen down to her chin. She gave it a push upwards with a wet and reddened hand then stepped down hesitantly from what Amy presumed was a box and sidled out into the mêlée to stand beside Cook, twitching at her skirt to get her attention. Cook stopped stirring and stared down at her in surprise. The girl had on a black dress which had obviously been cut down to fit her.

"What's up wi ye?" she said sternly, for skivvies, or indeed any servant in her domain, never left their post without her express permission.

The child lifted a stick-like arm and pointed at her mistress.

The servants had been subjected recently to another shock, one that affected them personally even more than the death of Prince Albert, when Mrs Armitage, the housekeeper, and Mr Holmes, the butler, gave notice to terminate their employment. There wasn't enough for them to do, they explained to Lady Blenkinsopp, both of them studiously avoiding looking at her ladyship's bulging stomach which was another reason they were leaving they admitted to one another. Things had never been the same since Sir Robert's accident. They missed the entertaining, the importance of their respective jobs, the bustle of callers, and if Sir Robert was a harsh employer it had not affected them in their elevated positions. They were of the old school and the way in which their mistress flaunted herself, which was how they saw it, in front of the servants, was not what they were used to. Ladies, when they reached a certain stage in their pregnancy, retired to their private rooms and stayed there until they were delivered, but the way her ladyship carried on it would not surprise them to hear she had given birth in the vegetable patch. Cavorting about with that child of hers who had got seriously out of hand since she had returned, and those dratted dogs which were for ever under somebody's feet and it was time, they agreed, to move on. They had been in Sir Robert's employ for many years but they had found good jobs, for they were highly skilled in their profession so if her ladyship was agreeable they would leave at the end of the month. That had been in November.

Amy had summoned Mrs Fowkes to her sitting-room.

"You have no doubt heard that Mrs Armitage and Mr Holmes are to leave us, Cook?" she began.

Cook said she had, her expression conveying that she didn't know whether to be glad or sorry. The pair of them had been strict and the house had been well run, but how would they fare under another housekeeper? Not that it would affect her, for she was a good cook, she knew that; she had been trained in a great house near the border between Northumberland and Scotland where her mistress, who was married to a member of the peerage, did a great deal of entertaining and was very demanding. She had started as a child of ten, scrubbing and scouring pans until her hands were red raw but she had worked her way up the chain until she became kitchen-maid to the chef himself who had taught her all she knew. She was happy here at Newton Law, for the lecherous ways of her master had never affected her. Mrs Armitage had made sure as best she could that Sir Robert had never interfered with the female servants and, knowing he had a treasure, not only in Mrs Armitage but in Annie Fowkes, he had more often than not kept his philandering ways outside his own home. She had been sorry for this lass when she came to Newton Law last year and like the rest of the women in the household had done her best to put out of her mind what was done to her in their master's bedroom. They had watched her wither and almost die and had wished they could do something to alleviate her suffering but they were only servants and wanted to keep their jobs.

Now, here she was, big with child again, the master shut out of sight as though he no longer existed, and what did she want with her? she wondered.

"Cook," her ladyship said hesitantly.

"Yes, m'lady?" Cook shifted on her aching feet and legs, for she had the chronic complaint that was the plague of those who spent all day on their feet, varicose veins. She longed to get back to her kitchen and her own chair beside the kitchen fire, a cup of tea in her hand, her feet up on her own special tuffet, Tibby on her lap, but her ladyship was speaking and when Cook heard what she had to say her face broke out into a gratified . . . well, you could only call it a grin.

". . . so do you think you could manage it, Cook? It would mean that you would be in charge of ordering provisions, paying the bills, in fact all the work that Mrs Armitage was used to doing, besides the cooking. You can read, I take it?" For so many servants today could not. Cook assured her that she could, her ma having sent her to Sunday school for that very purpose. "You would, of course, be given a raise and any new staff you might need you must employ, though when I am in the kitchen there always seems to be a plethora of girls to help you."

Cook was not sure what plethora meant, which was perhaps as well but she assured her ladyship that they, meaning her kitchen servants, would manage perfectly well. There were one or two of them who were shaping up well as cooks and with their continued training under her expert guidance there would be no need to employ more staff. She vowed she was capable of doing all that Mrs Armitage had done, for hadn't she watched her for years, and what with the food that was grown by Mr Weston and the other gardening staff, the milk and eggs and butter that came from what was called the Home Farm a mile or two down the valley, there was barely anything much she would need to order in from Allenbury.

"Then I will leave it all in your capable hands, Cook. I live a quiet life here and will be doing little entertaining, if any. I know the meals will continue as excellent as they have always been so shall we give it a try?"

They had given it a try and for the past fortnight, ever since Mrs Armitage and Mr Holmes – with one of the footmen – had departed, Cook had been in sole charge. The girls and Cameron, the remaining footman, had been somewhat apprehensive at first, for though Cook was known to be fair and good-hearted she was also strict; might it not all go to her head and turn her into a martinet? It was early days yet, but so far they had no complaints and neither did the family, for the meals were just as well cooked and served, and so what was her ladyship doing standing quietly just inside the door to the kitchen? they wondered, staring at her as though she were a being from another world. She had been down before, of course, mostly to bring her son to be petted by the servants but she was alone this time.

They all stopped what they were doing, on their faces an apprehensive expression, then her ladyship had smiled that sweet and gracious smile that was peculiarly hers and they relaxed. Anyway, they hadn't been doing anything they shouldn't, had they?

"M'lady," Cook offered, placing the bowl on the

table and moving forward, pushing the skinny child out of her way impatiently. "Was there something?"

"Oh, no, Cook, I'm just looking for something to occupy my time. You haven't a bit of chopping or kneading or whatever it is you do in the kitchen, have you? I can't get out" – indicating the rain that lashed against the window – "Robby is asleep and to tell the truth I'm going out of my mind with boredom."

She smiled round at the astounded faces. Chopping and kneading indeed! They were all appalled at the idea of this dainty little woman with the jutting belly being asked to do any of the tasks they did. They were preparing lunch, a nice piece of pork with fresh sprouts just fetched up from the garden and which the skivvy had been peeling, roast potatoes, apple sauce and Cook's incomparable gravy which she made with the juices from the meat. A plain meal followed by a mouthwatering apple pie and fresh whipped cream all come from Newton Law's bounteous orchards and farm.

"Eeh, gan on, m'lady," Cook said, so shocked she fell back on the north-eastern way of speaking, even if it was to her mistress she addressed it. "Yer canna do that, the day. See, sit yersen down an' Tilly'll fetch yer a cup of tea," waving an imperious hand at Tilly who left her chopping and rushed forward to reach down a cup from the dresser. When Cook frowned, for her ladyship could not be expected to drink from the sturdy stoneware cups the servants used, Tilly ran hurriedly to the stillroom where the "good stuff" was kept, bringing forth a bone china cup and saucer, a sugar bowl, a milk jug and a dainty little lace mat to put them on.

The trouble was, when her ladyship began to sip the tea, gazing around her with great interest, they none of them quite knew what to do. Should they ignore her, which seemed impertinent, and get on with their work, or should they stand politely by waiting for her to speak, which meant the lunch was not getting made?

"Please, do get on with whatever you were doing, Cook. I shall just sit here for a minute or two and then . . ." Her voice trailed away, for she had no idea what she would do next. She could hardly walk she was so bulky, and yesterday, when she had had the bright idea of taking Robby out in the gig, John-Henry had been quite rude in his determination to stop her. He had succeeded as well. She knew they were all watching out for her with the best intentions, concerned that she and the child were safe, but really, how was she to pass the time until the child was born? She was not allowed to walk, to drive the gig, to pick up her son and if this went on for much longer she would run mad.

The skivvy who had first seen her come in was still standing, her mouth agape, in the spot where Cook in her impatience had pushed her. Her red-raw hands, which made Amy wince to look at, hung down at the end of her scrawny arms, plucking at the sacking apron she wore. Her cap sat on the bridge of her turned-up nose but on either side of that nose two soft brown eyes, large and framed by sooty black lashes, watched her with bright intelligence. For a moment Cook was occupied and did not notice she was still there.

Amy smiled and beckoned the child to step forward. There was, despite her comical appearance, something appealing about her. Her nose was as red as the coals in the fire, and as Amy watched she wiped it on the back of her hand but she remained frozen to the spot where Cook had shoved her. Amy beckoned again.

"Come here," she said softly, but not softly enough for Cook to miss it and in a minute she turned on the girl and gave her a box on the ears which nearly had her off her feet.

"Ye sackless fool," she said tartly. "What d'ye think ye're doin', hangin' about like a line o' washin'? Get back to ye'r work unless ye want another bray."

Tears welled up in the girl's eyes and she held her fist to her ear. She turned and was about to run back to her hidey-hole when the imperious hand of the woman she knew was her mistress stopped them all in mid-stride.

"Mrs Fowkes, please, she is only a child. She was doing no harm, was she?"

Only hanging about where she shouldn't, Cook wanted to reply, ready to give the skivvy another "bray" about the ear but her ladyship only smiled at the girl and indicated that she was to come forward. The girl, with an imploring look at Cook as though to say it was not her fault, shuffled forward and stood before her mistress. She held her head up and bravely looked her in the face.

"What's your name?" Amy asked, her eyes soft and smiling.

The girl looked mystified.

"She doesn't understand, m'lady," Cook sniffed

disapprovingly, ready to be miffed, but then her manner softened, for wasn't her ladyship the kindest and most considerate of mistresses. Her problem was that she had nothing to occupy herself with until the bairn was born. The weather was bad and her ladyship so ungainly she couldn't even get about, so she supposed they would have to humour her though betimes it took all a body's patience.

"Why not? Is she a foreigner?"

"Oh no, m'lady. See . . ." turning to the girl. "What do they call ye? Tell her ladyship."

The girl was frightened but she bravely spoke up. "Rosy Little."

"Rosy Little, m'lady." Cook gave her a nudge which again nearly had her off her feet. "Go on, say it."

"Rosy Little, lady."

Cook sighed deeply. "Why aye, I don't know what they teach them in those places, m'lady, really I don't."

"What places are those, Cook?"

"Workhouse, m'lady. She came last week, her an' a lad. Lad's in the stables an' . . . well, Mrs Armitage wouldn't have had them, neither of 'em, but I allus feel sorry for't little beggars so I took them on. She'll be a grand little worker when I've finished with her."

"She doesn't look strong enough, Cook. Look at those arms." They all looked at those arms, even Rosy herself.

"Nay, when she's got a bit decent grub in her she'll start putting on weight. Her an't lad."

"Jumsie." Rosy smiled for the first time and a tiny spot of colour lit her cheeks.

"Jumsie?"

"Why aye, lady, him an' me's marras."

"Marras?"

"It means friends in these parts, m'lady," Cook explained patiently, her eyes wandering to the clock on the wall, for they'd never get lunch ready at this rate.

"I see, well, Cook, I'd like you to send Rosy up to me after lunch, if you please. I think I might have a job for her. And do remove that ridiculous cap before she comes."

10

The doctor had been shown out by the deferential maidservant and from the window of the bedroom where his master lay, Platt watched him climb into his gig and drive himself away down the curving drive. Doctor Parsons had just examined not only Sir Robert with whom he seemed satisfied, but also Lady Blenkinsopp, though whether he was satisfied with her Platt didn't know, nor care, if he was honest. The doctor had been with her ladyship for over half an hour, presumably taking tea as was his custom.

"Mumble mumble bloody mumble mumble gone?" the man in the bed said and Platt turned away from the window, dropping the curtain into place.

"Aye, bletherin' old bugger. We're well shot of 'im, an' all." He moved ponderously towards the bed, his enormous bulk, which had once been solid bone and muscle, hanging with loose flesh. Like his master, the inactive life he led and the good food he ate had made him put on a great deal of weight and the excess seemed to bounce as he moved.

"Mumble mumble right. Now, mumble mumble up mumble in mumble bloody mumble."

Platt seemed to know exactly what Sir Robert wanted

of him. The greater part of his speech consisted of quite unintelligible mutterings and splutterings and at first Platt had been forced to work hard to understand him, guessing at his meaning which had driven Sir Robert to the brink of raving violence. They never held a conversation, as such, but Sir Robert's system of mutterings, punctuated here and there by a few loud words, was quite adequate for the business of giving an order or asking a question. And Sir Robert had a lot of those, listening intently to what Platt had to say. There was not much that Sir Robert did not know of what went on in the house.

"Right, sir." He leaned over the bed and with scarcely any effort lifted the substantial figure of his master from a supine position until he was propped up, half a dozen pillows at his back.

"Howay man," he said cheerfully, for by now he and Sir Robert had formed a good if slightly uneasy relationship and his master allowed him many small privileges of speech as long as he didn't overstep the mark. If Sir Robert considered he had done so he could fly into a rage so maniacal Platt became dumb and cowed with terror despite Sir Robert being helplessly confined to his bed. He was able to perform several small services for his master which were a secret between them and he was well paid for them with the small but valuable ornaments and knick-knacks which, at Sir Robert's instigation, he took from the downstairs rooms and sold in Newcastle. On his last day off he had picked up some slut from the tavern in the next village, bringing her back to Newton Law and smuggling her into the house by a side window. She had been confused with the drink he had pressed on

her or, low as she was, she would not have performed
the tricks he and the master had forced her to in the
master's bedroom but both he and Sir Robert had
enjoyed it enormously. He was not so sure about the
lass who had been no more than thirteen or fourteen,
for Sir Robert had got a bit rough with her, held down
as she was by Platt but she had been well paid and
sent on her way over the moor back to wherever
she came from. Sir Robert had given what had taken
place a name, not that he could pronounce it, or even
remember it, but it was French for a "threesome" his
master had told him. Aye, a unique experience, since
Platt was used to feeding his lusts privately with just
himself and a woman present but it had forged a
strange bond between him and his master, and on
his next day off he had promised to fetch back another
lass and renew the pleasure.

"Will it be't newspaper then, Sir Robert?" he asked
amiably, and when his master nodded he slipped
silently down the stairs, for despite his bulk he could
be very light on his feet, yesterday's *Times* under his
arm. Peeping into the master's study where Lady
Blenkinsopp usually read the newspaper and, finding
it deserted, ready to dart back should one of the maids
be there, he picked up today's copy. It was slightly
crumpled so he knew her ladyship had done with
it and had left it for the parlourmaid to dispose of.
He had been performing this service for his master
for many weeks now, returning the old newspaper
to the study and, if it was obvious that her ladyship
had read it, taking the more recent copy upstairs and
none of them in the household the wiser.

There was a girl just going up the stairs as he peered

out from the study, a girl with a slight figure but with what Platt decided was a canny bum. Her head was bouncing with shining brown curls beneath her frilled cap and when she turned at the half landing he caught a glimpse of her young face. She was a bonny lass. He knew most of the maidservants by now but this one was new. His master would like to hear about this, he was sure.

The girl disappeared and, giving her a minute or two, enjoying himself enormously, for he loved these games he and the master played, he followed her quietly up the stairs and let himself into Sir Robert's bedroom.

"Theer's a new lass. Looks like she might be upstairs staff. A right pawky looker an' all. Nice little bum on 'er. About fourteen, I reckon."

Sir Robert raised his eyebrows which meant in their language to tell him more.

"I don't know owt else but I'll find summat."

Sir Robert gave what passed for a smile and slowly lifted his hand for the newspaper. Platt sat down beside the bed, holding the newspaper open and slightly up so that his master could read it, turning the pages when Sir Robert nodded.

Suddenly his master became agitated.

"Mumble mumble door mumble daft gowk."

"Jesus, I forgot." Leaping to his feet, Platt raced round the bed and locked the door. It was not likely that any of the servants would burst in unannounced, indeed the women crept hesitantly over the threshold as though there were a live tiger roaming loose inside, but Sir Robert was a stickler about the secretive nature of their relationship. Platt knew he intended something

dreadful for someone in the household and it didn't
need two guesses as to who it would be. One day
he would walk, Platt knew that, for he was the most
determined old bugger Platt had ever come across;
walk, or at least move in some way and he was waiting
with the patience of a spider at the centre of a web
for that day to come, and it would, with Platt's help.
In the meantime if they all believed that the master
was immobile in his bed, which of course he was at
the moment, they slept more easily in theirs! Even the
doctor had no idea of the slow but definite progress
that was taking place in Sir Robert's recovery and Sir
Robert did not mean him to know!

Platt wondered what his master was reading about.
Not that he cared much. Whatever went on in the
world was nothing to do with him so what was the use
of knowing about it. He'd heard the Queen's husband
had died but it didn't affect him so he took no interest.
As long as he was warm and his appetites fed, all of
them, he was perfectly content. No, he'd got a grand
job here and the longer it lasted the better!

To say that those who worked in the kitchen had
been flabbergasted by the elevation of the skivvy to
her present position could hardly convey their feelings
and it was talked about for days. They didn't begrudge
the poor lass her good fortune, for she'd had nothing
in her life but hard knocks and misery, hard work and
scraps to eat – and not much of them by the look of her
– until Cook had brought her and the lad back from the
workhouse. The pair of them had stood just inside the
door of the kitchen, huddled together as if they were
joined at the hip, the lad tall and thin and haunted,

the lass small and thin and haunted, since neither of them had been outside the walls of the workhouse since their respective mothers had given birth and died there. They'd cast furtive glances about them as though afraid if they were caught looking they might be punished, until Cook had beckoned them over to the table and sat them down in front of a plate each of mashed potatoes, cabbage and two thick slices of bacon, followed by baked jam roll and custard and a cup of tea apiece. Those watching were not to know that those plates held more than Rosy Little and Jumsie McGovern had eaten in a week at the workhouse table and though they had been hesitant and fearful they had tucked in and it had been a treat to see a little colour creep into their pallid cheeks.

The next hiccup occurred when they came to be parted. The girl began to cry without making a sound, which was most disconcerting, and the boy put his arm about her heaving shoulders and refused to let go.

"Now stop that sackless noise, the pair of ye," Cook told them sternly, though to be truthful neither of them was making any. "Lad, yer're only goin' across the yard to the stable where one of the grooms'll show you the way of things. Will ye not like workin' wi' horses? Gan on wi' ye. See, Tansy, take him across to John-Henry, and you, lass, away with Phyllis who'll show you how I like things done. 'Skimmering', and that means *clean*. That's the way of it and if I can't see me face in those pans when ye've done ye'll get a skelped lug."

After a day or two they had settled down, especially when they realised that they would see each other at every meal, sitting fastened together by some invisible bond, neither of them speaking except in whispers to one another. But they knew how to work, which they'd learned at the place in which they'd lived all their lives, and that was all that concerned Cook and John-Henry.

And now would you look at her. There had been no need to bath her, for, even had Cook not insisted on it, she herself was remarkably fastidious, but when her hair was rescued from her enormous cap, when it was washed and brushed by Tansy, under her ladyship's direction, it was like a living flame about her small, pointed face. It was the colour of a fox's pelt and just as burnished. It had been cut short at the workhouse but it was thick and curly, standing about her head like a dandelion clock. Her eyebrows were the same colour and her skin like rich cream scattered with golden freckles which, with the deep chestnut brown of her eyes made her appearance quite startling.

On that first day though, none of this was revealed, not even her hair, for Cook could not bring herself to send a servant up to see her mistress without a cap on her head. Amy wondered, as the girl stood shrinking in front of her, what had persuaded her to tell Cook to send her upstairs to see her. Then the girl chanced a glance from under her auburn eyebrows and she remembered what it had been. She had lovely eyes, a deep brown framed by long, thick lashes, but it was not that but the bright intelligence that glowed there. She was young, about thirteen, Amy decided, just the right age for what Amy had in mind for her, so all she had to discover was whether the intelligence in the girl's eyes was reflected in her brain.

"There's no need to be afraid, Rosy," she told her

gently. "I just want to find out if you're up to the job I have in mind for you."

Rosy stared at her, not defiantly, but with an expression on her face that seemed to say she was listening intently lest she miss something. Amy was not to know that Rosy Little and Jumsie McGovern had lived in the workhouse all their lives and had heard only the English spoken in the dialect of Northumberland which pronounced cake as "kyak", name as "nyam" and used the biblical "thee", "thoo", "thy", and "thine". The cultured enunciation of her mistress was difficult for Rosy to understand. She had managed well enough in the kitchen, for though the servants spoke somewhat differently to the way she did it was basically the same.

To her great consternation, before being presented to her mistress she had been put in a dress of grey cotton and over it she wore a plain cotton apron with polished black boots on her feet. In her hand she held a cap, small and frilled, and she was waiting patiently to be told whether she should put it on or not. The young woman who had washed her hair in an incredible room which the maid, Tansy she said her name was, told her was a bathroom, had given her no instructions. The room was all polished and gleaming with what looked like silver, so dazzling it almost hurt the eyes to look at it, but most startling of all, there was a basin with what Tansy called *taps* from which water actually ran. Wait until she told Jumsie about it. He'd never believe it! Just as the other goggle-eyed servants had not believed it when it had recently been installed on the orders of Lady Blenkinsopp!

But it was all so worrying, living among these grand

folks, in which she included even the scullery-maid,
and without Jumsie she would have been totally lost,
but she was eating better than she had ever eaten in
her life and that scratching emptiness that had been
part of her life for as long as she could remember was totally gone, leaving a lovely warm fullness
which she and Jumsie decided was what heaven, of
which they had heard a lot in the workhouse, must
be like.

"How old are you, Rosy?" lady was saying and she
only wished she could tell her, for she had such a
lovely face and the most beautiful eyes and Rosy
would have done anything to please her.

She shook her head helplessly, feeling the tears at
the back of her eyes.

Lady sighed and Rosy's heart sank then lady smiled
and Rosy's heart rose again thankfully.

"What did you do in the place you've come from,
Rosy?" she went on and this Rosy understood.

"Scrubbin', lady."

"Is that all?"

"Why aye."

"So you can't read or write?"

Again Rosy was bewildered. She twisted her hands
together imploringly, for whatever it was she would
love to be able to tell this beautiful lady who was huge
with a bairn that she could do whatever it was, and
would do whatever lady wanted her to do. She had
seen dozens of women like her in the workhouse and
helped at many of their birthings which was something
she *could* do. Anything to do with bairns was right up
Rosy's street.

"Well, never mind, I can always teach you. In fact

I intend to start at once. It will give me something to do in the next weeks and in the job you are to do you will need to read and write. I want someone . . . well, I'm putting the cart before the horse here so I'll say no more."

Rosy didn't understand a word but she wished lady would say some more, for it had such a lovely sound. She smiled, showing her even white teeth and at the corner of her mouth a dimple appeared.

"You really are a bonny lass, Rosy," lady said, smiling back, "and I'm sure my children will love you. I've only the one now but" – here she grinned engagingly and Rosy was enchanted – "I'm sure you've noticed there will be another soon. Now then, I shall send for Robby and Nanny Morag and we'll see how you get on with them. Especially Robby. I shall need a good girl, a girl I can trust. A girl who will love my children. Do you like children, Rosy?"

"Please . . . lady?"

"Children . . . oh, what do they call them up here? Bairns, do you like them?"

"Why aye. I minded 'em at the place the day."

"Really! Well, it seems you'll be just right for the job then. I'll give you a couple of months to see how you all get on together. Nanny Morag is wonderful with Robby so I must make sure she is happy with you as well as Robby."

Rosy, again not sure of what lady had told her, watched with silent interest as she leaned forward to pull at something that hung at the side of the fireplace. She heaved and stretched but could not quite reach it and at once Rosy leaped forward and with a little flourish pulled on it, looking at lady with a lift of her delicately arched eyebrows to confirm that she had done the right thing.

"Thoo's not ter stretch," she said reprovingly, then put her hand to her mouth in consternation, stepping back as though expecting a blow for her outspokenness.

Lady smiled. "I know, and thank you, Rosy. Now, let's see how long it takes that rascal of mine to get down here." And again, though Rosy was not sure what lady had said, when the door flew open and in a tumble of plump legs and dark bouncing curls a small boy entered she understood what lady had been telling her. With the toddler were two puppies who seemed to be in danger of tripping the boy up and in an instant Rosy caught him and lifted him up in the air, laughing, and, as he came down again, kissed him on his rosy cheek before sitting him gently on his mother's narrow lap. He stared at her solemnly, leaning on his mother's round stomach, then, struggling to get down again, lifted his arms to her and began to shout, "Up . . . up . . . up."

"Eeh, hinny," Rosy began, looking at her mistress in some apprehension but lady only laughed and indicated that Rosy might play with the boy while she herself held the puppies in check. But with a quiet word in the child's ear and another kiss on his round cheek, Rosy put him from her and, as she had seen the other maids do, sketched a clumsy curtsey.

"Go ter thy ma, hinny," she said.

Amy's eyes were warm and when she glanced across at Nanny Morag they exchanged pleased smiles as the child did as he was told.

*   *   *

They spent the next four weeks in the nursery, she and Rosy, Nanny Morag and Robby, and in that time though Nanny Morag had just as much opportunity to learn her letters as the new lass she did not get on as well. At the end of the first week Rosy could recognise her own name, *and* Jumsie's, though she didn't tell lady, or as she had now learned to call her "m'lady", that, nor that every night after they had finished their work she passed on all she had learned to him. As fast as she soaked it up, so did he. They pored together over the nursery primer, mouthing C.A.T. spells cat, and M.A.T. spells mat and after a few days the others took no notice, for the pair of them worked harder – or so John-Henry stated and Cook agreed with him – than any staff they had had under them before. Aye, Cook was fond of saying, it had been a bit of good luck that chance whim that had taken her into the workhouse that day on the lookout for a clean lass. The boy had come as an extra, so to speak, and would cost them nothing even if he did eat like one of the horses in John-Henry's stables. The lass, though she spent so much time with her ladyship learning to be a nursery maid, for Nanny Morag couldn't manage two, could she, was always willing when the bairn had gone to bed to give a hand in the kitchen, even with the onerous task of scrubbing the kitchen floor for the umpteenth time that day, since Cook never let up on her passion for "skimmering". Aye, Cook often thought in those first weeks, she'd taken a real fancy to the lass, bonny wee thing that she was and she could see her ladyship had as well. Teaching her her letters an' that, which not many ladies of quality would do. But then their mistress was not the usual run-of-the-mill mistress, was she? She'd been through a lot in her short life, for she'd not be more than nineteen now. No, a rare one was their ladyship!

They were all taken by surprise when, in the third week of January and five weeks before the date she was due, their mistress went into labour. John-Henry, not trusting any of the others with such an important task, flung himself on Prince, the fleetest among the horses, and rode post haste for Doctor Parsons, praying that he would be at home, for it was past midnight and wasn't this the time when most babies decided they might as well get themselves into the world. Alfred, the second groom, had gone off on Oscar, another of the stable's sprinters, to fetch the midwife who usually helped the doctor with his confinements.

They were all up, from Cook down to Phyllis, the scullery-maid, swirling round the kitchen, getting in each others' way as kettles were put on to boil, bumping in to one another irritably, and it was an indication of how concerned they all were when, at the sound of pounding hooves on the drive, they every last one of them jammed into the hall where none of them was supposed to be, to be reassured that the doctor had arrived.

It was John-Henry and he was alone.

"Dear God in heaven," Cook gasped, her hand to her breast, pushing aside the open-mouthed Phyllis who, like them all, was dressed in her night attire. "Tell me the doctor's right behind ye."

"He were out, Cook. Another confinement up at Longhurst Hall. Mrs Linton's bin took badly but I left a message with Doctor Parsons' housekeeper an' she'll get him ter come up as soon as he can."

"But what about midwife?" Cook protested. "Don't tell me she's out an' all?"

"Aye, she went wi' doctor. I just passed Alfred on't road. Oscar's gone lame, tonight of all nights."

Cook wasn't interested in Oscar's plight as she turned and looked about her at the circle of worried faces. Ten of them and not one of them a mother, so who was going to help her ladyship when she needed them most? They were all from big families, since their mothers, including Cook's own, had no choice but to bear a child every year so surely there was someone who knew about birthings? They had all left home at an early age, for that was what their sort did, pushed out of the nest as soon as they were able to earn a sixpence so was there some lass among them who knew which end was which, so to speak?

It was Morna who spoke. Morna was head house-maid and had been at Newton Law for ten years and if she had her way that was where she meant to remain. She was the sixth of fourteen and from the age of five or six years old had helped her mother through the birth of child after child until, at the age of twelve, she had left home, much against her father's will since she was a grand help to the family, and gone as a skivvy in the kitchens of a house belonging to a local mine owner. Not for her the life her mother led. Not for her the burden of a dozen children by the time she was thirty, and though she had had her opportunities she had remained steadfast to her resolution. She was more than satisfied with her grand position at Newton Law. She liked routine, order, cleanliness, her own bed in her own bedroom and the many little perquisites her position at Newton Law brought her. But she still remembered those days when, with her younger sisters, she had helped her ma to drag another unwanted bairn into the world even if it was twenty years ago. Mind you, by the time Morna had started her life as her ma's midwife, her ma had given birth to five others and almost did the job unaided. She was a labourer's wife, used to hard grinding work and certainly not the dainty little woman their mistress was. Still, how could she not help since no one else seemed to be offering.

"I'll have a look at her," she said gruffly, and everyone turned to look at her in amazement, for to them she was the stiff and starchy, prim and proper, demanding, nay finicky housemaid who had them all jumping to attention.

"I'll give ye a hand," another voice said diffidently, and again they turned to look in amazement at the new girl.

"We'll 'ave none o' that clish-clash here, man," Cook said to her sternly. When Cook was upset she used many of the old terms her own ma had used and clish-clash, meaning foolish talk, was one of them. "Her ladyship's in real trouble an' we need someone—"

"I 'elped out at work'ouse when there were a bairn ter come."

"Give over, yer'd only get in't road."

Rosy Little was ready to step back and keep quiet, for she was new here and wanted to keep her place, but suddenly the memory of that lovely smiling face, that kind and graceful way her mistress had of talking to you, her patience in teaching Rosy her letters which, in turn, was teaching Jumsie his, gave her courage and though her face was white with fear she spoke up again.

"No, Cook, I could just gi' Morna a 'and. She'll need a 'and . . . 'er ladyship bein' . . . as she is . . ." meaning not strong and healthy like most of the working-class women who gave birth in her world. Mind you, most of the women who had borne children in the workhouse had been none too strong or they wouldn't have been there in the first place. The workhouse was the last resort of the poor and needy, the weak and undernourished. She watched Cook's face anxiously.

"Why aye," Cook said hesitantly, "what d'you think, Morna?"

Morna drew herself up and reached for an old apron in which "dirty" jobs were done and which would envelop her from neck to ankle. "We can but try, Cook. See you, Rosy, get yersen into an old apron an' follow me. You, Clara, you stand on the top landing and you, Cissie, at the top o't stairs and Tilly by't kitchen door ready ter run errands. Now, where's Tansy?"

"She's with her ladyship, yer fool," Cook said irritably.

"Right then . . ." Morna drew in a deep breath, praying that all the little tricks her ma had known and taught her had not been forgotten. "Let's get up theer."

When Doctor Parsons and the midwife arrived at Newton Law he was amazed to find his patient sitting up in bed eating a large slice of Cook's coffee walnut cake, her hair brushed and tied in a scarlet ribbon, her mouth full of crumbs and with half a dozen assorted maidservants flitting about the bedroom, though it was pretty obvious who was in charge.

"We managed right nicely, thank you," the maid-servant who had apparently delivered her ladyship told him. "Me an' Rosy here," smirking at a young lass who was hanging over the cradle with a proprietorial air.

"Nevertheless I think I'll just examine my patient, if you don't mind, and what are all these women doing in here?"

He was surprised when her ladyship, who still had her mouth full of cake, told him in no uncertain terms that had it not been for "all these women" she doubted she would have managed.

The reason for their mistress's excessive bulk during the last weeks of her pregnancy was explained when it was revealed that she had given birth to twins. It also explained why the bairns had come five weeks before they were due, for everyone knew that twins were often early. Who would have thought it? Twins, but when Lady Blenkinsopp told Rosy and Tansy, who had helped Morna to deliver the babies, that she was one of twins it all made perfect sense.

What pandemonium there had been in the kitchen when the news was passed down to them. It had all gone like clockwork until the last minute. With Morna and Rosy and Tansy about the bed, with Cissie and the others in the background ready to run anywhere at a moment's notice, with the baby safely delivered, a small but strong boy with a pair of lungs on him like a young bull, to their consternation her ladyship continued to heave and push.

"Theer's another," Rosy had remarked in a matter-of-fact voice, taking the lad from Morna and passing her another square of clean towelling to catch the second child which came bellowing out with a roar of displeasure.

"A lass this time," she said, wiping round the bawling little face. Without even cutting the cord on the second child, Morna placed Lady Blenkinsopp's new son and daughter in her arms, for it had been her mother's contention that the sooner a mother and her newborn child, or children in this case, were united the sooner the love came. It always had with her ma.

Well, they all went a bit mad down in the kitchen when Cissie ran yelping down the stairs with the news, dancing and jigging about so that when the outside men, who had been hanging around in the yard, clomped over the doorstep to find out if it was a lass or a lad and it was revealed to be one of each it seemed a riotous party was about to break out. A quiet voice from the doorway asked the question that none of them had thought of they were so flummoxed.

"Her ladyship? She's . . . well?" it asked.

"Oh, aye," Cissie shrieked, "in fact she's asking fer summat ter eat, Cook."

The man on the doorstep turned quietly away and began to walk across the yard towards the back of the stables. When he found a patch of darkness he stopped and leaned his forehead against the rough stone wall.

"Thank God," he whispered, "thank God."

11

Duffy's cottage was set in a bit of garden at the back of the stables. It was, by the standards of the day, quite spacious with a parlour, a back kitchen which led out on to its own vegetable patch and a discreet "netty" which he shared with no one else tucked on to the back wall.

The cosy parlour was furnished with discarded bits and pieces from up at the house. A sofa and a wing chair, both the worse for wear, and a round table covered with a red chenille tablecloth. He had himself built shelves on either side of the blackleaded range on which was his large selection of reading matter. The range itself had a fireplace, behind the bars of which was a good fire and to the side an oven heated by the fire. The whole thing had a cast-iron surround and a gleaming brass fender on which Duffy often propped his feet to the blaze.

The rough flagged floor was covered with several worn rugs and at the windows were red woollen curtains to keep out the ferocious winds which swept across the moors from the far wastes of Scotland and beyond there from Siberia. There were several cheap prints on the walls, simple watercolours which seemed to have very little form, just an impression of flowers against water, a bird in flight, waves on a beach, images that had appealed to him and which he had picked up for pennies on a stall in a market somewhere and framed himself. In the centre of the table in a rough vase, probably purchased from the same source, was a mass of carelessly arranged holly branches and leaves adorned with bright red berries.

The crooked, narrow stairs from the parlour led up to two bedrooms, one furnished with a big brass bed with snowy linen which the laundry-maid washed for him, several warm woollen blankets, and a beautifully worked quilt. He often pondered on what woman had fashioned it, for it was obviously a labour of love, a pretty thing of hearts and flowers and twining ribbons. At the tiny window, which was almost at floor level, were a pair of bright red woollen curtains to match those in the parlour. There was a sturdy chest of drawers with more books standing on it and a big leather trunk fastened with straps and the initials A. M. cut in the lid. The second bedroom was empty.

He lay sprawled on the sofa, his stockinged feet to the blazing warmth of the fire which he had just built up with logs cut from the woodland at the back of Newton Law. One hand was behind his head, the other holding a copy of Melville's *Moby-Dick* which he was reading for the umpteenth time. At his side his dog snoozed, his big head on his paws, sighing now and again in his sleep. Over the fire, held securely on a swinging arm, a kettle was bubbling gently and on the table were a teapot, a jug of milk, a bowl of sugar and a cup and saucer, all of good-quality bone china, a sight that would have amazed his fellow servants, but perhaps not, for they admitted he was different to them.

For several minutes he continued to read, then, with a suddenness that made Dick jump to his feet and look at him reproachfully, he snapped the book shut and sat up. Getting to his feet he moved to the small window and drew back the heavy curtains, staring sightlessly into the scrap of garden at the side of the cottage. It was in a poor shape at this time of year and he knew that if it had been in Joshua Weston's domain he would have been mortified. Not that much could grow in January, if anything, but at least he could have turned over the soil ready for spring planting, old Joshua would have said. As he gazed out into the garden, his face set in lines of pensive sadness, it began to snow. He watched it indifferently, small, sharp flakes which tapped on the window but as the minutes passed the flakes became bigger, softer, landing on the bare soil as gently as a leaf falling from a tree. It took no more than five minutes for the flakes to cover the ground completely, form a white strip along the top of the wall at the side of the cottage and line the branches of the trees that stood against it.

He sighed heavily, turning away from the window and wandering to the fire where he picked up the brass poker and gave one of the logs a tap, sending a small shower of sparks up the blackened chimney. He leaned his arm against the mantelpiece on which a handsome strut clock stood on its own. The clock had been designed as a travel clock, being flat with a swivel stand hinged at the back of the case. It had travelled everywhere with him for five years, the only piece of "baggage" he had brought with him from the past. The dog watched him, swishing his tail on the floor, his head cocked to one side, his ears pricked as though waiting for a command.

"It's bloody snowing now, old chap," his master said, as though the precipitation was the last straw to afflict his black mood. The dog's tail moved faster.

"The truth is I don't know what the devil to do. You can see what a fix I'm in, can't you? I can't just keep hanging about here waiting for something to happen. God knows what I'm hoping for. The bugger to pop off, I fancy, but even if he did I don't suppose it would make any difference. Christ, but it will be bloody hard to leave her." He shook his head and sat down again slowly, his hand going to the dog's ears which he pulled gently.

"Perhaps now she's had the children she'll be able to live a life more suited to her status with her neighbours. She's only a young woman and shouldn't be shut up with no one for company but servants and her children but . . . oh Jesus, how am I going to go on without her sweet face turning to smile at me. Goddammit, it's tearing me to ribbons to think of leaving her."

The dog looked up into his face. Duffy placed his hands one on either side of his head, bending his own until his forehead touched the dog's as pain overwhelmed him, a wild pain and fury that the one woman he had ever loved was tied so irrevocably to another man. The dog's tongue came out and gently licked his cheek as though in sympathy and Duffy groaned out loud. There was no escaping it, the way he felt, he knew that. Even if he went to the ends of the earth he would carry it with him, but he couldn't stay here suffering the torment he had known for the past months. She was at the moment in no physical danger from that bastard who lay rotting in his bed but what would happen to her if he should recover? Could he go, chance that the doctor was right in his belief that Sir Robert would never walk again, leave her with no defence against him, for the servants would never dare to lift a hand against a man who . . . Damnation. Damnation . . . What . . .

He flinched visibly and lifted his head when some-one hammered furiously on the door. Dick leaped up and started to bark and at the same time to wag his tail vigorously, his rear end almost swinging him off his feet.

"Who the devil . . . ?" his master muttered. He pushed one hand through his hair which was already standing on end at the back where it had rested on the cushion and the heavy brown curls at the front flopped over his forehead. Dick was at the door, still barking, as Duffy pulled himself wearily to his feet and followed him across the room, wrenching open the door to what seemed a small blizzard which at once blew madly into his parlour. In it, barely visible on his doorstep was the boot-boy, Nipper. He had a piece of sacking about his shoulders and though he had come no further than from the back door of the kitchen, the snow had collected thickly on his wiry curls and along the slope of his narrow shoulders.

"Dear God, lad, what the dickens are you doing out in this? See, come in and warm yourself. You must be frozen. Haven't you a coat or something? Come in."

Dick was leaping about as though at the return of some long-lost traveller, doing his best to lick any bit of flesh on the boy that was within his reach, and it was not until Duffy bade him to "lie down and stay" which he had at last mastered that the boy could get himself over the doorstep and huddled against the fire.

"Now then, lad, what are you doing out in this? Surely whatever it is could have waited until morning. Unless . . . ?"

He was suddenly ravaged with the image of Amy Blenkinsopp lying ill in her bed, perhaps suffering with puerperal fever or any of the afflictions that can strike a woman after childbirth, but then why would they send for him, for God's sake, unless . . .

"Hell's teeth, lad, spit it out," he said savagely and the lad, who had been just about to sink on to the footstool by the fire to warm his hands, shrank back, a look of alarm on his face. He barely knew this man, for they worked in different areas of the estate. He'd seen him sometimes, striding across the yard, or making his way towards the woodlands that surrounded the house but he'd never actually spoken to him. They said in the kitchen that he was strange and he certainly looked it at the moment but his face suddenly softened and he laid a comforting hand on his shoulder.

"I'm sorry, lad, what is it? Have you a message for me?"

"Aye, Cook ses 'er ladyship wants a bit crack wi' ye." He even managed a cheeky grin and having delivered his message he turned back to the fire. The dog stood up, having done what he was told for a minute or two, wandering over to nudge him and the boy put an arm about his neck.

"A bit crack?" Duffy said incredulously, scratching his head. "D'you mean her ladyship wants to see me?"

"Aye man."

He almost asked the lad "what for", just as though a twelve-year-old boot-boy would be told what was in her ladyship's mind. Even Cook wouldn't know and if she did would certainly not tell the lad.

"Well, we'd best get over there," he pronounced, reaching for his boots and pulling them on. He draped his gamekeeper's greatcoat about his shoulders and with a word to Dick to stay where he was, he and the lad fought their way through the by now blinding wall of snow to the back kitchen door.

The twins were a week old, called David and Catherine but already known as "our Davey" and "our Cat" in the kitchen, when her ladyship sent a message to say that she wished to see Duffy if he could spare her a minute. *If he could spare her a minute!* Wasn't that just typical of her, Cook proclaimed to the astounded circle of faces about her, her mistress – and master as well – of this fine estate acting as though the gamekeeper were not a servant like them, but someone of importance in the same class as herself. As though he were so busy she did not like to intrude on his precious time.

"I know it's started to snow, Tansy," Amy had told her maid, "but it's not far from the house to his cottage and there's something I must discuss with him. It's most important. It's been on my mind ever since the twins were born and if I don't talk to him soon and get it settled I'll go mad. Ask Cook, would you, to send someone for him. He's bound to be in his cottage with this weather; at least, I *hope* he is . . ."

The strangest expression came over her face and as Tansy waited respectfully to see if her ladyship was going to add anything further, she wondered what the expression might be. There was a faraway look in her eyes as though she were looking at something Tansy could not see, something that was a dreadful worry to her.

Cook nearly had a fit! Her ladyship, though up and about in her sitting-room, against Doctor Parsons' advice she might add, was only a week out of her childbed and, though there were now two nursemaids in the nursery, and that Rosy was a godsend, Nanny Morag said, should not be having visitors. And certainly not gentlemen visitors, which was how Cook classed Duffy, though she was not consciously aware of it, even if he was Sir Robert's gamekeeper.

Her face lit up as he entered the room and he felt the air go out of his lungs and his heart beat to a frantic rhythm of joy. She was lying on the sofa which stood at right angles to the fire dressed in a loose wrapper the colour of which he could only describe as pearl. Tied at the neck and about the waist and wrists were ribbons of gold satin and there was another fastening back her hair from her face. It emphasised her delicate features and long slender neck. Her skin was flawless, her mouth a full and rosy pink curling up at the corners and her eyes glowed with some emotion he could not decipher. She looked no more than fifteen and yet there was about her a mysterious air of timelessness, of maturity, a womanliness that was ethereal. It was impossible to believe that she was the mother of three children.

She was radiant.

She held out her hand to him and in the doorway,

ready to close it with herself inside as was only proper, Tansy goggled in amazement.

"Duffy," she heard her ladyship say softly.

"M'lady," he answered, holding her hand in his, ready, Tansy believed, to bend his head over it as they said the gentry did, kiss it even, she thought.

"Thank you, Tansy, that will be all," her ladyship told her. "I'll ring if I need you." And Tansy had no choice but to bob a curtsey and leave the room, running down the stairs to declare to the open-mouthed servants that it was not fitting that a lady, a lady dressed in a garment only her husband should see, should receive a man who was not even related!

At last he found the strength to let go of her hand. He stood awkwardly, unable to tear his eyes away from her, until she indicated that he should sit down opposite on the sofa which matched the one on which she lay. They continued to look at each other in total silence, a silence that spoke volumes, their gaze locked in some indescribable way which neither of them knew how to break until at last he managed to squawk, or at least that's how it sounded to him, the polite remark that was expected of him.

"You look well, m'lady. The children are . . ."

"They are thriving, thank you."

"I'm pleased to hear it. Have you chosen names for them?"

"Yes. David and Catherine but I believe the servants have shortened them to Davey and Cat."

"Indeed, and do you mind, m'lady?"

"You called me Amy last time we met, Duffy."

His jaw dropped and he shut it with a visible snap, then gulped. "M'lady, I can't . . ."

"Can't what, Duffy? Call me by my name? No one has since I last saw you and I would take it as a kindness if you would do so now."

He wanted to bow his head and groan, for this was torture of the worst sort. Surely she was aware of what he felt for her? It seemed to him that everyone must know, for it appeared to shine out of him in a steady shaft of light that went before him and that was why he must go. Why he must pack his trunk and take himself off somewhere, God only knew in what direction, before he made a complete idiot of himself and her a target for gossip. The servants would not mean to harm her, for she held a special place in their affections, but if it was recognised that her husband's gamekeeper had tender feelings for her ladyship they wouldn't be able to keep it to themselves. Her reputation would be shattered and though he believed it would not unduly worry her she had her children to consider.

"M'lady, I'm sorry, but . . . really . . . is it wise for me to . . ." He tried to smile easily as though it were just a small thing but his face was stiff and he wished to God he had gone, packed his things and gone while she was confined to her rooms. He was not really needed now that Sir Robert no longer shot or hunted or fished in the busy river that ran through the valley below the house. He would get another job somewhere, something to do with the outdoors, he didn't care where it was but . . .

"Duffy, what is it?" she beseeched him, sitting up and swinging her feet to the floor. "There's something wrong, isn't there? I can tell by the way you're acting. I thought we were friends. I've asked you up here to do something for me."

"Anything, m'lady. I'll do anything for you, you know that" – his voice was harsh – "but you also know we cannot be friends."

Her voice was cool. "You led me to believe we could, Duffy. I was going to run the estate in place of my husband but with *three* babies, until they are a little older, I shall find it hard."

"And you want me to do it?"

"Yes."

"M'lady, please. There are dozens of men who are capable of doing it for you."

"No, not with your knowledge. You told me yourself that you know the farmers who are tenants on my husband's land. I want to know them too, and with your help I shall. This estate must be kept in good heart for my sons."

"They are well?" he asked in a strangled voice, forgetting that he had already enquired about them, attempting to divert her. "And the little girl?"

"Yes, thank you." She was hurt and she showed it; if he could have made it any different for her he would have done so, but this was crucifying him and he could only struggle on until the moment came for him to leave.

She stood up and at once he leaped to his feet. She moved slowly towards the window and looked out into the snow-shrouded world. He watched her. He was a tall man, lean and strong but he felt unsteady, vulnerable and this delicately fragile woman was the cause of it. There was a pain in his chest and throat and if he had been a woman he could have wept, but he had to keep a tight rein on his emotions, on his feelings for her, not let her see what was in him, for he had made up his mind to go and she might weaken him.

She swung round to face him, then, her lovely gown flowing about her like a pearly river, she moved slowly towards him until she stood directly before him. Short of stepping back he could do nothing to avoid her closeness. The fragrance from her hair – or was it her gown? – drifted faintly about him, settling in his senses and he knew he was lost even before she spoke.

"Duffy, I won't try to thrust friendship on you if you feel you cannot accept it even though . . ." She swallowed and he could have sworn there were tears glimmering at the back of her eyes. "But I really would be glad if you . . . if you – just for a few months – could take on the running of the estate. Things have been neglected since . . . well, messages have been left for me just these last few weeks, farmers wanting to see me about something or other, I don't know what, but I promised that as soon as I was able I would come and . . . But I can't go alone, don't you see? And my" – she smiled a little as though the words amused her – "my step-daughters, who have become active or so they say in the welfare of the tenants on the estate and the village since my husband's accident, tell me that some of labourers' cottages have fallen into a sad state of disrepair."

"Yes, m'lady, I know."

She sighed, whether at the state of the cottages, or his persistence in calling her by her title. "I want to go and inspect them and put right whatever needs putting right. Mr Sinclair did say that I had only to send estate bills to him and they would be paid. Surely

A Place Called Hope

my husband's tenants and estate workers fall into that category?"

Now that they were talking about everyday things he felt a little of the tension drain out of him though she still stood too close to him. He could see tiny grey specks in the blue of her eyes which must be why they sometimes looked blue and sometimes grey, depending on the light, he supposed.

Without warning she put her hand on his arm and he felt himself flinch. At once she removed it. He thought she was going to say something but his own movement must have changed her mind. She turned away and walked back to the window.

"Will you stay, Duffy, just for a while until I am able?"

"Yes, m'lady, I'll stay, just until you get to know the way of things, or until I can find you a suitable man to take my place."

There was silence for a moment or two while he gazed hungrily at her back, at the ripple of her gold and silver-streaked hair which fell down it, then: "How is it you have the knowledge to . . . to run an estate, Duffy? Have you done it before?"

"Yes, m'lady."

Her voice was very soft, so soft he could hardly hear her. "Dammit, Duffy, why the hell can't you call me Amy, and what is the mystery about you that you keep to yourself?"

"I think I must be getting back to my cottage, your ladyship," he said politely. "The snow is getting thicker and I would hate to be marooned in the kitchen."

"Of course."

"Perhaps I'll see you in the garden with your . . . children when the weather improves, m'lady."

"Perhaps you will, Duffy."

"Will that be all, m'lady?" His heart was breaking but his face and his voice were expressionless.

"For the moment, thank you."

The door shut quietly behind him and as she turned blindly towards the sound her hands rose to her face, crossing themselves over her mouth from which a tiny moan came.

"Oh, Duffy . . . Duffy," she whispered.

It was two weeks before she saw him again. The snow had come and gone in two days, but the ground was frozen hard and crisp with frost. The trees were all a-glitter in the winter sunshine and the two little dogs barked for the sheer joy of being out in the open air. They ran round in circles, and Robby, who was steadier on his feet now, ran with them. He kept his elbows up and out, like a pair of wings to help him balance and still moved with his feet apart. He fell over frequently but he was warmly wrapped and picked himself up cheerfully unhurt.

She had had a long argument with Nanny Morag who was of the opinion that her ladyship was out of her mind to take not only herself, who should still be in bed, but babies who were three weeks old out into the winter air. After all, they had been born prematurely and it was a well-known fact that babies born before their time were inclined to be delicate.

"Rubbish, Nanny. They're as healthy as two little horses," which everyone was agreeably surprised they were. In fact it was difficult to believe that they weren't full term for each had weighed in at seven pounds and were putting on plump, pink flesh at an amazing rate.

"I promise I'll take Rosy with me, Nanny, and between us we should all be safe and sound. Wrap the babies up warmly. You can even put a hot-water bottle in the baby carriage. With one at either end and well covered up they will come to no harm. I'll come back for them after they have had their feed."

She nodded graciously at the wet nurse who sat before the fire, a pleasant-faced, spotlessly clean farm wife who had a newborn of her own and, as she told Rosy cheerfully, had more milk than she knew what to do with. Feed a dozen, she could, and she and her Fred were glad of the extra cash, since she had six more under the age of ten at home. She was a kindly woman, singing numerous songs to Robby which her own children loved and even taking him on her knee before she left so that he wouldn't feel left out. Her bare and overflowing breast fascinated him and if Nanny Morag had not been there she would have let him have a suck as she did her own toddlers, since it would do him no harm. Instead she kissed him and nursed him for a minute or two before handing him to Nanny Morag or Rosy, or even his mother who came frequently to the nursery, and she was of the opinion that she had never seen a small boy who was so affectionately treated. She had heard that the gentry ignored their children, leaving them totally in the care of servants but not her ladyship.

She was trundling the baby carriage on the path that surrounded the lake, smiling indulgently as Rosy ran after Robby and the dogs, for the lure of water was strong in small children and animals, when Dick crashed out of the undergrowth and charged straight for the baby carriage, evidently looking for Robby who had once been its sole occupant.

"Dick," a voice roared, "come here at once, you fool. Lie down, I say," and to her astonishment the animal came to a halt and though he didn't relish it, lay down. He just couldn't manage to keep absolutely still, though, as he crept along on his belly towards her, and when Robby, who had turned at the sound of Duffy's voice, flew towards him with Bracken and Briar lolloping round him, the four of them were soon entwined on the ground. Robby was shrieking with joy, disturbing the rooks which were already beginning to build their nests. They circled the canopy of the denuded trees with a pleasing chorus of caws and croaks and when Duffy emerged from the woodland Amy felt her heart dip for a moment before it settled into the gentle, loving peace he had always awoken in her.

"Duffy." Her eyes narrowed a little in the brilliant sunshine which dazzled against the whiteness of the frost, her lashes meshing. Her cheeks were rosy with the cold. She wore no hat but Tansy had fastened her hair into a coil on her neck, kept in place with a bright scarlet knot of ribbons. She looked exquisite.

His eyes were filled with an incredible tenderness which she could not fail to see.

"Amy," he answered.

It was then that they both recognised, acknowledged and welcomed what was between them and knew that he would never leave her.

From her position along the path where she was

trying to separate the dogs and the child Rosy Little watched gravely and understood, for didn't she and Jumsie McGovern love one another and though she was young didn't she recognise it in others.

12

They waited until March when the weather was beginning to improve before they moved off the parkland
and on to the moorland paths which led to the six
farms that were rented from Sir Robert. It had been
a hard winter with frequent snowstorms, heavy frosts
and bitter winds which cut through to the bone, and
Duffy flatly refused to take her anywhere until he
considered it to be suitable weather for riding. He
had taken over the estate manager's office situated at
the end of the corridor that ran off the main hallway,
much to the amazement of the servants who were
struck dumb by her ladyship's announcement of his
promotion, and spent some part of each day in it.
The corridor had its own entrance off the herb garden
and at an agreed time they met there while he led her
through the complexities of the management of an
estate such as Newton Law. The office was something
like a gentleman's study, lined with books on every
aspect of country life from the study of insects, birds
and butterflies to the treatment of blow-fly in sheep.
There were ancient books on the breeding and rearing
of cattle, some of them in the hand of Sir Robert
Blenkinsopp's forebears, the rotation of crops, the

diseases of pedigree horses. The shelves on which they had been crammed and never touched since any of the servants could remember – for Sir Robert didn't like his things "interfered with" – lined two walls of the room. On the other walls, facing one another, were the windows that looked out on to the herb garden, and the fireplace. The door to the room that led into the corridor was cut out of one of the walls crowded with books, and any available wall space was taken up with maps of the estate, the parkland and gardens, and one that purported to be the original plan of the original house. The ceiling was high, the room tall and to facilitate easy access to the books on the top shelves a narrow wrought-iron balcony had been built round the walls just above the level of Duffy's head, reached by a narrow staircase. There was a comfortable leather swivel chair before a massive, leather-topped desk with a dozen deep drawers, so heavy none of the maids could move it when her ladyship requested that the room be given a spring-clean. The wrought-iron fireplace was blackleaded, shining with what Cook called "elbow-grease" and above it was a sporting print of the kind the master of the house favoured. In the fireplace a good fire was kept burning night and day, for it was never known when the mistress might be found working there. It was the job of Phyllis, the scullery-maid, to keep the fire stoked up, the coal scuttle constantly filled and the fire damped down at night with "clinkers" come from the ash-pan beneath. The room was always warm and Phyllis was heard to remark that she wouldn't mind spending *her* day in its cosy comfort. She got a skelp on the lug from Cook for that and was told to mind her own business and let others mind theirs!

He began by showing her the maps, for she should be aware of the boundaries of Sir Robert's lands. She memorised the acreage, not only of the estate but of each of the farms that lay within it. She was given a list of the names of the farms and of the farmers who tenanted them, their families and labourers, and the kind of farming that took place on each one.

He was meticulously polite and scrupulously proper in all his dealings with her. She was mistress of this estate and he was her employee and despite the bond, unspoken of but understood, that was between them, he never stepped over the line and would not allow her to do so. Whenever she entered the room he instantly stood up. He still wore the clothes he had worn as gamekeeper. He kept Sir Robert's grouse and pheasants in good order, he told her, his lips curling in what she knew wanted to be a smile. He set traps for foxes, since the land had not been hunted or shot over for nearly nine months. He spoke to the grooms and stable lads, being knowledgeable about horses, and when he began to ride out on her ladyship's business it was seen that he was a fine horseman. He made sure that the animals in the stables were exercised, well groomed and fed and if Sir Robert himself had got up from his bed and made his way to his stables he would have found everything as he himself would have wanted it to be.

She was busy in those first few weeks after the birth of Davey and Cat in the ordering of their young lives and that of her elder son who, if he was not watched, would soon become a little tyrant in the nursery,

Nanny Morag told her sternly. Where had that shy, diffident little boy gone, she said, who had been ready to burst into tears if a sudden noise alarmed him? Not that they wanted him back, she added hastily, for it was only normal for a lad to be noisy and demanding, but really, he did need a man's firm hand to guide him.

"Don't be silly, Nanny," Amy told her coolly, thinking of the hand of the man who was his father, and shuddering at the thought. She longed for the milder weather to come so that her son could once more be with Duffy who was not only kind, gentle with all living creatures, but would be firm. One day he would take over the training of both her sons, teach them to be gentlemen, as he was, but also to be productive members of the class to which they belonged. Robby was sweet-natured, if a bit headstrong and inclined to be jealous of the attention his new brother and sister received, but she was careful to take him to her sitting-room with the dogs and play with him on his own.

In the kitchen they talked about the new babies with a great deal of wondering curiosity. They were beautiful, both of them, with a head of silken fair hair which would darken to the colour of her ladyship's as they grew older. They had the flawless creamy skin of infants, with rounded pink cheeks and rosebud mouths but it was their eyes that confounded them, for they were brown, deep and smoky with green flecks in them and they slanted upwards at the outer corners. Her ladyship's were a lovely blue-grey, wide-set and smiling, and though it was months now since most of them had seen him, they seemed to remember Sir Robert's were green, as all three of his daughters' –

his older daughters – were green. A throwback to some ancestor, Cook wondered reflectively to Morna but who were they to speculate, since none of them had ever clapped eyes on her ladyship's family. They might all have brown eyes for all they knew!

They began by going to the stables and consulting with John-Henry on the best possible mount for her ladyship in view of the years it had been since she had ridden and the terrain she was now to undertake with her new estate manager. Also, though it was not discussed, since it was a delicate subject, it was only weeks since the birth of the twins. She needed a small horse but a strong one, a gentle, sweet-natured beast that could be trusted to obey her at once until she became more proficient. Her ladyship might, Duffy indicated to John-Henry, be taken out on a lead rein until he was satisfied she was safe. John-Henry was thunderstruck at what he thought of as Duffy's high-handed attitude towards her ladyship, acting as though he were her bloody guardian, or even her husband, he told Alfred on the quiet. He might be her new estate manager, and God knew she needed one, but did that give him the right to dictate to her on how she was to conduct herself and to talk to her as though they were equals?

"I never was much of a horsewoman before I married," John-Henry heard her say ruefully. "My father was a keen rider to hounds, and my brother, but my mother's side of the family were too busy with their collieries and numerous business concerns to have time for what my grandfather, my mother's father, called 'frivolities'. She didn't learn and saw no reason for me to learn so I rode round my father's estate on a quiet nag, that's all."

"We've none o' them 'ere, m'lady," John-Henry remarked stiffly. "Sir Robert was most careful when he bought an 'orse. 'An 'e knew what he were about an' all. Good stock, if ye know what I mean."

"Oh, of course, John-Henry, they are all wonderful, I can see that and your care of them shows. I want my Robby to be put up on a pony soon and I'm depending on you to look after him."

John-Henry, mollified, said he certainly would, and he'd the very mount for him when he was ready. Behind her back Duffy was seen to bend his head to hide his smile, for her way with the servants could not be faulted.

The name of her chestnut mare was Holly, a quiet, patient mount, John-Henry told her, as placid and reliable as any in the stable. He'd stake his life on her safety, he added, and was somewhat offended when the new estate manager nevertheless insisted that her ladyship be led like a child on a rein. He put her up on the mare's back, totally ignoring the help John-Henry – who was after all head groom and knew his business – was ready to offer. She rode side-saddle, of course, and was dressed in the most fetching outfit, or so the grooms, who watched the proceedings with intense interest, agreed, in a shade of deep blue. Her top hat and little face veil matched the colour exactly. The dressmaker who had come every day for a week to fit the riding habit had done her proud, and they were proud of *her*, their little mistress, for she had done well for Newton Law. Three children, two of them boys, in less than two years and now she was to take over the running of the master's estate and everything that went with it.

They moved slowly through the woodland, Duffy ahead, holding the lead rein attached to her mare. It was still cold, a fine, crisp coldness, tingling against their faces. They rode out on to the drive that ran down to the river, the hedges slipping by with the tall, leafless elms rising out of them and etching their lacy patterns against the paleness of the sky.

When they reached the edge of the moorland they were able to ride side by side, Duffy tall and straight on the grey stallion, Oscar, who stood at sixteen hands. He was a foot higher in the saddle than she was, moving easily, turning all the time to study her, not speaking, watching her every movement but not catching her eye and she was aware that he was doing it deliberately. She was so busy admiring the set of his bare head, the tumble of brown curly hair which looked as though it needed a barber's attention, the strength and yet delicacy of his brown hand on the reins, the silvery shine of his cat-like eyes as he turned to study the way she sat, the lean, flat plane of his cheek as it turned towards her, she scarcely noticed where they were going. She watched the shape of his well-cut lips that did not smile a lot but were inclined towards humour, she thought, until something in his life had made him as he was. She listened to the words he spoke as he pointed out a curlew in flight, its liquid, bubbling cry distinctive among the creatures that inhabited this part of the moorland. It was not until they clattered into a cobbled farmyard surrounded by a cluster of farm buildings that she realised they had arrived at their first destination.

"Home Farm," Duffy said shortly, "you remember, don't you?" as he swung down from his saddle and landed neatly on the cobbles. "Jack Elliott. The biggest farm and, in my opinion, the best run on the estate."

He fastened Oscar to a ring in the wall of the stable. Oscar, now that Duffy was off his back, was beginning to be skittish, flinging up his head and looking about him with great offence as though a creature of his pedigree should not be asked to mix with the chickens, the ducks and even a couple of geese which moved busily about him, stiff-necked and imperious. Duffy spoke sharply to him then smoothed his nose, softening his tone and at once the animal quietened.

He turned to her. "M'lady," he said, lifting his hands to help her down. She threw her leg over the pommel and with a graceful movement slid down into his arms.

It was as though a bolt of lightning had struck them both, a shock which spread through their bodies like the ripples on a lake. For an ecstatic moment she leaned into his embrace, ready to cling to him, blindly, senselessly, instinctively, and for another moment he responded, then, with a silent groan, he put her from him, steadying her, wondering who was to steady him. There were dogs barking from round the front of the farmhouse and as they stepped away from one another a little woman came hurrying round the corner, wiping her hands on her apron. She sketched an awkward curtsey.

"M'lady, Mr Duffy," she said in her broad northern accent, so broad and thick with "howays", "why ayes" and "gan ons", that later Amy had a great deal of difficulty in following the conversation. A lanky lad trailed after her, his boots almost to the knee in cow muck which, on seeing it, the little woman tutted at.

"Will, tha' boots, lad, an' all over me clean yard. Now don't stand there gawpin', tekk m'lady's horse, an' Mr Duffy's. Gan on, lad, howay wi' ye."

"Really, Mrs Elliott, the animals'll be fine where they are," Duffy said soothingly. "Now let me introduce Lady Blenkinsopp . . ."

"An' 'oo else would it be, lad," Bridie Elliott scolded him, sketching another clumsy curtsey, "an' 'er so bonny. Whist, man, let's get inside then. Tha'll both be needin' a cup o' tea, I shouldn't wonder," as though they had ridden over from Newcastle instead of three miles along the valley. "An' Will, fetch tha' Da."

They were drawn into an achingly clean little parlour shining with brass and pewter, smelling of lavender and beeswax and obviously never used except for special occasions such as this. For twenty minutes they drank Bridie Elliott's strong black tea and ate her cheese scones which were even lighter than Cook's, though Amy dared not tell her so in case it got back to Newton Law. Mrs Elliott was a garrulous little soul, starved of female companionship, for she had two sons and, naturally, word of the twins, such bonny bairns, she'd heard, had reached them. What a joy, but how sad for poor Sir Robert to be fast in his bed and did the doctor hold out much hope of him walking again? It was plain from the cold expression on her normally warm, rosy face that she sincerely hoped not, for he was a hard landlord, caring nothing for the state of the farm and those who worked it, for the farm buildings which had to be kept in good repair, as long as he got his rent on the due date. This was a farm in good heart with rich soil and Jack was a careful man where husbandry was concerned and they managed, but others did not fare so well. So what was to happen now that Sir Robert was fast in his bed? If it was true that Mr Duffy was to take over the running of the estate where would that leave them? Her ladyship looked kind enough, though Bridie found it hard to understand what she said, just as she did with Mr Duffy, but might she not be interested only in the rents with which she would buy the lovely clothes like the riding habit she wore? Well, only time would tell.

Duffy discussed crops and sheep and the price of wool with Jack Elliott, who it could be seen was longing to get back to whatever he had been doing before the arrival of the visitors, while Will adopted the attitude of a deaf-mute.

They went outside, to Jack Elliott's vast relief, to inspect his excellent herd of cows, his pigs, then his sheep, the broken places in his dry-stone walls where his animals would keep escaping, the state of his roof – Sir Robert's roof, after all – where the rain poured in to the lads' bedroom, the damp in the kitchen. With a promise to look into all these matters at once she and Duffy left to make their way across the river by a narrow bridge and up to Old Moor Farm.

He still led her by the rein, for the terrain was growing rougher the higher they climbed. The track was rocky, with sheep at either side, since Old Moor Farm was in sheep country. The animals stood to stare with curious eyes then lifted their heads to sniff the air as though they knew that spring was coming and their lambs would be here soon. There was the sound of water tumbling from a dozen burns, rocky courses, and from somewhere came the sound of a dipper's sweet, sharp music. The sunshine seemed to ripple over the hills as the clouds moved slowly from east to west, glinting on the water in the bottom of the valley.

It was the same at Old Moor. They were greeted with great hospitality and an apologetic list of roofs that needed repairing, windows that were warped and would not open, or if they did would not close again, of gates that hung askew. Sir Robert's neglect showed, not the neglect of the last nine months but of years.

"They lead a hard life up here, struggling to keep going, as their fathers before them did. Without the concern of a conscientious landlord they cannot keep up with the gradual erosion that takes place. Some are more capable than others and somehow manage to cope with the necessary repairs themselves, but unless they have sons or can afford to employ farm labourers they have time only to attend to their animals and the land that sustains them."

"It will be different now, Duffy. I promise you."

"I know and I'm glad. They're all decent folk whose families have farmed here for generations and don't deserve to . . . well, if the land and the farm buildings themselves are allowed to deteriorate Sir Robert will, in the end, lose money. Their rents are high now."

"Tell me what to do, Duffy."

"First we must have experienced men, builders and such, to inspect the properties; then, when we can estimate what it will cost confer with Mr Sinclair—"

"No! He will hum and hah and nothing will get done. Let's start at once and then, when the bills come in send them to him. That will be soon enough to let him know."

"M'lady, he won't like it." He turned to smile at her, that rare whimsical smile which because of its rarity was all the more enchanting. "And you haven't seen the worst yet. We don't have time to visit all six farms today but I want you to see the cottages in Hawthorne Lane where Sir Robert's estate workers and their families live: ditchers and hedgers and others who are employed about the place. It's half a mile from the house, you may have seen it when you go into Allenbury."

"Yes, a very pretty terrace of old cottages. I've often thought they would have an artist reaching for a sketching pad. Whitewashed with thatched roofs, rose-red bricks, lovely old chimneys and lattice-paned windows."

"Yes, and surrounded by marigolds and pansies, but wait until you see the insides."

The cottages had been built without foundations on to the bare earth as she found when she and Duffy bent their heads to enter the first one. The damp seemed to rise up and come across the sweated floor to meet them and the smell was enough to bring tears to her eyes. The walls ran with water in wet weather, rats lived in the roof space, and the ancient lath and plaster with which the cottage had been built was a haven for bugs. There was one netty for the whole row, an earth closet that did not drain properly but seeped obnoxiously beneath the cottages, which was probably where the smell, mixed with sweat, dirty bodies and lice, came from.

A small girl of no more than six or seven told them

that her ma was in bed. She stood on one dirty foot, rubbing the sole of the other on top of it, smiling nervously. Though she was pallid beneath the grime that coated her, her cheeks were a vivid scarlet and her eyes had an unnatural brightness.

Amy began to scratch before she had been inside the cottage five minutes. Her feet were inclined to slip on the wet floor and Duffy took her arm which she was glad of. There was no fire in the room though it was chilly as a tomb. In the chimney corner, crouched where the fire would be, were four other children younger than the girl who had opened the door to them.

"Is your mother ill? Er . . . what's your name, my dear?" Amy asked her gently, leaning for support on Duffy, for she really thought she might faint. The child looked confused and Amy remembered then how that question had gone over young Rosy's head and tried again.

"What do they call you?"

"Molly," the girl answered shyly.

"And your mother is poorly?" She was about to reach out a compassionate hand to the filthy child but Duffy pulled her back sharply.

"Don't, Amy," he said quietly. "Remember your own children. This one, and the others, probably have the consumption."

"Sweet Jesus, and the mother?" She put her hand to her mouth as though to stop any more of this contaminated air from reaching her own lungs.

"Your mother?" Duffy asked the child.

"She's just 'ad a bairn. Mrs Liddle's wi' 'er."

"I must go up," Amy began, but before she could

put a step on the bottom tread of the rickety stairs that led up into the gloom she was almost lifted off her feet by Duffy and carried outside into the clean, cold air which, gratefully, she dragged into her lungs.

"Duffy, let me go, if you please. I must help these people. Let me go."

"And so you shall, Amy, but you must think of your own babies. There are probably a dozen or more in these five cottages . . ." And indeed, alerted by the two horses tethered to Betty Long's tottering front gate, they had all come out in their rags and tatters, their enormous eyes in their pinched faces all agog, to see what was going on. "First of all we must get a doctor, someone who will be prepared to visit cottages like these. When you get home you must arrange for decent food, milk, eggs, fresh vegetables and fruit to be delivered here at once. Then, when the doctor's been and they have got some decent food inside them we will see to the repairs needed in each cottage. Do you agree?"

"Yes, oh yes," she answered feverishly, eager to start and alleviate the muck and muddle these poor creatures lived in. "We must do what we can and at once." She was scratching vigorously. "Oh, look, look, Duffy, at that poor child's face, the sores." And before he could stop her she had bent down to a scrap of bones and fluttering rags and lifted a small, astonished boy into her arms.

"Amy! For God's sake, put him down," he called out harshly. "Jesus God, I wish I hadn't brought you now. I had no idea myself or . . . Put him down, I beg you. Let's get home and begin where we can which is to send for Doctor Barrie."

"Doctor Barrie?" She placed the boy on the ground where he promptly clutched at her skirt with a claw-like hand. Duffy wanted to brush it off, brush the child away lest he transfer some dreadful thing to Amy, but she was smiling, putting out a hand to the boy's matted hair and he knew with a sinking heart that she was not about to alleviate these tenants of Sir Robert's from a safe distance but would be in the thick of it.

"Yes, he works with those who cannot afford Doctor Parsons' fees in the poorer quarters of Allenbury."

She turned to look at this man who never ceased to confound her. "How do you know that?"

He turned away to untether the horses, hiding his face from her. "I . . . heard about him when I was . . . well, I was in the bookshop in Hepple Lane, we got talking; he was looking for some book and, knowing the shop well, I was able to direct him. He comes from somewhere in Lancashire where his methods were not appreciated by those who believe the poor are poor through their own fault and should therefore be left to get on with it. He and his wife moved here a year or two ago and have done much good since. They are an enlightened couple and . . . I have dined with them a time or two."

Amy digested this in silence, this part of Duffy's life about which she knew nothing.

"Will he come? Tell him I will make sure he receives a decent fee."

"I'm sure he will. Even without the fee."

"Then let us get home and send for him right away."

"Will you promise me something?"

"Of course, anything." She turned a glowing face

towards him, a grateful expression on it as though she couldn't thank him enough for revealing to her this appalling state of affairs which, being her husband's responsibility, was now hers.

"Will you destroy that gown you wear."

"Destroy it!"

"Burn it."

"Burn it? Duffy, it cost a great deal of money and this is the first time I've worn it, for God's sake."

"Dammit, does that matter! Burn it and then have a bath with some . . . something in it to cleanse your skin and hair. Amy, don't be so obtuse, woman. God knows what you've picked up here today, so before you touch your children you must do as I say. Promise me?"

"I promise, then I must have some serviceable dress and apron made."

"What for?" But he knew the answer before she spoke.

"To wear when I come again."

It was as they turned away to mount their horses that a middle-aged woman came out of the cottage. She had on a white apron, heavily stained with blood, on which she was wiping her hands. She put one hand to her eyes and peered suspiciously from beneath it.

Amy turned back despite Duffy's detaining and exasperated hand.

"Good morning," she called out. "How is the baby?" She smiled, for surely babies were a great joy.

"Dead," the woman answered, "an' a good job an' all."

"Oh, no, and Mrs . . . the mother?"

"She'll do."

There seemed to be nothing else to say and Duffy

began to draw her away, thankfully, but she was not done yet.

"My name is Amy Blenkinsopp," she went on. "My husband is—"

"Aye, us know who thoo are."

"And you?"

"Jessie Liddle."

"I'm going to help, Mrs Liddle. With my husband . . . incapacitated, I'm taking over and . . . well, may I help?"

Jessie Liddle had no idea what incapacitated meant and no faith in what the gentry told her, especially dainty little things like this, but she had seen from the window how the lass had picked up Madge Dixon's little lad and it had brought her down for a closer look.

"Aye," she nodded, then went inside to tidy up the pitiable results of Harry and Betty Long's nightly encounters.

13

She met Andrew Barrie that same afternoon. As soon as she and Duffy returned to Newton Law, hardly before she had been helped down from Holly's back, she was giving instructions to John-Henry to send one of the grooms into Allenbury with a message to Doctor Barrie that Lady Blenkinsopp wished him to call on the row of cottages in Hawthorne Lane at the earliest possible moment. She would meet him there, she added. Duffy would give him the doctor's address.

Duffy did his best to be diplomatic, particularly as the grooms were all ears. "Really, your ladyship, another day will make little difference to them. Dr Barrie . . ."

She turned on him like a tigress, her face quite scarlet with indignation and both John-Henry and George, who was being given instructions to saddle up Oscar and take the strange message to the unknown doctor, blinked in amazement and stepped back a pace.

"How can you stand there and say that after what you and I have just seen?"

What him and her had just seen! And what in hell's name could that be? was written on both men's faces.

"Have you no pity for those poor creatures, especially

the children? They must be treated at once. Oh, and John-Henry" – spinning impulsively on her heel to the groom who backed off another step – "have you such a thing as a waggon, a cart of some sort?"

"A cart, m'lady?"

"Well, any vehicle strong enough to carry provisions will do."

"Carry provisions, m'lady? Where to?"

"To Hawthorne Lane."

"Hawthorne Lane?"

"John-Henry, I do wish you would not keep repeating everything I say. Surely it is plain enough. I want a cart standing outside the back kitchen door within half an hour and someone to drive it. I shall take the gig and lead the way but first I must speak to Mrs Fowkes and then get changed. And will you send word to Mr Wanless that I wish him to accompany me."

"Mr Wanless?"

"There you go again, John-Henry. I believe Mr Wanless deals with all the repairs that need doing about the estate."

"Yes, m'lady, but . . ."

It was at this point that Duffy, with what seemed to be great impertinence to John-Henry, interrupted by taking hold of her ladyship's arm and drawing her firmly away across the stable yard. It was a big yard with buildings on four sides and entered under a wide archway over which was a clock standing at twelve thirty. He could nor hear what Duffy said to her ladyship, which was just as well.

"M'lady . . . Amy, will you slow down. God's teeth, there is no need for this mad rush to save the inhabitants of Hawthorne Lane from what you seem to think is imminent disaster. They have lived as they live for years now, with nothing spent on their cottages, their welfare, or even the barest necessities of life."

"Which is why there is every need to begin at once. Those children will haunt me until I know I have done everything I can."

"Doctor Barrie will see to all that, Amy. Don't you see it would be most unwise for you to go careering off—"

Their faces were the exact same shade of fiery red as they glared at one another, she with outrage, he with fear, not for himself but for her.

"I am not careering anywhere, and if I am is it anything to do with you? These people are my responsibility."

"Dammit to hell, I wish I'd never taken you there. You made me your estate manager and it's my job to see that not only the estate but all those who work on it are—"

"Well, you did show me so let go of my arm and go about your business."

He had not been aware that he was holding her arm in a grip so tight he was lifting her up on to her toes. The grooms were staring in horrible embarrassment and mystification, for what the hell were her ladyship and her brand-new estate manager arguing about in the shadow of the archway?

"Well," she shouted to them, "are you to obey my orders or must I see to it all myself?"

They turned away hastily, wondering what the devil had come over their mistress who was as gentle as a dove, as delicate as a spring violet and as graciously spoken as royalty.

The maidservants were equally thunderstruck when their mistress, followed hot on her heels by her estate manager, strode into the kitchen. Cook had been leaning over the smaller range, the spoon with which she had been stirring something in a saucepan to her lips. She had tasted the mixture speculatively, her usually cheerful face set in deep lines of concentration, then, with the air of one who has just made a crucial decision upon which the life of every member of the household would depend, declared to Tilly who stood poised beside her that a further half-teaspoon of salt was needed.

"Not a dash more, Tilly, or we'll all suffer the thirst of the damned this afternoon."

"Right, Cook." Tilly, her eyes narrowed purposefully, measured the exact amount and tipped it into the saucepan.

The clatter at the door made them both jump and Cook put her hand to her bosom in a dramatic gesture.

"Oh, your ladyship, there you are," she spluttered.

"Yes, here I am, Cook, and I'd be glad of a word with you, if you don't mind." The other servants exchanged glances. What now, those glances asked, and from the scullery where he was busy with the boots, Nipper stood up and peered through the window in the wall that separated the small room from the kitchen.

"Of course, m'lady, but I'm just about to serve—"

"Never mind about that now. I want to know what provisions you have in your pantry?"

"Your ladyship, I beg you to listen to me," Duffy began, and all the maids who had been staring at their mistress, wondering what the dickens was going on, turned to look at him, then back at her.

"No, I will not listen to you, Duffy. It was you who brought the matter to my attention and if you are reluctant to help me I will understand."

"Goddammit, I never said that," Duffy roared and the servants flinched and fell back, just as John-Henry had done, stunned, not just by the ferocity of Duffy's voice but by what he had had the temerity to say to her ladyship.

"Then do something useful. Go and get the horse and cart ready while Cook sorts out the provisions. I shall need all the milk you have in the pantry, Cook, all the eggs and butter and whatever bread is available. And you, Tilly and Elspeth, I want you to bake another batch. Yes, of bread, if you please, and quickly. Ruth and Phyllis, put all the vegetables and fruits that are available in baskets and then run out to Mr Weston and ask him what is ripe in the hothouse, and . . . and . . ." She whirled to sniff at the lovely aroma that was floating from the range, the full skirt of her riding habit, which she had draped over her arm, swinging dangerously close to the fire. "What is that you are cooking, Mrs Fowkes?"

"M'lady, oh dear, m'lady . . . won't you," Cook managed to gasp, her hand still pressed firmly to her heaving bosom, "won't you please slow down."

Duffy put both hands flat on the kitchen table, leaning his full weight on them, and bent his head as though in despair, then, abruptly straightening up he whirled about and grasped their mistress just above each elbow.

"I won't have this, m'lady. I insist you leave it to me

and stay at home with your children where you belong. God only knows what's lurking in those cottages and I cannot believe you want to bring it home to the nursery. Please, be sensible. Doctor Barrie will do all that is necessary and Mr Wanless and I will attend to the cottages. We shall take cleaning materials for the women, and whitewash and lime for the men to use. We'll make sure that decent water is laid on, the privy seen to, perhaps build another and I promise you they will be as tidy and . . . and watertight as Newton Law."

"Duffy, I can't. I just can't stay at home. I must help. I've done nothing in my life that's worth speaking of, except my children. I've lived a life of uselessness and now I've the chance to do something for these people who depend on Sir Robert for their very existence. In his absence . . . Oh, please, Duffy, don't try to stop me. Help me to help them. There is so much to be done at Hawthorne Lane."

Her voice was soft and on her face was such a look of pleading, of compassion and a longing to be about something of which they in their ignorance knew nothing, the maidservants stood as though riveted to the flags. She put both her hands against Duffy's chest, looking up into his face and they were convinced she was about to weep. They hadn't the faintest idea what the pair of them were talking about but whatever it was it was upsetting them both no end. Hawthorne Lane had been mentioned which was where the estate workers and their families lived but as none of them had ever been down there it was all a bit of a mystery. But whatever it was why should the estate manager, or the gamekeeper as they still thought of him, have any say in the matter? Their mistress employed him and, like them, he obeyed her orders and yet here she was begging to be allowed to do something which, or so it seemed, he did not care for.

It looked for a mind-boggling moment that he was about to put his arms about her and draw her against his chest, then, so swiftly they knew they must have imagined it, they drew apart and her ladyship turned to Tansy who stood, her mouth open like the rest, against the dresser.

"Now then, Tansy, I want a bath immediately."

"A bath, m'lady? Now?"

"Yes, now. Run it for me, will you and then dash to the nursery and tell Nanny and Rosy that on no account are they to bring the children down to me until I tell them. Now this is most important. They are to be kept in the nursery. Yes, yes, they may venture outside into the garden but they are not to come near me. Is that understood?"

"Oh, m'lady," Tansy quavered, her hand to her mouth.

"Now stop that, Tansy, and all of you, jump to it and do what I've asked you. Has anyone any questions?" She looked enquiringly about the stunned group, then, as no one moved and no one spoke, for what were they to ask, she clapped her hands and, turning to Duffy, who was to jump with the rest of them, told him she would be no more than fifteen minutes and to see that the vehicles were ready.

"M'lady . . ." he began, then, in a voice so low none of them could hear him, "Amy, I beg of you, don't do this. If anything should happen to you I would never forgive myself."

"It won't, Duffy, I promise you."

The rest of the occupants of the room seemed to fade away, the whispers of consternation died and into her eyes came a brilliance which was reflected in his. She reached out a hand and blindly his groped for hers and their lives, already so irretrievably mingled, streamed together in a timeless tide.

Behind the door that led into the kitchen the bulky figure of Sir Robert's man slid silently towards the stairs as he heard the approaching footsteps on the flagged floor of the kitchen. With a speed and lightness surprising in a man of his size he was almost at the top of the stairs by the time her ladyship entered the hall and when she reached the top landing he was inside his master's bedroom.

His excitement caused Sir Robert to put down his newspaper, which he had learned to hold with one hand, and glare at him.

"Bye," Platt stuttered, "ye never 'eard such a clish-clash in yer life, man, an' I dinna kent what it's aboot so dinna ask me. Summat ter do wi' some cottages."

"Cottages?"

"Aye man, but dinna ask."

No one, as Platt should have learned by now, told Sir Robert Blenkinsopp what he was, or was not to do. Sir Robert lifted his head from the pillow and threw out his good arm. He lifted himself laboriously to his elbow and indicated that Platt was to pile up his pillows behind him.

"What mumble mumble are you mumble jabbering on mumble mumble. Sometimes you mumble talk mumble mumble bloody riddles . . ."

"Summat's gan' on downstairs wi' 'er ladyship an' that chap, 'im what were gamekeeper. They say 'e's bin medd up ter estate manager. I told ye, didn' I?"

"Yes, mumble mumble daft gowk get on with mumble or I swear I'll mumble mumble . . ." Sir Robert made a great effort to contain his temper which after over nine months tied to his bed and the sole company of this illiterate lout was just as dangerous as ever. To alleviate his boredom and frustration he had even done his best to talk to the maids who came in once a day to clean his room but all he did was frighten them even further, since they hadn't got the hang of understanding him as Platt did. His wife visited him rarely but when she did, stood at the door, or the window when it was open, asking him, or at least Platt, if there was anything either of them required, and once a week the doctor paid a call to check him over. Of course nobody, except Platt, knew of his slow but certain improvement. One side of his body was totally paralysed and, he realised, would never be of use to him, but with Platt's help the working side was becoming stronger. In his estate office hidden behind a cabinet was a locked safe and in that safe was a great deal of money which, when he was ready for what he had planned, would be used to bribe Platt, but until he could get at it himself he was not about to inform Platt of its existence. Platt continued with his little visits to Newcastle with the small objects he filched from the various rooms, and even the attic of the house, and which the maids had not noticed were gone, most of them worth very little but satisfying to the man who had never had more than a few shillings in his pocket at one time. But he would require a much bigger inducement to put into practice what Sir Robert had in mind.

Now and again he managed to bring in some whore from Allenbury who obliged them both and made a nice change. Of course, Sir Robert could not perform as once he had done but the whore, as whores do, knew a few tricks that satisfied him and it was always titillating watching her and Platt. Platt's plan to become friendly with one of the maids, especially the new one who was in the nursery, had come to nothing as yet. Each one he had approached had recoiled in horror, threatening to tell the mistress if he took one step nearer, and so for the time being they had been forced to make do with a trollop from the inn at Allenbury.

"Why aye, mistress's blatherin' on aboot summat. She's set on tekkin' summat, or doin' summat down at Hawthorne Lane."

"Wha'?" Sir Robert reared up awkwardly and his face took on an even more dangerous flow of blood beneath the skin.

"Why aye. She's beggin' that there gamekeeper ter 'elp 'er, tekkin' food an' such an' 'e's ter ask Wanless ter inspect the cottages an' daft gowk's ter follor an' there were talk of a doctor bein' sent for."

Sir Robert let out such a bellow Platt moved swiftly to his side to get a good hold of him in case he should take it into his head to wallow out of his bed in his attempt to reach his wife and stop whatever she was doing. Whatever it was it sounded as though it might cost his master some money. Platt was not an educated man, nor even a particularly bright one, but he had a sort of low cunning, a sly brain which could work certain things out for itself.

"Whist man, ye'll do yersen a mischief thrashin' aboot like that," he said soothingly, doing his best to force, without appearing to do so, his master back on to his pillows.

"Get mumble out of here mumble mumble mumble bloody fool. Mumble my wife mumble mumble mumble right away mumble. Tell her mumble mumble to see mumble today."

"Nay, man, ah'll gan doon ter fetch 'er but—"

"Don't you mumble mumble with mumble idiot. Fetch mumble mumble once or I'll mumble . . ."

"Right, sir, right, I'll fetch mistress but mind she'll know then ye can talk."

"Bugger it, mumble mumble spending my cash mumble the mucky hoit mumble and mumble mumble bloody gamekeeper . . ." He was gasping breathlessly with the effort of speaking for so long and with the madness that had taken him over. He and his minder lived a life separate from the rest of the household, with no contact between them apart from the daily visit of the maids who darted like scared rabbits from the room the moment they had finished and never, never spoke a word! He had lain bedfast all these months, working inch by inch to get some return of movement in his stricken body and for one purpose only: to get his hands on the bitch who was his wife. She had given birth to twins, got on her by himself during their last lusty encounter, proving herself to be fertile yet again, and if it was the last thing he did he meant to have her in his, and Platt's, hands again. His speech had to be improved since he must be able to communicate with those under him. He had to be stronger than he was now which was taking a long time to achieve, but that was all right, for so far she had done nothing to which he might take exception. But this, this determination, or so it seemed from what Platt was babbling on about, to spend his money on the bloody cottages in which his labourers lived was almost more than he could bear. He'd send for old Sinclair but the trouble was he knew, in the heat of his rage, he would not be able to communicate with the solicitor, who would go away thinking that poor old Blenkinsopp had gone completely off his rocker. The only one who understood him was Platt and so, until he was more in control of his damned mouth, he must bide his time.

"Right mumble mumble right but find out mumble what mumble mumble and tell me mumble."

"I will, man, I will, now get yersenn comfy an' I'll gie ye a drink. 'Ow aboot a sup whisky? Ye like that fine."

Of all the maidservants only Rosy, who had come down to the kitchen to see what was going on, offered to accompany her mistress to Hawthorne Lane.

She had scrubbed herself until she was pink in the tub brought up by the maidservants and placed before her fire; when she had changed into a plain and serviceable gown, tying up her hair in a bandana of cotton so that it was completely covered, she donned the enormous white apron she had borrowed from Morna.

The servants were quite horrified at the idea of their little mistress putting them all at risk by going into a place that must surely teem with every disease known to man. Their fears were worsened when Tansy, her face as white as a drawn sheet and holding her mistress's lovely new riding habit at arm's length, declared that she was to burn it.

"Saints preserve us," Cook whispered, backing away from the gown as though it contained the black death.

When the mistress bustled downstairs and into the kitchen where, outside the back door, her entourage awaited her, though they did not come near her, for hadn't she already been inside one of the malodorous cottages, they hovered anxiously, wringing their hands and bleating of their fear, especially Cook.

"Don't be so melodramatic, Cook," Amy said coldly to her, for as usual Cook was the spokesman. "There is nothing there that a decent roof over their heads, nourishing food and a doctor's attention cannot put right."

"But m'lady, the bairns."

"I've told you I shall not go near my children until I am convinced that I cannot carry anything that will harm them, and Doctor Barrie will advise me on that."

It was then that Rosy stepped forward and made her offer.

"Rosy, you are needed in the nursery and you know you can't go back there until we are sure there is nothing . . . horrid at Hawthorne Lane, don't you? There is . . . well, at least one of the women has consumption, we think, or so Duffy says, and I'm told it's infectious."

"M'lady, me an' Jumsie lived in't workhouse all our lives, man, an' there were plenty of it there. We catched nowt . . . caught nothing," for Rosy was doing her best to speak like her ladyship now that she herself could read. "Any one of t'maids'd be glad to 'elp . . . help out in't nursery while I'm gone. They love the bairns, all on 'em," she added wistfully, for she did herself. "Thoo canna go there by yersenn, hinny." Rosy was so fond of her mistress she often forgot herself. "Let me come wi' thoo. I'm strong an' . . ." She had just been about to say, "and you are not", as it was only a matter of weeks since the birth of her ladyship's babies but she stopped herself in time, for when you thought about it was there anyone stronger, in her will and temperament, than their mistress? She had been told by Phyllis when they both worked in the scullery of the bad things their master had done to his wife, not in any detail for Phyllis didn't know any details but it seemed the master was a wicked devil and had given her a black eye on the very night she had returned from wherever she had been. Phyllis didn't know where. And other things as well, Phyllis hinted, and yet here she was, sweet-faced, clear-eyed, a slender figure wrapped in an enormous apron setting off to give a hand to folk she didn't even know. If Rosy could help her she bloody well would, and nothing her mistress said was going to stop her.

Amy looked into the alert, intelligent eyes of the maid. Her bright curly red hair was severely restrained beneath a frilled cap. Her freckles stood out like small golden guineas across her snub nose and creamy white cheeks, and her mouth was set in a straight line of determination as though nothing that was said would make her deviate from her intention.

"I'm not afeared, m'lady," she said.

For a moment everyone in the room, including Duffy who had come to the back door, waited breathlessly, somewhat in awe of this good lass who had had such poor beginnings but despite them was prepared to risk herself, like her ladyship, in helping a group of feck-less, hopeless creatures who hadn't the gumption to get off their bums and help themselves. *They* wouldn't have sunk to such levels had they been in the same position, they told themselves, extreme poverty and privation unknown to them, for they came from decent folk. This lot at Hawthorne Lane were very evidently shiftless in the extreme and what her ladyship thought she was up to was an enigma to them. She'd even taken their *dinner* for God's sake, the dish wrapped up in a cloth and put among the heaped stack of food that had been loaded into the waggon. John-Henry was on the driver's seat ready for off, with Mr Wanless, somewhat mystified by the whole thing, beside him. The gig was there and the small pony who pulled it, with Duffy about to climb in and drive her ladyship. When he was told Rosy Little was to go he hastily ordered Oscar to be saddled, swinging into the saddle as her ladyship took the reins in the gig, clucking to the pony to walk on, with Rosy beside her. They were dressed so exactly alike in their plain gowns, their white aprons, their covered hair and the shawls which Cook, tearfully, had insisted they put round their shoulders, for it was cold out, that a stranger would not have recognised who was the mistress and who the servant.

Duffy led the cavalcade under the archway and out of the stable yard. The servants crowded at the kitchen window and the back door to watch them go and as they came into sight on the front drive the man at the window relayed to the man in the bed what was going on.

"Bloody 'ell, theer's dozens on 'em. They've a waggon piled up wi' all sorts an' 'er ladyship's drivin't wee gig. That lass is wi' 'er, the one what I were telling thee about. Smally bit lass wi' red 'air."

"Mumble mumble bloody gamekeeper?"

"Aye man, an' two other lads. Looks like a bloody—"

"Never mind mumble her ladyship mumble mumble . . ."

"Aye, she be drivin' gig."

"Mumble mumble mumble . . ." And here Sir Robert's mumbles became shouts of rage, so unintelligible Platt gave up trying to interpret them.

He continued to watch the procession until it disappeared round the bend in the drive, shutting his ears to the increasing cacophony from the bed. It went on and on, grunts and squawks and shrieks of rage until, his patience at an end, he reached for the medicine on the chest of drawers and, mixing up a good spoonful in a glass of water, he held his master's nose and poured it down his throat. Much as his master resisted it did him no good and the last thought in Sir Robert's mind as he sank into unconsciousness was that he would have to be more careful with his servant, for there was no doubt the man was beginning to take not only small liberties but big ones as well.

14

Doctor Barrie was a square-shouldered, blunt-spoken man, with a twinkle of humour in his eyes, probably around thirty-five or forty, it was difficult to tell. He was something of a radical, which was why he had made himself unpopular among the virtuous, narrow-minded folk in the district of Manchester from where he had come. His views on the practice of birth control, or such birth control as was available, views he aired freely among the labouring classes who were his patients and who had nothing to call their own but an abundance of children, were considered to be immoral. Surely, they proclaimed, those who were offended by his outspokenness, there was a solution of which God, and they, approved and that was for those who could afford no more offspring to put aside their lust and abstain from the sexual act. Doctor Barrie was forced to disagree and, in the end, to pack his bags, and those of his devoted wife, and leave for more enlightened parts.

Though it was never mentioned, since she could hardly *ask*, could she, Amy often wondered why they had no children of their own. They lived in a tall terraced house, the last in a row of twelve, in the centre of Allenbury where, Laura Barrie told her, it was convenient for the constant flow of men and women who pounded on their door day and night in search of the doctor. She herself was patient, competent, practical, showing the women who knocked timidly on her back door how to make a nourishing pan of broth from vegetables bought at the end of the day at the market when they were almost given away, and a pound of scrag end. She taught them never to throw away the water in which they boiled their potatoes, nor the dregs they discarded as useless, potato peelings, cabbage leaves and such which could help alleviate many of the diseases their children suffered, stunted growth, bad teeth, poor eyesight and bandy legs, which were all the result of a poor diet. Tasty stews and herb dumplings, the herbs themselves growing in abundance in her own back garden and to which they were welcome; constipation cured by an infusion of dandelion leaves, a clove of garlic simmered in milk which would do wonders for a cough. All milk, from whatever source, should be boiled, as should water that had not come from the town's new waterworks. Preventive medicine, she called it, and her gruff husband was inordinately proud of her.

It was all put to good use at Hawthorne Lane where Amy, with Laura Barrie to guide her, over the months, when Doctor Barrie finally allowed it, came to know the intimate details of unwashed children, sore eyes and running noses, the numerous women who were for ever pregnant and, because of it, had given up the fight. She learned how to scrub floors with hot water and lye soap – to Duffy's horror, ignoring his frantic pleading to let someone else do it – to decipher the almost unintelligible dialect of the north-east and hold earnest discussions with the women on what *she* herself had learned from Laura Barrie about the most economical way to feed a family. She came to know the simple remedies the doctor taught her for many of the children's ailments and she came to realise that it was not enough to feed them and nurse their bodies. They must learn how to continue in the way their lives were shaping, not just their bodies but their minds and not just those in Hawthorne Lane but all the children of her husband's estate.

When her little entourage arrived at Hawthorne Lane that first day Doctor Barrie was already there, tending to Betty Long, his voice kind and soothing as he bent over her bed, his stethoscope to her chest. He appeared not to notice the broad green stain on the low ceiling above her head, the dirty sheets and pillows, the stink of illness and unwashed bodies, the creeping things that scurried about the damp walls. Betty Long was perhaps twenty-five or twenty-six. She had borne eleven children and with her sunken cheeks, hollow eyes and missing teeth looked considerably older. Her husband, though a good-natured enough chap, was not quite right in the head and was given only the most basic of labour which he did to the best of his limited abilities. He stood at the end of the bed, his cap wringing in his hands, his loose mouth twisting in his unshaven anxious face, coughing now and again, the slow careful cough that pointed to the same fate as his wife.

The doctor turned as Amy entered the bedroom, bending her head, for even with her small frame the rotten ceiling touched it.

"Aah, Lady Blenkinsopp, I'm so pleased to make your acquaintance and glad to be of assistance. Duffy has spoken of you when . . . well . . . I'm afraid there is no time for niceties," he went on without giving her time to speak. "Mrs Long is not well and I have decided to move her to my small hospital in my own home where I and my wife can keep an eye on her. She needs careful nursing, you understand, and though I'm sure there are neighbours who are willing to help it is imperative that we get her out of this damp environment."

"Yes, Doctor," Amy answered, moving forward, meaning to take the hand of the sick woman who was plainly terrified, but a sharp word from Doctor Barrie stopped her.

"I beg you, m'lady, please . . ." He did not finish the sentence but his face was grave. "Now then, if you will fetch the woman . . . I believe her name is Mrs Liddle, who seems to be in some sort of charge of the family since the husband is . . . er . . . I will arrange Mrs Long's transfer and the care of her children while . . ."

"I'll care for her children, Doctor Barrie," Amy began eagerly but again the doctor interrupted.

"Indeed you will not, m'lady. I believe you have recently given birth. Twins?"

"Yes, that is so but I'm strong and—"

"Your own children must come first. My wife is driving over with our carriage and being accustomed to illness will arrange everything. She knows what is needed."

"But Doctor Barrie . . ."

She was preceding him down the rickety stairs which were scarcely more than a ladder, clinging to the wall for support, and was horrified when some small black thing ran over her hand. She drew it back in disgust and almost fell and had Duffy not been standing at the bottom of the stairs might have done so. It was as though he had been yearning to be upstairs with her, which she knew was true; in fact if he could have done so he would have ordered her to stay, not just downstairs and away from the patient, but outside where the air was pure and uncontaminated.

"Now m'lady, I'm afraid I must ask you to stay away—" the doctor was saying behind her.

"There you are, you see I was right," Duffy interrupted, giving her a little shake, looking as though, had there not been onlookers in the form of Doctor Barrie, Mrs Liddle and various women who hung about at the doorway, he might have dragged her into his arms for safety. His lean face was harrowed with deep grooves at each side of his long, humorous mouth and Amy took his hand and held it for a moment, the expression in her steady gaze telling him she understood.

Doctor Barrie if he was surprised did not show it. "Now, the most important thing is clean water of which there seems to be none. The barrel I inspected before I came in had a dead cat in it. Why there has not been an outbreak of cholera or typhoid is a mystery to me. You have a decent water supply at Newton Law, I believe . . . yes . . . then can someone arrange to have barrels brought over until something is done about putting in drains and piped water from the waterworks in Allenbury?"

Duffy stepped forward, putting Amy behind him as if to shield her from any more nastiness, and the women and children watched with fascination. They had a great deal of sympathy for Betty Long who had more to contend with than anyone in the row with her Harry a bit simple, but their main interest was the spectacle of her ladyship, who they had all seen going past in her carriage, concerning herself with them, and the man who was said to be the estate manager treating her as though she were made of bone china. Which she probably was by the look of her. They had not yet been confronted by her ladyship's strength, determination and courage. A couple of her men were unloading things from a cart, and, to their delight, when they turned to see what it could be they found it was food of a sort they had never seen in their lives. A young woman who was addressed as Rosy took a stance at the back of the cart and began to issue orders, lining up the children, of whom there were a great many, and, having looked them over individually, began to pour milk into the mugs they had been instructed to bring from their cottages.

"Drink that, lass," she told Ida Hodge's youngest who had never seen milk before, at least not milk like this that had not been watered down and she was not sure what it was, "then thoo'll grow up into a big girl. Now then, who wants some bread an' cheese . . . right. And stop that pushin'. There's enough fer all."

Within half an hour every last one of them, the adults included, were stuffing their faces with the best grub they'd ever tasted, their pinched faces beginning to smile, the children holding on to their stomachs which had never been so full in their young lives. Cook's casserole, which had been intended for the family's lunch, was fed in small spoonfuls to Betty Long, to her thin, pallid children and her half-starved husband before Betty was wrapped up in a warm quilt which John-Henry had dashed back to Newton Law to collect, since such a thing was not available in the cottages. With it he brought the fresh baked bread her ladyship had instructed the kitchen maids to bake. Betty was placed in the carriage with Laura Barrie and speeded on her way.

They waved her off fearfully, wondering if they would ever see her again, then fell on the rest of the provisions brought over by her ladyship's servants. They didn't know what the devil was going on and they didn't care. They didn't expect for a minute that it would last. The gentry were known for their impetuous charity to the "afflicted poor" which fell away when the novelty wore off but it seemed this was not to be like that. Sir Robert had three daughters who moved benevolently about the parish carrying calf's foot jelly and shawls for the old and infirm, with hand-knitted baby clothes and the like, but they did not concern themselves with such as them, only with what were known as the "deserving" poor.

Amy had noticed from the first that one of the women appeared to have an air of what she could only call *command* about her. The other women deferred to her, crowding round her as though for courage. It was a fine, warm day and they assembled on the strip of rough grass that lay at the front of the cottages, drinking the tea Amy had brought over and which the woman had made on her own fire, putting in a generous dollop of milk. They consumed the bread and cheese and cold ham though the fruit was not to their liking, since they had not been introduced to such things as peaches and pineapples and oranges in their deprived lives and were somewhat suspicious. They would eat an apple or a plum when they were available, since these things grew on trees in orchards with which they were familiar, at a distance, of course, but anything more exotic than that was viewed with mistrust.

Mrs Liddle, with her shawled head held high and her shoulders squared, moved across the narrow track and stood before Amy as though to barr her way. Amy had not been allowed to go back into the cottage from which Betty Long had just departed, nor into any of the other cottages in the row. Doctor Barrie and Duffy were deep in conversation just beyond the filthy stone step of the Longs' cottage on which the Long children sat, their bare feet in the dirt, consuming Cook's fairy cakes, a look of enchantment on their bemused little faces. Beside them stood their father who was still gazing after the carriage that had carried off his Betty, his face a picture of apprehension.

Amy smiled at Mrs Liddle and would have taken her hand, for these people were filled with mistrust and she longed to let them see that there was nothing to fear, but Mrs Liddle pulled it away and frowned. Jessie Liddle, despite her poverty, was a proud woman, she herself didn't know why, for she had known nothing but this life of hers since she was a bairn and that wasn't much to shout home about, but she'd not be patronised by anyone, even this woman on whose husband her Dinty relied for work. She did not smile.

"Mrs Liddle . . . I believe that's your name?"

"Aye, they call me Jessie."

"May I . . . ?"

"Aye." She crossed her arms over her breast, pulling her shawl more closely about her.

"I want you to know that I was unaware of the way you lived."

Jessie's frown deepened, for she did not understand. What was the way they lived to do with her ladyship?

Amy sighed. "My husband . . . he owns Newton Law, you know that?"

"Aye."

"He's . . . he's bedfast." An inspirational way of putting it and one that would be understood.

"Oh aye." Jessie shuffled her clogged feet in the dirt.

"Yes, so I have taken over, with Mr Duffy, the care of his estate, and the people who work for him. Mr Duffy brought it to my attention that you, and the others, were living in circumstances in which . . . well, to be frank, he would not keep his horses. My husband, I mean."

"Oh aye."

"Mrs Liddle, please do not take offence when I say I mean to change that. Doctor Barrie will tell me what is needed and I will make sure it's done. Do you understand?"

A gleam of something shone in Jessie Liddle's apathetic eye and she opened her mouth as though she would speak, then she closed it again and waited.

"Mrs Long is very ill but Doctor Barrie, if anybody can, will make her better. Now, are there any others among you who need to be seen by the doctor? The children, certainly. Have you heard of consumption?"

Jessie Liddle narrowed her eyes. "Aye, there's one or two like Betty but not as badly."

"Will you help the doctor?"

"Aye." And with that, as though there were no more to be said, since Jessie Liddle did not waste words when action was needed, she turned on her heel and marched to where the doctor and Duffy were still conversing.

Rosy, who had packed up the last of the empty food hampers on to the cart and was readying herself to drive back with John-Henry to the house, came to stand beside her mistress.

"M'lady, can I ask thee summat?"

"Of course, Rosy."

"Though I love lookin' after't bairns I reckon I'm needed 'ere. Well, someone is, until this lot get back on their feet. None of 'em could stand up in a strong wind and wi'out someone ter keep 'em at it'd fall back. Tansy an' them won't come an' I'm not blamin' them. They're not used to it, like me an' Jumsie. Jumsie's learned ter ride one o't 'orses. 'E could fetch me over every mornin' an' I could 'elp out 'ere until . . . well, wi' Mr Duffy . . ."

"And me, Rosy."

The expression on Rosy's face changed from one of earnestness to one of stern disapproval.

"Eeh, no, man. Duffy'd never allow that."

"I beg your pardon, what has Duffy to do with it?"

Rosy's voice was soft. "I reckon thoo know th'answer ter that, m'lady."

Amy liked Doctor Barrie. Once he had convinced himself that she was no ladylike member of the gentry playing at doing good works and that the danger of consumption, cholera, typhoid and all the other diseases with which the poor suffered was past he allowed her to do as she pleased with this scheme of hers. He made no fuss, as Duffy did, when she rode over in her little gig to see that *her* people were flourishing, though naturally she did not call them that to their faces. She had become, since her talk with Jessie Liddle, conscious of their northern pride which had taken such a beating over the years and treated them with sensitivity.

She liked the doctor's wife who worked beside him and in the next few months she was often to be found at Hawthorne Lane where, after the first few weeks and with Doctor Barrie's consent, she and Rosy took the gig several days a week. Duffy rolled up his sleeves and, under the direction of Mr Wanless who declared himself appalled at the condition the cottages had been allowed to fall into, spent most of his day sawing wood for new window frames and doors, for new floors which were to replace the bare earth; directing men who were renewing roof tiles and bad brickwork, demolishing the appalling netty and putting in two more, one at each end of the row, and contructing a track up from the road wide enough to drive a cart through to take away the night-soil and empty the netties. He supervised the digging of trenches to fetch clean water to two standpipes which would be available twenty-four hours a day. His lean face became as brown as a nut, as did his forearms, his neck and the portion of his throat that was exposed by his open shirt front.

They worked side by side and what was between them grew softly and silently, nurtured by their smiles for one another which they thought no one noticed, their exchanged glances, a soft touch of her hand on his arm as she sought his attention, his own lifting as though to enfold it in his own. Sometimes, when they found themselves alone for a moment it was as though the air became electrified, still and yet pulsing, and both would appear somewhat breathless. They both knew moments of intense joy, and then utter sadness and, at the end of each day, parted despairingly.

Betty Long, under Doctor Barrie's gruff but kind and experienced treatment, began to recover in the warmth, cleanliness and *dry* condition of his small hospital. She was returned to her own home which she scarcely recognised, and to her children who, after eating the good food sent down from Newton Law each day, began to thrive. As did the rest of the children belonging to Jessie Liddle, Ida Hodge, Madge Dixon and Patsy Williams. Between them they had almost thirty children and though they were stuffed like peas in a pod in their five cottages, sleeping three or four to a bed, at least those beds were now clean and dry, the cottages themselves free of damp, snug and sturdy ready for the onset of the winter. And with her ladyship breathing down their necks to make sure there was no backsliding they gradually clawed their way out of the pit of indifference and despair in which they had wallowed for years.

They began to bloom, men, women and children. Duffy organised the men, Dinty Liddle, Harry Long, Reuben Hodge, Peter Dixon and Manny Williams, into a routine of daily labour, which, with no one to supervise them, had fallen, like the lives of their families, into a slovenly laziness, making Dinty Liddle an under-gamekeeper. They said that the best game-keepers were men who had been poachers and, as he suspected they had all done a bit of that, he gave them permission to take a rabbit for the pot or a game bird for the oven, though what Sir Robert would have made of it he could only guess. Without the gentlemen who normally shot them during the autumn and winter the creatures were reproducing at an alarming rate and it was one way of keeping the numbers down.

There was also a great deal of activity at the six farms which were part of Newton Law estate, with men brought in from Allenbury and villages nearby to make right the leaking barns, the broken walls and all the other badly needed renovations Sir Robert had ignored for years. It was as though new life had been injected into the men and women who had plodded dourly on year after year, doing their best to produce what was necessary to pay the rents Sir Robert had demanded of them and barely managing it, but now, with Lady Blenkinsopp's encouragement and the knowledge of the latest farming techniques the new estate manager seemed to have at his fingertips, it put new heart in them. Their yields, of crops where they would grow, of lambs and calves, of eggs and milk and poultry, began to increase and there was much bobbing of curtseys and doffing of caps, of grateful smiles and warmly called-out welcomes whenever she visited them, which she did at least once a month. There was even talk, though it was probably a rumour, that she meant to build a school where, Dinty Liddle told Manny Williams, all the children on the estate would be taught to read and write and do a sum or two.

They told her she was doing too much, those who

served her, but it was said with deepening affection and respect, for who would have believed that the daintily turned-out, delicately slender, frailly beautiful creature who had stood up for her son on the first day of her return, over a year ago now, and who had been beaten because of it, could have turned out to be as brave as a lioness defending her own cubs. They were her responsibility now and she meant to see they were treated with the decency and respect they deserved, she told Duffy during one of their many and varied discussions on the running of the estate. The tenants lived hard, back-breaking, heart-breaking lives but for years had put the results of that labour into her husband's pocket. Now, with her and Duffy's help, not only were they reaping the benefit themselves with the growth of their endeavours but were still putting their rents regularly into Robert's pockets. Even Mr Sinclair and Mr Bewick, who had at first been horrified at the cash that flowed out of Sir Robert's bank account, were gratified by the way it was beginning to flow back due to the general improvement in the running of what was, after all, a business.

But, of course, all this took place over many months and during that period it was as though there were time only for her husband's tenants and what was left was given to her children. Robby was a noisy toddler of twenty months with dark, tousled curls, vivid blue-grey eyes very like her own, destructive fingers which, no matter how Nanny Morag or Lizzie-Ann, the new nursemaid who had been employed to replace Rosy Little, implored him, were for ever into mischief. He was spoiled, *ruined*, Cook declared sternly, though she was as bad as the rest, for he was always escaping from the nursery and tumbling in to her kitchen demanding immediate attention, having come to believe that he was the most important person in his mama's life, and indeed, in that of every person in the house. The babies, now seven months old and fighting with each other and their older brother for what they considered to be their due, rolled about on the floor of their mama's upstairs drawing-room, grasping in their chubby hands every ornament they could reach, tormented the dogs and were as beautiful as their mother with their silver-gold curls and their incredible deep brown eyes. Their mother could deny them nothing, for it seemed she would never forget that quiet child who had shrunk away from her when she returned from Liverpool.

During the fine weather she would romp about the garden with them and Lizzie-Ann, who was barely beyond childhood herself, an excited jumble of children and young dogs, the babies scrambling about the lawn and pulling up Mr Weston's fine bedding plants while Nanny Morag despaired of ever getting them calm enough to settle in their beds for their nap.

Lizzie-Ann had been a find. She was the eldest daughter of Jessie and Dinty Liddle, a girl of fourteen who had vast experience with children since her ma had given birth to twelve, seven of whom had lived. She was old enough to go into service and would have done so if Amy had not noticed her. Like the rest of them she had the pallid, flimsy look of the underfed but no sign of the brilliant cheeks and over-bright eyes of the consumptive. She had a chirpy look about her, cheerful despite the adversities of her life, and when given a good scrub, her hair washed, and her thin,

lanky frame put into the decent hand-me-downs that
Rosy and her mistress had found in the attic at Newton
Law looked as decent and trim as any maidservant up
at the house. She had never worn shoes and found
them difficult to get used to but, as Amy told Duffy,
she was a determined little beggar and would do in the
nursery to help out Nanny Morag until further arrangements were made. And there she had remained. She
was barely more than a child herself and sometimes,
Amy decided, led Robby and the babies into many a
noisy game which they would not have thought of for
themselves but they took to her and she to them. Amy
was satisfied. Her children were happy and Nanny
Morag was prepared to put up with Lizzie-Ann's high
spirits. If anyone gave a thought to the man in the
bedroom at the top of the stairs, or to his man who,
frighteningly, was often to be found lurking in places
he was not expected to be, they made nothing of it.
They became accustomed to it and, apart from telling
one another that, really, he hadn't half given them a
fright, they ignored him. The two chambermaids who
saw Sir Robert every day when they went in to clean
his room hardly mentioned him, for there was really
nothing to report. He lay in his bed as he had done for
over a year, lifting his lip in a snarl, dribbling down
his chin and staring blankly at the ceiling, as he had
always done. The doctor, who came once a week, had
been heard to report to her ladyship that there was
no change, and never would be now, in his opinion,
but thought it his duty to keep an eye on him, or at
least on the man who cared for him. Had her ladyship
noticed any improvement, or perhaps deterioration in
his condition? And Amy was forced to admit that she

had noticed neither, unwilling to tell the doctor, who she supposed must have heard of her work, that it was many weeks since she had even seen her husband.

It was at the end of October that Duffy, sitting stiffly in the chair behind the desk in the office where they had been discussing the improvement in the health of the children at Hawthorne Lane, told her ladyship in a deceptively casual way that for personal reasons he was forced to go away for a while.

15

She leaned against the window frame in the bedroom and listened to the night sounds, hearing the soft hoot of the owl and the barking of a dog fox from Newton Wood, but in her head there was no sound other than Duffy's voice telling her he was going away. He was going away tomorrow! *He was going away tomorrow!*

Tansy had left after tidying the sitting-room floor of the drums and balls and teddy bears, the books, the spinning tops and small horses on wheels, the railway engine and raggedy dolls which the children had left lying about. She had entered the bedroom, gathering petticoats and slippers, putting away the gown, an old one, for Amy found she didn't seem to have the time to order anything new these days, that she had worn to dinner with the girls. The girls were her step-daughters, of course, Agnes, Mary and Jane, whose lives barely impinged on hers but whom she met each evening at the dinner table.

"And how is your little . . . project at Hawthorne Lane coming along?" Agnes had asked her politely, exchanging glances with her sisters, for it was not, in their opinion, the sort of project their father's

wife should interest herself in. Good works, works of charity, visiting the poor and needy were all part of a lady's responsibility. They were involved in such things themselves, moving about the parish in the company of the local incumbent, baskets on their arms containing calf's-foot jelly, warm, hand-knitted shawls for the elderly and warm hand-knitted bootees for the newborn, but they certainly did not concern themselves with the life-threatening diseases, nor the question of clean drinking water with which their father's wife was obsessed. But then, without their father's guidance and under the influence of that man whom their father had employed as a gamekeeper but who was now, at *her* insistence, manager of the estate, it seemed to them she was taking her duties as the benevolent lady of the manor too far.

She had given them a graphic description of the state of the cottages, the health, or lack of it, of those who lived in them and had even shown them her hands which, she told them proudly, since she seemed to think it was the first *useful* thing she had done in her pampered life, had been immersed in a bucket of hot water and harsh lye soap up to a few days ago. Betty Long, she reported, the woman she had told them about who was recovering nicely from consumption of the lungs, was not quite up to scrubbing out the netty which was done in turns by the women in the row and so Lady Blenkinsopp, their father's wife, had done it for her.

"Good heavens, Amy," Mary had asked her, quite appalled, "is there no other woman to do it? Or even one of the men. I presume they all have husbands?"

"Oh yes, but I happened to be there as Betty was

trying to lift the kettle of hot water from the fire so I put on her apron and did it for her."

They all three had eyed her in open-mouthed wonder, for she herself barely came up to their shoulders and had a figure like a child's. Slim as a reed and as graceful as one and yet she was tackling jobs that were not only, they thought, far beyond her strength but beneath her as the lady she had been brought up to be.

She smiled as she remembered their horrified faces and their tendency to draw away from her as she left the dining-room, as though afraid she might have brought some loathsome thing with her from those low cottages and was harbouring it in the folds of her gown.

Now that gown was safely hung up in the wardrobe. Tansy had been inclined to inspect it to see if it needed the small attentions a lady's maid was expected to pay to her mistress's clothes. A tear in the hem, or a stain sponged perhaps, but Amy had sent her away, since she longed to be on her own to ponder out how she was going to manage without Duffy at her side.

"But your hair, m'lady?" Tansy had protested. Tansy was somewhat jealous of her ladyship's growing attachment to the new girl, as Tansy still called Rosy Little though it was ten months since she had been introduced to the nursery. Tansy had considered herself to be her ladyship's favourite. Look how she had sent her to be trained in her maiding duties. They had been, and still were, on good terms with one another and she knew her ladyship trusted her, liked her, she supposed, but she certainly was making a "marrer" of Rosy, as they said up here in the north-east corner of

the country. Thick as thieves they were over those folk at Hawthorne Lane where Rosy went most days, sometimes with her ladyship and sometimes on her own, to supervise the continued improvement in the lives of those who lived there. And what was she to do when they were living the decent lives her ladyship wanted for them? When their cottages were warm and sturdy, their menfolk strong and able to work as they should, when the women were able to look after their children as they should? When it was, in fact, the model community her ladyship had set her heart on? What then for Rosy Little? Was she to go back to the nursery and if so what was to happen to that Lizzie-Ann her ladyship had fetched up from Hawthorne Lane? It was all a mystery, not only to Tansy who brooded on it at times, but to the rest of the servants who often wondered if their little mistress had bitten off more than she could chew!

"I can brush my own hair, Tansy," her mistress replied, "so you can go."

"Very well, m'lady," Tansy had said, somewhat put out, bobbing a curtsey before closing the door and tripping down to the kitchen to tell the others that she really thought her ladyship needed a rest. Pale as a ghost, she was tonight, drifting about as though she couldn't rest and if you asked her she was heading for a breakdown if she didn't give up this daft idea of bettering the lives of those down at Hawthorne Lane. They all sighed, agreeing with her, knowing it did no good, for their mistress would go her own way whatever any of them said.

Amy sank down on to the little footstool before the fire and, clasping her arms about her knees, stared into

the glowing embers. It had turned colder as September moved towards October and though it was early for it there was a light coating of frost over Mr Weston's perfectly trimmed lawn. She shivered and laid her head on her knees, feeling the misery overwhelm her, misery and a despair she had not known in many months. There was a pain in her chest and throat which she knew were tears surging to get out but she must not cry, for she was afraid that if she did she would not be able to stop. Though the room was warm and the fire was blazing she felt the cold pierce her as though she were out there in the garden instead of snug here in her room. Though she was safe among her own people she was lost and frightened, and she knew why. She knew why she felt this way, oh yes, for had it not been growing quietly and lovingly for months, but what she couldn't understand, and was distressed by it, was why he did not trust her enough to tell her why he had to leave her. Of course, he wasn't leaving *her* since he did not belong to her. He was not compelled to tell her what had taken place in his past or what was to happen in his future, and the thought of it was almost more than she could bear. He had become a part of her life, a part on which she depended utterly and if he was to leave how was she to stand upright, to move about freely and confidently with the confidence *he* had given her? They had been partners in this enterprise, in the improvement of the estate and those who lived on it, and it frightened her to realise that without him she might not be able to go on with it. It had been hard won, the fight she had fought against what her husband had done to her, and she knew that without Duffy she could not

have done it. Oh, she might have done it, but would she have emerged as whole as she had?

Duffy . . . Duffy, her heart cried out silently, and across the roof of the house, the quiet yard, the stables and gardens, in a small, fire-glowed room a man raised his head and from him was wrenched a groan, and as the woman rose, moving across the room to stare blindly out of the window, so did he.

For five minutes he stood unmoving, his own face looking back at him from the reflection in the window. When the tap sounded on his door he was startled, and so was his dog who jumped up and began to whine. Not to bark, for he knew who it was. His tail moved in a circle and he put his nose to the bottom of the door and when his master opened it, instead of leaping on the visitor as was his custom, he moved back quietly and lay down on the rug before the fire.

For perhaps five seconds they looked wordlessly into one another's eyes then he put out his hands, taking hers, drew her inside and closed the door behind her. Without thought or word she was in his arms, trying to burrow herself deeper and deeper into his embrace, making soft little mewing sounds of comfort deep in her throat as she clung to him. He began to shake, for her touch was like an electrifying shock to him and the ripples spread through his body like those on a lake as a swan glides across the surface. They made no attempt to kiss, merely stood and trembled, their bodies pressed close, clinging to what both of them had longed for in all the months they had known one another. Not just months, but on Duffy's part ever since he had first seen her on the day of her return to Newton Law.

At last, gently, he put her from him, not far, his hands still on her, holding her shoulders, for he could not bear to let go. It was as though, now that this moment for which they had both waited, perhaps unknowingly, was here, they did not know what to do with it.

She spoke first. "I had to come. You see I don't think I can . . . go on without you. If you go away I don't know how I shall manage." Her voice was low but steady and in her eyes as she looked up into his was the profound truth of her love for him. Then she reached up and placed her lips on his. He took them reverently, gently as he knew how, for he believed she had known nothing of delicacy, of the sweetness and trust that are the mark of the true lover in her previous encounter with a man and he was afraid of offending her.

Their lips clung for a moment and when they drew apart his eyes were as steady as hers and filled with the deep and endless love which was for ever hers for the taking. It was all there for the taking, waiting, waiting, for the decision was hers.

Moving slowly they drifted again into a kiss but this time it was different. Moving their heads, their lips clung and trembled as urgency overcame them but once again he drew back, groaning. It was very evident she knew what she was about, that she wanted this as much as he did, but could he take what she was offering when tomorrow he was to leave her and God knew when, or even if, he would be back again.

"Darling . . . my dearest love," his mouth whispered against hers. She shifted her body, doing her best to get closer to him and her mouth became even more urgent, more demanding and, since he was a

man after all, with a man's needs and this woman in his arms was the woman he loved, *and willing*, could he resist. Her arms were about his neck but he reached up and brought them down, crossing them at her back so that she was defenceless, lifting her up against him, feeling the roundness of her small breasts pressed to his almost bare chest. He wore only a shirt pulled out of his breeches, fastened by just a couple of buttons. She had on her nightgown with a shawl wrapped about her and on her feet were thin satin slippers. The shawl slipped to the floor and with his free hand he opened the neck of her nightgown until her shoulders were bared, burying his mouth in the curve of her neck. His hand moved to the soft flesh of her throat beneath her chin, his thumb caressing.

"My love . . . my love," he moaned in the back of his throat, feeling her breath warm on the skin beneath his ear and the hot desire spiralled through him. She was so lovely, so fragile, her skin like satin and smelling of some fragrance he could not name but did it matter, for this was how he had imagined it to be and he could not stop had she wanted him to, which it seemed was the last thing in her mind.

"Darling . . . Duffy . . . I love you . . . I love you." Words he had longed to hear, and to say.

"I love you . . . you're my heart . . ."

"My love . . ." Her hands, which he had freed, went to his hair, his hair that she had hungered to touch; to cling to . . . beloved hair, beloved man . . . She laid her lips along the line of his jaw, letting them linger there so that she might retain the feel of him, the clean, sharp tang of his masculine smell, to carry it back with her to her home which would be dark and barren without

him, to hold it and cherish it, for in this uncertain world she might never see him again.

He placed his lips on hers for their third kiss and it was as sweet as the first and the second. Sweet and yet unfamiliar. He had studied her mouth many times in the past. It was as well known to him as his own which he saw in the mirror every day. The shape of it where it curled up at the corners, the upper lip longer than the lower. The colour, a mixture of rose and apricot, but now he knew its taste. It was like sipping warm dew. As sweet and warm as the syrup that made up the apple compote Cook sometimes sent over for him. In no way cloying but honeyed to the tongue. He wanted to lick her lips, as he boyishly licked the apple compote, but this woman in his arms who had known nothing but sexual brutality might not understand the delicate touch between tongue and lips, and be repelled by it. He was doing his best to hold himself back, to make his touch, his caresses, the length of his hungering body act in a way that would not be distasteful to her who was ignorant of true loving. But she would not have it so. To his amazement and delight she pressed herself against him, against his straining manhood which was rock hard, and seemed to feel, far from distaste a joyous sensuality to match his own.

"I'm not made of glass, Duffy," she murmured against his mouth. "I'm real. A woman who will not break nor wail that she misunderstood your feelings and is offended. I came here to speak to you . . . to ask you . . . to find out what you mean . . . *why* you have to leave, but that was not the only reason. I want this," pressing herself so forcefully against him it was

as though she were determined to get inside him. To make her body part of his so that they became one unit which would not function, one without the other. "I've known how you felt; how could I not, for my feelings mirrored yours."

She drew back slightly, *very* slightly, looking up at him with eyes luminous with that expression that is a sure sign of a sexually aroused woman, the pupils black as sable. Her hair hung down her back to her buttocks, the fire-glow and lamp-glow captured in it so that it rippled and shone like burnished gold. He put his hands in it, gripping it fiercely, forcing her head further back, then ran his lips down her arched throat, slowly, the tip of his tongue touching her skin lightly.

She moaned, then cried out with pleasure and at the sound the dog lifted his head, clearly puzzled, then lumbered to his feet and padded across to them, moving his tail questioningly. He butted his head against his master's leg and as though someone had walked into the room and called out in shock at the sight of them in one another's arms, Duffy lifted his mouth from hers and stepped away from her.

"Dear sweet Christ," he whispered, dragging one hand frantically through his hair, the other steadying her as, her support gone, she swayed against him. "What am I doing? You're another man's wife. I've no right . . . to offer insult to another man's wife."

"Insult! You think me insulted? After what was done to me . . . Duffy, I love you and where there is love . . ."

"Still, you are his wife and—"

"No!" Her voice was fierce. "I'm wife to no one. Never."

He turned away from her but she beat her fists against his back and the dog, sensing the tension, the violence even, cowered away, slinking back to his place before the fire. He lay down, putting his nose on his paws, his ears twitching, his eyes sad.

"Don't do this to me, Duffy. Don't turn away. I can't bear it. I have no one but you. You are my only friend and now you tell me you are to go away and I don't even know why. Duffy, please . . ." She laid her face against his stiff back. Her arms crept round him and overcome with despair he turned to her and wrapped her in his arms. Her face pressed into his bare chest. She clung to him and would have fallen but he held her fiercely, his cheek against her hair.

"Darling, darling . . . I'm sorry. There's nothing I want more than to pick you up and take you upstairs to my bed where I would . . ." He groaned and strained her to him. "I'm a fool. What man would turn away from a woman as lovely, as wonderful as you . . ."

"Fiddlesticks," she answered him, pushing him from her and twisting away. "This is you and me, Amy and Duffy, who have loved one another, don't deny it, for a long time. It was not the . . . the right time at first but now . . . don't push me away."

He was appalled. "Sweetheart, I'm not pushing you away. You mean more to me than my life but . . ."

"But you find you cannot take another man's leavings, is that it?"

"Sweet Christ, no . . . no." He dragged her back into his arms, his face as grey as the ash on the hearth, his eyes almost black in the deep hollows beneath. "Damn it, can't you see I want to do the right thing, the gentlemanly thing. What man would take another man's wife when her husband is ill in his bed and unable . . ."

"Don't be absurd, Duffy. Take another man's wife! Shall I tell you what my husband did to his wife?"

"No . . . no," he howled and the dog shivered. "Don't you think I haven't imagined it a hundred times since that night you came home. I saw your face . . . and could picture the rest and I wanted to kill him, would have done if he had not already been injured. I was maddened with rage and abhorrence . . . to see you standing there, your face mutilated. If he had not already fallen down the stairs I would gladly—"

"He did not fall." She stepped out of his arms and moved away from him, standing before the fire. The dog sniffed at the hem of her gown and moved his tail slowly as though telling her that whatever she had done it meant nothing to him, but the man did not move. His shoulders sagged and his face, already pale, whitened further.

"Amy." His voice was barely above a whisper and in his eyes was an expression which, had she turned and looked at him, she would have found difficult to read.

"Yes." Her own voice was vague and she stared with unfocused eyes into the leaping flames of the fire. "He had done . . . performed . . . one of the worst acts a man can perform on a woman. I was in agony . . ."

"Amy, I cannot stand it."

"Neither could I, Duffy. I had already been . . ."

"Don't!" He turned wildly away, almost falling as he reached for some support against the table. His face was twisted with anguish but she would not spare him.

"I was . . . I wore nothing. He had ripped away . . ."

"Sweet Jesus . . ."

"I ran on to the landing but he followed me. He caught me at the top of the stairs. We were both as silent as the grave, which seems strange since I know I was screaming inside and I'm sure he wanted to roar with insane rage. We struggled; he caught me by the hair and . . . swung me. His back was to the stairs and, quite deliberately, I pushed him. He let go of me and tried to save himself by grabbing the banister but he missed and . . . he went down. I stood and watched him go, hoping he would break his neck. I wanted him dead, you see. I had come back to him despite what he had done to me after Robby was born. I was not healed after the birth but within days he was demanding his . . . his *rights* as he called them. He tore into me, my body, and I ran away from it, from him and from my son. My family, my cousin and . . . and her husband were kind to me. They helped me to recover and I came back, but this time I was determined, for Robby's sake, to put up with him, to make a life, but even when I had been in the house no more than a few hours I knew it was not possible. Women will put up with many things for the sake of their children but . . . Well, you know now, Duffy, and if you are to turn from me, then so be it. You deserve the truth before you go away."

With a sound in his throat like ripping cloth he turned and blundered across the room to her. He was weeping and as he put his arms about her, turning her towards him, the tears flowed on to the fabric of her gown. She was stiff, unresponsive. His wet face rested on her shoulder and he shook so violently she shook with him, but gradually he felt her relax against him.

"Forgive me . . . forgive me," he mumbled, pressing her closer, and with a gentle sigh she lifted her arms and put them about him, her hands in his hair. "I knew that he had . . . but I had no idea . . . I'm a man, you see, but the violence done to you is beyond comprehension. I would have willingly done him harm, so I understand, I cannot blame you. I love you."

"I did it deliberately, my darling. You must understand that."

"I do, and I cannot find it in my heart to judge you. Does that sound pompous? I didn't mean it to be. It makes no difference. Dear God, I sound . . . I don't know how to explain what I mean, I only know that you're the most courageous woman I know. I respect you. I love you, and I want you but . . . it cannot happen now, my love. Not here. Do you understand?"

"I think so. He would come between us."

"Yes. Come and sit down. I'll make us a cup of tea." He smiled as he took her hand and led her to the chair by the fire. "A cup of tea, supposedly the panacea for all ailments and troubles, or so I'm told," and it also would give him a moment to recover himself. He needed to have her some distance from him, since his male body, no matter what he might say, didn't give a fig for the fact that she was another man's wife. His fine honourable mind did, he thought wonderingly, but his body wanted nothing more than to lay her down wherever was handy and make love to her until she was totally satiated, and him with her. He realised that her revelations about the way her husband had met with his accident didn't actually concern him overmuch. It had been a shock that so lovely and fragile a creature would have the strength, and the strength of will to do such a thing, but would he not himself have done Sir Robert Blenkinsopp an injury had he had the opportunity? So did that make Amy, because of her sex, any the worse for it? It did not. She had been defending herself in the only way she could.

Her shawl lay on the floor where it had fallen. Her nightgown, though high-necked and long-sleeved, was of fine lawn, insubstantial, the light from the fire shining through it and revealing every curve of her slender but shapely body. It fell away from one white shoulder and he hastily retrieved the shawl, draping it about her as she sat down in the chair, doing his best not to touch her.

She noticed. "Don't worry, Duffy, I'm not about to seduce you."

"Don't, my darling. Don't say such things. You know I love you, don't you?"

He had made the tea in the sturdy brown pot and now he poured the rich liquid into a dainty cup which he placed on an equally dainty saucer, adding milk and sugar. He passed it to her before pouring one for himself and sitting down in the chair opposite hers.

She took a sip then looked up at him, her gaze steady.

"I know, my love, and the remark was not worthy of either of us. It's just that . . ."

"I know, darling and . . . when the time is right we will; but with my going away tomorrow and . . ."

"Perhaps never coming back?"

"I'll come back. I promise you."

"I don't even know why you must go." Her voice was forlorn and the dog sat up and nudged her hand. She put it on his broad head.

"It's something I must do."

"Can't you tell me? I know there is something in your life that you prefer to keep secret, but surely you can trust me to keep it secret, too. Please, Duffy, so that I may understand why you must go. Duffy—"

His quiet voice interrupted her. "Alec," he said, his eyes brooding into the fire.

"Pardon?"

"My name is Alec. Alec Murray."

She was clearly confounded.

"Alec?"

"Mmm."

"But why call yourself Duffy if . . . ?"

"It was a name I got at school. I am Alec Duff Murray. Duff was my mother's maiden name so, when I went to school . . . you know how boys are."

"No, not really, though I had a brother."

"It was considered smart to have a nickname. Mine was Duffy so when I came here and at other places I called myself that."

"Why?" She leaned forward, her eyes glimmering into his. She had not re-buttoned her nightgown and the firelight turned the skin at her throat and down to her breasts to the sheen of gold. He wanted to reach out to her, to lay his hand on the warmth and colour and beauty of her but he knew if he did he would be lost, and so would she.

He took a deep, ragged breath.

"I wanted to hide my identity."

"Why?" she repeated. "Had you done something wrong, something illegal?"

"No, nothing like that."

"Well then?"

"I had a disagreement with my father. He wanted me to do one thing, I another, so I left. I did not want to be found."

Suddenly he rose from his chair and retrieved *The Times* which lay on the table. He opened it and sighed, pointing to a paragraph on a page inside.

"It was this. I'm afraid I'm needed at home."

It was the obituary page. It was a simple paragraph reporting the death of Lord Richard Murray, tenth baron of Ladywood in the county of Cheshire.

She read it several times, the newspaper trembling in her hand as the implication of the words became clear to her, then she looked up at him and he could see the fear start in her eyes.

"No, my darling, no." He kneeled down at her feet. He took the newspaper and threw it to the floor before drawing her into the protection of his arms. "I won't desert you. I'll come back. This makes no difference. I have to go, you do see that, don't you? My mother and sister will need me but when everything is settled I'll come back to you. Oh hell, what a bloody mess." He dragged his hand through his hair in a way that was becoming increasingly familiar to her, then closed his arms about her again, kissing her passionately on her closed eyelids from which tears squeezed. "I'll come back . . . I'll come back."

"To be estate manager at Newton Law! You who are

the eleventh baron of – where is it? – Ladywood in the county of Cheshire."

"It doesn't matter. I love you. One day you will be my—"

She pushed him away and sprang to her feet, her face wet with tears and twisted in despair.

"Don't say it, Duffy, don't say it. I can't bear it. You know we can never . . . please, let me go."

Savagely she pushed him from her and darted for the door. Before he could stop her she had it open and had fled into the darkness.

Platt was breathing hard as he pushed the trollop from the Three Feathers through the dining-room window and into a spiky bush that stood beneath it, unconcerned with her protest that, along with the other injuries she had received that night, she was being bloody scratched to buggery.

"Howay woman, yer've bin well paid fer it," he was whispering, for if he wasn't careful the whole house would be roused. She was as drunk as a lord, which was the state they were forced to get her into in order to persuade her to what they wanted from her.

When the back door, the kitchen door into the yard, banged to, he stiffened and put his hand over the woman's mouth as he listened intently. He turned in the direction of the hallway and was just in time to see, in the light from the dying fire, her ladyship, dressed in nothing but her nightgown, flit like a ghost along the hall and past the open dining-room door to the bottom of the stairs. He was so astounded he let the trollop fall into the bushes where she seemed to drop off into a drunken snooze. Bugger it, bugger it, he'd have to climb out after her and get her on her way, because the last thing he and Sir Robert wanted was for one of the gardeners to find her the next morning.

When he had finally escorted the floundering woman off the premises, through the garden and on to the moorland path, he could hardly wait, in his excitement to get back to his master and report that his wife had been out of the house in her nightgown and it didn't take much reckoning to know who it was she had been with!

16

He was gone the next day. He went without saying goodbye and she was glad, for she knew it was beyond her strength, which was at its lowest, to see him go.

He had said goodbye to no one, it seemed, which threw the servants into noisy consternation. Where had he gone? Why had he gone? Did her ladyship know and what would she do without his help, they asked each other, their faces perplexed, and if she didn't already know who was to tell her the news?

It was Phyllis who discovered he was not in his usual place behind the desk in the estate manager's office. She had gone in to fetch the coal scuttle which it was her job to replenish, and to stoke up the fire if it was needed. Mind you, Mr Duffy, as they had begun to call him when he was promoted, was not the sort of man to ring the bell to summon someone else to throw a bit of coal, or a log, on the fire when he was perfectly capable of doing it himself, he told her. He had smiled when he said it in that lovely way he had, a half smile really, just a twitching of his mouth which had most of the maidservants in love with him, relieving her of the heavy scuttle and placing it beside the hearth. She and Ruth often argued over who was to take in his coffee which he liked early, long before her ladyship joined him in their morning discussion and on this day Cook had almost skelped the pair of them, sending Ruth into the scullery and Phyllis with the coffee. She remembered she had thrown a triumphant look at Ruth who, behind Cook's back, had pulled her tongue at her.

"'E's not there," she had proclaimed a few minutes later, her face a picture of consternation, the tray on which the coffee pot, cream, sugar, cup and saucer were arranged trembling in her hands.

"What? Who?"

"Mr Duffy, 'e's not there."

They all stopped what they were doing and turned to stare at Cook as though she had the answer. Mr Duffy was so regular in his habits, always to be found in the office no later than eight o'clock of a morning, and to be told he wasn't there at nine was a bit of a facer.

"Well . . ." Cook was for a moment nonplussed, but for goodness' sake, it wasn't the end of the world, was it? The chap had probably decided to have an extra half-hour in bed so why was everyone standing about with their mouths open as though . . . as though . . . well, she didn't know what to say, or to think, but there was an easy answer and that was for Nipper to run over to the cottage and find out. They weren't prying, or anything like that, were they? Just concerned. He might be poorly, in which case Cook would send him across one of her potions, something for his chest, or his throat, or his stomach, whichever he needed. Perhaps some of the casserole she was about to put in the oven. She might even go herself and take a look at him. Men were notorious for not looking after themselves and he was a bit of a favourite with her.

Nipper was gasping for breath when he tumbled into the kitchen and it was evident he had raced there and back in his eagerness to tell them the news.

"'E's gone. 'E's not there an' neither is Dick. Place is tidy as anyfink an' . . . an' . . . empty," which was the only way the boy could describe the echoing quiet of the gamekeeper's cottage.

There was silence, a thick silence, just as though they all knew there was something wrong, for one of the things they liked about Mr Duffy was that he was most considerate in letting the kitchen staff know where he was off to the day. He'd no need to, for it was nothing to do with them where he went on estate business but then that was him and to leave without a word made them uneasy.

Cook turned to Morna. "Nip over there and have a look round, like, there's a good lass. See if . . . well, see if everything's there. His books and what-not. Perhaps he left a note the day."

What she was telling Morna was to look the cottage over and give her opinion as to whether Mr Duffy had just gone off for the day without telling them, or . . . well, she didn't know what she had in her mind, or even why she should feel so disturbed, but Morna was sensible, sharp-witted, and would recognise the difference between a place left for the day and one in which the occupier was no longer in residence!

What Morna told them could only bring them to the realisation that Mr Duffy had gone for good. Or at least for the foreseeable future. His books were still on the shelves, his pictures on the walls but every stitch of clothing and that big leather portmanteau he owned was missing, as was his dog. So what were they to tell her ladyship, that's if her ladyship didn't already know? Surely Mr Duffy had informed her that he was to be off, but if that was the case why hadn't her ladyship told *them*?

It seemed, when Morna questioned Tansy and Tansy hesitantly put it to her ladyship, hesitantly, for her ladyship wasn't at all herself that morning, that the mistress *did* know that Mr Duffy had gone but she gave no explanation as to why, nor even seemed inclined to speak about it. In fact she was sharp with Tansy, which wasn't like her, not exactly telling her to mind her own business, but coming close to it. She thought she might stay in her bed this morning, she told her maid, and would Tansy ask Nanny Morag to keep the children upstairs for the time being. She felt the need of a rest and no, she didn't want any breakfast, just a cup of tea perhaps and then she wanted to be left alone. She'd ring when she needed her, she told Tansy, and Tansy and the rest of the worried servants were left to whisper over whatever could be wrong, not only with her ladyship but with Mr Duffy that he had to leave so suddenly without a word to anyone.

When Tansy left the room, her honest, rosy face screwed into an anxious frown, Amy rose from her bed, the bed where she had tossed and sleeplessly turned all night. She felt as insubstantial as a wraith wavering on a ripple of air; as though her body were transparent, flimsy and ready to collapse into a trembling heap of chilly bones and flesh. Although Tansy had built the fire up into a cheerful pyramid of crackling coal, throwing off a splendid heat, she felt cold and, yes, frightened. The world was empty without him, empty and hollow and meaningless. What should she do now? She was aware that her expression was haunted; she had seen Tansy stare at her in dismay. There was a pain inside her so deep it came from a part of her she had not known existed. She had never known such despair, even in the days when her husband had overwhelmed her mind and body, the very soul of her with his abuse. She had thought then that she would never escape it, that she would never know the simple, uncomplicated life of a wife and mother, which was all she asked. She had been wrong. She had, for almost a year, been content with her children, with the days of peace Robert's descent into obscurity, his absence from their lives had brought her and she had gloried in it. And she had found love. She had found Duffy, loved him and lost him again and how was she to survive without him? It seemed, at this moment, that everything was in ashes and ruin. Nothing would be the same again. Once again she had lost faith and for this day, this moment in time, she let herself give in to it. Soon she must drag her tattered life about her again, for her children's sake she must, but for this small period, this day, this day that was to be her first without Duffy, she would allow herself to grieve for him.

He had promised her he would come back. *Promised her*, and she was aware that when he made that vow to her he had meant it, or at least believed he meant it. He had become, on the death of his father, a baron, a member of the peerage. He had inherited the ancient seat of Ladywood in the county of Cheshire and though he had gone into no details on its size or wealth she understood from his manner that it was not one that could be left to the management of a steward. He had a mother living, and a sister, people who were dependent on him and how could a man, a man of integrity, with his own estate to manage, return to help her with the one she held in trust for Robby? Her son would one day be Sir Robert Blenkinsopp, since the baronetcy was hereditary, and the estate must be kept in good heart until Robby was old enough to oversee it himself.

She leaned listlessly on the window frame and stared out into the garden. It was a soft grey day, damp and cool. She could smell rain through the half-opened window and hear the noise the swans and ducks made on the small lake. At its edge stood Nanny Morag and Lizzie-Ann, each with a hand on the handle of the perambulator, deep in some nanny-like conversation but at the same time keeping a watchful eye on their charges, especially Robby. The babies, both with a frilled bonnet on their head, were doing their best to stand up and leap from the perambulator, eager to join their elder brother and the two dogs as they scampered beside the water. Robby was enthusiastically flinging lumps of bread on to the water and just as enthusiastically Briar and Bracken were doing their best to retrieve them without actually getting wet. At any other time she would have laughed out loud at the sight, but now it only pierced her with a knife-like thrust, for Duffy was not here to laugh at it with her.

She bent her head and put her face in her hands, not weeping but making a sound which, if Tansy had heard it, would have alarmed her. The devastation tore at her and she trembled like a leaf on an empty branch, a leaf waiting for that final swirl of wind to bring it spiralling to the ground. Today was hers, her to mourn in, and hers to get to grips with the plans she had made, with Duffy, and which she had expected to put into operation with him beside her. Now she must do it alone. It would be a start, or rather a continuation of the fine project they had begun together and which she had believed they would see to the end, together. Perhaps . . . perhaps . . . dare she hope that he would come back for her? Dare she, but did not that route spell disaster. A false hope. Dear sweet Christ, how was she to bear it if . . . ?

She lifted her head and sighed, a long shuddering sigh of hopeless despair, for, should he return, what was there in the future for her and the man she loved? She was married even though she was not a wife, and never would be, at least to her husband. Duffy was the holder of a hereditary title for which he would need a son to carry it on. He would need a wife and she could be wife neither to her husband, nor to Duffy. She was condemned to live a sterile life, for even if Duffy did return what could she offer him, or he her?

With a soft but savage sound in the back of her throat she flung herself at her wardrobe, wrenching from among the neatly arranged clothing a warm, sensible dress and a hooded cloak of wool, both in a shade of practical grey. Divesting herself of her night things she donned her undergarments, the dress and the cloak, pushing her feet into woollen stockings and a pair of stout boots. Quietly she let herself out of the bedroom and slipped down the back stairs, along the passage that led to the office – from which she turned her face in anguish – and let herself out of the side door and through the herb garden. She could still hear the noisy play of her elder son and the excited barking of the dogs but, keeping to the trees, she avoided the little group, striding through the familiar woodland towards its edge where the moorland began. She crossed the stream over which once Duffy had lifted the perambulator, and began to scramble up the path that she and he, with Robby on his shoulders, had climbed so many times; the path on which she and Duffy had urged their horses when they had visted Berry Hill Farm, Bilberry Farm and the rest of her husband's tenants. So many glorious memories of a time which, she had thought, if she had thought at all, would go on for ever.

It was a day of autumnal coolness, inclined to be damp, and as she forced her weary way upwards through the dying bracken her mind was almost numbed by recollection. Here she had stopped to catch her breath, leaning against a mossy, waist-high stone with Duffy's hand hovering at her elbow ready to catch her if she should stumble, for she had been with child. Here they had stopped to admire a great patch of moorland speedwell and higher up the purple stretch of heather which had blazed in the summer. She remembered days of gathering blue bilberries, the basket carried home to Cook for her jams and pies. They had climbed almost into the clouds, dodging those that scudded across the blue just above their heads. She had shrieked when an adder streaked across her path and found comfort in Duffy's strong arms, then bent to study the sundew plant which stickily entangled, then consumed insects. They had watched the swallows gathering for flight and listened to the haunting cry of the curlew. She had been transported into another world, a world of enchantment and joy, a world that had awakened in her the supreme rapture of living, of just being alive and now every step she took she seemed to be walking on her own heart.

The Weeping Stones. How appropriate that name was now. It was said they had been called that for a girl who had lost her lover and who had shed her tears into the tough moorland grass, as she herself was doing now as she stared with blind eyes over the valley through which ran the most beautiful river in Northumberland.

For a long time she stood, her back against the pitted stones, her hands thrust deep in the pocket of her cloak, her chin buried in its collar. Her heart broke a dozen times as she stood there and she wanted to shut her ears to the sound of its shattering but she knew she must listen to it, accept its fragile state and go on. Go on until, though it would never be whole again, it would be mended sufficiently for her to live her life as she had planned it with Duffy at her side. He would no longer be a part of it but it must be done, for what else was she to do with it?

The two men watched from the bedroom window as the slight figure of the woman dragged across the garden. She was hatless and her hair lay limp and bedraggled down her back. It had begun to rain quite heavily and there was no one about to see her, not a gardener or any of the men who worked around the house and grounds. Her cloak, which was grey, was heavy and darkened with rain about its hem and her whole demeanour seemed to convey a melancholy which was almost tangible.

"Mumble mumble bitch looks as mumble mumble lost a guinea and mumble mumble sixpence," the man propped in the chair snarled. His eyes conveyed some dreadful emotion, an emotion in which were mixed loathing, frustration, bitterness and a venom so implacable it seemed to say woe betide her if she ever fell into his hands. He seemed to swell with some dreadful thing which even the lumbering brute beside him flinched away from. His lips stretched, and his teeth, yellowed and stained, for it had not occurred to the man who was hired to look after him to give them a clean, bared like those of an animal, and about his mouth a foaming kind of spittle formed. Encompassing him was a deep and terrible malevolence and at the same time a kind of pleasure as though in anticipation of something sweet to come.

"'Appen tis 'im what's gone, the mucky hoit. 'Appen tis 'im she's upset about the day, like. If 'im an' 'er were . . ."

The man in the chair flung himself round, aiming his good arm at his minder's head but the minder, well used to his master by now, ducked nimbly to one side, grinning foolishly, showing his own set of decaying teeth.

"Mumble your bloody mouth, you ignorant mumble mumble. They might mumble mumble but it's not up to mumble mumble mumble the likes of you to mumble mumble. She's a mumble whore and she'll bloody mumble pay for it in my good time but mumble mumble mumble . . ." Here he became so incoherent even Platt, who had become adept at understanding him, could not make out what he was saying though he could guess. Platt was of the opinion that the only thing that kept his master alive, and not only alive, but improving, was what foul thing he had in mind for his wife. He blamed her for his accident which had imprisoned him in this room for the past sixteen months and it was his dedication to the revenge he intended for her that kept his deranged mind and damaged body ticking over. Not that Platt applied such words to his master's condition, for he was an uneducated man but he knew nevertheless what Sir Robert was.

The vicious snarl on Robert Blenkinsopp's face faded away and was replaced by a contemplative expression, almost a smile, dreamy and yet at the same time demonic, if such a thing was possible, and Platt hoped that when the time came he would be there to see what was to happen. Lady Blenkinsopp held him in contempt, he knew that, shuddering when they met, and it would give him a great deal of pleasure to be involved in her . . . well, he could only think of the word, *come-uppance*!

As her ladyship disappeared round the corner of the house Sir Robert relaxed. His face slipped into its usual insensate expression. His mouth, half open, drooled saliva at one corner and his eyes drifted into a dazed, unfocused stare.

"Time's come to start to mumble mumble, Platt. Something mumble mumble small, I think. Mumble mumble that will give her mumble mumble mumble a shock but mumble mumble nothing to what she'll mumble mumble in the end."

He smiled, then, lifting his good hand, he indicated

that he wished to be carried back into his bed, and without effort Platt heaved him up into his arms, a more difficult task than sixteen months ago, since his master had become grossly obese.

"Now listen," Sir Robert slurred. "This is mumble mumble what mumble I want you to mumble mumble. Unnerstand?"

Platt indicated that he was all ears, listening carefully to his master's snuffling instructions.

Amy had finally fallen into a light doze. The previous night she had not slept at all and her climb up to the Weeping Stones, her aching journey through the past she had shared with Duffy, had wearied her, stunned her almost into a state of semi-consciousness which was not unpleasant. Tansy had tiptoed round her when she returned, begging to be allowed to bring her a boiled egg, a sliver of toast, some of Cook's light and appetising broth which would put heart in her, but she had been refused. They had deliberated in the kitchen, the older women and Tansy, since she was the carrier of news, what could be upsetting their mistress so and, not being daft, had come to the conclusion that it must be something to do with Mr Duffy. Not for a minute did they believe that anything improper had gone on between them, since for nine months her ladyship had been pregnant with the twins, but you had to admit that she and her estate manager had been inseparable since they had undertaken the renovation of the cottages in Hawthorne Lane. They had been of the same mind over its residents, determined to better their lives and they had succeeded beyond all recognition. The farms on Newton Law estate had not been forgotten and her

ladyship, with Mr Duffy alongside her, had ridden up
on to the moors, visiting each one and making herself
known and respected by Sir Robert's tenants. They had
been of one mind, it seemed, and as Mr Duffy had
been of the same class as their mistress could they
be surprised they had been drawn to one another.
Who else had her ladyship been able to converse
with on matters of which they, as servants, were
ignorant? There were, of course, her step-daughters
but . . . well, to be honest, they said to one another,
the Misses Blenkinsopp were old maids and not of the
same nature as their young and beautiful mistress. She
liked a bit of a laugh, did her ladyship. You only had
to see her with her children, and though you couldn't
exactly call Mr Duffy a *merry* person, he was of a
humorous turn of mind and he certainly seemed to
make her ladyship laugh. They still had no notion of
why or where he had gone and they couldn't ask her
ladyship, could they, though Tansy, at the instigation
of the others, had hesitantly asked her ladyship if
another estate manager was to be employed.

Her mistress had turned on her quite tartly.

"I suppose you and the other servants have been
gossiping in the kitchen, is that it?"

"Oh, your ladyship, we only—"

"I don't care to hear what you have been saying,
my girl, but you can tell them, so that there will be
no mistake, that I myself am to run this estate. Mr . . .
Mr Duffy has taught me all there is to know and I shall
proceed in the . . . in the same way."

"We was only . . . oh, your ladyship, we care about
thi' an' . . . ." In her distress Tansy reverted to the way
she had spoken before her ladyship promoted her to

lady's maid and which she had been doing her best to correct.

Amy relented, doing her best to smile though her face felt stiff and unyielding.

"I know, Tansy, I know, and you may tell the others that . . . that Mr Duffy" – it was agony just to say his name – "has been forced to return to his home on family business."

"And, is 'e ter return, m'lady?" Tansy asked cautiously.

"I . . . I don't know, Tansy. I don't believe so."

She was restlessly turning, in a state of half waking and half sleeping when the noise began and for a bewildering few moments she merely lay there, clutching the sheets about her chin while her heart pounded in terror. It was a kind of wailing, a tearing, shrieking wail of what seemed to be agony and it froze her to her bed, for she recognised that it was some dreadful thing that might destroy her. Dear Lord, what? where? who? Who was it in such appalling pain? For that was what it was, a scream of pain that echoed about the house, and already she could hear the sound of voices, of feet running past her bedroom door.

The children! Sweet Jesus . . . Oh dear God, the children . . . And yet it had not sounded like a human voice but an animal . . . animals howling, a wolf. Didn't wolves howl like that in the night? But there were no wolves . . .

With a strangled cry she leaped from her bed and flung herself at her closed bedroom door, wrenching it open so fiercely she fell back into the room. She was amazed when, dressed roughly in nothing but his breeches and an open shirt, no boots to his feet, his braces flying, John-Henry flew past her and began to leap, three steps at a time, up the stairs to the nursery. He said something to her as he passed but she couldn't make out what it was, for at that moment the shrill sound of a terrified child rent the air and she felt her heart stop, distinctly come to an abrupt halt before racing on at a speed that made her gasp.

"What . . . John-Henry," she managed to shriek at the groom's back and was again made speechless by the realisation that there were men behind her, and on the top landing where the nursery door stood open was a crowd of mute, white-faced maidservants, all in their nightgowns.

"What is it? Dear sweet Lord, what is it? Nanny . . ."

Nanny was on her knees with Lizzie-Ann beside her and both of them were weeping. Nanny Morag had said more times than Amy could remember that "them dratted things" were more nuisance than they were worth, for they were for ever under her feet, but she was distraught now as the two young dogs died in agony, vomiting their brave hearts out, both of them, with their cheerful faces – cheerful no longer – in her lap. Lizzie-Ann was stroking first one head then another, saying the words of comfort that woman say to all creatures in pain. "There, there," she repeated time and time again and then stopped as she realised that both of the little dogs were dead.

In the doorway of the night nursery was a small figure in a white nightgown, one foot on top of the other, one thumb plugged securely in his mouth. His eyes were blank with shock and he had wet himself.

"Robby," his mother whispered. In one bound she was across the day nursery, leaping the still tableau, lifting him into her arms where he rested, stiff as a plaster doll, his eyes still staring at the horrendous scene before him.

A murmur of horror began to whisper through the small audience and Ruth and Phyllis, unable to hold in their anguish, began to weep noisily, but at once Cook, who stood no nonsense at any time and was not about to let it begin now, no matter what had transpired, put an arm about them both and chivvied them towards the stairs that led down to the main bedrooms.

"See, you two, this is nowt fer you. Go an' put kettle on and mekk a big pot of tea. I reckon we could all do wi' one." She turned to the rest. "You can all go with them but fer pity's sake make yourselves decent first. Now go on, the lot of yer. I'll be down in a minute."

Amy remembered little of the following hour. Small events remained in her mind. A big mug of scalding hot tea, much sweetened, put in her hands, Robby's heavy body relaxing against her as she sat, still in her flimsy nightgown, in Cook's chair by the kitchen fire. John-Henry and Alfred slipping tactfully through the kitchen after Robby slept, a pitiful bundle in each pair of strong but tender arms, for though they'd all complained about the harum-scarum puppies, they'd been fond of them.

And finally, of being placed carefully in her own bed by Tansy, Robby still in her arms. Duffy, her heart was murmuring, oh Duffy, I need you now, now and always, and how am I to manage without you? Come home to me, come home to me.

17

For several days she remained in her sitting-room, her children about her, the two babies who had slept through the horror of the small dogs' deaths crawling about the room and doing their best to stand, and when they did, climbing on to the chairs and sofas, turning to look at her with proud baby smiles, seeking her approval which she gave gladly. They were noisy and cheerful and though she was aware that they missed Briar and Bracken, who had been a part of their nursery world ever since they were born, they were too young to voice it. They babbled and laughed, or yelled for their mother's attention, their destructive fingers grabbing for everything within their reach while she and Robby, who was still quiet and inclined to cling to her, sat by the fire and read his favourite books. Simple tales of the farmyard and the woodland with brightly coloured pictures which he gazed at solemnly, reminding her of the infant who had gazed at her from his nurse's arms almost eighteen months ago. He who was the noisiest of the three of them had been badly affected by the deaths of the dogs and the violence and sound of their suffering, and Amy was at her wit's end as to how she was to return him to the merry imp he had been. The child had had a poor beginning to his young life, from which she had rescued him, and now for this to happen – happen being a foolish word, for it had not just *happened* – seemed destined to set him back again to the withdrawn child he had been when she returned to Newton Law.

She was startled, though why she should be she couldn't imagine, for the child had loved the man, when Robby turned a trusting eye on her and said, "Where Duffy, Mama? Duffy gone?"

Her heart lurched painfully and her mouth became dry, for how was she to explain to this damaged little boy the absence of the man whom not only she had loved but so had he.

"He . . . he had to go home to see his mama, darling. His mama was all alone and . . . needed him. His mama lives a long way away so it . . . it will take him a long time to get there."

"Duffy home soon, Mama?" he asked hopefully, ignoring, as children will, the reference to Duffy's mama's home, for this was where Duffy lived. With Robby.

"I hope so, sweetheart."

But even at almost two years old Robby recognised the hesitant nature of his mama's answer and his face took on an anxious expression. "Soon, Mama?"

"Oh my darling." Amy laid her cheek on the child's glossy dark curls, evading the searching gaze of his blue eyes which were the exact colour of her own and, though she was not consciously aware of it, held the exact expression of loss. She held him close while the twins who, as long as they had one another were perfectly happy to allow their brother exclusive rights to their mother's lap, wrestled with each other fiercely until they disappeared under the flounces of their mama's sofa.

The boy was silent for a moment or two, then: "I yike Duffy, Mama." He sighed forlornly.

"I know, darling."

"You yike Duffy, Mama?"

"Yes, sweetheart, I do."

Briar and Bracken, in John-Henry's opinion, had been poisoned and she was not surprised by his words.

"I'm that sorry, m'lady," he said, twisting his cap between his strong brown fingers, fingers that could hold a self-willed horse to his command and yet had been as gentle as a woman's on the night the dogs had died. His expression said that he would give an arm or a leg to save her the dreadful news. It was almost as though he blamed himself, for the dogs had been accustomed to taking their meals in the stables after a run in the fields with one of the grooms. They were then returned to the nursery where they spent most of the day with the children. When Nanny Morag and Lizzie-Ann took their charges for their daily walk, they frisked alongside Robby who steadfastly refused, at almost two years old, to be put in the perambulator with David and Catherine, or even to hold Lizzie-Ann's hand. A right little "rattle-scawp" he had become, but now would you look at him, sitting on his mother's knee and refusing to sleep in his own little bed in the night nursery, his eyes enormous in his pale face and what was to be done about it, the worried servants asked one another, for they loved the little scamp.

"Who on earth would do such a thing, John-Henry?"

Amy was aghast but of course it made sense, for would two healthy little dogs both die at exactly the same time and in the same way?

"Nay, m'lady, I wish I knew for by God I'd wring 'is bloody neck," the groom answered savagely, then begged her pardon, quite horrified by what he had said.

"No, John-Henry, I'd do the same if I had the chance. Who could possibly do such a thing to a child, let alone two young animals? Robby is . . . well, you've seen the way he is," nodding her head in the direction of her bedroom door which stood open and beyond which her son slept restlessly in her bed.

"Aye, m'lady, an' I 'ope yer don't think me ter be steppin' outer me place, like, but I wondered if this might 'elp." And with the air of a conjurer producing a rabbit from a hat he withdrew from his deep pocket a sleepy kitten. It was a tiny striped tabby with markings of grey and transparent aquamarine eyes blinking from a head of grey velvet. It curled itself up on the groom's hand, quite at ease it seemed in its strange surroundings, ready to go to sleep wherever it happened to be. "I were in two minds whether ter fetch another pup. I know a chap what breeds right nice little beagles, like. Then I thought 'appen another dog might, after other two, might remind t'lad, so . . . Well, stable cat 'ad a litter, which she does regular, like, an' so . . ."

He held out the kitten, his embarrassed expression and shifting feet telling her how badly this had affected them all, not just "lad".

"Oh, John-Henry, how lovely, and I'm sure Robby will be delighted." For a moment, quite bewildering John-Henry, she turned away, taking a step towards the window. She was, in that moment, overwhelmed by a grief so fierce she was sure that John-Henry would recognise it and wonder. The little dogs, a gift from Duffy, had been a link with him, a memory that was precious as all her memories of the days she spent with him were precious. He had been an integral part of not only her life, but the children's, and the dogs were part of it all. Now they were gone, as he was, and though John-Henry, whom she had asked to come up to her sitting-room to see if he could shed some light on the young dogs' appalling deaths, was offering this pretty kitten as a substitute, it only seemed to renew, in a wave of pain, her loneliness and despair.

She turned back and managed a smile and the groom's smile in response was relieved. He moved from foot to foot, plainly uncomfortable in this pretty sitting-room which was totally out of his experience, then, clumsily, he held out his big hand with the kitten still occupying his palm. She took the small animal and held it to her face, then smiled genuinely, for it was the daintiest, most charming little thing and so utterly unlike the two robust dogs, which was a good thing, she thought; it might just do the trick with Robby. Another dog, a dog that would not be Briar or Bracken, might be turned away from but this little thing which would need his protection could be just what he needed, and the groom had, with great delicacy, recognised the fact.

"Thank you, John-Henry, this is most kind of you."

"No, no, m'lady, it's just . . . well, I'll not forget little lad in a 'urry, like. What were in 'is face when them pups died. Why aye, if it does trick I'll be suited, me an't rest o't servants. An' if we find out 'oo the . . ." He had been about to use some strong language but, remembering who he was with he merely said, ". . . chap what done this 'e'll live ter rue t' day 'e were born."

It did the trick, for when Robby awoke the next morning to find the dainty little kitten dancing on the counterpane, playing with a small ball of wool which Tansy had produced from the kitchen where much knitting went on, he was enchanted. Nothing would suit but that he took Kitty up to the nursery to show his brother and sister and from that moment he slowly began to return to the ebullient small boy he had been before the deaths of Briar and Bracken. It did not happen overnight but the kitten which, his mother impressed on him, was his and his alone, his to feed and groom, went everywhere with him, tucked unceremoniously and uncomplainingly under his arm. Even later, as it grew so that he was no longer able to carry it, wherever he went the cat went too, as though it knew its purpose in life, following him even into the garden and the woodlands surrounding the house where, with a great show of indifference which is the nature of a cat, it idled along behind him.

It was Rosy who forced Amy to pick up the threads of her life without Duffy, for didn't Rosy know what ailed her mistress since was she too not suffering . . . well, not *suffering* because Rosy's love was returned and the lad she loved was with her every day but she knew, since she had seen them together as they worked side by side on the Hawthorne Lane project, how it had been between her mistress and Duffy. She supposed the other women, those who lived in Hawthorne Lane, for women noticed these things, had had some suspicion but they were too busy with accustoming themselves to the wonderful new life Lady Blenkinsopp had introduced to them to take much heed. What the gentry did was nothing to do with them, only in the way it affected them. They could not get over the change in their lives since her ladyship had shown an interest in the way they had lived: the appalling conditions, the inability of their menfolk to provide decent food and warm clothing on the pitiful wages Sir Robert paid them. Their children had begun to thrive. Their husbands were in secure employment bringing in a wage which, if not excessive, was enough to ensure they were decently clothed and fed. Their cottages had been restored to a comfort, a cosiness, a sturdiness, to sheltering homes so that they felt they had died and gone to heaven, they told one another. Jessie Liddle, who was spare with her compliments, if indeed she paid any, had given her opinion that without her ladyship the coming winter would have brought many deaths, one of them being without a doubt Betty Long, who now tramped every day into Allenbury to help Mrs Doctor – as they called Laura Barrie – in her small hospital. Who would have thought it? Betty Long who had not had the strength to drag herself to the netty a few months back, working alongside Mrs Doctor, light work to be sure, mixing potions and such under Mrs Doctor's supervision, but enjoying herself, earning a few bob and, what's more, gaining a feeling of self-worth she had never known before. The rest of them worked at the casual labour that was to be found in the big houses and the industries that went on in these parts, scrubbing or doing a bit of laundry, which was now within their strengthening capabilities. Her ladyship still sent down gallons of milk which the children had to drink, eggs, even butter from the Home Farm which not one of them had ever tasted in their lives. Aye, life was good and they only had her ladyship to thank for it, and they had begun to wonder why she never came near them these days.

The farming community, now that their farm buildings were repaired and their farms becoming more profitable, gave heartfelt thanks to Mr Duffy who seemed to know about such things and had passed on many a helpful bit of advice to Jack Elliott, to Edwin Berwick, William Dawson and the others at Bilberry Farm and Breck Farm. Though they had farmed all their lives none of them could read or write, apart from awkwardly signing their names and adding up a column of simple figures, and they were quite amazed at the modern methods, or what they called "new-fangled" ways, Mr Duffy told them about and had at first been reluctant to try them out, but they had to admit that what came out of them books of his were proving to be bloody marvellous.

Amy had been for a lonely walk that morning, again retracing her steps up to the Weeping Stones and sitting for an hour with her back to the grey, lichen-covered rocks, huddled in her warm cloak, her arms wrapped about herself. It was nearly into December and it was cold and bleak. She had been so still, her breath wisping round her head in a white vapour the only movement, that a sheep had grazed almost to her boots before it had realised that she was a living creature. Bleating, it had shied away, scampering to join its fellows who were pulling at the tussocky grass. The moors were a patchwork of dull colours, browns and fading green, shades of grey and even a touch of dark purple blending into the pewter of the sky, the waters of the river a flat metallic grey in the valley bottom; and though she had not wept, the tears inside her had torn her badly bruised heart to shreds, her heart that seemed destined never to heal. She had had no word from Duffy since he had left in October and though he had not promised to write she had thought, *hoped*, that he would. She had anguished over it, broken and wounded, knowing that she could really not go on this way if she was to survive. She had told herself weeks ago that she must straighten her burdened back and square her drooping shoulders and damn well get on with her life if only for her children's sake. So far she had, she knew it, indulged herself in a swell of self-pity and it just would not do, but somehow there seemed to be nothing and no one who could drag her out of it. The servants, bewildered but reluctant to penetrate the wall that she had erected about herself, crept round her quietly and waited for her to recover from whatever it was that ailed her. The departure of Mr Duffy, certainly, and the horrible deaths of the two dogs and, of course, having that dreadful old man cooped up in the bedroom at the top of the stairs didn't help.

A woodpecker was hard at work on the cracked, gnarled bark of an old oak tree as she walked back through Newton Wood, the floor of which at this time of the year was covered by a drift of leaves which were wet and sodden beneath her feet. The light was diffuse from the low sun, casting long shadows across the worn path along which she and Duffy had once strolled. Hastily she twitched her mind away from the thought, making her way through the rickety gate that led in to the orchard, across the vegetable gardens where Mr Weston and Purvis, accompanied by the "lads", were digging in a good dressing of rotted manure ready for the planting of winter-growing vegetables. She felt too shredded by her misery even to ask what they might be and scarcely returned their polite greetings and doffing of caps.

She was crossing the stable yard, oblivious to the sympathetic glances of the stable lads and grooms, when she felt a light touch on her arm. When she turned, startled, she looked into the glowing face of Rosy Little who, though her mistress was not aware of it, had just spent a satisfying five minutes being kissed behind the barn by her Jumsie which was perhaps why she found the nerve to do and say what she did.

"Oh, Rosy," Amy said vaguely, smiling a little as she continued to walk across the yard going she knew not where.

"Yes, I've just bin up to 'Awthorne Lane, m'lady. They was all askin' after yer."

"Well, thank you, Rosy. Tell them . . ."

"Yes, m'lady?"

"Well, I'll be over to see them soon."

Rosy put an impertinent hand on her mistress's arm, indeed she held it in a firm grip. Amy glanced down at it in surprise.

"An' when'll that be, like?" Rosy asked, her young face a bit nervous but in her eyes a determined gleam.

Amy frowned. "I beg your pardon?"

"When'll tha' be over ter see 'em, m'lady, only it's bin weeks now an' they're askin' me all kind o' questions."

"Questions?"

"Aye. They keep gan on about what tha' promised 'em fer them bairns. They know tha's done more than most, man, an' they're grateful but now tha've gorrem goin' they want more."

"More?" Amy's delicate eyebrows shot up almost to her hairline and she turned truculently to the maid. "They can say that after all that I and . . . and . . ." She could not pronounce his name and Rosy took her cold hand in her warm one, her eyes filled with her understanding and affection.

"Duffy, m'lady?"

Amy threw off her hand ferociously, turning away to hide what was in her but Rosy would not be put off. Skipping nimbly, she placed herself in front of her mistress and her face bore an expression that said now she had made this start she intended to finish it. She might not have another chance. She had been trying for weeks to get up the courage to speak to her ladyship but the stark misery that hung like a shroud about her was such that she was afraid to disturb it. To disturb her. To upset what she recognised as the sorrow that Duffy's going had planted deep in her ladyship's heart. The other servants, who weren't blind, for God's sake, knew that their mistress was deeply unhappy and had whispered and worried over it but what could they do? She needed something to buck her up, but short of fetching Mr Duffy back from wherever it was he'd gone it seemed to be hopeless. And only a few months ago she'd been radiant with happiness, busy and humming all over the place as she made her plans for her husband's tenants and busied herself with carrying them out. Dear Lord, she'd even seemed to be happy scrubbing out Betty Long's netty, and now would you look at her, drifting about like a ghost, hardly speaking, only coming alive when she was with her children and even then she didn't romp with them as once she had done.

"I'd be obliged if you'd get out of my way, Rosy," she said coldly.

"Would yer?" Rosy answered, just as bitingly, and the grooms, who had been listening to this conversation while they swept the yard or cleaned the little gig which her ladyship never used these days but which was cleaned nevertheless, stood with their mouths open, brushes and cloths hanging from their hands

"Yes, and you had better watch what—"

"I'll not watch what I say, m'lady, 'cos if I don't say it, who will, like? Thee an' me's goin' ter 'ave a bit crack an' if tha' want all an' sundry ter 'ear it" – glaring round at the frozen figures of the men – "then that's all right by me. I'm gonner say it."

"Are you indeed, then I suggest you pack your bag and leave my house, for I will not be spoken to—"

"Aye, tha' will. An' if, after I'm done tha' want me ter go, then go I shall, but I can't stand by an' let tha' fade away ter nowt. Tha' mun pull thissen together. Howay, woman, theer's folk dependin' on thee, women an' bairns, yer own included."

"Nay, lass," a deeply disapproving voice said from the doorway of the stable. "Tha mustn't speak to 'er ladyship . . ."

Rosy whirled, her face the bright, fiery red of a holly berry, the golden freckles across her nose blending in with the colour so that they were almost invisible. Her eyes, a glowing brown so dark they were almost black, flashed a look of menace at John-Henry and he was later to think to himself that Jumsie McGovern would have his work cut out keeping a restraint on this one.

"Someone 'as ter before she goes inter a bloody decline."

It was as she spoke these last words, among which was a swear word she herself would not allow, that Rosy came to her senses and with a strangled gasp of horror turned to her mistress and began to weep. She hung her head and wept as though her heart were broken, for she loved this woman almost as much as she loved Jumsie. She could not bear to see her in such a deep trough of despair but just the same she should not have spoken as she had; but then, if she didn't, who was to help her ladyship to find herself? It might not be Rosy Little's place to speak up as she had done but – lifting her wet and dripping face to her mistress – she was defiantly glad she had.

"I'm that sorry, m'lady, but I'm not tekkin' it back. It 'ad ter be said. By someone."

The men about the yard gasped and exchanged amazed glances, and in the doorway of the tack room Jumsie McGovern, still holding the bridle he had picked up when his Rosy had slipped from his embrace and raced after the mistress, took a step forward, convinced she would need his protection. All the outside men were right fond of her ladyship and he had to admit she deserved their affection, but Rosy had been worried for weeks over the way she had been since Mr Duffy left and now would you look at her. His Rosy, he meant. She'd get the bloody sack, sure as eggs is eggs, and him with her, for where she went so did Jumsie McGovern.

But her ladyship didn't look as though she were going to give her the sack. She was looking at her with wide and wondering eyes, her own mouth open in a little sigh of understanding. She shook her head then took Rosy's hand in hers. There were faces at the kitchen window, for it did not take long for some unusual event to be noticed and as Rosy and the mistress moved slowly into the warm, fire-bright room Cook had a right old how-d'you-do getting the maids back into their proper places. Their eyes followed the mistress and the girl who was her servant as they walked through the kitchen, their hands clasped, would you believe, and when they had vanished through the door into the hallway they turned as one to gape at Cook as though to ask her what the devil she made of that.

"Now then, sit down and tell me what all this is about, if you please," her ladyship said, throwing her cloak carelessly to the sofa where it slipped off and fell, all crumpled, to the floor. Rosy remembered thinking that Tansy would not be best pleased about *that*. She was pushed gently into the chair by the fire and her ladyship sank into the one opposite.

"I think we'll have some hot chocolate while we talk. Ring the bell, will you, Rosy."

Morna took advantage of her authority as head parlourmaid to have a fascinated look at what was going on in her ladyship's sitting-room, bringing up the tray of hot chocolate and the plate of Cook's almond macaroons her ladyship had ordered, reporting back to the others, who were all agog, that that there Rosy Little was sitting down beside her ladyship as bold as you please and what the dickens it was all about was anybody's guess.

"It's about t' school, m'lady," Rosy mumbled, her face in the tall beaker of hot chocolate which was absolutely delicious.

"The school?"

"Thoo did say . . . before Mr Duffy went," watching in a sorrowful way the sudden crumpling, that was the only way she could describe it, of her mistress's face at the sound of Mr Duffy's name. "Thoo did say there were ter be a school. That bairns were ter be taught ter read an' write. Like I was. They're a grand lot, them folk at Hawthorne Lane, m'lady. Grand now thoo've given 'em opportunity, like, ter mekk summat . . . something o' themselves the day. The bairns're bright an' . . . well, their ma's especially, want them ter gerron."

"So they want me to provide them with a school?"

"Aye, they do that." Rosy leaned forward eagerly. "The men've offered ter build it if thoo can provide the materials, the books an' whatnot. I know thoo'll 'ave a schoolmaster ter pay but they said they'll put a penny or two aside each week, or more if they can, ter pay summat towards it, like."

"They are very keen—" Amy began but so was Rosy, so keen she had the audacity to interrupt.

"Oh, m'lady, thoo . . . *you* don't know the 'alf of it. They want ter keep their bairns outer't mills an' mines an' they know only way is ter be educated. Even if 'tis only their letters an' 'ow to add up an' such."

"Like you, you mean?"

"Ay, like me. Like me an' Jumsie. Dost thoo know

297

that Jumsie reads ter't stable lads of a night? When thoo've ... *you have* finished with newspaper he reads to 'em. 'Alf of 'em didn't know what went on in't world until Jumsie told 'em. All about this war in America what's been goin' on now fer over a year an' they're right interested, m'lady, an' little lad, 'im what they call Nipper keeps beggin' Jumsie ter teach 'im an'—"

"And who taught Jumsie, my dear?"

Rosy looked surprised. "Why, me, m'lady. I told thoo. When you taught me I passed it on to 'im."

"So." Her ladyship was smiling. "There you have it, Rosy."

"What, m'lady?"

"Why, there we have our schoolteacher. If you can teach Jumsie to read and write in the evening after you've both done a hard day's work, you can certainly teach a dozen or so children if you have them five days a week for five hours each day. And to tell the truth I think I might fancy helping you out."

18

The schoolhouse, after much discussion with everyone concerned and a heated argument with John-
Henry who swore the children would interfere with
his horses, had been built to the side of the paddock in a little plot of land which, Amy said to him
patiently, was used for absolutely nothing, surely he
would admit that. There was just enough room beyond
the hawthorn hedge that surrounded it for the plain,
four-square school building, a netty shared by both
girls and boys tacked on to the schoolhouse, and a
bit of soon-to-be-trampled grass where the children
were allowed out to play.

It had taken a month to build, the venture shared by
all the men on the estate, even those without children,
John-Henry included, built in their spare time, which
wasn't much at this time of the year with the short
days and long nights. Inside was a long, lofty room
with a dais at each end and in the centre a fireplace
stove. The stove consisted of two open fireplaces set
back to back, the flue of which passed through the
floor into the foundations. Amy had taken advice
from a master-builder of Sir Robert's acquaintance,
who was vastly amazed at the task Lady Blenkinsopp

had set herself. But notwithstanding his disapproval, for surely a "ragged school" would suit the children of estate workers, there had to be ventilation, he had told her, which would allow a bright and cheerful fire to warm the room. A schoolroom, he murmured, unbelievingly, wondering if Sir Robert knew anything about it, or indeed if he was still alive, for no one had seen the poor old chap for many a long month. But still, it was none of his business and her ladyship had insisted that he must send his bill to her banker, Mr Bewick, and since it was paid promptly he supposed it was all in order.

Facing the fireplaces there were two table desks, one for herself and one for Rosy, and ranged on either side of the table desks were the rows of children's desks with a bench running behind each row. The wall space between the windows, which were large to allow in plenty of light, were occupied by bookcases which Amy meant to fill with books and on top of the bookcases, which were set no higher than five feet so that a child might reach the top shelf, were an atlas and boxes for pens, paintbrushes, paints, pencils, slates and chalk. On the remaining walls would hang blackboards, maps, and pictures of countries and their inhabitants painted in bright colours. There was to be a piano, for Amy believed music should be a part of every child's life. Her own Robby could sing, slightly off-key and with a slurring of some words, all the nursery rhymes and even a verse or two of "Are You Going to Scarborough Fair?" which she had taught him.

Thomas the coachman, dressed in the immaculate Blenkinsopp livery of dark blue and maroon – which he had little occasion to wear these days – had driven Rosy and Amy in the splendidly gleaming carriage pulled by the equally splendidly gleaming coal-black carriage horses to Alnwick, where his mistress and her maid were to get the train to Newcastle. The purpose of the visit was to purchase everything that might be needed for setting up the school. The desks and benches, as many as would be needed for at least thirty pupils, since those to be taught included some of the children from the estate's farms, such ones as their parents could spare. Most of the farm children, of course, were a much needed source of labour to their fathers and worked as long as there was light, even the youngest doing their bit with stone-picking and rook-scaring, but Lady Blenkinsopp had extracted their promise that at least on one day a week, even if it was a Sunday, they would send them down for a bit of book learning.

There would be slates and chalk for the beginners – which in fact was all of them – but there would be those who progressed more quickly than others and she meant to promote those to exercise books and pencils as a reward for hard work and diligence.

Rosy, a brave and willing girl who had survived the rigours of the poorhouse and her transfer to the frightening – to her who had known nothing like it – and gruelling work of skivvy at Newton Law, shrieked almost as loudly as the engine's whistle when the train thundered into the covered station at Alnwick. She hung back, clutching at her mistress's arm, repeating again and again that she was sure they would all be smashed to pieces by the monster into which she was expected to climb; and all the way to

Newcastle, a journey of some thirty miles, which they covered at a terrifying speed, she huddled up to Amy and refused absolutely to look out of the window at the fields and rivers and cows and sheep which flashed across her vision.

They were both dressed faultlessly according to their station in life. Amy had summoned a dressmaker by the name of Rosamund Ashworth, newly set up in Allenbury in Hepple Lane next door to the book-shop and recommended by Laura Barrie, a clever young lady who was capable of making the plain garments required by a doctor's wife, as well as the more fashionably elegant outfits of someone like Lady Blenkinsopp. Lady Blenkinsopp, who had excellent taste, was somewhat of a catch for Miss Ashworth, since it did no end of good for business when it became known that a member of the aristocracy was catered for at her salon.

Amy was dressed in a fine woollen gown the colour of burned almond, in a fabric known as mousseline-de-laine which resembled muslin in texture but was warm enough for winter, Miss Ashworth told her. The crinoline skirt was wide and flounced, each flounce edged with narrow velvet in the same shade as the dress. It had pagoda sleeves which were narrow at the shoulder and wide at the wrist, again with nar-row flounces edged in the same velvet. The bodice was neat, plain and well fitting, curving to her small rounded breasts and narrow waist. Over it she wore a paletot in a warm wool the same colour as her gown, a loose, wide-sleeved, three-quarter coat lined with a pale fur which edged the cuffs, the hem and the collar. Her bonnet was of a cream silk, small and tipped forward, disregarding the current fashion for the "spoon bonnet" which Amy considered unflattering. On the small brim of the bonnet was pinned a bunch of miniature bronze rosebuds cleverly fashioned by Miss Ashworth from silk. Her boots were a pale brown and of the finest kid, and she carried a fur muff to match the lining of her paletot. It was some time since she had taken any interest in her appearance but it was reported by Tansy, who had access to such things, that there were no fewer than four new gowns, two for evening, three bonnets and two walking-out outfits in her ladyship's wardrobe, so was her ladyship coming out of the melancholy that had gripped her for so long? In fact, though this was not dwelled upon, since Mr Duffy had left for parts unknown last October.

Rosy was just as charmingly rigged out, or so Rosy thought. She who had never had a new outfit in her life, wearing other lasses' cast-offs through her days at the poorhouse and even, though of a better quality, when she began work at Newton Law. Her gown was of a dove-grey wool, her long coat, somewhat similar to her ladyship's though not lined with fur, a shade darker, the hem and sleeves edged with the pale grey of her dress. Her bonnet, small and tipped to the back of her head, since it would not do to copy her mistress, was lined under the small brim with white lace. But nothing could dim the brightness of her vivid auburn hair, nor the glowing intelligence in her deep brown eyes. Though she was as ... well, one could only describe Amy Blenkinsopp as delicately exquisite, a slender loveliness of the sort to make the male sigh with longing and yet be aware that she was too frail for the likes of masculine ardour, Rosy had a wholesome bloom, a glossy look of a woman who was made for loving. They would have been wrong about Lady Blenkinsopp but they were right about Rosy Little.

It had been believed, first by Cook and then by Amy herself that when Rosy was brought from the poorhouse, her small size resulting from a poor diet, that she was probably about twelve or thirteen, but in the past twelve months or so in which she had learned how to read, write and add up a column of figures, not only her mind had developed but also her female body. The good food she ate at regular intervals every day had turned her from an ill-nourished scarecrow of a child into a well-rounded young woman. She had begun her monthly courses which, though she had early been introduced to the bloody battle of childbirth in the poorhouse where she had often given a hand, had terrified her until Cook explained the way of it. She and Jumsie had blossomed into young adults who, in Cook's opinion, must be at least sixteen. Something else had blossomed as well. She and Jumsie had been inseparable from their early years, or as inseparable as a boy and girl are allowed to be within the walls of the poorhouse, but now that childish dependence on one another they had known for so long had altered into something else. The others took it for granted that the maidservant and the stable lad spent hours after their work was done poring over books and the newspapers their mistress let them have. They were only a couple of bairns after all and what was the harm in the pair of them being alone up in the little room Jumsie had made for himself above the tack room.

It had taken them both by surprise, that first soft kiss, that first meeting of their innocent young mouths, but within days the kisses had changed in character, for they were not bairns but a young man and woman and when, following their instincts, the softly swelling breast, the rosy peaked nipples of Rosy Little were revealed, to the delight of them both, who had no idea that this between them could be so enchanting, they were lost in the wonder of it. They had seen lust, they had witnessed the rutting of male and female in the dark corners of the workhouse, and the results of it in the puny infants that were born, but it had nothing to do with them. Their naked young bodies loved one another as sweetly as their young minds had done and Rosy Little and Jumsie McGovern were just waiting for the right moment, perhaps when the school was well and truly launched, to inform her ladyship that they meant to marry soon. Jumsie McGovern, though not as clever as Rosy, was a hard-working young man and was thought a lot of by John-Henry. He was good with the horses. He could turn a hand to anything, really, and was willing to help out wherever he was asked. He *liked* work, he was fond of saying, to the other men's amusement, and the only time he wasn't mucking out the stables, digging a row for Mr Weston, even giving Nipper a hand with the boots, he was reading or fast asleep in his bed. Aye, they agreed, a grand lad was Jumsie, tall and lanky, but strong. He and Rosy had their dreams. Simple ones. Perhaps they could take over the small cottage where once Mr Duffy had lived, for it seemed to them that he would never live in it again. Even if he came back . . . well, their thoughts never went further than that, for they could not look into the future, could they?

The bustle of Newcastle was alarming, not only to

Rosy, but to Amy who had, for the most part, travelled all her life by carriage. Central Station was a vast, airy – Amy could not bring herself to call it a *building*, since it was like being in some magical bubble. Great pillars at regular intervals along the railway track held up an incredible glass roof, arched, delicate and looking so fragile both the young women, their necks painfully craned the better to view it, thought that even the alighting of the pigeons that swooped over the roof might cause the structure to come crashing down. There were great piles of boxes, crates, expensive leather luggage, wickerwork baskets, all waiting to be carried by dozens of porters who were dressed in smart uniforms of navy blue, and top hats. Men, and women, many of them ladies accompanied by their maids, for ladies, real ladies, never travelled alone, hurried here and there on what seemed to be business of a vastly important sort. Compartment doors were flung open for them, then banged shut by uniformed officials to the sound of shrieking whistles and all taking place in clouds of steam drifting from the snorting engines. There was an enormous clock beneath which, it was said, was a favourite meeting place for travellers, and certainly it seemed to be thronging with impatiently waiting, foot-tapping figures.

With Rosy's arm through hers, since Rosy in the whole of her life had never seen more than a couple of dozen people together at one and the same time, they ventured cautiously into the wide space beyond the portico which announced itself to be Carlton Square. A street singer was intoning a popular song of the north-east and Rosy relaxed, for it was the first familiar thing she had met since leaving Newton Law.

"Me an' Jumsie used ter sing this," and to confirm the statement she began to sing along with the enthusiastic warbler. "Aw went ter Blaydon Races, twas on the ninth o' Joon," she began, then bent her head in a shy smile as her voice tapered off.

The ballad singer, delighted with her response, called out to her. "Yer a canny lass. 'Ow aboot 'Durham Gaol'?"

"When ye gan inter Durham Gaol," he began, but Rosy shook her head, smiling, for what would her ladyship think? Her maid singing in the street!

"You and Jumsie are . . . close, are you not?" her ladyship asked her gently, pausing for a moment on the pavement to look into her face, her own saddened by some memory, and gentlemen passing by paused too, unaware that they were doing so, for the two women made a charming picture. The singer winked at Rosy who was blushing furiously, then Amy laughed and, still holding Rosy's hand in the crook of her arm, began to walk in the direction of a narrow lane which she had been told by Andrew Barrie, led to Pilgrim Street and then to Grey Street where the better-class shopping area was.

The streets were cobbled and the din was ear-splitting as great waggons piled with goods clattered up from the dock area. A Northumberland long-cart stacked with hay, the body of the cart lighter than most but the shafts broader to allow for the lurch of the Clydesdale horse that pulled it, turned into the yard of an ancient inn. Carriages driven by uniformed coachmen drew ladies of the gentry towards the best shops in town and carts and hansom cabs vied with one another for an inch of road. Carriage horses brayed their displeasure at being held up and dogs barked at the horses. Barefoot children shrilled and street musicians did their best to outdo one another to gather a penny or two from the passers-by. A performing bear, a chain so tight about its neck it had worn a groove in its dusty fur, pranced listlessly to the command of its owner, who played a penny whistle. Both Amy and Rosy hurried on, their faces averted, for children, knowing no better, were poking the animal with sticks in an effort to make it more lively. Then, to the astonishment of the crowd, and to her mistress, Rosy, her face as rosy as her name, turned violently, letting go of Amy's arm.

"Thoo should be ashamed o' youselves, the lot o' thi'. Poor beast don't deserve it," she said sternly. The children gaped and the man smirked and the bear snarled, for it was frightened by the sudden interruption to its well-known routine.

"Only tryin' ter earn an 'onest penny, lady," the man protested. For a moment it looked as though Rosy Little, protector since her childhood of those less fortunate than herself, and there weren't many of those, was about to clout him but Amy took her arm and drew her away.

"It does no good, Rosy."

"I've a mind ter call't polis."

"They would only move him on and the bear would still be made to perform."

"Aye," Rosy said sadly, then brightened as her mistress led her across the road to inspect the windows of the better shops that lined Grey Street.

Rosy was inclined to linger, her mouth agape, for she had never seen such lovely, incredible and expensive goods as were on show in every window. Gowns and hats and jewellery, dainty shoes and sumptuous furs, French corsets and glowing furniture, silver plate and French flowers of silk, cheeses, something called *vermicelli* and Indian tea, photographers and opticians. They moved slowly past the grand building of the Theatre Royal with its six fluted columns, staring in awe, even Lady Blenkinsopp, at the fashionably dressed crowd of ladies and gentlemen who, they heard it whispered, were to put on a performance of a Shakespeare play that very evening; and then, at last, when Rosy's head was spinning with the need to retain the splendours of what she had seen today so that she might repeat it all to Jumsie, they came to the vast emporium, as it was called, where everything for the schoolroom might be purchased.

Spending what to Rosy seemed more money than the world could possibly hold, Lady Blenkinsopp airily commanded the manager of the emporium, who had taken over from his assistant and who practically bent himself double in his pleasure at serving her, to send the bill to Mr Bewick, banker of Alnwick. If he could himself have paid for the desks and pens and exercise books, the slates and blackboards and every other article her ladyship purchased that day, the manager would have gladly done so, for in all his life he had never met a lovelier and more gracious lady, and even her companion was a real looker. The pair of them caused a sensation wherever they went in the store, gentlemen stopping to stare and bow hopefully, but Amy Blenkinsopp had been brought up in the privileged classes, bred from birth to have that quiet air of natural grace and authority which, though not offensive, knew exactly how to put the importunate in their place. It was unconscious and without vanity. Her curls were of spun silver and gold in which sunshine seemed to be caught, or so Rosy decided though she knew it was fanciful. A flawless skin of rich cream and rose, and, ripe and glossy, an innocent child's mouth which looked as though it had never known the touch of a man's lips. She drew the male sex to her like bees to honey, and always would.

"Now then, Rosy Little," she announced as she took Rosy's arm and they were bowed out of the emporium, "we have worked hard for a long time, months now, and I've no doubt we will work harder still when the school opens and I think we deserve a treat, don't you? We have a couple of hours to spare before we catch the train and I believe I spotted a hotel as we came along where I'm sure we can take luncheon. What d'you say? Are you hungry?"

The County Hotel was the finest in Newcastle and was situated on the corner opposite the Theatre Royal. It was a splendid building with fluted columns to match those of the theatre and broad shallow steps which led up to the wide, glassed front door where a top-hatted doorman opened the door to the two ladies, bowing deeply as he did so. When he bent his head to the two ladies he actually meant a lady and her maid, for though the maid was neatly and fashionably dressed it was obvious to him, who opened the door to the lowest and the highest, mostly the latter, that there was a difference in their station. He was quite astonished, as was the head waiter in the elegant dining-room who hurried forward to greet them, when the lady asked for a table for two.

"Of course, madam, please follow me." He led them to a table which, though pleasant, was somewhat hidden behind a luxuriant palm tree. A small group of musicians was playing nearby and though they played valiantly on, the rest of those lunching, ladies and gentlemen one and all, stopped nibbling on their poached salmon and sipping their champagne to stare surreptitiously at the gorgeous creature, beautifully dressed in the latest fashion – except for her bonnet which they had to admit suited her – wondering who the dickens she was.

They were astounded when, in a clear voice, she asked for another table.

"My companion and I have no wish to be tucked away in a dark corner, if you please. This table will do nicely," pointing to one exquisitely laid in the centre of the room where they could see everybody and where everybody could see them. This was a special occasion and she wanted to enjoy every minute of it. Rosy Little, though she was quaking in her boots, rose admirably to the challenge but in her heart of hearts she wished that her ladyship had been satisfied with the more discreet table. She had never sat down to eat with gentry and though she was what Cook called a "dainty eater", not like some of them who sat down in Cook's kitchen, she was not sure she could manage the alarming array of silver, the row of crystal glasses, the beautifully arranged napkin in which a rosebud nestled, nor the little bowl with scented water in it, its purpose a mystery to her.

"Sit down, Rosy and do everything I do," her ladyship told her, and when the waiter, his nose in the air, held her chair for her she sat in it with the same ease and grace that her ladyship adopted. She ate what was put before her, some sort of clear soup, not as good as Cook's, a sliver of something with sauce on it which was quite delicious and which her mistress told her was fish, and several other courses, watching assiduously and using the same silver utensils as her ladyship did, the same glass which contained wine, or so her ladyship said and which she could have drunk gallons of if her ladyship hadn't told her it would go to her head and she was to sip it, not drink it straight down like water.

They both were enjoying themselves immensely, for Rosy Little, as her mistress had known she would be, was quick to learn, clever and proud of what she had achieved since that day her mistress had summoned her to her sitting-room. Had she been dressed as her mistress was dressed and not in the quiet, neat gown of a servant, and had she not spoken, she would have been taken for a lady of the same class as her mistress.

They both looked up with the same expression of polite disapproval when a voice with the cultured drawl of the pedigreed class spoke to Amy from just behind her left shoulder.

"I do beg your pardon, madam, but have we not met before? I must admit that your name escapes me but if you would just remind me I'm sure we would both remember where it was. Are you acquainted with . . . well, perhaps with . . ." He smiled charmingly and bowed gracefully. Though neither of the women was aware of it, unlike the waiter, he was a member of the cast of the players who were to perform that evening. His manners and the way he spoke had been learned on the stage. He was tall, young, handsome with that air of self-esteem that said that he had from birth been told he was everything that any woman could desire, that any man could admire. He had come from a table at which three other gentlemen were seated and they were all watching with what looked to be sly artfulness. One of them actually winked at Rosy.

Lady Blenkinsopp, who was not the same woman as the one who had once been called Amy Spencer, looked him up and down as though he might be some drunken ruffian who had stepped in her path and would do well to get out of it. On her face was an expression her husband and her husband's man might have recognised: a look of utter contempt, cold and dismissive, then she turned to the hovering head waiter, beckoning to him.

"I would be obliged if you would ask this . . . this gentleman to remove himself from my table. I was under the impression that this was a place of some refinement, a place where a lady might safely take luncheon without being accosted as though she were . . . well, I will say no more since I'm sure he, and you, will understand. Now then, my dear," dismissing the young man as she might any riff-raff, turning back to Rosy who sat with her mouth agape, "would you care for some strawberries? I see they are on the menu."

The man's face was a joy to behold, so thought many of the diners, as he was led, barely protesting, back to his friends who were doing their best not to snigger at his discomfiture. The head waiter was beside himself, fulsome with his apologies and hoped that . . . that . . . fishing for her name.

"Lady Blenkinsopp. Of Newton Law," Amy said

casually, smiling under her long feathery eyelashes at Rosy, for the head waiter was ready to lay down at her feet and let her wipe her smart boots on him he was so mortified. Not only a lady but a *real* lady married to a baronet, and one of his diners had done his best to pick her up as though she were a common tart. He hoped Lady Blenkinsopp would do him the honour of allowing him, and the hotel, to treat her as a guest at the hotel's expense.

They were still laughing when Thomas picked them up in Alnwick, though what the dickens there was to laugh about, Thomas said to the other servants, he was at a loss to understand. Anyway, whatever it was it certainly seemed to have done her ladyship a power of good.

Several days later there was great excitement, shared by them all, when the purchases made by her ladyship in Newcastle arrived in several laden waggons, brought from the station at Alnwick to where they had travelled by rail. Knowing how much this meant to everyone on the estate who had children she excluded no man or woman who wished to be involved in the setting up of the schoolroom. One or two of the servants, the younger ones such as Nipper, Jimmy and Herbie and Henry who worked in the garden, had shyly asked if it would be possible for *them* to be taught to read and write and do sums. Even John-Henry, who was thirty-five and courting a housemaid at Ashington Priory, the home of Mr Thomas Henry the banker, drew her to one side and privately – and very diffidently – told her that he wished to . . . well, learn a bit of summat. When he was wed, as he hoped to be, and which seemed likely, he wanted his children to get an education, for only in that way would they become summat in life, he told her simply.

It became apparent to Amy that this was going to be a bigger undertaking than she had imagined. It had not occurred to her that there were grown men and women who wanted the same opportunities that she was offering to their children. There were many, of course, women like Betty Long and Patsy Williams, good women, hardworking and honest, who aspired to be nothing more than decent wives and mothers, but there were a few, such as Jessie Liddle and Rosy Little who, though born in abject poverty with no hope of ever dragging themselves very far from it, would, given the opportunity and a sliver of hope, grasp at the chance of learning. In every heart there is a place called hope and she was to give it to them.

But where, she thought sadly, was *her* place of hope?

19

The sound in the classroom reminded Amy of a swarm of bewildered bees doing their best to buzz in harmony but failing dismally. Not one voice sang in time or in tune with another and though the children had all started the song at the same time, the last to finish was at least ten seconds behind the rest.

A partition had been erected to separate her class from Rosy's, and on the other side all was quiet but for the soothing sound of Rosy's voice reading from *The Swiss Family Robinson*. The story was somewhat bemusing to children who had been brought up in the environment of Hawthorne Lane and had never seen a ship or the sea on which it sailed but, as Rosy said, it kept them quiet and appeared to be a delight to some of what she called her more "promising" pupils. Though Rosy herself had been "eddicated", as she described it, for only just over a year, she had the rudiments of reading, writing and a capacity to do sums and, more to the point, seemed to have the knack of passing what she knew on to others. Look at Jumsie who was a constant source of admiration and amazement to his fellows in the stable! In her class were several children with open, enquiring minds who appeared to enjoy what they did and though she often wondered what these children were to do with the knowledge they soaked up – she had started them on a bit of geography when they began to read *The Swiss Family Robinson*, hoping to show them on the atlas, which totally baffled most, the whereabouts of the place where the family fetched up – she persevered gamely.

It was May and from where Amy stood at the front of the class she could see a dazzling lacework of blossom, pink and white, of apple and pear and plum trees, as ethereally beautiful, as fragile as a froth of gossamer as it stirred in the morning breeze. Beyond the neatly trimmed hawthorn hedge, beyond the orchard, was the kitchen garden where Mr Weston was bent industriously over row upon row of asparagus and artichokes, the divided roots of rhubarb, French beans and runner beans, peas, celery sown in March, carrots and onions, leeks, parsnips and potatoes, and many more vegetables put in over the months of winter and spring by the patient efforts of the head gardener, by Mr Purvis, the under-gardener, helped by Jimmy and Herbie and Henry. Her attention wandered from her class as she wondered idly who would eat all this magnificent harvest when it came to fruition, for it seemed to her that there was enough to feed an army, or a village, or even the row of cottages in Hawthorne Lane. She supposed it would never be wasted, not with the mouths that needed to be fed in the cottages.

She had walked that morning with her children, the twins, almost eighteen months old now, as active as their elder brother. The three of them had tumbled and jostled and raced and shouted along the neatly raked paths beside which bright ribbons of flowerbeds stretched, where the trumpets of daffodils had recently flaunted their golden beauty but which now blazed with the bright azure blue of anemone, the bold yellow and red of tulips and the pink, purple, crimson and scarlet of clarkia. Clustered among them was prince's feather, the deliciously fragrant mignonette, the deep red of antirrhinum, all spilling riotously over the edges of the paths, but it was the water that drew them, as it draws all children. Each one was eager to be the first down to the small lake where the ducks swam lazily, and into the woodland which was their favourite place, revealed to them by Duffy who the twins did not remember but who was still spoken of wistfully by Robby. Kitty-Cat, as she was known, followed by an assortment of the kittens to which she gave birth with alarming regularity – to the children's wondering delight – flirted along behind them, her tail straight up in the air until Robby picked her up in a stranglehold of devotion. Not to be outdone Catherine and David swooped on the kittens, clutching two apiece, one under each arm until the lake was reached where they were dropped unceremoniously at the water's edge to spit at the ducks.

The lake had shimmered in the morning sun which lay in a golden path across the waters where the ducks swam, leaving behind their own widening path. The children had shouted, twisting and turning in some game of their own devising. The animals, abandoned, still followed huffily as the little retinue vanished beneath the trees.

She had felt old that morning, despite the laughter

and energy of her young family. It was here that she remembered him most strongly, for it was here that their love had begun. Was she old? Was twenty *old*? It felt like it sometimes. She would catch sight of herself in a mirror unexpectedly as she happened to pass one and was startled by the utter sadness she saw there. Though her flesh was taut and young there was about her a look of maturity which alarmed her, and yet what else could be expected of a woman who had been married for three years and had borne three children? She was no longer youthful. Her girlhood had fled on the night her husband had brutally raped her, though, for a time, despite her pregnancy and the child she already had, she had felt a girl again: the time when Duffy was with her. She liked to tell herself that her love for Duffy – or should she call him by his true name of Lord Alec Murray, eleventh baron of Ladywood? – was dead. That his absence of seven months without a word has killed that love, buried it and it was lost for ever but she knew it was not true. Her love for Duffy was not dead nor consumed to ashes but flickered wilfully in her bruised heart and she knew she would never be free of it, ever. She tried, dear God she had tried by throwing herself into the building of the school, the hours of teaching, not just the children during the day but those servants who had begged to be included of an evening.

She visited the farms, lonely visits despite John-Henry's presence, since he would not dream of allowing her ladyship to ride without someone beside her, he had said sternly. She had braved the muddy yards full of boisterous bullocks, landing on the farmhouse doorstep to be greeted with consternation, she was sure, by Lily Gledson or Mary-Ann Berwick. The parlour was not swept and there was only a spoonful of tea in the house but the inside of the kitchen would be fragrant with the smells of pies and pastry on the table and three or four little Gledsons or Bewicks ranged on a settle licking the jam spoon.

"Oh, forgive me," Amy would cry, "I have interrupted your baking."

"No, no, m'lady, sit yer down an' 'ave a tartlet an' a drop of gooseberry wine." Which she did, and for half an hour her heart would be soothed by the simple goodness and pleasure of these women whose lives, she hoped, through Duffy's beginnings and her own continuing concern, might be made more comfortable.

She remembered those days since they were bright candles in her dark life without Duffy, for they were filled with the goodwill of those she visited. They were independent, respectable small farmers and she was gentry, the representative of inherited wealth and frivolous idleness which they knew nothing about. She was a lady, by birth, but she was also a lady in the truest sense of the word, as Mr Duffy was a gentleman, and they were grateful, though they would not dream of harping on it, for what she and Mr Duffy had done to improve their lives.

She was a regular caller at Hawthorne Lane where the women gathered her in, pressing cups of tea on her, begging her to sit beside their good coal fires and their shining hearths, to admire their children, those too young for school, longing to show her how their lives had been bettered, thanks to her. She sometimes drove the gig into Allenbury, for she and

Laura Barrie had become friends, steadfastly keeping her face impassive when Laura spoke of Duffy, wondering where he had gone, and why.

"Do you . . . or Andrew not hear from him, then?" she had asked at first, since they had been friends and one might expect friends to keep in touch, but it seemed not.

It was at night that he came to her, smiling that kind and whimsical smile of his in the dark of her bedroom as soon as she laid her head on the pillow, slipping into her dreams so that when she awoke her face would be wet with tears. She wanted more than anything in the world to pluck him from her heart, for her life among her people, the school, her work with the farmers, was fulfilled. She had taken an interest in the recently formed Northumberland Agricultural Society and through the society had found invaluable help for the hill sheep farmers. She had sent away for a book, Bailey and Culley's *General View of the Agriculture of Northumberland* which she read to William Dawson of Hill Farm, Ted Humble of Bilberry Farm, both hill sheep farmers. With the help of books loaned to her and letters received from the Agricultural Society she had been able to give sound advice, which she had offered diffidently and which had at first been received suspiciously, on many aspects of sowing and reaping the hay, a staple crop on the lower slopes of the hills, and had it not been for her memories of Duffy would have found life satisfying.

Why, dear God, could she not pluck him from her heart? Why did her body still remember that brief moment when he had held her in his arms, touched her with hands that trembled, making *her* tremble, even now. Why did her flesh remember his touch . . . why, why?

". . . ter do now, lady?" a voice was piping, and she became aware of a general shuffling and scraping as the class, who had been doing their best to learn the song she had been attempting to teach them, stared at her apathetically.

> Early one morning, just as the sun was rising,
> I heard a maiden sing in the valley below . . .

She had thumped the piano keys vigorously, sung the words enthusiastically and two or three had made a valiant attempt to do as she did. That was all. Two or three. Molly Long was one, bright and eager and already the top of the class. Gracie Hodge was another and the third was Christabel Dixon. All girls, and she often wondered if their parents' longing to give their children an education stemmed more from their mothers' ambitions than their fathers' gratitude. Harry Long, Reuben Hodge, Peter Dixon and Manny Williams were decent and on the whole hardworking, though Harry Long, being a bit simple, had to be supervised, but it seemed to her they could see no advantage in having a son who could read and write when all he would amount to in this world would be a farm labourer, a collier or a mill worker. They were willing to let their sons come to school, since Lady Blenkinsopp had been so good to them, but the lads, taking the hint from their da's, made little effort to accept the learning she offered them. Only one, Hughie Long, a lad of about seven or eight – Betty wasn't sure – had taken to the schoolroom with enthusiasm, since it meant he had access to paints, paper and a paintbrush. He would sit for hours with a pad upon his knee, splashing the paper with brilliant colours which drew gasps of astonishment from all and sundry, especially his ma and da who had no idea they had harboured such a genius in their midst.

"Look, 'tis orchard an' theer's Mr Weston wi' Jimmy," they told one another when their Hughie brought home another of his masterpieces. "Eeh bonny lad, 'tis canny," almost speechless with wonder that between them, especially with Harry being as he was, they had produced such an artist. Not that their Hughie would ever do "owt" with his talent, or so they thought, but it was summat to preen over when his "pickshers" were pinned up on the wall, not only of the schoolroom, but their back kitchen. In all the years they had lived in their mouldering cottage they had never had a bit of paper or a pencil so how could they have guessed what was in the bairn's fingers?

Now Amy pulled herself together with an effort.

"Very well, Molly, pass out the slates to those on the front row" – the slow ones – "and I shall write the alphabet on the blackboard and they will copy it. Sit down, if you please, Dicky, and leave Alice alone. She does not wish to have her plaits tied together. Now, those in the second row stand up in an orderly fashion and go and get your exercise books. There is no need to push, Andrew Williams. Now, I want you to sit down, all of you, please, George Dixon, and with your new pencils which I sharpened last night . . . yours is broken already, Paulie, well bring it to me. No, stand there and keep still, and I will sharpen it for you. Now, write down, in your best writing, what you had for tea last night. Surely you can remember what you had for tea last night, Reuben? Well, think hard. Now then, third row, Christabel, hand out *Easy Reading Lessons* and begin to read from page six where I believe we left off last night. Do you understand?"

"Yes, lady," which was what they called her in their childish lack of understanding of her position. They knew she lived up at the big house and they knew she frequently brought them good things to eat, even at Christmas, presents of dolls and engines, books and jigsaw puzzles which they had looked at in bemusement, but the concept of her being a baronet's wife was beyond them. Rosy was "miss" and she was "lady".

After a great deal of shuffling, of banging of desk lids and crashing of benches, they settled down and Amy was able to sit behind her own desk and begin marking the exercise books of her brighter pupils, those who had been promoted to paper and pen instead of the chalk and slates of the less interested, and who, with encouragement from their mothers and because they genuinely enjoyed it, did "homework". Like Molly Long who, she and Rosy had agreed would, when the time came, make an excellent teacher herself.

Lost in thought, she found herself gazing distractedly out of the window, seeing not just the orchard, the kitchen garden, the paddock to the side, but the sweeping hills beyond the River Coquet which reflected the blue of the sky except where protruding rocks made small diamond splashes on its surface, gently rising to the north-west until they reached the untamed, natural beauty of the Cheviot Hills. She had walked with Duffy, ridden with him up to the hill-farms on her husband's land but had gone no further and, with her chin in her hand and her eyes clouded with images, she left behind the rising babble of voices, for children will take advantage of any slip in their supervision, and climbed higher and higher in her imagination. With Duffy beside her, of course, for her life had begun with Duffy and when would she—

"M'lady . . . m'lady, is there anythin' wrong, m'lady?" an anxious voice asked her. Her eyes faltered and her chin almost fell off her hand as she turned her head quickly to the source of the voice.

"Only there was a right blather comin' from here." Rosy turned a stern and admonishing face towards the children who, but for Molly Long, Christabel Dixon and Gracie Hodge, were clattering about in their sturdy boots doing what seemed to be a northern sword dance. They all immediately sat down, for even though Rosy Little was barely seventeen, if that, she was "miss" and they'd get a right "bray" from their ma's if she was to report them. They had been told a dozen times, even if they were not happy about it, that they were very lucky to be given this chance to learn their letters. But even so, wouldn't they rather, now that they ate well and were freed from the poverty and hardship they had known up to six or seven months ago, be racing over the hills, playing the games that had been played for decades before them. Kitty Cat was one, handball was another played against the gable end of the cottages, the wall roughly marked out in chalk, the ball, called a tuppeny ball which was what it would have cost if it had been purchased from a shop, a tightly rolled-up unwanted garment; skipping or hopscotch, bays which was similar to hopscotch.

"M'lady," Rosy asked gently, "would you like me ter tekk over? Gan on, I can manage this lot." She turned to glare fiercely at the children, all except Molly, Christabel and Gracie. These three with saintly expressions on their faces were describing, laboriously, what they had had for their . . . well, lady had called it "tea" but they supposed she meant the supper their ma's prepared for the whole family. Mostly stews, rabbit stew perhaps, for rabbits were plentiful now that Mr Duffy had left, or happen a bit of bacon, mostly fat but very satisfying, with potatoes and the leeks that were sent down on a regular basis with other vegetables from the big house.

Amy shook her head vigorously. "Oh no, I wouldn't dream of it. You have as many in your class as I have in mine."

"I dinna mind, m'lady. These sackless wights'll be no trouble ter me. Why aye, they know they'll ger a brayin' the day if they don't be'ave."

The children sat as still as mice, their eyes enormous in their faces which, though they had filled out in the last six months, still wore the pinched look of the underfed. And the strange thing was Amy knew they understood exactly where they were with Miss Little. Though she was young she was a more astute teacher than Amy was or ever would be. For a start the bairns, as Rosy called them, understood exactly what she said. She spoke the same language as they did, the same broad dialect. They were not quite at ease with "lady", for often they could not understand the words she spoke, or the tones of what were known as the "leisured" classes which were totally out of their sphere. They were somewhat overawed by her, for she was the lady from up at the big house and they knew what that meant. Hadn't their ma's dinned it into them a hundred times how grateful they should be, but like children everywhere they would rather play than learn. Amy had been pondering for several weeks now whether she had taken on a bit more than she could manage with these lessons, for she realised that her own children were being sadly neglected. Robby was heated in his demands that Mama stay and play with him and Cat and Davey, with Kitty-Cat and the as yet unnamed kittens. Perhaps, she had thought, she could take on some educated young woman of the same class as Rosy, if such a person could be found, to teach the children in the classroom the elementary basics of what were called the three "R"s while she continued with the music, singing, and painting classes, which would give her more time to be with her own children and help them to develop. There was so much to do now that she had taken on the welfare of the people on the estate which she had been glad of since it took her mind off her grieving for Duffy but sometimes her life was so . . . so . . . joyless she felt she could bear it no longer.

"Gan on, m'lady," Rosy said gently, turning her back on the class who were watching with avid interest, knowing something was being discussed that concerned them. Perhaps they were to be "let out" they thought hopefully.

"It's a canny day ter be out in," Rosy continued, "an' I can tekk on this lot," nodding her head in the direction of the quiet class. "They'd be no trouble."

Rosy knew what ailed her ladyship, and what's more

she was aware that her ladyship knew that Rosy knew and because of it Rosy was gentle with her. Not that the other servants were anything other than kind, respectful, affectionate even, but there was something in Rosy's manner that spoke of her understanding of the way it was with her.

It was weeks since Amy had been in to see her husband and even the doctor, believing that there was nothing further to be done with him, called only once a month. Somehow she found it almost impossible to go into that room and look at that bitter, glaring, dribbling face, that grotesque shadow of a man who was keeping her and Duffy apart. Though she had said nothing to Rosy it was as though Rosy could read her mind, could look into the innermost secret heart of her where her longing for Duffy and her loathing of Sir Robert Blenkinsopp lay side by uneasy side. There seemed to be a strong bond between the two women, unspoken and somewhat astonishing considering the difference in their station, but Amy was aware that, should she need it, Rosy would stand in staunch defence of her and, if it *was* spoken of, keep any secret Amy might divulge to her.

"I will perhaps take the gig down to Hawthorne Lane then," she said at last. "Ida Hodge's baby is due any minute and I promised her some of the twins' clothes they've grown out of." It was as though she were determined to do something that might still be called her "work". Something useful. That she was making it clear that she would not just pass the sunny afternoon away in idleness. As if Rosy cared if she did, but at least she felt her conscience to be clear.

Alfred harnessed up the gig for her, putting Buttons

between the shafts. He had helped her to pack the boxes of baby garments, all the while admonishing her to do this or that, to take care and not go too fast as though she were a child.

"Watch 'im when thi' go through that gate, m'lady. 'E's tekken a dislike ter that bit o' parsley grass in't ditch fer some darned reason. Talk about a daft gowk."

"Oh come now, Alfred, Buttons! He's the best-natured animal in the paddock. John-Henry intends putting Robby up on him shortly."

"Aye, so 'e ses but keep a tight fist on 'im. 'E don't like bein' parted from Jason, neither." Jason was Sir Robert's hunter who was getting fat and lazy in the lush paddock and if someone didn't take him out with the hunt soon, in Alfred's opinion, he would be past it and him only five years old. It was a right shame, for he was a fine animal, well bred from good stock, and it was in his and John-Henry's mind to talk to her ladyship about selling him and some of the others as well, for it wasn't fair on the beasts to be shut up with the gentle mare her ladyship rode, the two ponies and the couple of hacks which were kept for visitors. Not that there were many of those now either. And this was such fine hunting country, too. The countryside from the borders of Scotland to south of Durham was park-like in appearance, well-wooded valleys and gently rolling hills, ideal for the hunting that took place from October to the spring. There were numerous recognised packs of foxhounds within the boundaries of Northumberland, and the horn of the huntsman was often to be heard as the hunt, following the fox, led the dogs over Sir Robert's land. But it was almost two years since Jason or the other hunters had been with them. They would often throw up their heads and whinny at the sound, galloping furiously from one end of the paddock to the other, with Buttons bravely attempting to keep up with them. But for the exercise the grooms gave them, they were reduced to the placid grazing in the paddock which filled their days.

Alfred watched her ladyship as she manoeuvred Buttons through the gateway, satisfying himself that the pony was behaving hinmself, then rejoined John-Henry, squatting down on a bale of hay and lighting his pipe, indulging with the head groom in a bit of nostalgia about the old days when the yard had been filled with fine horses and jovial gentlemen, with noise and bustle, with the dogs and the jokes, a man's world which, though Sir Robert had been a bugger of the first order, had at least been *their* world.

Another pair of eyes followed her ladyship's progress down the well-tended track towards the gate at the bottom that led out into the lane to the row of cottages.

"'Er's gone," a voice said triumphantly. "'Er's off ter them mucky 'oits at 'awthorne Lane. By, she gotter a surprise in store fer 'er."

"She's in the trap?" another male voice asked.

"Aye, that she is an' goin' at a fair lick, an' all."

"Silly cow, I hope she breaks her bloody neck."

"'Appen she will."

"Not that I want her dead, you understand, just fastened to her bloody bed like mumble mumble."

Sir Robert Blenkinsopp glared malevolently at his manservant, the manservant who had been his only companion for almost two years and the madness in his eyes, which he kept well hidden in the passive role he took on when the doctor visited him, was as hot and hating as a caged tiger, one that has been wild and free for all of its life and was now destined to dance to the tune of others. They were the only part of him that could be said to be truly alive. For some reason of his own, not even revealed to Platt, he had kept his slow improvement not only from the doctor, but from the maids who still came in daily and dutifully at her ladyship's behest to clean his room, to change his bed linen, to take away his soiled body linen and to empty his – and Platt's – foul slops. Unless he was in one of what Platt called his lunatic moods, which frightened him half to death and from which he kept well away, Sir Robert could now talk with a fair degree of lucidity. He could not walk and was aware now that he never would, for though his broken legs had mended, his long imprisonment in his bed had wasted his muscles to stringy threads. His "good" side was terribly weakened and the other wasted away to bone covered by flabby flesh, but with Platt's help he could get out of his bed and *crawl* about the room like some venomous spider. He made Platt think of a blackclock, the name given to a cockroach in Platt's world. The first time he had managed it Platt had watched with a spine-chilling horror, thankful that his employer's hatred was not aimed at him. Imagine seeing this monster crawling across the floor towards you! Cripes, it fair gave him the willies and sometimes, though she treated him as though he were a bloody blackclock himself when she came to look Sir Robert over, he had it in him to feel sorry for the woman.

20

She felt a slight lifting of her spirits as she and Buttons bowled along the well-used track between Newton Law and Hawthorne Lane. It was downhill all the way following the route which, in the other direction, if she had turned right instead of left as she left the grounds of Newton Law, would have taken her across the lower moorland and up to Weeping Stones. Turning her gaze, and her heart, which yearned towards the moors, away in the direction she had to take, she clucked to the eager pony, twitching the reins to guide him towards the river, gleaming in the sunshine, moving between drystone walls above which, perched high on the seat of the gig, she had a fine view of the valley.

It was one of those unexpectedly warm and lovely days of May when summer seems to have finally decided to come to the high Northumberland moorland. A light, westerly breeze blew the infrequent cloud wisps towards Cheviot and both she and the pony lifted their heads and sniffed the champagne quality of the air. The silence of the moor was impressive.

Suddenly, an unaccustomed sound broke the stillness, the deep, throaty *cronk* of a hunting raven, and once again her heart was ready to break, for it was Duffy who had taught her to recognise the sound, not only of the raven, but of many of the birds that flew across her vision on the downhill journey.

A hedgehog plodded ponderously along in the middle of the track and, as it scented danger, curled itself up into a defensive ball directly in front of the trotting pony. For a moment she thought Buttons was going to balk at it but he continued along the grassy track and when she glanced back she saw the hedgehog, unhurt, begin to uncurl itself.

It was as she was about halfway to Hawthorne Lane that she felt the sudden lurch of the gig. It seemed to shift slightly to the left from its steady downward path, then, barely noticeable, come to the centre again. The movement was so slight she and the pony, after a fraction of a second's uncertainty, unsure that it had even happened, forgot about it.

"Get on, Buttons," she called out, more from habit than from any need to chivvy the animal forward since he was already going at a steady gait. Alfred, had he been there, would have called it *wild* and put a stop to it at once but Amy, who was fairly new to this form of transport, slapped the reins on Buttons' back which encouraged the pony to go even faster.

The sharp crack made them both flinch it was so unexpected and for a moment Amy glanced round, for it had sounded just like the crack of a gun. It was not yet the hunting season, she had time to think, and then her thoughts were no more than tangled skeins, like silks in a carelessly kept sewing box. How blue the sky was as it toppled over her head like an umbrella caught in a high wind; how sweet the smell of the burgeoning heath; how glossy was Buttons' coat as he disappeared into the ditch at the side of the track and who on earth could that be screaming in such agony. The gig tipped violently to the right in a welter of cracking, snapping wood, the reins flying from her hands in an amazing loop of whirling leather and, as she flew up and then down, how incredibly hard was the tufty grass on which she landed and how black was the pit into which, as she landed, she fell.

Alfred Ridley was, like most men who worked with horses, wiry, compact but very strong. Well, he would be, the good food he'd eaten for the past twenty-two years, ever since he had been brought by his da, shivering with fear, to be stable lad for old Sir Robert. He had been ten years old then, accustomed to hard work since he was a babby, unable to read or write, and still couldn't. He was thirty-two years old, time he was thinking of getting wed, his old ma kept telling him, and he agreed with her. He had had his eye on Tansy Moore, who had been made up to lady's maid when her ladyship returned from wherever she had been the year before last. He had high hopes of Tansy, who seemed to favour him, but it had been a bit of a facer when Tansy had stepped out of her lowly position as chambermaid, since there was a big difference between lady's maid and chambermaid. So, like the true northern countryman he was, he was taking his time in progressing further with his courtship. After all, Tansy was ten years younger than him so there was no rush. There was an unoccupied cottage beyond the orchard and when the time came he was pretty certain her ladyship would be agreeable to letting him and Tansy move into it. When they were wed, of course.

Though he couldn't read he could tell the time and he frowned as he glanced at the clock over the entrance to the stable yard. Turning back to her ladyship's mare whom he had been grooming, he gave her a final polish then led her into her stall, threading her lead rein through the ring in the wall.

"Theer, my lass, tha' look right bonny. 'Tis a pity tha're not rode more often, a fine mare like thoo." He rubbed his hands on a bit of straw, then stepped from the stable and into the yard where John-Henry was turning a piece of harness over between his fingers.

"'Er ladyship's tekkin' 'er time," Alfred said to no one in particular. Thomas, the coachman, who had little to do these days since the coach was rarely taken out, was sitting on an upturned bucket drinking from a mug of tea he had just cadged from Phyllis, and the other lads, Jumsie among them, were larking with a football. It was almost the end of their day and soon they would be either on their way home to their wives or clamouring into the kitchen for the good food Cook put before them three times a day.

Alfred lit his pipe, puffing several times until he was satisfied it was drawing well, then, clenching it between his good strong teeth, shoving his hands deep into his breeches pockets, he wandered down to the gate that led from the stable yard and on to the lane. He leaned on the top of the gate, drawing on his pipe and enjoying the warm sunshine on his back and the musical sound of the woodpigeons which were the bane of Mr Weston's life. They were destructive to the gardener's young vegetables and seeds and he was often to be heard saying to anyone who would listen that whoever brought a dead one to him would get sixpence from him. They roosted in the trees at the edge of the woodland and at this time of the day would be leaving their feeding ground – Mr Weston's newly growing peas – to return to their nests.

Alfred sighed, and, shading his eyes with his work-seamed hand, looked down the track from where Lady Blenkinsopp would return. There was no sight of her so, sighing again, he wandered back up to the stable where John-Henry had begun mixing a feed for Holly, her ladyship's mare, who had a finicky appetite.

"Theer's no sign of 'er." He took up a stiff buzzum made of heather and began, to John-Henry's amazement, for it was the stable lad's job, to sweep the floor of the stable, which didn't need sweeping anyway since it had been done that morning.

"'Oo's that then?"

"Barmy bugger," Alfred snorted. "'Oo the 'ell dost think? 'Er ladyship, o' course. She's bin gone three 'ours the day."

"Dinna fash yersel, lad, tha' know what women're like when they get tergether. They'll be 'avin a bit crack an' 've not noticed time."

"A bit crack! Not 'er ladyship. She's not one fer blatherin'."

The back kitchen door opened and Tansy stood on the step, clean and bright and very attractive in her black cotton dress and pretty frilled apron. Her hair, which had a tendency to curl, escaped in endearing tendrils from beneath her lace-trimmed cap and Alfred for a moment forgot his anxiety about her ladyship. She was a bonny lass, was Tansy, and he made up his mind that he'd ask her this very night if she was willing. An autumn wedding which would give her a chance to get together all the fancy bits and bobs on which women set such store. He smiled in anticipation, his blue eyes gleaming in his weathered face, then turned away, looking towards the gate.

The call came that food was on the table and the lads were jostling and laughing as they crowded at the entrance to the kitchen. Tansy pushed her way past them and stood by the step shading her eyes, pretending not to but surreptitiously looking for Alfred, since it seemed she was as smitten as he was. Lady's maid she might be but she was a strong, healthy girl and it was time she was wed and starting a family. Alfred was a good catch for a girl like her, honest, decent, in regular work, well thought of by her ladyship and his fellow servants, and not bad looking into the bargain. He'd make a good husband, a good provider and she was doing all she could to let him know she was ready when he was.

But strangely, Alfred, who she knew favoured her, was not making his way to the kitchen door, nor even looking in her direction now. He had wandered down to the gate again and was gazing uneasily down the track. The pleasant warmth of the day was fading. There was a bit of a nip in the air and the birds were beginning to settle in their nests, twittering and fluttering in the branches of the newly leafed trees, but still there was no sign of his mistress. It'd be dark soon and he didn't like it. He didn't know why he felt so anxious, for after all it was a straight and easy drive down to Hawthorne Lane. He was very fond of her ladyship, they all were, and very protective of her, which it was not really his place to be, but after what that sod of a husband had done to her what man wouldn't feel a sense of outrage and a need to watch out for her. She was such a slight little thing, frail and lovely as the lily of the valley and . . . well, Alfred didn't know the meaning of the word *chivalry* he only knew that he felt a great need to watch out for her, and the rest of the men were the same.

Turning on his heel and taking no notice of Tansy's obvious wish to see him seated under her benevolent eye at the kitchen table, he strode into the stable where Holly was just about to tuck in to *her* meal and to the astonishment of John-Henry, who was watching her fondly, he backed her out. She did not wish to be parted from her meal and showed signs of temper but with a stern word and a strong hand he led her out into the yard and without even saddling her leaped upon her back.

"Open t'gate fer me, lad," he shouted to John-Henry, and so bemused was the head groom, who had not been called "lad" since he first came to Newton Law twenty-odd years ago, that he did so, scratching his head and watching Alfred and Holly as they set off at a gallop towards Hawthorne Lane. Tansy watched too, her mouth open in astonishment, then she slammed indoors and though they didn't know why, glared at the men and women about the table.

The pain was so excruciating when she came to that she lapsed off again into a kind of semi-consciousness, moaning feebly in the back of her throat. She was aware of where she was and who she was, but her mind still seemed to be floating somewhere off a way, she didn't know where. She didn't know that this was the result of shock and the agony she was in. She could hear someone, or something, making the most awful noise somewhere but she seemed to have fallen in a ditch, or at least off the track and could see nothing of the gig, or the pony who had pulled it. She tried to cry out for help – surely there would be someone using the track down to Hawthorne Lane? – but her brain wouldn't work properly and all she could see was Duffy's face and she knew damn well that there was no possibility of *him* passing by. Not now, and not ever . . . Duffy . . .

"Duffy, if you're there, will you please come and help me," she whimpered, she didn't know why, and was astonished when he was there, his face creased with concern.

Alfred couldn't for the life of him understand why she was calling him by the gamekeeper's name but perhaps it was something to do with the state she was in. She didn't seem to know where she was, or who he was, but his one thought was to lift her out of the hollow in which she crouched and get her back to Newton Law. Jesus, he wished he'd insisted one of the others come with him, for he was going to need help. He couldn't leave her now that he had found her, and he couldn't simply crouch here and watch her. She was sitting in a ghyll, a bit of a hollowed-out ground just off the track with her knees drawn up to her chest. Her face was as grey as the ash in the fireplace of a morning and around her eyes were great black circles brought about by shock. There was blood on her face. Her left arm lay across her waist and she held the elbow of that arm cupped in her right hand. Her left shoulder was so distorted it looked as though the bone was about to break through the material of her cotton gown.

"M'lady . . . Dear sweet Christ . . . m'lady. What in 'ell's name 'appened?" He turned to look about him distractedly, running his strong hand through his wiry curls. The gig lay on its side just a little way off the track, minus a wheel and just beyond it was Buttons, also on his side, quivering, dying, his chest heaving and from his mouth came the sound of an animal in agony. His leg must be broken, Alfred thought dazedly, his instincts as a man who deals with horses urging him to go to the animal and try to comfort it and why the hell hadn't he brought a gun so that he could put it out of its misery? Of course he hadn't known he'd need one. Bloody hell, what was he to do?

"Duffy," her ladyship said to him, her eyes huge and glittering with shock. He was in shock himself but he couldn't hang about here, could he? He must get her back to the house, get John-Henry to ride for the doctor; get Cook to bring . . . well, whatever was needed, bandages perhaps, hot water, brandy, but when he reached out to pick her up she screamed in pain as he touched her and he fell backwards as he tried to lower her again to the ground.

"Ah'll go an' fetch 'elp." His face was as pale as hers. "You sit there, my lass, an' try not ter move."

She shook her head very carefully as though the slightest movement was likely to send her spinning off into that agonising void. Her lovely blue-grey eyes were nearly black with pain and already one of them was closing up where she had apparently crashed it against a rock.

"I can walk," she said through gritted teeth. "Don't leave me here . . ."

"But m'lady . . ."

"Help me up. I can walk, Duffy."

Alfred put a hesitant arm about her waist and she got slowly to her feet. Her left arm moved a little as she did so and she moaned, biting her lip so hard it began to bleed. Her eyes turned up and with a little sigh, she fainted. Taking advantage of her unconscious state Alfred picked her up – she was as light as a bit of swansdown – making sure that the grotesquely distorted shoulder was turned away from him. Doing his best to shut out the sound of the injured pony he began to stride out across the moorland, taking a short cut towards the house. Her ladyship was still unconscious, her face nestling into his shoulder. His heart, in which Tansy aroused the fundamental feeling of a man for a woman, was filled with tenderness and he knew that no matter what happened he would never feel for any woman what he felt for her ladyship. He thought the world of Tansy. She would make him a splendid wife and mother for his bairns but Tansy was strong, uncomplicated, and what he felt for her was just as strong and uncomplicated. He wanted a woman to make a home for him, to warm his bed, to give him children, and Tansy would do just that. She was a grand lass with a bit of spirit and yet with kindly good sense. But there was none of the almost reverential devotion that he felt, he admitted it only to himself, for Lady Blenkinsopp. She was like a creature from a world as far apart from his as the angels in heaven and, quite literally, he would die for her had the need arisen.

But he had no time to dwell on these thoughts. While she was unconscious he meant to get her as near to the house as possible, with as little pain as possible. It was about three miles, he thought, praying she would stay as she was, for it tore his heart to hurt her as he had done.

Holly, her reins trailing, her head down, began to follow him back to the stable and her feed.

"Almost there," he kept whispering to her ladyship in the panting whisper her weight, which seemed to have doubled since he picked her up, caused in him. He wanted to shout, to yell at the top of his voice to anyone who might be in the vicinity and come running to help but there was no one about. It was the end of the day and those with homes to go to were in them.

His shoulders were on fire when he came at last, panting and red-faced, to the gate that led into the yard. He had a fleeting image of John-Henry who had eaten his meal in the kitchen and was hanging aimlessly about by the stable door as though he hadn't the faintest idea what to do with himself, he who never wasted a minute in his busy day. John-Henry had been vexed with Tansy who had been fretful, petulant even, asking where on earth Alfred had gone, and when told, informing the rest of them that in her opinion Alfred took too much on himself, for what harm could her ladyship come to on the short ride to Hawthorne Lane.

"Well, if tha' asks me it were only sensible o' Alfred ter go lookin' fer't mistress. She left schoolroom three hours ago an' 'oo knows what's 'appened to 'er. I'm right worried meself." Rosy Little glared at Tansy.

Tansy returned the glare, for there was a small amount of jealousy between her ladyship's maid and her ladyship's choice of schoolteacher. She didn't like the inference that she, Tansy, was uncaring of what happened to their mistress.

"An' are thi' sayin' I'm not," she snapped, bristling dangerously. She was still smarting at Alfred's apparent dismissal of her when she had called him in to his supper.

"Eeh, stop blatherin' on the pair o' ye," Cook intervened, moving to the window and looking out over the stable yard. Alfred was just coming through the gate which John-Henry had flung open for him, a bundle in his arms which Cook, at first, failed to recognise.

When she did she began to scream, waving the wooden ladle she was just about to dip into a crock of cream, and for several moments there was pandemonium as the crock was dashed to the ground, the cream spreading in a ripple on Cook's clean flags. Rosy, Phyllis, Maddy and Dulcie, who had sprung up at Cook's cry, knocked the bench on which they were perched backwards, narrowly missing Cook's fat tabby cat who ran screeching for the door, and all about the room women put their hands to their breasts and men glared about them as though looking for an intruder.

"What's up?" cried Elspeth, who shed easy tears and was ready to shed them now, and it was several minutes before her ladyship, just coming out of her swoon, was placed tenderly in Cook's chair by the fire. She began to moan, holding her arm and doing her best not to move but it was a rocking chair and had a will of its own.

"Please . . ." she whispered. "Get me up. The bench

. . . straight upright." She winced at every touch as hands were tenderly reached out towards her, for they all longed to help. In the doorway Alfred was having an urgent conversation with Thomas and George while all about her ladyship her servants stared in horror at the shape of her arm and shoulder.

It was Morna who took charge, sensible, practical Morna who, with Rosy Little at her side, had brought her ladyship's twins into the world.

"It's dislocated," she told them all sternly, pushing them back to give her mistress a bit of room. "It'll 'ave ter be put back."

"Dislocated," Cook said tremulously.

"Aye, I saw me brother with just like it. 'E fell outer't hay loft. Me da thought 'e were deed until 'e began ter scream. Has doctor bin sent for?"

Alfred, from his place by the back door, his face as ashen as that of his mistress, nodded his head.

"Aye, George's just set off."

"Well, theer's nowt ter be done until he comes. 'Ow did it 'appen?"

"God knows. Gig's all smashed up an'—"

"What dost mean?" Rosy quavered, putting out her hand to her ladyship then drawing it hastily back as her mistress recoiled from her touch.

"What ah said. Wheel's off an' Buttons is . . . well, John-Henry'll see to 'im."

Jumsie, in whose heart Buttons had held a special place, creased his face up in what, in a younger boy, would have been a readiness to weep, but instead he ran from the room and though Alfred, knowing the lad's fondness for the cheerful pony, tried to stop him, he was off and across the yard at a fair lick.

They watched, for what else could they do, since her ladyship said she could not bear to be moved to her bedroom, while the doctor examined her. Tears ran down her face and several of the younger women servants began to cry silently, for her arm looked as though it had been half torn out. The men had been sent out into the yard while the doctor, as gently as he could, removed her ladyship's blouse, cutting it away from her with scissors. The bruising to her arm and shoulder had gone a deep and lovely violet colour but her face was like suet.

"I'm going to have to put it back, my dear. It's dislocated." As the doctor spoke Morna nodded wisely as though in total agreement with the medical opinion. "And it's going to hurt. A really bad hurt but I promise you that as soon as the bone goes back you should be as right as rain. You have no other injuries apart from the graze to your face but you'll need something to bite on while I put the bone back in its socket. Perhaps Cook . . ."

He turned to look at the pitying face of Mrs Fowkes who silently handed him the wooden ladle that was still in her hand. All the while Doctor Parsons' gentle hand was stroking Amy's arm from the elbow to the wrist and she was quiet, just as though his eyes and the gentle hand were hypnotising her, relaxing her.

The wooden ladle was put between her teeth, the handle sticking out at one side, the ladle end at the other. Elspeth had begun to weep loudly now in her sympathy for poor Lady Blenkinsopp but the doctor turned to her, frowning, and she gulped, for it was not her he was about to hurt even more, was it?

"Here comes the pain," he said, almost conversationally as though he were talking about the arrival of an expected guest. One of his hands was on the point of her ladyship's shoulder, the other on her wrist and when, so quickly it took them all by surprise, he pushed at one and pulled the other, the creaking pop was as loud as the crack of a log in the fire. Amy opened her mouth to scream shrilly, the ladle fell out and the shoulder suddenly looked the same as anyone else's.

A concerted "aah" breathed round the room and the figure of their little mistress became as soft and boneless as a rag doll.

"It's gone," she whispered wonderingly. "It doesn't hurt anymore."

The women turned to each other and smiled in relief. Cook nodded at Tilly to make her ladyship a pot of tea in which she meant to put a tot of brandy; in fact they'd all have one after their mistress had been tucked up in her warm bed, for they were all of them in a fine old state. Dulcie was sent scampering to see to the fire and draw down the bedcovers in her ladyship's bedroom, and word was passed out to the men that their little mistress was going to be as right as rain.

"Now then, Mrs Fowkes," the doctor admonished her. "Lady Blenkinsopp's not out of the woods yet. That shoulder's going to be sore for a couple of weeks and I want you to make sure she rests. No more driving about in that gig of hers."

Hardly, thought Alfred when he was told what the doctor had said. The gig, whose wheel had unaccountably come off, was beyond repair and poor little Buttons, whose leg was broken, had been put out of his misery. It'd be a while before another gig and a decent pony were found, but what he'd like to know, and John-Henry had felt the same, was who the hell had tampered with the gig in the first place. That gig, like all the vehicles that he and the other grooms and lads looked after, was checked at regular intervals and there'd been nothing wrong with it last week. Summat funny was going on and he and John-Henry agreed that it needed looking into.

"'Er's dislo . . . diloscat . . . dixolated . . ."

"Are you trying to say dislocated, you daft wight?"

"Aye, that's it. 'Er shoulder, they said. 'Tis a bloody wonder tha' didn't 'ear 'er screamin'. I were stood at door ter't kitchen an'—"

"Perfect, perfect," Sir Robert interrupted his minder rudely, smiling grotesquely out of his ruined face.

Platt, wanting a bit more of the limelight, interrupted his master with a fresh description of her ladyship's screams and was rewarded with a stream of osbcene abuse which roughly translated meant that if Platt didn't shut his mouth he might be sorry.

Platt shut his mouth.

"Now then," Sir Robert declared softly, "I think it's about time her ladyship and I became reacquainted. Became . . . friends, so I want you to knock on her door and ask her—"

"That there maid's ter be with 'er. Doctor did say she were ter rest."

Sir Robert made a great effort not to lose control again, though it was very hard when you were forced to live, night and day, with a halfwit. He could barely handle the frustration he felt but his patience was to be rewarded at last, and what was another week or two. All the weeks and months of learning to talk and move and at last he was to get his just desserts. And so was the whore!

"I'll give her rest," he hissed. "She'll know none when I get hold of her. When *we* get hold of her, aye, Platt. What do you say to that?"

Platt didn't know what to say so he kept his mouth shut, listening with something that he didn't recognise as pity as his master described in detail the "fun" he and Platt were to share when her ladyship fell into their hands.

"We'll give her a week or two, shall we. Make sure she's in good health, otherwise she might not give value for money, eeh, Platt?"

He began to laugh, the high, hysterical laughter of a man who is totally insane.

21

The young girl sitting across the desk from her was obviously very nervous but she had a steady gaze, her clear blue eyes looking bravely into Amy's. She sat bolt upright, her spine three inches from the chair back and Amy recognised the years of training at the hand of a strict nanny, the sort she herself had had. But when the girl spoke it was not with the cultured tones of the privileged class to which Amy belonged. So much for the nanny, Amy thought. Her accent was as broad as any of the servants at Newton Law, though she did use words that Cook or Morna or any of the others would not normally use. She was not of the so-called "leisured" classes, that was apparent, but neither did her appearance place her among the ranks of the workers. She was plainly dressed, neat and immaculately turned out in a serviceable grey, the touch of white on her collar like the driven snow.

They were seated in the estate office, the one in which she and Duffy had passed so many pleasant and productive hours and where even now his half-smiling, whimsical ghost still lounged against the fireplace. She could almost believe she could smell the aroma of the cigar he had sometimes smoked, the cigar that was a throwback to the days when he had lived the life of the gentleman he undoubtedly was. It was eight months since he had left Newton Law to attend to his family's business, eight months and she had heard no word of him, and though the first raw savagery of the pain of his going had not left her it had eased somewhat into a dull ache that was constantly with her. Something like the dragging of her dislocated shoulder which nagged at times like a toothache. It was worse when she was in the schoolroom, just as though the noise and ceaseless movement of the children, who seemed incapable of sitting still for any length of time, the commotion with which they seemed unable to perform the simplest tasks, reverberated through her. It was this that had decided her on the course she was undertaking. In her anxiety to improve the lives of the children on the estate, to the detriment of her own children, the realisation that unless she took the doctor's angry advice that she should rest more if she wanted that shoulder to recover, she had finally been brought round to the decision to employ another teacher.

Rosy, who would be the most affected, agreed with her.

"That there tumble took it outer thi', m'lady. I know thoo's still in pain at times. No, don't try ter tell me different 'cos I've seen thee when thee thinks no one's lookin'. Them bairns is a handful at best o' times an' need a firm 'and. Most of 'em don't want ter be there," she added shrewdly. "Tha' knows that, don't thi'?"

"Yes, I know. I'm well aware that they would rather be playing Tarsy or Striddly-Pigeon or some such activity," she said, laughing. "Oh yes, Rosy, I'm becoming acquainted with all the games they play and I know that if it wasn't for their parents, their mothers to be precise, they wouldn't come at all. But I don't care about that. I'm determined that in one way or another these children are to be given an education of sorts and for the moment I must admit I can't manage it. It needs someone who can give her whole attention to it. Someone who is . . . dedicated, as you are."

"An' where willta find such a person, m'lady?"

"I'm not sure. Perhaps if I were to advertise in the Allenbury *Clarion*." Her voice was hesitant and Rosy took the opportunity to speak of what was in her mind.

"I've a feelin' there's no need fer that. In fact I've a feelin' there's someone who'll know the very one tha's looking for."

"Oh, and who might that be?"

They were sitting side by side on one of the benches in the schoolroom after a particularly hectic afternoon on Amy's part of wrestling with Francy Long, Dickie Hodge, George Dixon and the two Williams brothers, Andrew and Paulie. The boys were restless, filled with the pent-up energy of healthy boys, the energy brought about by the improved diet that she herself had instituted. They weren't impertinent or disrespectful, since they knew that if "miss" didn't give them what for, their da's would, but they squirmed in their seats, teased the girls when "lady" wasn't looking, and tittered behind their hands at what they considered to be a good joke, which, as lads do, was anything and everything that "lady" said and the funny way she said it!

Rosy had made a cup of tea from the kettle which was kept simmering on the fire and the pair of them were sipping from the sturdy mugs that Rosy considered suitable for the schoolroom. The tea was hot, strong, sweet and, though it was not to Amy's taste, she found it invigorating.

Rosy placed her mug on the desk beside her.

"Mrs Barrie."

"Mrs Barrie?"

"Why aye. Doesn't she get round Allenbury all the time an' doesn't she know everybody who lives there. She an' doctor are in an' outer every hoose."

"Only of working-class folk, Rosy."

Rosy bristled. "An' what's wrong wi' that, pray? There's many a lass'd be glad ter gerr a chance like I did. Mrs Barrie'd know."

Amy sighed and gazed out of the window up to the far horizon where Bilberry Farm lay in the sea of bilberries from which it got its name. Below that was a heather moor where ling grew in profusion and where, before his continued seclusion in his sickroom, her husband used to shoot the grouse that proliferated there. Since Duffy left the moorland had not been burned off and purple bell heather spread its carpet of colour as far as the eye could see, patchworked with the glorious golden brown of springing bracken. She had not been up there for a long time, admitting to herself, though she did her best to keep thoughts of him at bay, that it was because of Duffy. Shaking herself, at least mentally, she brought herself back to the question of caring for the land that would one day pass to her son. She supposed she should be attending to the burning off, which she had been told heartened the moorland, or at least she should be talking to the farmers about what should be done, but she knew little of such things and her days were so busy filled with the school, with her own children, with her household, with her tenants, that, leaving aside the misery it caused her to dwell on memories of Duffy, she had let it slip away as painlessly as possible. Perhaps one of the men at Hawthorne Lane might know what to do about it. After all they were country men and . . .

"M'lady." Rosy's gentle voice interrupted her thoughts and she came back to the problem of where and how she was to find a teacher for her school, which, if it was not helped, would founder. Rosy, despite her enthusiasm, was not capable of carrying on alone. There were thirty-six children on most days, though some of them were absent when it was a busy time on the farms, which would be busier still at harvest time. But still Rosy needed help and she herself seemed no longer able to provide it. The poisoning of the young dogs, the accident with the gig, Buttons' death, her own injury had all combined to make her feel sadly weakened, dissipating what strength she had, especially when Alfred had insinuated, not on purpose, of course, that none of them was an accident. He had been mortified when he realised what he had said to her about the gig, proclaiming angrily that the thing had been checked only the week before and it was not until John-Henry had nudged him warningly that he had clamped his mouth tightly on what his thoughts were. But it had been too late then. The misgivings she had harboured had been given form, though it was still a mystery who could have been so spiteful, if that was the word, not only to kill two small and innocent dogs who had harmed no one, but to tamper with her gig. It had taken its toll, the worry of it, and with Duffy gone, the only person to whom she might have taken her fears, she had become woefully out of sorts.

"Very well," she said now. "I'll ride into Allenbury tomorrow and speak to Mrs Barrie. It can do no harm."

And here was the result sitting opposite her. A small, fair-haired girl of about sixteen, she thought, who looked as though she couldn't keep a basket of kittens in order, let alone the boisterous high spirits of Francy Long and his contemporaries. She wasn't even sure where to begin, since she had never interviewed anyone for a job before. Servants were employed by the housekeeper, or, as was the case at Newton Law, by Mrs Fowkes the cook, by John-Henry the head groom or by Mr Weston in his capacity as head gardener.

She plunged right in, for what else was she to do? "Now then, Miss Blamire, Mrs Barrie tells me you are looking for a post as a teacher and as I have such a post available I feel we may be of some help to one another."

"Aye, m'lady, that's true enough. I've ter support meself now me da's gone. I don't fancy bein' a governess, which I doubt I'd get any road, not wi' my accent." Miss Blamire spoke with a warm frankness that Amy found she liked. "But I've 'ad a good education from me da an' it seems a shame ter waste it," she continued.

"Your da . . . ?"

"Aye. Me da were a parson. Or as good as. 'E found himself a little chapel in the gift of Sir Alfred Ashworth over by Whitton. Dost know it?"

Amy admitted that she didn't.

"'E was a good marra ter me da, was Sir Alfred, considering Da never had any proper qualifications fer a parson. But he was a good, simple man, me da, and folk came for miles to listen to 'im preach. Mind, 'e didn't preach, not as such. 'E just talked to them and when one of 'em was in trouble he turned out, rain or shine an' they loved 'im fer it." As though suddenly aware that she was becoming tearful and such a thing was not in her nature, Miss Blamire cleared her throat, straightened her already straight back and continued steadily. "Any road, though the livin' wasn't much it kept food in us bellies and put a clout on us backs an' what me da knew 'e taught me. Someone taught 'im ter read an' write when he was no more than a bairn an' from then on 'e taught himself, like. Read! 'E never 'ad his nose out of a book an' he taught me ter be t' same. 'E were a good teacher," she finished simply. "I canna speak like thou does an' I reckon I never will now, just like thou could never learn ter speak like me but I can teach bairns ter read an' write an' 'appen a few other things an' all."

For some reason she could not define, perhaps recognising the sort of woman she herself would like to be – and not recognising that she already *was* that sort of woman – Amy leaned over the desk impulsively and reached for Miss Blamire's hand which lay tightly clasped by the other in her lap.

"Give me your hand, Miss Blamire."

Miss Blamire hesitantly and wonderingly put out her

357

hand and was quite astounded but strangely moved when Lady Blenkinsopp clasped it firmly. She smiled uncertainly, the smile lighting up her rather plain face and putting a glow of something in her long, pale-blue eyes which were her best feature. They were intelligent eyes, somewhat anxious at the moment since she desperately needed this job. Ever since Mrs Barrie, who had sometimes visited her da with the doctor in his last days, had told her of the school at Newton Law and of Lady Blenkinsopp's need of a teacher she had prayed to her da's God that she might be given the chance to show what she could do. She had taught one or two of the children of her da's parishioners, those who had eager, questing minds, which was difficult to achieve in the circumstances in which they were reared, and she knew she was capable of taking on a classroom of children, given the chance. And here was her chance. Lady Blenkinsopp seemed kind though somewhat distracted, not the sort of woman who had built a school, taught in it herself, run her husband's vast estate, cared for that husband in his illness, put decent roofs over her tenants' heads and was rapidly doing away with the consumption and rickets that had afflicted the children of the estate for decades. She was pale and delicate-looking, quite beautiful in a frail and ethereal way. She reminded Abigail Blamire of the dandelion clocks that trembled in the fields in summer. Creamy white, insubstantial, unspoiled until some breeze came along to blow the flower to pieces. But then the dandelion clock, when it was blown away, took root elsewhere and became a sturdy dandelion again, bright-hued and long-lasting, in fact difficult to quench, so perhaps this lovely woman was the same. She did hope so.

"Miss Blamire." Lady Blenkinsopp smiled, a bright smile of genuine pleasure. "I think you are just what I'm looking for."

Abigail Blamire's heart lifted joyfully in her breast and her joy showed in her bright eyes.

"In fact I'm sure of it. I don't wish to . . . offend, but you are just what the children need. I've often wondered if it's the way I talk, a foreign language to them, I'm sure, which is what holds me up when I try to teach them." Her smile broadened. "You would be the first to admit, in fact you already have in a way, that up here in the north-east you have a way of expressing yourselves that is hard for those not of this area to understand at times and I suppose the opposite is true. Frankly, I find the accent and dialect attractive if somewhat . . . problematic to grasp. 'Gan on', they say to me, which I found bewildering at first and only the other day I heard Betty Long, one of the women from Hawthorne Lane whose children you will teach, say to one of them 'Ah'll skelp thy lug' and until Rosy, who is the other teacher and also from these parts, explained to me what it meant Betty might have been speaking double Dutch."

All the while she was speaking Amy held Abigail's hand, not realising that she was recruiting another to the band of devoted women she had gathered about her. First there had been Tansy who, though she was free with criticisms of her mistress, it was only to the other servants who were, after all, family, but who would lay down her life in her ladyship's defence should someone *outside* the family threaten her. Then there was Rosy Little who would never give over thanking, not the fates that had brought her to Newton Law, though they had been more than kind, but the woman who had seen something in her that even she had not known was there. And now, right out of the blue, so to speak, here was another. Another strong woman and Amy was the only one of the four of them who was not aware of her own strength which drew them to her.

"So, Miss Blamire, what do you think?"

"Me name's Abigail, m'lady." Abigail's face was flushed and almost pretty in her excitement. She made no attempt to withdraw her hand from that of her new employer. She and her da had been devoted but not demonstrative. Now she found she liked the touch of another human being, the warmth and friendship which Lady Blenkinsopp seemed to hold out to her. She didn't know what was to happen next but she was sure this woman opposite her would have it all arranged and she was right.

Within a week Abigail Blamire was installed, not only in the class once taught by her ladyship where she immediately sorted out the rough from the smooth, as she called it, but given one of the empty estate worker's cottages that stood in a row at the back of the stables. She was not to know that it had once belonged to the gamekeeper. She and her pa had had little in the way of worldly goods but her ladyship had taken her up to the tall and overflowing attics at the top of the house and told her carelessly to pick what she wanted. There was already a bed and several bits of furniture in the cottage, she told Abigail in a strange, toneless voice, but she was sure Abigail would want to set it out to suit herself, which Abigail did, and before a month had gone by it was as if she had always been a part of the household. She ate with the servants, for that was what she was, and because she was so obviously of the same background as themselves they accepted her as one of their own. She was quiet, reserved, but she put on no airs nor graces and except for her rather confounding habit of bending her head before each meal and quietly thanking her God for what she was about to eat, which was a bit unnerving at first, made no ripples in the smooth surface of their lives.

It was up at the school that she made the ripples, and Rosy Little reported that the class was totally transformed by her presence. Even Francy Long, who had been the spirit behind most of the disruptive influences, had actually learned to read a word or two, much to his mother's delight. Miss Abby, as they learned to call her, wore plain, unadorned grey, or sometimes on a Sunday a muddy brown when she went to the chapel where her father had once preached, but always with a little white collar which was band-box fresh every day. Her fair hair, which was almost white, was smooth and gleaming, well brushed into an enormous coil at the back of her head and her boots, which often paddled through the muck and mire of the yard before it was swept by Jumsie McGovern, were polished each day to a bright and lustrous shine. She was a credit to her upbringing, whatever that might have been, Cook was often heard to say approvingly.

Amy continued to show an interest in the classes, both of them, for neither Abigail nor Rosy could play the piano, nor could they apply themselves to the painting and drawing that were taught to all girls of good family in childhood. Amy was no genius, either at the piano or with a paintbrush, but she believed the couple of hours she spent each week singing the songs she sang to her own children, encouraging the estate children to sing with her, and the attempt she made to involve them in putting colour on to sheets of paper showed them that there was more to life, and to school, than the repetitious chanting of "one and one is two", "two and two is four", "C is for Cat and D is for Dog" which Abigail and Rosy dinned into them. Mind, she knew that both of them tried to put life into their lessons; to add something that the children knew from their own lives and on the whole she believed that this scheme of hers was a success.

She was in her sitting-room when someone knocked at her door. It was several weeks since Abigail had settled in at the school and had become the tenant of the little cottage that had been Duffy's. That had been hard. Amy had only been in the cottage on one occasion and that was the last night Duffy had been there and the image of the kitchen and the memory of what had happened in it was still strong and whole in her heart. They had never made love. She had not belonged to him as a woman belongs to a man, which she had longed for with a passion that consumed her, which she still yearned after, but in that room all her hopes and desires had blossomed and then shrivelled away like summer flowers when winter nips. She had not known really what it was she had hoped for, but whatever it was Duffy had taken all that with him and gone from her life. Though she knew she could not hope to keep that warm room, those warm hopes, that lovely moment enshrined for ever as though in a place of sacred worship, it had torn her to ribbons to let Abigail take up residence there. But she had done it, as she had learned to do all the things that were painful to her but which had to be done just the same. She walked alone with her children through the woods where once Duffy had walked with her. She had even climbed up to the Weeping Stones in an effort to exorcise him from her soul but it did no good. He was gone, leaving a huge hole in her life and though she wanted to squat down in the sweet-smelling heather, put her arms about herself and wail of her loss, she strode on down to the life that was hers and which waited for her at Newton Law.

She lifted her head from the book she was reading, sitting with her feet up on her chaise-longue as she had been ordered to do by Doctor Parsons for an hour each day, her arm propped on a soft pillow.

"Come in," she called, her finger in the book to keep her place. It was *The Woman in White* by Wilkie Collins, a book recently published and which she was reading for the second time.

The door opened slowly and as she watched curiously, wondering who it was who was creeping with such hesitation across her threshold, when the widely grinning face of her husband's minder appeared – dear sweet Jesus, she didn't think she could remember his name even – she recoiled as though a live and snarling wolf had entered her room. That was what he looked like, a wolf, a wolf with great rotting teeth – fangs, not teeth – and what appeared to be saliva dripping from his lips, which was absolutely ridiculous for he was only a man, a nasty, unsavoury unclean man, it was true, but human and no more than a servant in the house of which she was mistress. It was just the shock of seeing him there when she had expected Tansy or Morna or Nanny Morag with the children. Of course there would have been a lot more commotion if it had been the children, for she could hear them coming from as far away as the nursery door as they galloped down the stairs and along the landing to her room.

The man, Platt, that was it, that was his name, sidled into the room and she had a distinct desire to tell him not to close the door, for the idea of being alone with him behind a closed door filled her with revulsion. Dear God, don't let him come any nearer, she whispered silently as he took several steps away from the door. She wished she was closer to the fireplace where the bell was that summoned one of the maids but it was a warm day, the window was opened wide and her chaise-longue was placed beneath it.

Though her throat was suddenly dry she managed to lift her head imperiously and pronounce one word.

"Yes?"

"M'lady, I'm ter say sorry ter trouble tha', like, but Sir Robert wants a crack wi' thi'."

"I beg your pardon?" she managed icily.

"'E's clever now . . ."

"Clever?"

"Why aye. 'E's ready fer a bit crack if tha' could spare time, 'e ses."

"Are you trying to tell me that my husband wants to talk to me?" she asked incredulously. She sat up and placed her book on the table beside her, then swung her feet to the floor, noticing that the man's eyes flickered from her face to her bare foot and ankle. He licked his lips and she felt her flesh creep.

"Why aye, diven't I just say soo?"

"Don't be impertinent with me." Her eyes flashed and Platt's small brain was filled with images of what this woman would be like if – when – his master got his hands on her. Sir Robert spent many an hour dwelling on what he would do to her when the time was right and it often inflamed Platt's mind to such an extent he had a hard job not to blunder from the room and carry off the first maid he came across. The slut from the inn came up now and again but as she was so well paid she was acquiescent, submissive, and it wasn't the same as having a struggling, unwilling victim like the one his employer's wife would make. Her shoulder had healed according to the gossip he heard about the place and it seemed that Sir Robert was about to implement – though Platt did not use such a word – the next part of his plan. By gow, he'd been patient, him and Sir Robert both, and her bleedin' ladyship was in for a bit of a shock when she entered his master's bedroom.

Amy pushed her feet into the house slippers that lay beside the chaise-longue and though Platt didn't notice it particularly, took a wide circle away from him to reach the fireplace, where she rang the bell. He waited indifferently, for he knew that his master was in command now, no matter what her ladyship said or did, and when Tansy knocked on the door, entering it at Lady Blenkinsopp's order, he was quite tickled at the way she flinched and gasped when she saw him. Her hand went to her mouth and she scurried like a frightened rabbit round the periphery of the room until she stood by her mistress.

"M'lady?" she quavered, almost hiding behind her ladyship's wide skirt, but her ladyship, after that first shock, was in full command of herself. Something told her that there was a surprise in store for her and though the man appeared harmless enough she didn't trust him, or Robert, incapacitated as he was. Best to have Tansy with her.

"We're to go and see my husband, Tansy," she said firmly. "I think it best you come with me then if there is anything . . . needed, you can run and get it."

"Oh, m'lady," Tansy almost wailed, for only the girls who did the cleaning went into Sir Robert's bedroom and they brought back tales of such a nasty nature the rest of them were thankful they didn't have to go. Pay them a king's fortune, they said to one another, and it wouldn't get *them* in there.

"Come along, Tansy. It will only take a minute or so and then . . ." She nearly said "and then we can escape" but with the great hulking brute who looked after her husband watching them both with enormous interest, at the same time scratching at the sagging crotch of his greasy trousers, she felt it was somewhat beneath the dignity of Lady Blenkinsopp. She didn't want to go but she was not about to let this brute see her fear.

"Lead the way . . . er . . ." Why in God's name did she keep forgetting the man's name? She didn't know, only that she felt a great fear growing inside her, and when she and Tansy, shoulder to shoulder and almost holding hands, stepped into her husband's room, she realised why.

22

At first she did not recognise the man sitting in the chair by the window. He wore a smoking jacket of blue velvet with a loosely tied cravat at the neck and he was smoking a cigar. He was washed, shaved and his sparse hair had been brushed. Across his knees was a rug which was tucked completely about his legs and feet. On his lap was a copy of *The Times* and, apart from the rug, he looked the picture of a country gentleman enjoying a moment of respite before jumping up to be off about his gentlemanly pursuits.

"Good morning, my dear. Lovely morning, is it not? I am just enjoying the summer air and the view from the window. And, I may say, listening to the sound of the children's voices as they toddle off with their nursemaids is a delight. Enchanting, really enchanting. I even managed to catch a glimpse of them as they crossed the lawn and can't believe how they have grown. My Robert is quite the little man now. I believe the image of me at the same age, or so the painting my mother treasured tells me. But the twins . . . well, I must admit I can see no family likeness at all. So fair! What a pity I have missed so much of their babyhood, but then that can be easily rectified now that I am up and about again, so to speak. What was it you called them? I have quite forgotten. That's if I ever knew, since you have been most remiss in visiting me lately. So remind me, will you?"

He took a deep drag on his cigar, relaxed and perfectly at his ease as though this moment in the day was one to which they were both accustomed, then blew the smoke into the air before smiling with such malicious enjoyment Amy felt her heart fall, quite literally, before rising like a storm-tossed balloon into her chest. It pounded furiously against her ribs and beside her she heard Tansy moan and felt her hand slip, like that of a terrified child, into her own. She was glad of it. They both stood in the doorway, their faces the colour of unbaked dough, she was sure of it, for she had felt the blood drain away.

"Well, dear wife, have you nothing to say to your husband on the miracle of his recovery? I'm not yet able to walk but that will come, I'm certain. Platt and I have worked hard these last months, over a year now in order to give you the pleasant surprise of a husband restored to his former health . . . and capabilities. So come over here and give me a kiss. In fact I do believe we may send Platt and that servant who hides behind you away and have a small reunion of our own. What d'you say to that, wife?"

Platt smirked and his face flushed with some perverted image that was evidently filling his mind and he began to edge towards Tansy, perhaps believing that while his master played with the mistress he might do the same with her maid.

Both Amy and Tansy cowered back, so shocked

by what was taking place their wits had deserted them, leaving them only with the blind instinct of an animal, the instinct that told them to run . . . run to get out of this place of menace, of great danger, to twist and turn as fleeing animals do to avoid the predator. Amy's head was filled with a great swirling mist, not just of terror, the terror this man had always invoked in her ever since she had first been introduced to him as her future husband in her mother's house, but of despair. How was she to live her life, give her children the stability and love they needed if they were to be under the charge of this monster, which if he was truly recovered they would be? If he had them under his control again, not just them, but herself? These thoughts had no coherency to them. They were no more than flashing pictures that darted across her vision. This loathsome man recovered with his brutal and befouled hands; those hands once more on her; his voice to be heard in the house again giving orders, countermanding hers; her school demolished, for there was nothing more certain than that he would not be prepared to spend good money on what he considered to be a waste; her children reduced to the timid ghosts her elder son had been when first she returned! It didn't bear thinking about.

It could have been no more than thirty seconds, thirty seconds of orderless, frenzied madness, before reason seeped slowly back into her brain enabling her to stiffen her spine and pull herself together. It was as though some voice had spoken in her head, untangling her thoughts and placing them in perfect order so that she could look at them, study them and rationally dispose of every challenge this foul beast had flung at her feet. She heard the voice in her mind, a silent voice that no one could hear but herself, in the mind of the woman she had become, first in the peace and recovery of her cousin's home in Liverpool over two years ago, then in the love and warm strength given to her by Duffy. It rose quite smoothly to the surface of her brain but behind that smoothness that she showed to her husband was the savagery of a lioness defending her young. A savagery that said she would protect herself, her maid, her innocent children who had no one but her, indeed everyone in this house, this *home* of hers and woe betide anyone who tried to stop her. She didn't know how this horror had come about; well, she supposed she did if she was honest and at least she must be honest. She had slept away the last eight months since Duffy had left, neglected those in her care, ignored this room and the man in it and allowed him, unseen, to rise again like a phoenix from the ashes.

"I have this to say, Sir Robert, and it is that I have never heard such nonsense in my life."

He hadn't expected that and she watched the complacency slip away from his face, noticing beyond the neatness, the cleanliness, the blue velvet jacket, the cravat, the cigar and the newspaper, which after all were only camouflage, that her husband was still crippled. That one side of his body was still paralysed, that his face, though shaved, still drooped, one eye lower than the other, or so it seemed, that that eye was inclined to water and that from his mouth on the same side saliva dribbled. With his good hand he held a cloth which he used constantly to wipe his mouth. In fact he had only one hand, for the other, on his paralysed side, lay covered beneath the rug.

She smiled and Platt, who had been just about to move across the room towards the two women, with what in mind he really had no idea, faltered, then came to a stop. She wasn't supposed to smile, his master had told him so.

"She'll be bloody terrified, Platt, when she sees me up and about. She'll be so bloody terrified she'll do just what I tell her to do. If I threaten her with her brats she'll jump to like a trained dog. A bitch and by God I mean to make her pay for what she's done to me. When I get her in this room she'll wish she'd never been born and when I've done with her you can have her."

But it seemed her ladyship *wasn't* terrified. Far from it. Leaving go of her maid's hand she twitched her skirt and began to saunter across the room towards her husband, keeping out of his reach, to be sure, but facing up to him unafraid and contemptuous.

"Tansy," she said to her trembling maid, "I want you to go down to the stable yard and bring Alfred and John-Henry into the kitchen. If I'm not down in ten minutes send them up here. Tell them that my husband is having . . . a nasty turn and that they are to be ready to . . . restrain him."

Though her face was still pale she was smiling and Tansy was seen to shake her head slightly in great admiration. By gow, she was a one was their little mistress, her expression said, to face up to that devil in human shape who was her husband. You had to hand it to her, she had guts, even to stay in this room with not only Sir Robert who looked as though he was *really* going to have a nasty turn, but that shambling halfwit who was scratching among the tangled hair on his head in great confusion. It took enormous courage and Tansy knew she couldn't do it. In fact she was not awfully sure she should leave her to the mercy of these two terrible creatures.

She said so bravely.

"It's all right, Tansy. He can't hurt me. You can see how he is. Just do as I say."

"M'lady, shall I not . . . ?"

"Tansy!"

Tansy went but she left the door open and in her own mind she decided she wouldn't leave Alfred and John-Henry in the kitchen but fetch them up to the top of the stairs so that, should things turn nasty – and she wasn't sure what she meant by that – they would be in a handy position to control Sir Robert. The other chap was nothing without his master to lead him and if she knew the two grooms, and she did, for wasn't she to marry one of them, they wouldn't allow a hair of their little mistress's head to be harmed. Mind you, she didn't for a moment believe that the master could walk, or ever would, else he wouldn't have been sitting in that chair, would he? No, it was all in his head, the daft gowk.

"Now then, husband," Amy said lazily, smilingly, eyeing him with a scornful expression, lifting her eyebrows. "What is it you wanted to say to me? I feel I would like to understand completely what it is you have in mind for the future. Your future, not mine, for I am perfectly content with the way things are now."

Sir Robert Blenkinsopp's face flooded with the bright puce of his venomous anger. His almost colourless, though bloodshot eyes strained out of his face and his mouth opened in a roar of rage. His fouled tongue quivered over his bottom lip and he dribbled so violently his smart cravat was soon soaked through. His good hand lifted and clenched and Amy noticed that though he had been washed his fingernails were black with grime and she wondered how such a thing could happen to a man who never left his room. His hand reached out for her but she was too far away and he thrashed about in his chair in his effort to get to her. His proud boast that he would soon be walking was seen to be nothing but a charade, for he was stuck fast in the chair. One leg twitched and the foot attached to it kicked out at her. Disturbed by his movements the rug slipped to the floor and she saw that under the smoking jacket he wore nothing but his nightgown which had worked up above his knees. One leg, the good leg, looked much as normal, though painfully thin; but the other was nothing but a withered stick. As he jerked and twisted, howling indistinguishable mouthings to his servant, the nightgown hitched higher and the shrivelled worm of his dead manhood was revealed. For a sick, horrified moment Amy stared at it and then began to laugh.

"Is that what you mean to use in the renewal of our relationship, husband? Do you seriously believe that you and I could be husband and wife again, perhaps have more children? I honestly think you did and really, I am astonished that even you, who are known to be arrogant, could believe that such a thing could happen. You had best make up your mind that you are confined here for the rest of your days and . . ."

"You whore . . . we . . . mumble . . . mumble . . . saw
you . . . mumble with that . . . sod . . . mumble mumble
mumble . . . Jesus, Platt . . . mumble mumble . . . cover
. . . mumble . . ."

In his fury and frustration, his defeat in what was
to have been his moment of triumph, a moment
towards which he had worked for months, all he
had painstakingly struggled for left him and he was
once again the gobbling idiot of his early days. He
had been speaking slowly and clearly to Platt for a
long time now, savouring the day when he would do
the same with *her*, when he would demand to have
his lawyer summoned and once again take command
of his own life. Now, with a few jeering words she had
reduced him to gibbering and gesturing and, should
she agree to let him see Sinclair, which she might if
only to prove to the lawyer that he was still not fit to
be in control of his money, his estate, his children, *her*,
she would make sure that the man saw him like this.

"I am not the woman you married, Robert, even you
must see that," she was saying quietly as Platt carefully
tucked the rug about him, hiding the shameful thing
that peeped from the thicket of dark hair between his
thighs. "I have grown, become strong and confident,
and despite what you did to me I no longer wish you
harm. The people who work for me respect me and
are grateful for the change in their lives. Their children
are learning to read and write and have been given the
chance to make something of their lives. So I will not
let you take control of me or my children, or this estate
which will one day belong to my son, *your* son. And
yes, you are right about . . . well, perhaps you might
send your man from the room while we talk about the

twins who are called, by the way, David and Catherine *Blenkinsopp*. David Conal and Catherine Jenna, after my cousin and . . . and her husband. No, you mean you don't wish to hear or you don't care if *he* knows who . . . aah, I see . . ."

She thought he was about to have another apoplectic fit similar to the one he had suffered on the night she returned from Liverpool and, turning to Platt, was about to ask him to send one of the grooms for the doctor when something stopped her. She had told her husband she wished him no harm and she supposed that was true. Providing he was kept shut away from the children and providing she could continue to live the life she had made for herself he might do as he liked, or what he was able. But, having seen the way he had looked earlier when she first came into his room, might not the doctor be impressed should he see him the same way? He had carefully hidden his improvement from everyone for months now, even the doctor, presumably so that he might get her into his clutches again, and his children. Convince the doctor and the lawyer that, apart from actually walking, he was himself again, that he was once again master of Newton Law. The thought of him perhaps being brought out into her home filled her with horror; allowed into the dining-room to eat with her and the girls, who, like her, scarcely visited him now, indeed seemed to have forgotten him, as she had for weeks, perhaps into the garden where he would frighten the children, was more than she could bear. He must be kept in this room, even *locked* in if needs be.

"I'll . . . get . . . you . . . mumble mumble for this . . . mumble bitch." With a great and sustained effort he managed to say those few words so that she understood them but she knew she had only to taunt him and he would go off ranting and choking and dribbling again which would be understood by no one. He must be kept here and when the doctor called she must impress upon the servants that he was not to be allowed in here unless she was present. She must make up some story of violence, threatening behaviour, which after all would not be a lie and which would explain her actions.

He watched her, his eyes flamed in his face, red hot and hating malevolently but he was still now, quiet, though she could tell it was taking a great deal of control on his part.

"You can longer hurt me, Robert. Today has proved that. Surely you agree. You are confined to this room and must make the best of it. I won't allow my children near you and you cannot move from this room."

"No," he said clearly, "but Platt can."

She was surprised when she left the room to find Alfred and John-Henry at the top of the stairs, both smelling strongly of the stable and beside them was Tansy.

"I know tha' said in't kitchen, m'lady," Tansy said stubbornly, "but I didn't like look of t'master. By't time we'd got up from down below 'e could 'ave murdered thi'."

"Well, he didn't, Tansy, and is not likely to so there is no need for melodrama, but thank you just the same, and thank you, John-Henry and Alfred."

The two men shifted uncomfortably, conscious all of a sudden of their rough appearance in this dainty woman's presence. It didn't seem to matter in the stable or the yard but up here amidst the comfort and luxury of her home, in this part of their world where they never went, they felt out of place. But their mistress wouldn't allow it.

"I just don't know what I would do if I didn't have the friends I have found here at Newton Law," her ladyship continued. "Your help is a great comfort to me. Sir Robert is . . . not himself today and Tansy was right to alert you. I may have to call on you again should he need restraining."

"M'lady, tho've only t'er say't word an' me an' Alfred'll . . ." John-Henry began eagerly, appalled that she might find herself in danger from that bugger who seemed to menace her even from his bed. "When Tansy said . . ."

"Now you mustn't go about telling the others what you see in Sir Robert's room, Tansy," she said mildly, reprovingly. "We don't want to alarm them, do we? John-Henry and Alfred can be relied on to . . . look after things should the need arise."

There, she'd put the idea in their heads that her husband was not to be trusted, which, from what he'd said as she was leaving the room, was true. These two servants, neither of whom was a gossip like the younger ones, would keep it to themselves and she felt better knowing they would be on the lookout for her if what Robert had said about Platt was to be believed. She was beginning to realise now who it was who had poisoned the dogs and done something to the gig so that the wheel had sheared off which, though he hadn't said it in so many words, Alfred had implied.

Her shoulder, as though at the unaccustomed stress, was aching, and with a smiling nod at the two men she dismissed them and she and Tansy entered her sitting-room. She had meant to go up to the nursery and play with the children for an hour before their bath but somehow she felt weakened, weary, somewhat frail and, she admitted it, yearning for a good cry. A good cry! As if that would do any good!

"Why don't tha' lie down fer a bit, m'lady?" Tansy asked her soothingly, leading her unobtrusively towards the chaise-longue from where she had risen when Platt knocked at the door. "Tha' don't look too clever an' forty winks'll do tha' the world o' good. See, I'll put rug over thi'."

Amy did as she was told. She was just dozing off, half asleep and half still awake, when she rose up in a sudden dread.

"'Tis all right, yer ladyship, I'm 'ere," said the quiet voice of her maid from the fireside chair and, reassured, she fell into a restful sleep.

"What's up?" Cook asked Tansy when, later, her ladyship had gone up to the nursery to play with her children.

Tansy looked furtively about the kitchen where, in various parts of the big, high-ceilinged room, the other maids were going efficiently about their business. Clara and Cissie, the parlourmaids, were readying the cutlery and crockery, the place mats and napkins preparatory to setting the dining-room table. As usual there would just be the four ladies, three of whom were in the drawing-room placidly embroidering as they had been taught to do as young girls. Agnes, Mary and Jane's lives were very pleasant since their father had had his accident and their step-mother had taken over the running of the house, which was her right, and the estate, which wasn't, but, since they were incapable of doing it, they made no objection. They had heard that their father had sent for her this afternoon, which was unusual in itself, but they would not ask why, since they did not care to be involved in case it made a ripple on the surface of their uneventful lives. They had accepted that Amy, Lady Blenkinsopp, was an energetic, efficient and intelligent woman who seemed to know what she was doing; the workers on the estate confirmed this. They themselves only visited the "deserving poor", as they called them, those women who wore a clean apron when they called and sent their children to Sunday school, where they, of course, read the Bible to them, but there seemed to be a general feeling that the estate was faring well, which was quite splendid. It left them feeling graciously benevolent with no effort made on their part.

Tansy drew Cook into the empty stillroom after furtively looking about her to see that none of the others was watching. Tansy was a good, kind girl who wouldn't harm her mistress, or indeed anyone. She loved Lady Blenkinsopp and would have done her best to defend her this afternoon if Sir Robert, or that monster who looked after him, had turned nasty, but she was totally incapable of keeping the thrill of it all to herself. To do her justice she wouldn't have dreamed of blabbing to any of the other maidservants, but Cook was older, and could be trusted to keep things to herself.

"Well, 'e sent fer 'er. Said 'e wanted a bit crack."

"Who, not the master?" Cook whispered, drawing Tansy deeper into the stillroom.

"Aye, well I gan wi' 'er, 'im not bein' all there, like, an' that chap of 'is . . . well, tha've seen 'im."

"Why aye."

"Well, there 'e is, large as life an' twice as nasty."

"Who?"

"Sir Robert."

"Not . . ."

"Why aye. All dressed up like a dog's dinner, sittin' in chair readin' paper an' smokin' a cigar."

"Niver."

"Why aye. Dear knows what 'e were up to. Well, me an' 'er ladyship just stood by't door, frozen-like an' 'e ses I'm ter go . . . aye, he could talk proper an' all. Not that mumbo-jumbo 'e's bin mouthin'."

"Dear God above!"

"Aye, until 'er ladyship started on 'im! She's nowt but a pawky little thing but she stood up to 'im."

"Give over!"

"Aye, and that daft gowk just stood there."

"So that's why she wanted Alfred an' John-Henry."

"Aye, but the man canna walk an' that minder of 'is 'asn't the brains 'e were born with. Mind, me an' 'er ladyship were afeared at first but I reckon there's nowt to be bothered about."

"Is 'e ter come downstairs then?" Cook whispered.

"Eeh, noo," Tansy cried scornfully. "Mistress wouldn't let 'im, not wi' bairns growin' up. Best where 'e is I reckon, an' that's where 'e'll stay."

Tansy would not have been quite so cheerfully complacent if she could have overheard another conversation – if the monologue that was taking place in the room at the top of the stairs could have been named such. With his wife gone and his composure regained, Sir Robert was talking coherently and rationally to Platt, though it is doubtful Platt understood half of what he said. He listened for hours to his master doing what Platt called "babbling", disclosing his plans for his wife, his estate, his horses, since he seemed to think one day he would ride again, for his son, and the two babies whom he had never once seen. Once, when Platt had had a glimpse of them in the garden he had tried to describe them to his master, for surely a father might be expected to take an interest in his family, but Sir Robert only flew into one of his dangerous rages, losing the coherency of his speech and gradually it began to dawn in Platt's slow, treacle-like brain that his master did not believe the twins were of his get. Of course, Platt had not been here on the day that had seen the return of her ladyship from her journeying, nor that evening when Sir Robert had fallen down the stairs and become as he was now. But from what he had heard, and there were always snippets of gossip to be picked up, even by someone like him who the rest of the servants avoided, it appeared that the master and mistress had spent the night together. The mistress had been given a good braying, she'd a black eye and a bruised face to prove it when first Platt had seen her, so those bairns must have been got on her by the master.

"Those brats of hers'll go, that's the first thing. No, don't ask me where" – though Platt had not spoken and had shown no interest – "but I'll find somewhere. Poorhouse, I reckon, or to some chap, and there are plenty about, who deals in child flesh. There are men who . . . well, let's say a good price is paid for children in certain places. By Christ, she's a hard-faced cow. She gives herself away by the bloody names she's called them. Jenna and Conal! Get that, *Conal*! She must think I'm half-witted. But the lad, *my* lad, and I *know* he's mine, will be taken in hand and taught how to be a *man*. Not the namby-pamby weakling she'll make of him. But she's got to be taught a lesson, that hell-cat, and soon. She thinks she's got me trapped here but by God, I'll show her. I'll admit to you, man, while I'm fastened in this bloody chair she's got the better of me but there are ways and means and she'll find out to her cost that I know 'em all. She took me by surprise just now but she'll not do it again. I'll have her eating out of my bloody hand before long, just you wait and see. Now, listen, this is what I want you to do. Are you listening?"

Platt said that he was.

23

She remembered the first time of terror, as if she could ever forget it, because it happened on the day after what was the last moment of peace and a certain contentment she was to enjoy, though she was not aware of it at the time. A happy day, a joyful day for them all, the day on which Rosy Little and Jumsie McGovern, or James as he begged to be called, at least on that special day, were married.

It was a Saturday in July, a gentle, sunny day with a slight breeze which lifted the bride's small veil as she stepped from the carriage in which her ladyship had insisted she be driven to the tiny village church in Alwinton, accompanied by her ladyship herself. Rosy was dressed as a bride should be, though she was no virgin which was a state only she and Jumsie were aware of. Her ladyship had provided the bridal outfit – and Jumsie's new suit as part of her wedding gift – bearing in mind that the gown the bride wore had to be of a style and simplicity that would serve Rosy for many years, probably to the end of her life, as an outfit for special occasions. It was in figured muslin with a high neck and long sleeves, not overly full in the skirt, the waist tied about with wide, white satin ribbon on which were pinned peach-coloured rosebuds. She wore a wreath of rosebuds and white gypsophila, called, appropriately, Rosy Veil, on her bright copper hair which had been cleverly arranged by Tansy. In her gloved hands she carried a small posy to match her wreath, all from Mr Weston's garden and tied about with narrow satin ribbon. She looked quite radiant as she walked up the aisle on John-Henry's arm towards her bridegroom and Alfred, who was best man.

They were all there, crammed like peas in a pod in the pews, the house servants and their spouses, those who had them, farm tenants, those who could get away, and their wives, the folk from Hawthorne Lane, the women inclined to shed a tear, for was it not customary at a wedding. If the farmers were surprised by the fuss made of a girl who was no more than a servant they were quickly made aware that the bride was a great favourite with the mistress and indeed was the very young woman who was attempting to cram a little learning into the indifferent heads of their own children.

Cook, from her place in the pew behind her ladyship where she sat with the upper servants, murmured that "wor" Rosy had turned out right well but then if a girl couldn't look bonny on her wedding day when could she? And wasn't she a lucky lass to have such an indulgent mistress. Normally on these occasions the lord of the manor, or lady in this case, looked in and nodded benevolently at the lower classes enjoying themselves, but her ladyship treated Rosy as though she were a member of her own family and as such was deserving of this ostentation.

In the dim church which she seemed to light up, Jumsie watched Rosy come towards him, his mouth agape, evidently unable to believe that this glorious creature was his good and wholesome Rosy, and it was not until Alfred nudged him that he closed his mouth and turned to the minister who was waiting to get on with the service.

The ceremony over, the newly wed husband and wife were not surprised, since it was an old custom, to find that the church gates had been tied with string and until Jumsie paid a "toll" to the cries from the children of "Hoy a penny oot" the new wife and her husband could not get out.

Cook and the rest gathered in the churchyard to watch, Cook remarking with great satisfaction, as though she had arranged the whole affair all by herself, that "Married in white, she'd be all right" and that since Rosy was wearing a blue garter, carried a handkerchief borrowed from her ladyship and wore a new dress the marriage had a fair chance of success.

They danced until almost midnight, the fiddler, helped out by a man on a flute, played the lively jigs and reels, while the booted feet of the revellers stamped out the steps with great gusto, aided by the lavish supply of ale and a heady wine that their mistress had provided.

There was a display of northern sword dancing, an elaborate formalised performance by five men holding "swords" or "rappers" which were an integral part of the dance. The group was accompanied by a musician and a "Betty", a male dancer dressed in women's clothes who normally would walk among the spectators with a box collecting money, but it seemed her ladyship had already paid the group most generously. The guests roared their approval and one or two of the men who had imbibed rather unwisely did their best to join in, but with great good nature they were restrained and the performance continued unhindered.

An open-sided tent had been erected on the wide lawn at the front of the house, since the weather in the Northumberland fells could be unpredictable, but as it turned out it was not necessary. The tent had been hung with fir and copper beech and tied up with yards of bright ribbons, again provided by her ladyship. Amy sat at the top table in a place of honour beside the bride and groom, and next to her were Doctor and Mrs Doctor Barrie. The three Misses Blenkinsopp had condescended to be present, looking somewhat startled by the extravagance of the whole affair as they sat at the top table beside the upper servants, one of whom was Cook. Morna, as head housemaid, and Mr Weston and his pleasant-faced wife were included along with John-Henry and Alfred, who had played an important part in the ceremony. Jumsie was quite overcome and held on to his new wife's hand beneath the table, making it difficult for either of them to tuck into the good food. Cook's best damask tablecloth which, in fact, actually belonged to the house, was laid along the length of the table and from the top table, forming a T, ran a long trestle table about which the rest of the servants, indoors and out, were placed, taking it in turns to serve and partake of the feast. In the middle of this table sat farmers in their rusty best, then finally, at the bottom, the cottagers from Hawthorne Lane dressed in their old-fashioned finery, thinking themselves to be in heaven, not only with the good food but with the smartness of their appearance which came from the boxes, or so she said, that her ladyship had found in the attics.

Mr Weston had excelled himself, almost stripping his flowering borders to provide bright centrepieces down the length of each table, the bowls of flowers themselves joined by long trails of ivy, all arranged by her ladyship, which, apparently, she had been taught as a girl. There was a vast sirloin of beef roasted to a brown glaze on the outside, succulent and pink within, a huge ham, garnished with parsley, a whole loin of pork, two great steak and kidney puddings, pickled onions, cheeses, golden-crusted home-made bread, fruit pies, bowls of fresh cream brought down from the dairy, which all began to disappear like snow in summer, while Cook's cowslip wine for the ladies and ale for the men was disposed of in great quantities. Amy had been told on the quiet by Cook, when she had suggested more delicate dishes such as salmon, asparagus and the sort of dishes that would be served at a wedding in her world, that these simple folk would be suspicious of such things.

"Give 'em something they understand, m'lady, something they can get their teeth into."

They certainly did that, losing their diffident shyness as the feast, and the drink, was disposed of, becoming rowdy, laughing and calling to one another across the tables. There were toasts and rambling speeches, some of them inclined towards coarseness, for these were country folk who were close to the earth and the basic instincts that this implied. When Jumsie was beseeched to kiss his bride, which he did shyly, some wag called out, "Tha'll 'ave ter do better 'n that ternight, lad," and was nearly flung out for his impudence.

Amy took a turn about the floor with Doctor Barrie, then with the bridegroom, who was red-faced and sweating with the pride of it, then with Mr Weston, who was still rather distracted by the raiding of his flowerbeds.

Mr and Mrs McGovern had long gone to their small cottage next door to the shy, new schoolteacher's, who also made her excuses early, relieved that her ladyship had expressly forbidden any of the rough customs that had in the past been part of any wedding. Crude, most of them, such as seeing the newly wedded pair not only into their bedroom, but into their bed. Those who could still stand lingered on, drinking some of them, others, young men and women who saw no one but their own family from one year's end to the next and were loth to end this wonderful day and the opportunities it had brought, finding sheltered nooks and crannies under bushes and in the woods.

Amy confided to Laura, who was staying the night at Newton Law, that she hoped nine months from now there would not be an unwanted crop of illegitimate babies, then smiled a goodnight and was helped to her bed by a solicitous Tansy who had come to regard her ladyship as her own private possession. She was weary but it was a good weariness, for all about her had been a feeling of cordiality which had nothing to do with the free-flowing drink. Everywhere she went she had been greeted with great warmth and kindliness, by a show of shy affection and gratitude, and it had soothed her heart which often these days was sore and troubled.

She lay in her bed and, as he always did in a quiet

moment, he came to her, smiling his wry smile, and with all her heart and soul she wished he could have been here today to see the peace, the joy, the goodwill, the content which he had helped to build at Newton Law.

Laura and Andrew had been gone no more than ten minutes when she heard her name being called. It was another warm summer's day and as the carriage bearing her friends turned out of the gate towards the road to Allenbury she lifted her head and took in a great draught of the warming sun-filled air, dragging it down into her lungs. The men were busy on the lawn dismantling the tent, Mr Weston peering in growing horror at the holes in his lawn where the tent pegs had been. She could hear him moaning to Mr Purvis as though it were a wound to his own flesh that "it'd tekk a fair deal o' doin' ter put this grass back inter some sort o' heart an' would Purvis look at them 'oles where some bugger'd stamped 'is bloody boots," before he suddenly noticed her idling down the path towards the shrubbery. At once he clamped his mouth shut, for after all he'd been one of the buggers who, with a great deal of ale inside him, had ground his own boots carelessly into the grass.

He and Purvis and the other men lifted their caps respectfully, wishing her "good morning", nodding and smiling, though most, including Mr Weston, had heads that could do with being kept still.

The shrubbery was in full summer bloom, the tall spears of foxgloves and columbine standing proudly among the vivid greenery. Thrushes and blackbirds sang for joy and it was so quiet she could hear a woodpecker hammering away at a trunk deep in the woodland. There were dozens of brilliant butterflies, red admirals, peacocks, tortoiseshells and common blues, named for her last summer when she had walked these paths with Duffy. There was that smell of summer, a smell of cut grass, of turned earth and distant fires as the gardeners disposed of rotten wood cut from the trees. She could hear the clatter of the lawnmower, the chink of a spade, the scuffle of boots on the path leading from the yard at the back of the house to the lawns at the front and the metallic snick of handshears, hard at work on Mr Weston's already perfect privet. She opened her heart to it, and felt a warm current of content ripple through her, unaware that it was for the last time.

She had reached the edge of the wood when she heard her name being called. At the sound of the frantic voice, a female voice, the men had stopped what they were doing, some beginning to move forward anxiously, for the caller sounded as though she'd gone out of her mind, her voice high and hysterical. It was Lizzie-Ann, from the nursery, and she was lolloping down the drive as though the devil on horseback were after her. She was a well-built lass and her rounded breasts were bouncing about in a way that momentarily fascinated the watching men, until they began to realise that the girl was scared out of her wits.

"M'lady . . . oh, m'lady, tha're ter come at once. Please, oh, please come quick. 'E's got 'im. 'E come an' took 'im an' Morag ses . . ."

Amy had turned back, standing quite still like an animal that scents danger but is not sure from which direction it is to come. She had on a plain day dress of rose-coloured batiste. It had short sleeves above her elbow and a deep, square neckline which revealed a fraction of the rounded tops of her breasts. About her waist was a sash in the same colour. She wore black boots, sturdy and made for walking, for she meant to take the children through the wood and up partway on to the moorland. Robby was two and a half now and the twins eighteen months but all were sturdy, well used to walking and liked nothing better than to escape Nanny Morag and Lizzie-Ann, who were both aware of the responsibility of caring for their charges and therefore were inclined to be restrictive. Their mama, just as careful but, as they were her own children, more indulgent, allowed them to run like the wind, or, in the case of the twins, toddle and fall over, pick themselves up and toddle on, allowing them the freedom they needed to grow. When the two nursemaids were with them it was "Mind the stones, Master Robby", "Watch where you're going, Master Davey", "Don't plodge in that water, Miss Cat", and to be alone with their mama was a great treat, for she loved to run with them, to "plodge" in the water, to climb up on rocks to "the top of the world". Exciting stuff to young children and she knew they would be plaguing Morag as to when Mama was coming as she had promised at breakfast.

Amy's hand went to her mouth as the most appalling sense of dread trickled icily through her veins and she began to run, Lizzie-Ann at her heels. Lizzie-Ann, now that she had delivered her message, had begun to weep, her breath rasping painfully in her chest as her legs propelled her in the wake of her mistress. Amy took the steps at the front of the house from where she had just waved Laura and Andrew off two at a time, crashing the door back on its hinges, astonished, with the part of her mind still functioning on a day-to-day level, to find the wide hall full of servants, not just the kitchen-maids but also the men from the stables.

"Oh, m'lady," Cook quavered as though already some dreadful apparition were staring her in the face. The poor little mite who had screamed so shrilly, but not for long, dead perhaps, or worse, in the hands of that dreadful beast who lived in the room at the top of the stairs. The grooms and stable lads, who had heard the commotion from the back nursery window, open owing to the heat, muck on their boots and bits of dust stuck in the sweat on their troubled faces, shuffled their feet, wanting to throw themselves up the stairs, just waiting for her command. It was not their place to venture upstairs, not without her say-so and they turned pleading faces towards her. Nanny Morag was crying as though her heart would break, Cat, who was in her arms, as quiet as a rabbit confronted by a stoat, Davy clinging to Morag's skirts.

"Mama," he wailed when he saw her, running across the hall, expecting to be picked up and kissed and petted as she always did when he was upset, but his mama brushed past him and flung herself to the bottom of the stairs.

As she hurtled upwards she was conscious of the eager men at her back, all of them longing to . . . well, to do whatever was needed, hoping it would involve fisticuffs, for they had all loathed the man who looked after their master ever since he had been seen snooping round the maidservants, frightening them with his dirty mouth. Alfred and John-Henry were convinced that the bugger had poisoned the dogs and who else would have interfered with her ladyship's gig but him, and now, or so it seemed from the garbled tale the maids had babbled, the man had come along to the nursery and, taking the terrified nursemaids by surprise, had plucked the master's son from the nursery floor where he was playing and hoisted the child into his arms.

"'Is da wants ter see 'im the day," he said, smirking triumphantly, for both these hoity-toity bitches, one of them no more than a lass from the workers' cottages, had refused even to speak to him when he had tried to pass the time of the day with them.

When they reached the open door of the master's bedroom the sight that met their eyes brought them all, Amy included, to a floundering stop, jamming them in the doorway, and had it not been so terrifying it might have been comical. They almost pushed her over, the men at her back, so keen were they to get at the bastard, meaning Platt, but it was not Platt who had the little lad but the little lad's da, and what could they do about that?

He was sitting in the bay of the window as he had been the last time Amy had seen him. He was in the same blue velvet smoking jacket with a silk scarf tied casually at the neck. Across his knees was a rug, just as before, tucked firmly about his legs. He was washed, shaved, his hair brushed neatly and he was smiling.

On his lap was his son, his small body rigid, his blue-grey eyes, so like his mother's, a deep pewter grey, for already he had sunk into a kind of shock, so great was his terror. Sir Robert had his arm about the boy, his good arm, the other hidden beneath the rug. The men stared at their master and their master's son, frozen behind their mistress, for though they would have had no compunction in laying hands on the paralysed beast of a man they had last seen when they laid him in his bed over two years ago, this was Sir Robert Blenkinsopp, their master for many years and when he spoke they shrank back in confusion.

"Well, well, that brought you here quickly, my dear, as I hoped it would," he said, smiling but not smiling they were to tell the others afterwards. His face was still all lopsided and his mouth still dribbled down his chin and into the silk cravat, but his eyes were steady and knowing, and the bastard, whom they had been told could do no more than mumble unintelligibly, could speak. He was their master, the owner of this great estate, a baronet, the father of the boy on his lap and what could they, servants after all, do to him? Her ladyship was swaying like a bit of smoke in a breeze, looking just as insubstantial, and every man at her back, one of whom was Jumsie McGovern, though they longed passionately to defend her and the young master, with the inherited habit of many generations of serving, of obeying orders, began to back away.

"That's right," the master suddenly shouted, "you lot can bugger off and don't let me see any of you in this part of the house again. My wife and I would be glad of some privacy, so get back to your duties and leave us alone."

He smirked and in an obscene way began to bounce his son up and down on his knee in a parody of a loving father. He even leaned forward and pressed his foul mouth against the child's cheek and it was this that released Amy from the frozen desolation she had found herself in ever since Lizzie-Ann had uttered the words " 'E's got 'im."

"Take your hands off my child," she snarled. "Put him down and let him come to me or by God I swear I'll kill you with my bare hands. Put him down; put him down." Her voice began to rise into a shriek in her horror but her husband only laughed, jerking her son up and down even more enthusiastically.

"Tell those men to get out of my sight, if you please, madam," he said, for the grooms still hung indecisively at her back. They were afraid now, afraid as all men were afraid in this era of poverty and hardship brought about by unemployment. Hadn't they seen with their own eyes the cotton workers of Lancashire, where mills were at a standstill for lack of cotton as a result of the American civil war, tramping here and there and everywhere looking for work? Hadn't they had the Irish, emaciated children clinging about their legs, knocking on the back door for a job, for a crust, for a drink of water? These were unsettled times. Work was hard to come by and it seemed to them, with Sir Robert in control again, which he appeared to be, they had better watch themselves. Dear sweet Christ they longed to stand by their little mistress but if *he* was back in charge of Newton Law, which it seemed he was, then he was the one to whom they must listen.

They still waited and it was not until her voice, soft and despairing, her flash of defiance defeated before it scarcely began, told them to get back to their work that they reluctantly shuffled down the stairs and, drawing the women with them, walked slowly and sadly through the kitchen. They didn't speak, for what was there to say, but their men's minds dwelled in horrid fascination on what was to happen to their little mistress.

"Well, that's better." Sir Robert handed the boy, who seemed to have slipped into an unconscious state though his eyes were open and staring, to Platt.

"Hold him, Platt, that's right, sit down and give him a cuddle and I shall do the same with my wife. Come here, my love, and sit on your husband's lap."

Amy bowed her broken head though from beneath the curtain of her hair which had come loose on her wild gallop from the garden she watched her son. She did not take her eyes off him as she sat down obediently on her husband's lap. She flinched and trembled as his hand plunged down the front of her gown but made no resistance when he exposed her breasts to Platt's mesmerised gaze. Cruelly he pinched and bit at her nipples until one began to bleed but she made no resistance, continuing to watch her son as though, should she take her eyes off him she would go whirling away in a squall of horror from which she would never return.

"Now, my dear, I think you may disrobe, don't you, Platt? We've waited for this mumble mumble for a long mumble, haven't we, mumble mumble."

She barely noticed that in his excitement he was beginning to lose control of his speech. She was dead, frozen in the horrific filth her husband was slowly dragging her into, and with steady hands, for dead women don't tremble, she began to pull her gown off her shoulders.

Rosy McGovern, still warm and dwelling in the delight of her new status, in the loving of her new husband and the night they had spent together, was still somewhat bemused in the wonder of waking that lovely morning with Jumsie beside her. It was a Sunday and her ladyship had given them both a day off, so when they could pull themselves from the deep bed their ladyship had given them they had decided they would go for a tramp across the moorland, take a picnic, lie in the sweet-smelling heather and watch the skylarks wheel about above their heads.

The commotion that had startled the grooms, the shouts of "What's up" brought them both to a sitting position and then abruptly from the flushed state of loving which had them in its spell. Rosy's heart was pounding in her breast as though already it knew the catastrophe that had overtaken them. They leaped from their bed and with Abby beside them, who had clattered out of her next-door cottage as they did, their clothes hastily flung on any old way, they had run across the yard and into the kitchen which was empty and out into the hallway just as the grooms were heading up the stairs behind their mistress.

"Worris it?" Rosy was so terrified by the tension in the house and the maids swirling about as though the end of the world were upon them, she reverted back to the accent she was trying so hard to eradicate.

"'E's gorrim," Lizzie-Ann moaned.

"What tha' talkin' aboot?"

"'Im. Maister. 'E's got little lad."

She didn't know who had spoken and she didn't care. Pushing through the press of servants in the hall she followed Jumsie, who had started up after the men, crowding at his back, for if her mistress or her mistress's bairns were in danger, which it seemed was the case from the weeping, speechless women below, Rosy McGovern would have something to say about it. Next to Jumsie she loved Amy Blenkinsopp more than anyone and them bairns meant all the world to her mistress, for who else had she to love since . . . since that chap had gone.

Unlike the men Rosy was not afraid of losing her job or of what her master would do to her and she peeped over the men's shoulders, and her eyes, which had been drooping with the aftermath of the loving she had enjoyed for the past ten or twelve hours, became sharp, clear, steady. The door was shut suddenly on the dreadful scene within but she knew as if the door had been made of glass what would be happening on the other side.

Grasping her bewildered husband, who was not as quick-thinking as she, by the arm, she dragged him across the hall and into the master's study.

With a word or two to Jumsie who once he knew what she was about, sprang to like a good'un, they ran downstairs, made a rapid choice and with their trophy in Jumsie's hands flew up the stairs again and crashed through the door into the master's bedroom. So sure was he that the servants would do his bidding as they had done over two years ago, Sir Robert had not even locked the door.

Amy had on nothing but her drawers with which Sir Robert was giving her a helping hand and when Rosie and Jumsie McGovern almost fell into the room Platt, in his eagerness to share his master's prize, had put the boy on the bed where he sat without movement, tranfixed with fear.

The gun in Jumsie's hand was a sporting gun, a

Purdey which had cost Sir Robert a great deal of money. It was a handsome thing with a walnut stock and had been used on many occasions to shoot Sir Robert's grouse and pheasants. It was cocked and ready to fire, for Jumsie McGovern, along with Alfred, had used it to bag a rabbit or two. Well, it was no use letting the thing go rusty, was it, and her ladyship didn't seem to mind. Besides, all of them in the kitchen were right fond of a rabbit pie, especially the way Cook made it.

At the sight of it Sir Robert, who knew its power, slowly took his hand from between Amy Blenkinsopp's legs and fell back in his chair.

"The boy!" he roared at Platt, since his young son was his weapon against his wife but it was too late, for Rosy had swept the child into her arms. Jumsie, to give him his due, though he was aghast at the sight of his mistress as near as made no difference naked, did not let the gun waver and Platt lifted both his hands to shoulder level, for there was no way he was about to offer himself as a target to satisfy his master's perverted wishes.

Amy was shattered from her hopeless, detached and insensible state, her own mind now as sharp as Rosy's. She wanted to moan and whimper. She wanted to turn and attack the man who had once more done his best to abuse her. She wanted to drag the gun from Jumsie's hand and turn it on her husband, have the thing over and done with for good but the sight of her son safe in Rosy's arms would not allow it. She was her children's protector, their provider and she'd be no good to them in prison, or on the gallows, would she?

Thank God for Rosy. Rosy! Dear God, what a good day that had been when Cook brought Rosy to Newton Law. The others had tried to help, she knew that, but this courageous woman, not forgetting Jumsie, had dared to defend her and, dear God in heaven, she had been given a second chance. He wouldn't catch her again if she had to hang him in chains to contain him.

"I won't forget this," she whispered harshly to him as she dragged her clothes about her and took her son in her arms.

"Neither will I," he hissed.

24

She was quite astounded to find that the sun was still shining, the swallows still swooping and squabbling in the purple blue of the wisteria which grew against the house, that in the rose garden where Nanny Morag and Lizzie-Ann had taken a tearful Cat and Davey the roses smelled as sweet and looked as lovely as they had this morning. Was it only an hour since she had wandered down the path to the shrubbery after seeing Laura and Andrew off? Was it only an hour since her life, the life she had painfully built up, brick by patient brick since Duffy had gone, had been savagely kicked down again by cruel and evil feet? She had believed that she was safe, that her children were safe, that her household was content and would go on being so, that her husband's estate was thriving under her careful and hardily learned management and in a moment of horror she had been dragged from what she now saw as complacency and her world turned upside down.

She stood by the lake, Robby in her arms and watched Nanny Morag and Lizzie-Ann shepherding the children down the path towards the lake and wondered why she was allowing them, and the rest of her household, to remain in such danger. Her mind struggled to find some way out of this net of despair that had her trapped but there seemed to be none short of . . . of . . . short of actually getting rid of Platt. It seemed to be, when she studied it rationally – why had it not occurred to her before? – the only solution. But dare she do it? Could she take the chance that Platt would keep the true state of affairs at Newton Law to himself? Might he not go blabbing all over the county that Lady Blenkinsopp kept her poor crippled husband a prisoner? That she had deliberately kept hidden the fact that he was talking, that he was quite capable of having visitors, that he was his old self in all but the functioning of his legs. And what about her and Duffy? And at least Platt managed the horrendous task of caring for her husband with what seemed to be equanimity and which no other man in the household would take on. Would it be a question of out of the frying pan and into the fire? Sir Robert, and Platt, had this hold on her, through her fear for her children. Dear Lord . . . oh dear Lord, what was she to do?

The babies were clumsily gathering rose petals as they had seen their mama do, placing them in the basket at Nanny Morag's feet, looking up into Nanny Morag's face and grinning broadly, waiting for her approving nod as young children do. Amy had been in the habit during the summer months of making pot-pourri, starting with roses for their colour and scent. The deep pink of Beauty, the soft yellow of Mermaid, cabbage roses and damask roses, all the lovely colours and perfumes mixed so that the garden came into the house during the dull winter months. She had picked peony heads, delphiniums, pinks, larkspur

and night-scented stocks, all under the diligent supervision of Mr Weston, but the children cared little for Mr
Weston, their chubby hands and clumsy fingers doing
untold damage to his pride and joy.

"Mind the thorns, lambkins," Nanny was saying and
had Mr Weston been there Amy didn't think he would
have protested, for the whole house was now aware
of the nightmare these babies, their brother who clung
round her neck, and she herself had gone through in
the past hour.

Robby, for the third time in his young life, had
been badly affected by the experience he had been
put through by the savage brute who was his father.
She remembered when she had come home just over
two years ago to a withdrawn six-month-old infant
cowering against the flat and heartless bosom of the
dried-up woman in whose charge her husband had
put him. Amy had rescued him, gradually coaxing him
out of his shell with loving patience and a great deal of
gentle laughter, which he didn't understand nor even
know how to *do*. And then there had been the puppies
he had loved. He had seen them destroyed, heard them
scream in agony before it could be prevented and,
but for the kindness of John-Henry who had brought
him a kitten and the warm affection with which the
servants surrounded him, who was to say he would
ever have recovered from such a trauma. But he had.
With the resilience of a child, one who knows he is
valued, one who knows those about him think he is
worthwhile, he had emerged whole again, and now
for this to happen. Of course, it had not just *happened*.
It had been deliberately planned and carried out, not
to hurt the child, that was clear, but he had been hurt

nevertheless. The terror of the past hour was still deep within him and it would take careful, loving, protective hands and hearts to deliver him safely again.

He would not let her go. When Rosy had placed him in her arms, in his mother's arms, his had gone round her neck in a stranglehold and he simply would not let her go. She wanted to bathe herself, to spend hours in the tub before her fire and scrub off the evil with which her husband had once again coated her. Her breast was throbbing in agony and certainly needed some cleansing treatment, for that filthy mouth and those rotten teeth had actually mauled it. Tansy, weeping still, wringing her hands inconsolably, had begged her to let her fill the bath and "see" to her, for it had not taken long before what had happened in her husband's – why could she not even *think* his name, let alone say it? – bedroom had got round the house. She should feel humiliated, ashamed, but she had other things on her mind besides her own pain. She had no time for self-pity. She had no time to dwell on what had been done to her. All she could think of was the safety of her children, the safety of her servants, especially the women, the containment of the madman in the bedroom at the top of the stairs, for surely, *surely* he had lost his mind. There was so much to be done. Within minutes of her leaving that room she had sent for Mr Wanless, the estate carpenter and odd-job man, and a bolt had been fixed on the outside of *that* door. It had taken several of the grooms to hold it shut while he did it, for Platt, fetched from his usual vacant indifference, had protested strongly at being fastened in with his master, and she'd have to do something about that, she supposed. Was her husband in the right hands? Would she send for Doctor Parsons who had not been near the house for a month and seemed to have washed his hands of her husband's welfare?

She sat down on the carved wooden seat, smiling reassuringly at Nanny Morag and Lizzie-Ann, aware that they were looking everywhere but at her. They sympathised, of course they did, but they were embarrassed, not only for her but for themselves. They didn't know what to do or say, for they were both innocent women neither of whom had known the touch of a man, any man, good or bad, and what she had suffered was beyond their comprehension. And it was they who had let that man, that beast, take their darling, take her ladyship's beloved son from the nursery. Master Robby had been in their charge and they had allowed the beast, which was how they saw him, to pick the bairn up and take him, wailing with fright and shock, into that room which all the servants were beginning to think had a bad spell cast on it. But it was his father who had sent for him and what could they have done about that, even had the whole thing not taken them completely by surprise?

"You mustn't blame yourselves," were the first words her ladyship said to them. "If I had been there it would have made no difference. You do see that, don't you? I could not have stopped that . . . what happened."

"Oh, no, m'lady," Nanny Morag protested, tears seeping from the corners of her eyes, and both babies, who were now huddled up against their mama's knee, longing for a place on it if only there had been room, looked at her, their lips beginning to quiver.

"We cannot speak of it here, not with . . . later, perhaps." She kissed her son's pale, rounded cheek. "See, darling, won't you sit on Nanny's knee, or Lizzie-Ann's? I know, perhaps if Lizzie-Ann was to ask Cook for some crusts we could go and feed the ducks. Would you like that?" But the child shook his head and burrowed deeper into her breast and the twins, bewildered and anxious, for they had never been denied their mother's lap, stuck out their bottom lip and tears welled in their golden-brown eyes. She was at a loss, for her elder son needed her desperately at this moment and at the same time her babies could not understand why their usually lively brother would not play, or come down to the pond to feed the ducks, nor why their mama would not lift them on to her lap. Davey, though so young, could not forget how his mama had ignored him when he ran, frightened, to her in the hall where all the dreadful commotion was. She had never, *never* pushed him aside before and he was confused and a trifle wary.

They were diverted by the sight of the grey-haired, thickset gentleman who was walking towards them accompanied by a smiling, slightly old-fashioned-looking lady of about forty. When Amy saw who it was she felt a great lifting of her heart. It was no more than an hour and a half since they had left in her carriage and, knowing they were the only people she could bear about her at this moment, apart from her loyal servants, someone, probably one of the grooms, had been sent to fetch them back.

"Oh, Laura . . . Andrew . . ." She was ready to weep now, she knew she was. She who had been strong was suddenly weakened and hardly before she knew what had happened Laura, good, kind, sensible Laura whom Robby loved and trusted, had swept him into her arms, kissing his cheek, giving him no time to protest and, nodding to the nursemaids to do the same, began to run with him down the slope towards the pond.

"Wheeee . . ." she was crying, as women do with a child, gathering speed so that her hat flew off and Amy could hear her talking to him, asking him questions, pointing out this and that, holding him close in loving arms, lightening the sombre, unnatural expression of dread on his face and though he glanced back fearfully towards her, his mama, now that he was off on some pursuit that he normally loved, he made no protest.

"Amy," Andrew said gently. "My dear Amy, I have spoken to Rosy and you really must let me look at you."

She hung her head then, for surely she could not bear this kindly man to see what another man had done to her. While she could cover it up she had managed to put it to the back of her mind, to dwell on all the steps that needed to be taken to safeguard all those at Newton Law. Protection for her children, her servants, herself, a way of living with this nightmare constantly hanging over, but now, with the goodness and kindness that beat in his crusty, well-hidden heart, this man, and his wife, had gently turned her away, momentarily, from others and directed her towards what she herself was in need of.

"Come, dear lady," he said, "while Laura distracts the children you and I and your good friends, for you have many, will attend to you. You need to rest and—"

"Andrew, I cannot leave Robby . . . he needs me,"

she protested, at the same time allowing him to lift her from the bench and lead her towards the house.

"Robby needs to sleep, Amy. I shall give him a draught and in your arms he will nod off and when he awakes you will be there and he will recover. He will, I promise you, my dear. I shall tend to your . . . wounds, for I know you have some. Yes, Rosy told me and you must forgive her but she loves you, as we all do. And then, when you are feeling more composed we shall talk about Sir Robert."

"Sir . . ." Even then she could not bring herself to speak his name.

"Yes, what is to be done about him. You cannot go on like this. I'm surprised Doctor Parsons did not prescribe a . . . a decent nursing home."

"You mean a lunatic asylum?"

"No, I don't. There are places . . ."

"But he is coherent, Andrew. Lucid, articulate and he would soon convince the authorities that he does not belong—"

"Amy, Amy, first things first. Now come, let us fetch Rosy and your maid and get you right. A bath, I think, and then I will dress your . . . wound."

A stitch had to be put in her breast where Sir Robert's teeth had worried it, and the whole time Andrew was with her in her bedroom, with a distraught Tansy standing by ready to run for hot water or whatever the doctor might need, they could hear Sir Robert bellowing. He swore he would have the law on her, and everyone involved in this heinous crime, for that was what it was, he shrieked. A wife's duty was to obey and honour her husband and there was not much sign of either that he could see in *his* marriage and by all that was holy if the bloody door was not unbarred, and at once, his wife would regret to her dying day what she had done. She was to let him out *now*, this minute, did she hear? He was not a well man. He needed sustenance if he was not to have a relapse. He needed a brandy to steady his nerves which were torn to tatters by her treatment of him and she was to send up one of those idle women of hers to fetch it for him. And she wasn't to think he was afraid of that bugger with the gun, for as soon as he was free he would see the young sod behind bars.

He, or it was assumed Platt, battered so hard on the door they were convinced he would come through it. The maids cowered in the kitchen. The men hung about in the yard lest they be needed, since it seemed, if not himself, he would do someone an injury. Surely he couldn't go on like this much longer, they murmured to one another. Honestly, you wouldn't believe that a man as weakened as he had been could have the strength to go on and on as he was doing, and it was not until the doctor and his good wife had gone that the reason for it and the cunning with which it had been carried out was revealed.

Amy had been bathed, her hair washed, the wound on which the doctor had put a dressing, saying he would be back tomorrow to look at it, carefully kept dry. She was in her warm, quilted bedrobe by her fireside, her hair hanging down her back in a cloud of silver, gold-streaked curling disorder as it dried. Robby was asleep, in the deep, healing sleep into which Andrew's mild sedative had eased him; the babies, having spent an hour with her and the books she read to them and fallen asleep on her lap in the process, had been tucked up in the nursery, when Tansy tapped on her door and with round eyes and a fearful expression on her face, announced that Mr Bewick and Mr Sinclair were downstairs in the drawing-room.

For a moment her astonishment kept at bay the implication of what this call meant.

"Mr Sinclair! Mr Bewick!" She sat up slowly, her drying hair catching the glow from the fire and turning it to a pale copper.

"Yes, m'lady and" – Tansy's face was ashen as she stepped closer to the lamplight – "and . . . and . . . oh, m'lady, that there monster's wi' 'em."

"That there monster?" She stood up, holding for support to the arm of the chair, since she knew there was disaster coming and she'd had so much of that today she didn't know if she could stand any more.

"Man," Tansy whispered, forgetting herself in her agitation, "I'm that sorry."

"What . . . what . . . who is it?"

"'Tis Platt, m'lady."

"Platt?" But Platt was safely bolted in the room with her husband. They hadn't heard him but then her husband was making such a row, still was, she could hear him through the door which Tansy had left ajar, that any sound Platt might have made would be completely drowned.

"Platt is downstairs?" she mumbled. Her tongue felt too big for her mouth and her lips were stiff so that she could barely speak.

Paralysis seized her and her heartbeat roared in her ears. Her eyes were those of a woman who has seen something terrible moving and shifting in the shadows and though she didn't know what it was she was aware that Tansy's words spelled out something that she was not sure she could cope with.

"Aye, 'e came in't carriage the day. Wi't gentlemen."

"But he is . . . upstairs with . . ."

"No, m'lady, why aye, isna 'e wi't gentlemen in't drawin'-room." Tansy lapsed further and further into her natural northern dialect in her distress.

"How?"

"Ah dinna ken, m'lady, but 'e's norr upstairs."

Amy moaned in the back of her throat, so softly it was barely discernible but Tansy heard it. She moved swiftly forward and put both her strong young arms round her mistress and for a moment Amy allowed herself to fall against her, her forehead pressed into the hollow of Tansy's shoulder.

"Tansy . . . Tansy, what are . . . Sweet Jesus, what am I to do?" It was no more than a momentary lapse, a fraction of a second in which she faltered, then her head came up and she stood away from Tansy.

"Get me dressed, Tansy. No, no, don't bother with my hair, a ribbon will do and . . . and . . . is Rosy in the kitchen?"

"Aye, m'lady." Tansy was busy pulling a simple afternoon gown of rose silk about her mistress and fastening it down the back with weak and clumsy fingers. A ribbon was found to match and in five minutes Amy was presentable and not only presentable but composed. Her face was like alabaster, even her normally rosy lips colourless, but her head was erect and her back was straight. She walked with her usual natural grace to the door which Tansy held open for her.

"Run and get her for me, will you, Tansy."

She and the astounded Rosy moved into the drawing-room together, Amy slightly ahead of Rosy. Rosy in her position as schoolteacher wore a plain grey gown in her work, and she had it on today. Her wedding finery had been put tenderly away for wearing on special occasions, along with Jumsie's good suit. She was a bride of one day but no one who had seen her on her wedding day would have recognised her today. Her flaming red hair was dragged back from her wide brow giving her a scraped, bony look, accentuated by her high, prominent cheekbones. Her brown eyes were narrowed menacingly, almost yellow, cat-like, a cat that knows it is about to get into a scrap, of what sort Rosy didn't know, but when she saw Platt smirking at the back of the two gentlemen, though her heart lurched sickeningly, her shrewd intelligence told her what it was, and why she was here. In the background the hullabaloo from upstairs could still be heard.

The two gentlemen, who had been sitting side by side on the sofa, at once rose to their feet, and Platt, who was lounging in a chair by the window, slowly did the same.

"Mr Bewick, Mr Sinclair," Amy murmured graciously, though her heart was pounding so hard she was sure the gentlemen could hear it knocking against her ribcage. "This is a surprise." She held out her hand and the two gentlemen took it in turns to bow over it, before, having her permission, they both sat down.

"May I offer you some . . . tea?" For a moment she was confused, since she had no idea what time of day it was. Should she offer morning coffee, afternoon tea, or a before-dinner drink, perhaps of brandy? It was still light, being just past midsummer, but the day had been such a nightmare she had lost all track of time.

"No, m'lady, there is no need. We have come to see Sir Robert. At his request, you understand. His urgent request, or so he says in his letter brought by his man." Mr Bewick looked distastefully over his shoulder at Platt who was sprawled in his chair where, thinking himself unobserved, he was exploring the contents of his nose.

"His letter?"

"Yes, m'lady." His voice was apologetic, for the young woman before him *was* a lady and the things said about her in the letter were quite incredible. He accused her of . . . of adultery, of scheming to swindle Sir Robert out of his property and wealth, of cruelty, not only to himself but to his children whom she kept from him. She had him locked up and tried to starve him and had it not been for his faithful retainer who had been forced to escape through a bedroom window he was sure she would succeed. He was quite recovered from his fall, though he could not easily get about, and therefore wished to take control of his estate once more, so if his lawyer and his bank manager would come at once, when they would see how he was treated, he would be most obliged.

"It seemed of the utmost urgency, m'lady, if only to verify the falseness of these foolish accusations. The last time we saw Sir Robert he was . . . well, he was not himself and that being the case we wanted to . . ."

"To see for yourselves that he was still . . . not himself."

"Exactly, m'lady. There seems to be some . . . commotion upstairs." Mr Bewick paused delicately, for

the noise coming from the floor above this gave him
reason to believe that Sir Robert was still in the state
of . . . well, he would hesitate to call it madness, but
what other name could he give it. It was unbelievable
that this lovely, fragile woman was capable of the
frightful things her husband was accusing her of. They
had had several dealings with her over finances, for
the school she had built, for the improvement to Sir
Robert's properties which seemed not unreasonable.
Every penny she spent was vetted and agreed upon
by himself and by Mr Sinclair and she was certainly not
extravagant. She had a decent dress allowance which
was only right. Her children were well provided for
and she paid her servants decent wages, all accounted
for in a ledger she kept scrupulously and presented to
them every three months. She was well thought of in
Allenbury and as for the accusation of adultery, that
was laughable. Who with, for God's sake? She mixed
with no one, none of the gentry in the area who would,
the two gentlemen were sure, be glad to entertain her.
There was not an iota of gossip or scandal attached
to her name, but they could not ignore the perfectly
sensible letter, sensibly written, that is, that had been
delivered into Mr Bewick's hands an hour or so ago.

"You had better come with me, gentlemen," Sir
Robert Blenkinsopp's lovely wife said calmly, but
there was an air of hopelessness about her, of despair
that they could not account for, and as she stood up
they both noticed that she winced as though in pain.
Her companion – for what else could the plain young
woman be? – stood up with her.

They followed her up the stairs and behind them
came a smirking Platt. Rosy, who had really no idea

why she had been included in the events in the
drawing-room, followed behind Platt, turning her head
away from the sour smell of his unwashed body.

The door was still bolted and behind it Sir Robert
still ranted and raved. In the kitchen the servants stood
about, unable to bring themselves to do any of the
ordinary, everyday tasks that they would normally be
doing at this time of day. Dinner should be being
prepared. Cook should be directing this kitchen-maid
and that to beat sauces, baste meats, vegetables, skin
the nice piece of sole for the first course, set the dining-
room table elaborately, with the flowers her ladyship
liked to see on its shining surface, and the other
hundred and one jobs that made up this part of the
day. Upstairs in their rooms the three sisters, cowering
themselves at the sound of their father's voice, not
prepared to become involved in what seemed to be
another drama, pretending therefore that it was not
happening, were silently dressing for the dinner that
should be on the table in an hour.

"Unbolt the door, Platt, if you please," Amy Blenkinsopp told him calmly, stepping back to allow him
to do so and, when he did, indicating to the two
hesitant gentlemen that they were to proceed her into
her husband's bedroom.

He had moved away from the door, how she didn't
know, unaware that he could crawl like some squat
and ugly slug across the bedroom floor, dragging
himself and even undulating as a slug does on a
garden path. He had hauled himself back into the
chair by the window where he normally sat during the
daylight hours and the fading light fell on his perfectly
composed figure. His hair was in slight disarray but

his blue velvet jacket and the silk cravat he affected were in place and the rug, though slightly askew, was wrapped about him, covering him from his waist to his ankles.

"Well, and about bloody time too," he said clearly. "I've been banging on this bloody door for hours but that bitch must have left instruction that I was to be ignored. I've had nothing to eat since my damned breakfast and I'd be obliged if someone would fetch me up something to eat. See, send that slut." He pointed to Rosy who was keeping as close to her mistress as was possible without actually holding on to her.

"I'll have some chicken and whatever pie Cook has in her pantry. No pobs, girl, you understand. Good solid food and a bottle of that claret I laid down before my . . . accident. Accident! By all that's holy, that's a good one, isn't it, Bewick? I'm in this bloody state because of her." He lifted a slightly shaking hand in Amy's direction. "Ha, you don't believe me, Sinclair, I can see it on your face, but let me tell you there's more to this prune-faced woman than meets the eye. But you'd have to ask her lover about that, wouldn't you?"

"*Sir Robert*, please, I cannot believe you know what you're saying."

"Oh, be quiet, you fool, it's you who don't know what you're saying. The gamekeeper, it was, or so I'm reliably led to believe, but the bugger seems to have tired of her and gone to fresher pastures. But that's water under the bridge and there's nothing to be done about it now. Except to *her*."

Sir Robert Blenkinsopp's eyes slid from the open-mouthed, disbelieving figures of his bank manager and his lawyer, smiling, his mouth loose and wet and still inclined to dribble, and Amy and Rosy stood as though turned to stone, white-faced, both of them, in the doorway, while just inside the door Platt turned to look speculatively, not just at the mistress's maid, but at the mistress. She'd not get away with it this time, his porcine eyes told her.

"Well, girl," Sir Robert suddenly roared, "what are you standing there for? I gave you an order and by now it should have been carried out. By God, there's to be some changes made in this house now the reins are firmly back in my hands. Go on, and don't look at your mistress, for she don't give the orders here. I do. Now then, Platt, slip down to the study and fetch me a bottle of brandy. You know where it's kept. Sit down, Bewick, sit down, Sinclair, there's a good fellow. We've a lot to discuss."

He turned his malevolent gaze on his wife. "You can go, woman. This doesn't concern you. I'll tell you what's been decided. Now then, gentlemen, let's get down to business."

25

During the next few months she often felt like one of those tightrope walkers she had seen pictures of in a book. Those who performed in circuses up and down the country. It was all in the balance. One slight lurch to the left, or to the right, and you were done for, hurtling down and down into the blackest pit of hell and there was no going back to try again. Once you were off the rope, that was it.

The rope, of course, was the life she led in her husband's house as the summer months turned cooler and became autumn. That was what she called it now, her husband's house. It was not her home, not her children's home but her husband's house where she stayed because she had nowhere else to go.

Mr Bewick and Mr Sinclair had come down the stairs that merciless day with their heads and backs bowed in what seemed to be the deepest sorrow, just as though the life sentence *she* had had imposed on her committed them to the same cell. They had been upstairs for more than two hours and though she knew for the sake of hospitality she should ask them to stay for dinner, since it was dark by now, she had led them into the drawing-room and offered them, calmly, as though this were the most normal of evenings, a brandy.

"No, dear lady, thank you, but we must be getting back to Allenbury. My wife . . ."

"Of course, Mr Sinclair."

Mr Sinclair thought he had never seen a woman as calm and dignified as Sir Robert Blenkinsopp's wife, wondering, as his appalled mind struggled with the orders Sir Robert had given him, how she would manage. She was to be confined, no, *fettered* in the life her husband dictated, her management of the estate which she had made such a success of, to be taken from her and put in the hands of the man who was her husband, and, of course, no one could deny it, the rightful owner of Newton Law. Sir Robert was an important man in these parts, a prominent landowner with many acquaintances – but no real *friends* let it be said – and though he might be crippled as he so obviously was, there was nothing wrong with his mind, as he had demonstrated to him and Mr Bewick.

"What has my husband to say, Mr Sinclair?" Amy asked him, addressing the lawyer, since he seemed to be the spokesman. Inside, she could feel herself breaking up, her heart threshing about in her chest so that she felt the need to put a hand to it to calm its terror. Though neither of the gentlemen had actually said anything to frighten her, one look at their faces was enough to tell her that her husband was not going to let her get away lightly. It would be bad, she knew that, but just the same she would not give in to him without a fight. She didn't know how she was to do it, for as yet she didn't know what his demands would be. He had the law on his side. Women had no rights, no legal redress to any cruelties they might suffer at the hands of the men they married. She belonged to her husband. Her children belonged to her husband. Anything she brought with her to the marriage belonged to her husband and should he keep a mistress, should he keep his wife in tatters to hang jewels on that mistress, the law looked indifferently the other way. Whatever her husband decreed would be done, or so these men thought, since they were husbands too.

"He wishes you to go up, Lady Blenkinsopp. I believe he has . . . has many things he wishes to discuss with you."

"Discuss? Surely you mean dictate to me, Mr Sinclair?"

The lawyer had the grace to look shamefaced, but after all she could not blame him, or Mr Bewick, the banker, for they were employed to do their client's bidding and her husband was their client, their wealthy and influential client.

"Then I had better do what I am bid, gentlemen."

"M'lady . . ." Mr Bewick began, then turned away unhappily, longing to get away, she could see.

"Please, Mr Bewick, don't concern yourself. I am a . . . a strong woman and . . ." She didn't know how to finish what she was saying, since she could hardly tell the concerned gentleman that no matter what it took she would not be beaten by the savage devil upstairs. These gentlemen were not privy to the dreadful acts her husband had performed on her, nor to the scene that had taken place before they arrived so how was she to tell them that none of it would ever happen again, she would make sure of it. The warning of how her husband and that foul brute who was his servant had meant to treat her, though it had been bestial, would stand her in good stead. There was a saying up here in the north-east, though God knows how she had come to hear it, but in her case it was true.

"Every dog has its day, and a bitch two afternoons." It was really a term of abuse but she would have her two afternoons and get the better of the man upstairs if she died doing it.

The two gentlemen climbed into their carriage after bowing sorrowfully over her hand, the expressions on their faces identical. Poor soul, poor lamb, what she was to suffer. A black eye by nightfall at the least and then what? They didn't care to guess, and since what a man did with his wife was not their concern, nor indeed anybody's, they indicated to the coachman that he was to drive on.

She went into the study and stood for probably fifteen minutes staring about her musingly before ringing the bell.

She smiled brightly at the scared housemaid who bobbed a curtsey from the doorway as though afraid to come any further into the room. The atmosphere of fear in the house was a tangible thing, for the bolt that had been put on the master's door and which had for the first time given them a feeling of security had been ripped off by that monster who looked after the master and who, they thought cringingly, was now free to roam the house. So who was it ringing the bell in the study, they had cried to one another, each whimpering that she would not go, not unless she was accompanied by one of the men. Even now Jumsie lurked just outside the door, ready, should it be needed, to protect poor Clara who had answered the bell.

"Will you ask one of the men to come to the study, Clara?" Amy asked the cringing maid.

"Which . . . which one, m'lady?" Clara quavered.

"Any will do."

Clara inclined her head furtively and Amy was filled with sorrow that just one man could inspire such terror in her servants.

"Jumsie be outside," Clara whispered.

"Outside?"

"Aye, in't hallway."

"Bring him in, Clara, and then go back to the kitchen. Oh, and in future you are to go about in twos," she added.

"Twos, m'lady?" Clara's eyes goggled.

"Yes, wherever you are, whichever room you are cleaning you are to do it in pairs. I will be along to the kitchen shortly and speak to you all about it."

Clara's eyes were like saucers in her pallid face. "Outside men an' all?"

"Yes. Now send Jumsie in."

Jumsie, his thin, honest face clouded with fear, not for himself but for his mistress, his new wife and indeed for all the defenceless folk in this house of terror, walked quietly into the study. He was a peaceable young man, good-natured, easy-going, willing, but without the sharp and intuitive brain his Rosy had, though give him a task, a command, an objective to be carried out and he would see it through to the end.

"M'lady?"

"Come in, Jumsie."

She smiled at him and his stout heart almost burst

with his devotion. He had seen what the master had done to her and it had shocked and angered him to the core. For a gentleman, for that was what his master was, to do what he was doing to a lady was past his understanding and if her ladyship asked him to take the sporting rifle he still had in his possession and go upstairs and shoot both her husband and his minder, he would have done so. He could, as well, for the rifle was one that could fire six shots and if he missed with the first shot, which he was not likely to do, for he was an expert rabbiter, there were always five more.

"Jumsie." She paused and Jumsie inched forward, longing for her to ask him to do something incredibly dangerous so that he could prove to her what she meant to him and Rosy. Had it not been for her there was no doubt in his mind that he and his brand-new wife – if she had been his wife! – would be living in some slum in Newcastle or on the tramp looking for work. Of course, his Rosy, being a clever lass, would have found something for them, but would either of them be in the position they were now in? Not only decent jobs and a cosy home in which to bring up the children they would have but they could both read and add up which meant their children, when they came, would have a grand start in life. Not like him and Rosy and it was thanks to this woman.

"Yes, m'lady?" he breathed.

"I was wondering . . ."

"Yes, m'lady?"

"You seem to have an interest in guns . . ."

"Why aye, m'lady. 'Course, I never seen one until me an' Rosy come 'ere but betimes I bin out shootin' wi'—"

He stopped suddenly and blushed, since he was not a lad to get anyone else into trouble.

Amy smiled gently and was tempted to move forward and take this boy's hand, for that was what he was, no more than a boy. A married man he might be, but without Rosy he was still a boy. Rosy was a woman, mature and understanding. He was older in years but he was still only a cheerful, willing boy. Loyal though, and she trusted him.

"I am not about to . . . to reprove you, or indeed anyone, at a time like this. You see, I am in a . . . a great deal of trouble. To be blunt I and my children are in a great deal of *danger*. Do you understand?"

At once he sprang to attention like a soldier who has been given a perilous task and will do it or die.

"Why aye, man, there's no need ter be afeared. Me an' t'others wouldna let an 'air on tha' heed be harmed, nor t' bairns. That bugger . . . eeh, m'lady, I'm that sorry. I shouldna . . . but tha's not ter be feared the day. Me an' Alfred, 'e knows about guns . . . more'n me, well, we talked on it an' if tha' were ter ask 'im . . ."

Jumsie might be an unworldly lad who relied on his Rosy to make the decisions for both of them, but he was sharp enough to be aware what her ladyship was asking of him. He certainly knew about sporting rifles, for had not he and Alfred been out a time or two, or more if he was honest, shooting over the moors like the gentry did, and they had used Sir Robert's guns, but that was all he knew, sporting rifles, and that was not what his mistress was asking him about.

"Fetch Alfred, will you, Jumsie."

They were both back in two minutes, the maids in

the kitchen watching them dash past them with their mouths agape and their eyes wide. What the dickens was her ladyship up to, wanting the stable lad and the under-groom in the study? Well, Clara had said her ladyship would be down to the kitchen to talk to them so it would all be explained then. They might have been easier in their minds, or perhaps not, if they had been privy to the conversation in the study.

"I want a gun, Alfred, a small gun that I can hide about my person, and I want you to show me how to use it."

Alfred did not even blink. "Yes, my lady."

"Then I want every other gun in the house, of any sort, to be taken to . . . to a place of safety, a well-hidden place of safety that only you and Jumsie, and perhaps John-Henry, know about. Do you take my meaning?"

Alfred smiled, his lean face taking on a foxy look. "Why aye, m'lady."

She took her time. She had changed into a plain dove-grey gown of batiste. A serviceable gown with deep pockets which she sometimes wore when she visited the school at the back of the house. It was cool enough for the warmer weather but was full in the skirt and not too tight in the bodice. Not a gown to turn a man's head with its high neck and elbow-length sleeves.

She opened the door to her husband's room and walked in unannounced, causing her husband and the man who lolled in a chair by the unlit fire to start and sharply turn their heads.

Platt stared but did not stand up, for this woman was

nothing now in this household. She was the master's wife but, taking his lead from his master, he meant to treat her with the contempt with which she had treated him in the past. His slow brain did not think exactly in these terms, since it was not capable of forming the thoughts or the words in his head, he only knew that he could stare rudely at her as he did at the other women in the house. The master meant to use her hard and perhaps he might get a "go" as well, and of course the rest of the servants, for that was all she was now, would be available. The thought of that made his crotch suddenly swell and he fondled it lovingly.

"Well, look who's here at last. You took your bloody time about it, madam. I told those fools to send you up at once and that was more than an hour ago." Sir Robert's mouth curled in a snarl of vitriolic menace. He was in charge now, he had made that plain enough to the two buffoons earlier. They would be back tomorrow with papers and God knows what else was needed so that madam here could no longer draw on his accounts, but until then he meant to make it plain to her what he wanted, not just from her but from the rest of the men and women who were his to command.

"I had things to do," she answered him coldly, and for a moment he felt a sliver of doubt prick him somewhere in the region of his chest, since he had expected submission, not defiance. Still, defiance was good, for it meant the quelling of it would be all the more enjoyable.

"Did you indeed?" he sneered, prepared to enjoy himself. "Well in future, when I ring my bell or send one of those bloody idle sluts to fetch you, you are to come at once."

"Really, well, I'm sorry, but that might not be possible."

Platt sat up and his mouth dropped open, as did his master's. Neither of them had particularly noticed that she had remained by the door which was slightly ajar and that one of her hands, the right one, was hidden in her pocket.

"*What did you say?*" It was more a hiss than a collection of words, like a snake rising slowly from its coils and facing up to an adversary.

"I think you heard me. I will certainly make sure that the maids answer your bell, and in pairs, I might add, and do their best to bring whatever you need but I have other duties that cannot be interrupted."

"*What did you say?*" he repeated, but this time it was a roar, and at the top of the stairs where she had stationed him Jumsie flinched but did not move. She had told him to stay where he was. She had told him not to reveal his presence unless she signalled to him, and so far she had not even come out of the room. Of course, that hulk could have overpowered her but he did not think so. His mistress had been warned by the last attack and he didn't think she would be taken by surprise again. She had the small "pepperbox" revolver, a six shot with an ivory handle in her pocket, which she had told him she would use if she had to.

Just to be on the safe side he crept closer to the door where he could hear what was being said.

"I am here to make a bargain with you, one that I hope will suit your . . . needs."

"Blast you, woman, I'm master in this house and I have no intention of making bargains with you or anyone. If I give an order I expect it to be obeyed, by you, and by the servants. Now then, *I* will tell *you* what is to happen. First of all your allowance is to stop. I will check every penny that is spent in this house, including the household bills, the servants' wages which I'm sure, knowing your propensity towards weakness, will be far too high, and my son's clothing. That bloody school is to be closed since I refuse to spend good money on a bunch of snotty-nosed brats whose parents are of no more use to me than the bloody sheep up on the moors. Less, for the sheep will fetch a good price at the markets. I've been told you have hired a schoolmarm . . . yes, well you can get rid of her, and that pauper woman who fancies herself a teacher. By God, woman, the ideas you have put in the heads of these people who haven't the brains they were born with. Well, it's over now, your little experiment in the betterment of the poor. The money you've squandered on the farms . . . well, I suppose there's nothing to be done about that and the properties are mine so it's still in my hands, I suppose, but that's the last of it."

His narrowed eyes glared vindictively at her and she had time to thank God that he couldn't get at her. The man, Platt, seemed to be mesmerised, paralysed, but she had no doubt that at a word from his master he would lumber forward and do his best to get hold of her. She gripped the small handle of the gun fiercely, then relaxed, for it would do no good if her fingers were frozen about it.

"Have you finished?" Her tone was glacial and her husband reared up in his chair as though he were about to walk, but his struggle was to no avail and he sank back, breathing heavily.

"No," he purred, though it was not a pleasant sound, not at all like the warm purring of the amiable cats who lay before the fire in the nursery. "I've not finished, not by a long way. The carriage that you make free with is to be shut up in the coach house and if I hear that it's been got out I'll sack every last man in the stable yard, tell them that. There's to be no more gadding about visiting those bloody quacks you're so friendly with in Allenbury. Oh, yes, Platt here keeps me up to date with your comings and goings."

Platt smirked as though the praise of his master were well deserved.

"And last but not least that lad of mine is to be put in the care of a decent woman. A woman who knows the way in which I want him brought up and when he's a bit older, a tutor will be found."

"Oh, no . . . no." She began to shake her head wildly and almost moved into the centre of the room the better to emphasise her determination to protect her son from this beast and his accomplices, but some instinct, perhaps a small sound that only she could hear from Jumsie, stopped her and she became still, wary, but *very* alert.

"No . . . no, you dare to say no, my dear?" Sir Robert was pleased by this first sign that his new order had at last brought a response from her, but it seemed he had not yet finished. She had begun to tremble, he could see it, and he liked that.

"And last but not least you had better make some arrangements for those brats of yours. Oh yes, indeed, I am fully aware that they are not mine though whose they are is anybody's guess. Not that bloody game-keeper's, that's for sure, since they could only have been got on you while you were absent from this house. But let me tell you this: I'm having no bastards, no other man's by-blow living in my house. I had intended giving them to Platt to dispose of but I'm willing, if you're amenable . . ." He smirked and turned to wink at Platt who began, ludicrously, to giggle. "If you're amenable to being . . . friends, I will allow you to put them elsewhere, I don't care where, as long as they're not under my roof. Now, come here and . . ."

With a steady hand she withdrew the revolver from her pocket and aimed it at her husband. Alfred had told her exactly how to cock it, how to put pressure on the trigger, in other words how to fire it, though she had no intention of doing so. She merely wished him to know that she was not to be trifled with, which seemed a foolish choice of words. He was not trifling with her. He was destroying her life and that of her children, and surely he was not fool enough to think she would allow him to do that.

Strangely, he smiled, though Platt looked as though he were about to jump out of the window. Of the two men he was perhaps the only one, being of an animal-like nature and with an animal's instinct, to realise the true strength and purpose of this woman who was his master's wife.

"My dear, how melodramatic. But do you honestly believe that small revolver, an old revolver which probably wouldn't fire anyway . . ."

"Oh, believe me, it does. It has been checked in the wood at the back of the house" – which was a lie – "and has been found to be accurate. I can hit a tree further away from me than you are sitting and there are six bullets in it, as I'm sure you well know. I mean to defend myself. I mean to defend my children and I mean to help my servants to defend themselves. There are a dozen men working in the area of the house and each one will be taught to use one of the guns in your study. Most know how to already, since they have been beaters and loaders on the shoots you and your friends attended. The rest of the guns have been hidden away where neither you nor this . . . creature of yours can find them. The maidservants will do your bidding. They will look after your needs but they will be constantly guarded. This house will be like a fortress except that the enemy will be within. There will be locks put on doors where it is necessary and I think I may safely say you will be hard pressed to . . . interfere with anyone. As for my children, though the law is on your side, they will remain under my guidance and under the care of the nursemaids they love and who love them. Believe me, sir, I, and they, have the sympathy and protection of every person in this house."

"You bitch . . . you whore, I'll have the mumble mumble you, see if mumble mumble . . . Jesus mumble . . ." Sir Robert's face took on the colour of a ripe plum and he looked as though he were about to have another stroke. He hated her, loathed her, and if he could have got his hands about her neck would have taken the greatest pleasure in throttling her to death, but the terrible affliction that came on him when he was driven into a wild rage – by this one woman – had struck at him again and he knew that he must have time to recover. Jesus God, she had got the better of him again but he would have her, by Christ he would have her . . .

"I see you are . . . not feeling yourself again but you brought it on yourself. But I have not yet told you of my part of the bargain. You have let me know what you wish *me* to do, which I'm afraid is out of the question." The gun in her outstretched hand did not waver. "I shall keep away from my friends in Allenbury if you wish it, though what good it does you I cannot imagine, and in exchange you shall have *your* friends to see you. All those men and . . . women, who used to fill this house before your accident. You may have your parties and do all the wild things you did then, or at least as far as you are able, but you will stay away from my part of the house. If you wish I will prepare a set of rooms where you can . . . do as you like, but you, and them, will keep away from me, my children and my servants. That is my offer. But let me say this. Should you, or they, or this imbecile here overstep the line I shall draw I shall have Doctor Barrie and Doctor Parsons up here and I'm certain both of them will certify that you are insane and need to be put away."

Sir Robert's face contorted and a long string of saliva fell from the corner of his mouth on to the cravat about his neck. His eyes darted from her to Platt as though judging the distance between them, but she had opened the door wide and stepped just outside. She made some movement with her hand and silently the young man who had threatened him earlier was suddenly beside her, the Purdey, which had been Sir Robert's rifle, in his hands. Somehow it made it seem worse, to be threatened with his own favourite rifle. His eyes, unblinking, stared at them both and Jumsie was to say later to Rosy, when he was safely wrapped in her arms, he nearly dropped the bloody thing, turned tail and ran.

"I shan't lock you in. You are free to go wherever you want except where you find the door barred to you. That means the nursery, the kitchen, the maids' bedrooms and my bedroom. If you would care for it I will order you a chair with wheels so that your man can push you round certain parts of the grounds. Dine with your daughters if you wish but you will not find me at the table. Visit your friends now that you are able to . . . to communicate but never, never attempt to meddle with my staff. Both Doctor Barrie and Doctor Parsons have seen the injuries you have inflicted on me, the recent ones included, and on your son, though he is not physically hurt, and I think they would have no difficulty in convincing the authorities that you are insane. So, that is what I offer you. Complete freedom to live the life you desire in exchange for my own and my children's safety. I don't trust you, of course, whatever you agree to, but at all times I and my children will be guarded. Think about it, and one more thing. If that man of yours attempts to touch any female in this house I shall have him removed and leave you to fend for yourself. Or, worse still, employ a man of my own choosing to look after you."

She whirled about and, with a small cry which neither man in the room heard, fell against Jumsie's chest. Murmuring softly, as he would to an injured animal, he led her down the stairs and into the circle of the wondering women in the kitchen.

26

The two gentlemen collided violently with one another, since neither of them was looking in the direction they were going. One of them, who was just leaving the elegant and expensive fur shop of H.G. Ireland in Bold Street, was accompanied by two ladies and he had bent his head to listen to what one of them was saying to him. The second gentleman, who was alone, was glancing down at a paper he had in his hand. The gentleman with the ladies was tall and dressed as a gentleman dresses in a pair of immaculately tailored dove-grey trousers, a fine, worsted, plum-coloured morning coat which reached his knees, a beautifully laundered white shirt with what was known as a Shakespeare collar, turned down in the very latest fashion, and a necktie to match the colour of his coat. His elastic-sided boots were polished to a glowing shine and he carried a top hat. The sun, which slanted over the tall roofs and into the shadowed canyon that was Bold Street, was captured in his well-brushed brown hair, putting a touch of copper in its dark depths. It was inclined to curl over the collar of his coat as though the man were due a visit from his barber.

The second gentleman, older and not so tall nor so

distinguished as the man with whom he had collided, though his dress was clean, tidy and well pressed, was somewhat shabbier and his hair, beneath his top hat, was greying.

At once they both began to apologise profusely, almost clinging together as though each was determined to give the other some support, but their spluttering protestations of regret died away as they stared at one another in what seemed to be incredulous astonishment. Each was still clasping the other's arm and the crowded pavement began to clog up with the surging shoppers who were somewhat irritated by the hold-up.

At last they pulled themselves together and again they started speaking at the same time, the expressions on their faces turning from amazement to pleasure. In the manner of gentlemen, friends, who have not met for a while they began to pummel one another in the forearm and about them passers-by stared in astoundment.

"Andrew. Dear God, is it really you?"

"It is, in the flesh. By heaven, you have no idea what a pleasure this is. I thought . . ."

"What the devil are you doing here, my friend?"

"I might ask the same of you."

"I live in Cheshire now."

"Do you indeed! We had no idea, Laura and I. How long is it since you disappeared, and not once did you get in touch to let us know . . ."

"I must apologise."

"And so you should, Duffy. To leave as you did . . ."

"I know, I'm sorry but circumstances . . . I can't apologise enough."

"Merciful heaven, if we apologise any more . . ."

For an embarrassing moment it looked as though the two men might embrace so great was their pleasure, but a voice with the cool and cultured tones of the upper classes interrupted their boyish delight, boyish even though they were both above thirty years of age.

"Alec, my dear, it is very obvious that you and this . . . gentleman are pleased to renew your acquaintance but you are blocking the pavement. Perhaps we might step to one side. And might it not be polite to introduce your friend?"

At once the two men turned to the lady who had spoken. She was probably about fifty years of age, elegantly and expensively dressed in the very latest fashion of the day and, despite her age, still very handsome. It was an era of vivid colours, purple and emerald green, magenta and scarlet, of yards of trimmings, flounces, velvet bands, ribbons, bows, ruching, braids and tassels. Seventy or eight yards of trimming might be employed in a skirt alone but the lady who had politely interrupted the two gentlemen was in grey, a pale-dove grey which was almost silver, her stylish gown wide-skirted and tight-bodiced, showing off her still tiny waist and rounded breasts. Her sleeves were wide at the wrist and from the fullness cascaded a froth of snowy-white lace which was repeated at her throat and beneath the brim of her small bonnet. Her kid boots and gloves were the exact shade of grey as her gown. She looked quite exquisite. Beside her was a young woman, no more than a girl really, dressed in white muslin with a pale pink velvet bolero. Again her gown was wide-skirted and about her waist was a broad pink velvet sash from which hung a tiny posy of fresh, tightly furled rosebuds. Her bonnet was of cream straw decorated about the crown with the same pink rosebuds. She looked charming, shy, pretty and innocent as she peeped from beneath it.

"Mother, I do beg your pardon," the younger man declared, "in the confusion—"

"Yes, yes, Alec, I saw the confusion," the pretty woman interrupted, smiling, though her face did not really lose the somewhat frosted look she had assumed as she took in the shabby, one might almost say *casual* dress of her son's acquaintance.

"This is an old friend of mine, Mother. May I present Doctor Andrew Barrie from Northumberland. Andrew, this is my mother, Lady Murray, and my sister the Honourable Augusta Murray."

Andrew Barrie bowed politely over the hands of the mother and sister of his friend, his face quite blank with astonishment, only his eyes, as he turned back to the friend he had known simply as Duffy, revealing his consternation, but Lady Murray, who had been taught by her mother the correct and expedient use of her fan, tapped him on the arm with it, drawing his attention away from her son.

"So you are the reason for my son's long absence, Doctor Barrie. I can only hope, now that he is returned to his duties once more, you are not going to persuade him to run away again."

Andrew's mouth fell open and he lifted his bushy eyebrows in surprise while beside him he heard Duffy – or should he call him Alec as his mother was doing? – sigh with exasperation.

"Come now, Mother. Do you honestly believe that

Andrew was the reason I stayed away from Ladywood? You know the reason why."

Lady Murray smiled sweetly and put her arm through her daughter's. The Honourable Augusta Murray had not spoken a word during the whole incident and now, with a quick peep at Andrew from beneath her long eyelashes, she obediently prepared to be led away by her mother who evidently was of the opinion that this acquaintance of her son's had taken up enough of their valuable time.

"Yes, my dear, I suppose I do but I hardly think this is the time or place to discuss it," Lady Murray murmured. "But had we not better be getting on. I'm sure Doctor Barrow has urgent matters to attend to. We live over the river, you know, Doctor Barrow. Our train to Runcorn leaves at three and as we are to take luncheon at the Adelphi first we cannot tarry." Her girlish smile dimpled her cheek. "My son likes to spoil me, Doctor Barrow, especially since . . . the death of my husband. Aah, I see, you knew nothing of . . . Really, Alec, did you not tell even your friends of your father's death?"

Andrew watched this little scene between the man he had known only as Duffy and who now turned out to be a member of the peerage, and his mother, still with his mouth open. He felt a surge of laughter wash over him, for Duffy seemed not to know which way to turn in his embarrassment; then, as his mother was ready to bow graciously in Andrew's direction and move on, Duffy became the man Andrew had known in Northumberland.

"Perhaps you would care to join us for lunch, old fellow." He smiled imploringly and Andrew, who had taken Lady Murray's measure by now, and was aware she had taken his and found him wanting, shook his head politely. He could not imagine sitting down to luncheon with this pretty, helpless, or so she would have her son believe, woman and her speechless daughter, and having the sort of conversation he and Duffy had once enjoyed. He was delighted to see his old friend, though he would have liked to ask him bluntly what the devil he was up to, fleeing Newton Law without a word to a soul and leaving poor little Amy Blenkinsopp, of whom he and his wife had become increasingly fond, in the lurch. She was managing reasonably well, damn well, in fact, and her tenants were in good heart, but it had done neither her nor the estate any good losing Duffy like that. Especially in light of recent happenings. At the time he and Laura had made up their minds the man was not worth considering, but perhaps he had good reason to leave and who were they to judge him. This mother of his, even after such a short acquaintance, was enough to try a saint, and perhaps one of the reasons Duffy had made his own life so far away. Now, with the death of his father, or so Andrew had gathered from the recent conversation, he had been forced to return home.

"I'm so sorry, Duffy, but I'm due to attend a lecture at the Medical Institution on Hope Street. It concerns the effect of poor nourishment and deprivation on the minds of – Oh, I beg your pardon, Lady Murray" – as her ladyship made a moue of distaste – "I had not meant to distress you but . . . well, I will say no more."

"Where are you staying, Andrew? Perhaps we could

meet later. There are so many things I would like to discuss with you—"

"Now, Alec, you know the Archers are dining tonight," his mother interrupted coolly. She smiled at Andrew, her long silvery eyes, so like her son's, narrowing ominously. "I am only just out of full mourning, Doctor Barrow, and this will be the first time I have entertained since my husband died. I do hope you will understand."

"Of course, Lady Murray. I understand perfectly."

But Duffy was not prepared to let him go. "Andrew, I must talk to you, I must." His voice was so vehement even the docile Honourable Augusta turned her limpid gaze on him and his mother looked vastly displeased. "When are you to return to Northumberland?"

"Come now, Alec, cannot you see that Doctor Barrow—"

"It is Doctor Barrie, m'lady." Andrew Barrie could be just as frigid as her ladyship.

"Of course, Doctor. I really do apologise. I have an appalling memory for names, have I not, Alec?" She tapped her son's arm playfully.

"So you say, Mother. Now then, Andrew, you have not answered my question. How long will you be in Liverpool?" Again his voice was urgent.

"I leave the day after tomorrow."

"Then if you will tell me where you are staying I will come into town and meet you. We could dine—"

"Alec, darling, we have been invited to—"

"I'm sorry, Mother, but you must make my excuses."

"I cannot be rude to—"

"Then I will be rude to . . . whoever it is. Tell me and I will ride over tomorrow."

"Alec, please, you are embarrassing your friend."

"Oh, don't mind me, Lady Murray," Andrew remarked distantly, "but if Duffy can spare me an hour or two I should be glad of a chat."

At once Duffy savagely took hold of Andrew's sleeve, so savagely he almost pulled him over, his face creasing into such deep lines of anxiety his mother and sister stared at him in bewilderment.

"What is it, Andrew? Is everything all right at . . . ?"

"Not now, lad, your mother is eager to get away. I'll meet you . . . where?"

"Andrew, I cannot possibly wait until—"

"I'm afraid you must. Your mother" – bowing slightly at the bewildered Lady Murray – "is in a hurry so tell me where to meet you."

"Very well. I shall have to . . . At the Adelphi tomorrow night at seven?"

Andrew grinned mischievously. "I'm not sure I can afford—"

"Bugger what you can afford, Andrew Barrie," Duffy snarled menacingly. "Be there."

"*Alec!*" his mother wailed and Andrew was even more convinced that this woman was one of the reasons her son had left home.

Duffy rose from his seat by the entrance to the bar lounge as Andrew, who was late, strode passed the magnificantly uniformed doorkeeper and into the wide and busy entrance lobby where crimson-coated porters hurried hither and thither at the command of the desk manager. The lobby was bustling with ladies and gentlemen, all of them expensively dressed, the ladies trailing their furs, for it had turned cold on this

September evening. Everywhere was stacked luggage of the most costly sort, waiting to be taken up to one of the many suites of rooms of which the hotel, the best in Liverpool, boasted three hundred. Private rooms, bedrooms, parlours, dining-rooms, grill rooms, rooms for private parties, all taken care of in the most superlative fashion by one hundred and seventy staff, thirty of whom were chefs. One frock-coated gentleman was frantically dealing with telegrams, letters, applications of some sort or other, for the business world and those in it did not stop when night fell. There were princes of industry, princes of royal blood, men of great wealth and talent all partaking of food the writer Charles Dickens, on one of his stays at the hotel, had described as "undeniably perfect" and which had become a byword of the hotel.

Duffy had obviously placed himself so that the moment his guest arrived he would see him. He was drinking brandy, and as Andrew threw off his cloak, which was instantly whisked away by an attentive waiter, Duffy snapped his fingers to order a drink for his friend.

"Thank God you're not in full fig, lad," Andrew exclaimed as he took a sip of his brandy. "I wasn't expecting to be dining in such splendour. Not that my evening suit would stand up to such an occasion nor the visions of gentlemanly attire that are drifting about here. Is there some event taking place?"

"Oh, it's always like this. A ship's just got in from New York and all the first-class passengers stay here, and I believe that the Channel Fleet is paying a visit to the Mersey. There are balls at the Town Hall and I must admit the ships at anchor in the river are a fine sight. I . . . while I was waiting for . . . this evening I walked down there to look at the squadron."

Andrew looked at his friend in great sympathy, for it was only just now becoming apparent to him that Duffy, Lord Alec Murray, to give him his correct title, was under a great deal of strain, though he did his best to keep it hidden.

He cleared his throat, then, giving Duffy a moment to collect himself, stared about him with great interest. He was not accustomed to such luxury, nor to those who availed themselves of it, which it seemed Duffy was. But he was not a man to be overawed by the greatness or otherwise of men more fortunate than himself. Indeed it was doubtful he considered himself less fortunate than any man in the room.

"I've booked a table for us in the grill room," Duffy told him, doing his best to appear relaxed, at ease, with nothing on his mind but entertaining his old friend, but his old friend was not taken in.

"Very well," Andrew said, "let's go and eat then. I'm famished, and anyway, as they say in Northumberland, it's time we had 'a bit crack'."

They had barely been seated in the crowded grill room when Duffy leaned forward eagerly, pushing to one side the beautifully arranged bowl of flowers so that he could see his friend's face more clearly.

"And how is it in Northumberland, Andrew? Is everybody . . . well? How is Laura and – what's her name? – Betty Long? Do you see anything of . . . those up at Newton Law?" His face was pale, his eyes haunted. It was obvious he had a hundred and one questions he wished to ask but was doing his best to appear no more than politely concerned, as someone who has once been friendly with these people would be.

"Laura is thriving, Duffy, thank you, as is Betty Long. She is a great help to Laura now that she has recovered from her illness of last year."

The waiter placed a bowl of the turtle soup for which the Adelphi Hotel was rightly famous before each gentleman and Andrew picked up his spoon and began to eat. Duffy watched him for a moment, his face working with some deep and painful emotion, then: "I had to leave, Andrew. I had no choice."

"It is entirely your affair, old chap. You owe me no explanation. We were just sorry to lose your friendship. If you had written . . ."

"I couldn't, Andrew. Bloody hell, man, I knew if I kept in touch with . . . with anyone, I would be done for."

"Done for?" Andrew placidly spooned the soup into his mouth. "This is bloody good soup, Duffy. Why don't you try some?"

"Sod the soup, Andrew. Just tell me how she is." His voice had sunk to an agonised whisper.

"By she I assume you mean Amy? I thought . . . *we* thought you were no longer concerned."

"No longer concerned! Jesus Christ, she is the most important . . . Don't you know how much she meant to me? I *had* to leave, first because my father had died and I . . . I inherited his title, but do you think that would have mattered if . . ." His voice was ragged in his agony. "If she had been free," he managed to whisper. "I would take her away tomorrow, anywhere . . . damn the land, the title, but I couldn't ask her. She has *him*, her children, the estate and all the people on it for whom she believes she is responsible. I too have responsibilities similar to hers. My mother – you see how she is – my young sister, people on the estate, farms and the land. I meant to keep in touch with her, with you, but I knew when I got home that it would do no good. As long as she is safe, safe from that monster they married her to, I felt I could ask for no more. Tell me about her. Is all well? You seemed to imply that . . . Hell and damnation, man, put me out of my misery."

"I'm afraid I can't."

Duffy sank back in his seat, his face ashen. "Can't?" he whispered.

"We haven't seen Amy since July."

"July!"

"I'm afraid not. It seems her husband does not care for her to 'traipse', that is the word he used, all over the county and has forbidden her the use of the carriage. She wrote us a note which Rosy Little brought us."

"God almighty." Duffy stood up so savagely his chair crashed backwards, almost hitting a passing waiter who leaped to retrieve it. The lady and gentleman at the next table both rose to their feet, the gentleman hurrying to put an arm round his companion, who seemed to believe Duffy was about to launch an attack on them and the head waiter darted across the room, threading his way adroitly through the tables of horrified diners.

"Is there anything wrong, sir?" he begged but Andrew shook his head.

"Sit down, Duffy, there's a good fellow," he began, but Duffy was beyond such peaceable exhortations and with an oath grabbed Andrew by the arm and hauled him to his feet.

"Sir, I beg of you," the head waiter began but without another word Duffy sprang towards the door into the entrance hall, taking Andrew with him. The head waiter, after a nod at the next waiter in the chain of command who could be relied upon to put everything in the grill room to rights, followed them into the crowded entrance hall.

"Sir, please . . ."

"My friend is not well," Andrew managed to gasp. "Have you a room?"

"Lord Murray has a room booked, sir, on the third floor."

"Take us there at once, if you please."

"I'm not going to any bloody room, Andrew. See, you" – gesturing to the hovering waiter – "find out when the next train is to . . . to Carlisle."

"Duffy, old chap, won't you come with me to your room." Andrew looked enquiringly at the head waiter.

"Room 301, sir."

"Where we will discuss this in private. There is a lot to tell you."

"I must go to her, Andrew. If she is in the hands of that devil again, d'you think I'm about to leave her there to be abused and debased?"

The head waiter, torn between his duty and his fascinated desire to hear the details of this woman the gentlemen were talking about, hovered beside them, his face quite anguished, and was vastly relieved when the older gentleman managed to persuade Lord Murray towards the stairs.

"Bring brandy," he said curtly and the waiter was only too happy to pass the order on to the appropriate member of staff.

"Tell me," Duffy ordered the moment the door was closed behind the waiter. "Tell me now or I swear I'll strangle you." He was close to tipping over the edge into a pit of madness, and Andrew wished he had brought his bag with him, for by God he'd make it his business to slip a small amount of something in Duffy's drink to calm him.

"If you strangle me, old chap, you'll never hear the truth," he answered mildly, ready should Duffy take a swing at him.

But Duffy sat down obediently enough in the chair by the dressing-table when Andrew told him to.

"Tell me."

"I don't know any details, old man, only what Rosy could pass on. Amy begged us to believe that she was in no danger but that for . . . for the moment she must comply with her husband's wishes. It seems he has . . . recovered."

"Sweet, sweet Christ." It was no more than a tortured moan.

"He won't allow the doctor to visit him so I couldn't even beg professionally for news of Amy, or him, but Amy beseeched Rosy to tell us that . . . that she was . . . unhurt. I beg you not to be distressed, but I believe that Sir Robert is . . . no longer a man, if you take my meaning."

Duffy bent his head into his hands and groaned. "I'm inclined to believe you but there are other ways of abusing a woman than . . ."

"I realise that but we have a good ally in Rosy who, I believe, would die for Amy. As would the other servants. You know how she has endeared herself to them all. I can only think of one way the man would have a hold on her and that is through – I hate to say it – through her children, but Rosy reports that so far they are . . . unharmed. The man is deranged, but I think even he realises that should he do harm to his children, and such young children, he might be in trouble with the law."

Duffy lifted his head and stared with haunted eyes into Andrew's. "Do you honestly believe that? A man's wife and his children are his property to do with as he pleases. But how has this come about? The man was paralysed, unable to walk or even talk. How has he recovered enough to regain his hold on his household, on . . . on his wife?"

"I believe that if a man is determined enough, has a strong constitution and, even more importantly, a strong incentive, then he can perform wonders. And that man of his is . . . well, Rosy says he terrifies the maidservants and all these things added together are enough to . . . to keep . . . I hate to say it, old chap, but to make Amy tow the line. Fear, not for herself but for her children and the women in the household. I believe she would get rid of them if she could, for their own safety, but they won't leave her, so Rosy tells us. But that is not all."

"In the name of all that's holy, don't, I beg of you."

"No, it is perhaps for the best."

"What is it?"

"It seems he has . . . women . . ."

"Women!"

"Yes, the sort of women who will do anything a man asks, and there are tales of wild parties, drinking, so perhaps, with a bit of luck, he will kill himself."

"I must go to her." Duffy stood up abruptly, tipping the remainder of the glass of brandy down his throat.

"D'you think you should? Rosy said that . . . well, Sir Robert speaks quite openly about . . . indeed, shouts it from the rooftops really, that you and she were . . . you can guess the rest. He shames her, Duffy, but it can do no good for you to be seen."

"D'you think I give a damn about that?" Duffy snarled.

"No, but she might if it affects her children."

"I must go. I trust I can stay with you and if I can't there are inns."

"Of course you can stay with us, but please, Duffy, think about it."

"I have."

By noon the following day Lord Alec Murray and his friend Doctor Andrew Barrie were in a first-class railway compartment on a train to Preston and from there to Carlisle where they would change for Alnwick, taking a carriage to Allenbury.

27

There was a burst of hysterical laughter followed by a scream which had a touch of fear in it. A man shouted and from above there came the thunder of men's feet. "Catch her, she's getting away," another bellowed and again the laughter rang out, a door crashed to, then there was total silence and Amy was left to dwell on whatever mad game was going on in her husband's quarters. She was glad of it, since, for the time being, it was keeping him occupied and away from her, her children and her servants. The novelty of having *guests* once more under his roof, even if they were the sort no decent folk would entertain, of having women continuously available to him, of the fun and games imagining which made Amy shudder, seemed to occupy him totally and neither he nor his minder came near *her* side of the house. For weeks now, ever since she had delivered her ultimatum to the livid, gobbling man who lived in the bedroom at the head of the stairs, this had been going on and though at the time she had thought it was the only way onwards, the only way to keep herself and her household safe, she did not know how much longer she, and the household, could carry on with it. But then what alternative did she have? What else could she have done? Packed her bags and her children and gone . . . *where?* Her mother had washed her hands of her when she ran away from Sir Robert years ago, saying, not to her, though it had been passed on, that a wife's place was with her husband, whatever the circumstances, and that her daughter was not to think of coming to her since *she* would not take her in. Her own brother, her twin, would have helped if he could but he was dominated by a wife whose only desire was her own gratification, her own position as Lady Spencer and would not offend society by housing her husband's runaway sister and her children. Two, almost three years ago her cousin Jenna who had taken her in, and Jenna's husband, Conal, dear Conal with whom she had shared a moment of love, though they were both good people, would not care to repeat the experience and so she had no choice but to make the best of the situation at Newton Law. Which was what she was attempting to do.

There was another crash and she thought she heard her husband's voice, his words slurred with drink. He was no longer accommodated in the bedroom at the head of the stairs, at least not until he was heaved into his bed in the early hours of the morning by the wordless hulk who still looked after him. The small dressing-room in which Platt had slept, and still did, had, on its far side, a door knocked through and the two bedrooms beyond, all on the first floor and at the front of the house, had been turned into a splendid drawing-room and dining-room in which Sir Robert entertained his friends.

A great deal of time and money had gone into

planning and carrying out the alterations which had been put in the hands of an architect of Sir Robert's acquaintance, a young man who seemed to understand exactly what Sir Robert needed and, indeed, was often a guest at the parties he gave. When it was completed almost every night there was wild revelling, with a good deal of roaring and shouting and stamping of feet, high, drunken laughter, and it was not unusual to find some wandering, often lecherous gentleman staggering along the upstairs hallway that led to her bedroom. She had a stout bolt on her door as did Nanny Morag in the nursery and every female servant on the next floor, but she knew the maids lived in a state of constant alarm, afraid to venture out of the safety of the kitchen when Sir Robert's guests were about.

And they were offended, as any decent woman would be, by the kind of females Sir Robert entertained. Gaudy creatures with painted faces and bosoms practically exposed to any man's sight. Colourful, most of them pretty in a tawdry sort of way, brought from God knows where in carriages ordered by Sir Robert and accompanied by the kind of males the servants were well aware were not gentlemen. They had money, that was evident by the magnificence of their dress, and where they got it was a source of constant speculation, but it was known that card games went on well into the night. Sir Robert had employed a young man of a very strange sort, as pretty as the women, Morna was heard to say when he came into the kitchen to fetch the food Cook and the kitchen staff had prepared for Sir Robert's guests. Apparently he served the food, since her ladyship had decided not to allow any of *her* staff, male or female, to enter Sir Robert's rooms and as to where he slept, they shuddered to think!

It was all most disturbing and Amy was aware that, had she not been held in such high esteem by the members of her household, many of them would have handed in their notice in that first week.

Sadly, it was Sir Robert's three daughters who suffered, if not precisely the most, then very near it, from the change in the arrangements in the working of the household and in the rowdy goings-on which, naturally, shocked them to the core. Their pleasant, placid lives were shattered beyond repair, since they could not, in all conscience, invite such persons as the minister and the ladies of the church to a place of such debauchery. They were forced to keep to their rooms, since none of them wished to be accosted by the strange men and appalling females who roamed about the place, not just after dark, but in the mornings, for many of them stayed overnight. They complained bitterly to their step-mother who told them patiently that they must take their grievances to their father but, knowing it would do no good, and terrified of the man who looked after him, they drew the line at that.

The overnight guests made more work for the maid-servants, and more problems for Amy, since she had to protect her maids from the unwelcome attentions of her husband's guests. A great deal of scurrying around took place, watching from windows, counting the revellers in and out again so that, when the place was emptied, the maids could scamper to change beds and empty slops and clean fireplaces. So far there had been no breakdowns, nor upheavals in the smooth working of this procedure, but it would only take one gentleman to corner one of the maids and there would be a catastrophe. It wasn't fair, she was well aware, to expect these good and decent women to put up with the dreadful tension in the house and she knew it was only their loyalty to her that kept them here.

It was the end of September and although it was early evening the darkness outside was already laying its cloak over the garden and beyond to the woodland and lake. It was quiet tonight without the usual wild shrieks and unhinged laughter that so often pervaded the house and they were all enjoying the peace. She was in her sitting-room, the lamplight and firelight putting a glow of false colour in her pale cheeks, when there was a tap at her door which, as usual, was bolted.

" 'Tis Clara, m'lady," the quiet voice beyond the door answered when questioned. "Clara an' Maddy."

It was strange how quickly the servants had become used to the new routine and how, instead of the brisk cheerfulness of previous days they spoke almost in whispers as though afraid they might be over-heard by the master and his minder. They scamp-ered about the house in pairs, almost holding hands, and had it not been so tragic it might have been comical.

The three children and the kittens, now young cats, were playing some complicated game under the floor-length cloth that covered the round table in the bay window. At least the children were playing, and the long-suffering animals roped in against their will were wearily submitting to being "tigers" in the game Robby had thought up. He was an imaginative child, fond of being read to, and the pictures of animals prowling about forests and jungles on his nursery wall fired him up to what he called "ventures". There were squeals and infant roars and a great deal of rather garbled conversation which the children seemed to understand and Amy wondered, and not for the first time, at the resilience of the young. They, like the servants, had become used to being locked in, to being hemmed about by protective staff. Never allowed to roam about, which Robby, at almost three years old, would have been allowed to do in the old days, perhaps down to the kitchen where he would have been made much of; to his mama's room where he would be loved and petted and allowed the privilege of having his mama's undivided attention. Everywhere he went out of the nursery he was accompanied by one of the men, and when he and his nursemaids took their daily walk with his brother and sister in the gardens or in the bit of woodland by the lake there were *two* grooms lurking about, both with hidden firearms. She knew she was obsessed with the need to keep her babies safe, particularly the twins, who could be spirited away and never be seen again and sometimes she thought she would go mad with it. And this was only the first few weeks, and as far as she could see it could go on for ever, or until Sir Robert had that fatal apoplectic fit which surely he was due, particularly with the life he led.

Clara and Maddy sidled into the room and Maddy at once kneeled down by the table, lifted the cloth and said "Boo!" into the children's startled faces. At once they screamed with laughter and attempted to drag the maid under the table with them.

"Bless 'em." Clara smiled. "Thank t'dear Lord they know nowt."

"Indeed, Clara."

Clara continued to watch the high jinks under the tablecloth for another fond moment, then Amy touched her arm gently.

"You wanted me, Clara?"

"Why aye, m'lady, beg pardon." Clara turned to her apologetically. It was not often laughter was heard in this house, except the drunken kind, of course, which went on most nights.

"Young Dicky Hodge's at back door, m'lady. 'Im from 'Awthorne Lane. Now what 'e were doin' in't woods at this time o' night I wouldna like ter say," Clara added sternly. "Probably after a rabbit fer 'is ma's pot. Anyroad, 'e come tappy-lappy up 'ere wi' a message for thi'."

"A message for me? At the back door?"

"Aye, m'lady, we thought it strange an' all, an' Jumsie ses tha's not ter go in case it might be a trick o' that black limb o' Satan."

"Not to go where, Clara, and who is the message from?"

"Well, that's it, m'lady." Clara looked apprehensively over her shoulder while Maddy appeared from under the table minus her cap and her hair all over the place, accompanied by strong protests from the "venturers". "Us don't know," she whispered. "A chap, Dicky ses, an' 'e's by't 'edge o' wood, tha' know, by't bench an'—"

"What sort of a chap, did Dicky say?"

"Oh, a gentleman, m'lady. Dicky knew right off, an' what's more 'e thought 'e knew 'im though 'e were all muffled up. 'E give 'im sixpence an' all. Now Jumsie thinks it might be a trick, like, an' tha's not ter go. At least norron tha' own."

"But . . ."

For some reason a tiny ripple of luminous joy ran through her veins, warming her blood and bringing a flush to her pale cheeks.

"Oh, an't chap said we was ter tell thi' 'e come from Cheshire. Aye, that's right. Cheshire."

The tiny ripple of joy burst in a great explosion of gladness, a feeling almost of exultation, of glory, and Clara was quite astounded as her mistress, her face the face of a woman who has just had a vision, a vision of such rapture she could not contain the wonder of it, spun round and lifted her hands to her mouth, then her face to the ceiling. Her eyes were closed as she whispered some words Clara could not hear though it did seem as though it might be a prayer.

"Stay here, Clara, or send for Nanny Morag to fetch the children. Maddy, Maddy. Dear God, don't leave them. I'll be back as soon as . . . He's here . . . he's here . . . Why did I ever doubt it . . . why?"

She ran to her wardrobe and rummaged about inside, selecting her warm, hooded cloak, flinging it out and round her shoulders like the wings of a bird. Her face was rosy, her eyes glowing with some magical emotion, her lips parted and ready to smile, to laugh even and the two maids stared in amazement, for this was their little mistress of the old days. Who was this man from Cheshire though, wherever that might be, and why had he such an effect on her ladyship? And was she to go without the protection of one of the men, and in her house slippers into the bargain?

"M'lady, tha' shoes," Clara said reprovingly. "Ista go in—"

"Oh, Clara, Clara . . . never mind my shoes."

"But tha' canna go on tha' own."

"Mind the children for me, Clara. I don't know when I'll be back."

"M'lady!" Clara was shocked.

The door, which had been bolted carefully behind the two maidservants as they entered, was unbolted and torn open, and without another word their mistress raced along the corridor, her cape and her unbound hair flying out behind her, down the back stairs, past the open door of the estate office in which no one had set foot for weeks except to clean it, out of the side door, through the herb garden and on to the lawn that led down to the lake.

He was there, just inside the woodland and when his arms lifted and opened wide to receive her she flew blindly into them. They closed about her as she returned to the place her heart knew as hope.

It was a long while before either of them could speak. They stood quite still in those first precious minutes, clinging, clinging so tightly they hurt one another, for they were both home at last, safe, loved and where they rightfully should be. There was stillness and silence, every living creature in the woodland holding its breath as though the wonder of this moment had them in thrall as it did the human creatures. A vast sense of peace enveloped them both and then, as though they beat as one, their hearts tripped and hammered and they parted a bare inch to look into one another's eyes. She shivered and once more her body surged with enchanted delight against his and she smiled and his own mouth responded. Suddenly, what might have been a moment hedged about with solemnity, with quiet reverence, such was the deep nature of their love, became light and joyous just as it had been on so many occasions in the past.

"Where . . . why?" she asked him, watching his mouth, seeing the curl at its corners and the deep grooves on either side of it which had not been there when last she saw him.

"I met Andrew. He told me . . . about . . ."

"Andrew . . . where?"

"It was in Liverpool. Sheer bloody coincidence. I was coming out of a shop and we collided. We could have so easily missed one another but . . ."

"But you didn't." She sighed at the perfection of it, though she knew it was far from that. He was here, just when she needed him the most and for the moment that was all that mattered.

"Come, let's get away from the house." He held out his hand and she put hers in it and they began to run through the little coppice, the walk they had known many times. Though it was almost dark he seemed to find his way with ease, guiding her thinly shod feet over twisted tree roots and shallow dips in the ground, across dense patches of wood sorrel, avoiding brambles and prickly holly which did their best to tear at her cloak. Leaves had begun to fall and there was a thin carpet through which their feet rustled, and the night creatures, those that ventured out at this time, shrank back and were silent and still. He helped her over the bed of the stream which had dried up in the summer months and with her hand still in his led her up the dark track on to the edge of the moorland. There was a fingernail of moon and the sky was a silvery blue fading in the east to black, but where the sun had gone down it was still lit to pale apricot and golden lemon on the horizon. She could smell the heather, the rich earth, a fragrance of the wild flowers that still bloomed in every crevice of every rock, and when they reached one that was tall and sheltered he leaned her against it and put his mouth to hers. It would be time to talk later, his manner said. Their flesh met, ice-cold cheeks and warm lips as their bodies pressed together, two bodies long starved of one another. There was no thought of despairing regret at what might have been, no talk of the future, for who knew what it held for them. There was just now, just this magic moment neither of them had expected, this warmth which both so badly needed, this closeness which could end almost before it had begun, so best make the most of it.

"My lovely girl," he murmured, his mouth hot on hers. His body was hard and yet tender against hers and his lips dropped to smooth the skin along her jawline. Her body was enclosed by his, the sudden trembling of his limbs awakening hers so that she was certain she could feel the deep-rooted rock shake with their love and passion.

"I love you."

"I love you."

"I know . . . I will not leave you again."

"Ssh, my darling, don't speak of what is to come, only what we have now. Hold me . . ."

"Darling, darling, I will never let you go, not this time. Jesus Christ, you're so beautiful . . . I want to make love to you . . ."

"I know . . . where?"

He groaned and his lips moved across her eyelids and cheeks and then to her mouth again which was full and moist and ready for love. They held on to one another with frantically growing need. His mouth was soft as silk but hard and masculine and he began to look about him for somewhere to lay her, for though in his mind he had not meant to love her tonight at this, their very first meeting in almost a year, his body, his male, demanding body cared nought for his gentlemanly intentions. His earlier scruples about making love to another man's wife seemed to have vanished. His body knew she was willing and as eager as his to be about the satisfying of its own desires.

Every inch of their bodies strained one against the other. His arms crushed her, hurt her and she felt the agonised need in him and longed to assuage it. His legs pressed against hers, one between hers and she could feel the strong outline of them and the hard jut of his manhood even through the layers of her clothing. His face buried itself in her neck, into the hollow beneath her chin and he groaned when she sank her hands into the thick depth of his hair and dragged him closer to her. She whispered his name over and over again, "Duffy . . . Duffy . . . Duffy," and the softness of their lips became hard, almost cruel in the savagery of their need.

They sank down slowly on to the earth from which the warmth of summer was almost gone. The thick tufted grass was soft and deep and the bed of it was enough. His lips still held hers and his tongue was warm against hers as his hand drifted to the buttons of her gown, undoing them one by slow one until her breasts were in his hand. First one and then the other, the palms of his hands gently pressing against the hardened rosy peaks of her nipples.

"Dear God . . . aah, my dearest, dearest love," he murmured, placing his mouth in the hollow between the soft white mounds, smoothing and caressing, then lifting his head to look into her eyes, his own filled with marvelling love. She put her hands in his hair again and pulled his face down while he took first one nipple and then the other between gentle lips, then with a fiercer bite which made her cry out, not in pain but in rapture.

"Is it to be here?" he almost snarled, for like all men in love he wanted the first time to be in some special place, perhaps with candlelight, soft music, flowers, a deep bed, but this was all they had and she, the more realistic of the two, knew that it must be this, or nothing.

"Yes, here, my love . . . here." Fiercely he pushed her skirt up about her waist, adjusted his own clothing and at last Amy and Duffy loved one another in a way that had been denied them for so long, and which they were both convinced was their right, their destiny, the fate for which life had intended them. She was at last bound with the ropes of love for which she had waited. Bound not by marriage or duty or obedience but by the simple truth of loving. She loved this man and always would. And he loved her and she was overwhelmed with the enchantment he gave her, for when, dear God, when would she have it again? As his body entered hers, the strokes of him, long, hard, insistent, she threw back her head, her arms clinging round his neck, her legs about his body and when the white-hot, ice-cold joy raced through her she cried out loud, the sound echoing from rock to rock. It was their first time as she arched her back to meet him and the honey-sweet kernel of delight his hands and mouth and fierce masculine body had awakened in her burst in an explosion of joy as he groaned, then fell heavily on top of her.

For a full five minutes they remained fast together, their hot, sweated bodies rapidly cooling and when she shivered he sat up and lifted her against him, wrapping them both in the ankle-length, double-collared cape he wore. His mouth smoothed her brow and her hair and they were so still and quiet that finally when they did move they badly startled a rabbit as it nibbled on the grass at Duffy's feet.

At last he spoke. "I tried to stay away. I meant to come back when I left you. You needed my protection, I thought, but then I convinced myself that with . . . with Sir Robert fastened to his bed, for life, at least I imagined so and it seemed likely, you were safe. I could offer you nothing, my sweet, sweet love. I had no rights to you. You were his, the law said so. Your children were his, at least . . ."

"Yes?"

"Forgive me if I say . . . Robby . . . I believe Robby is his but . . ."

"The twins are not."

She could just make out the pale blur of his face and the deep gleam of something that might have been a tear in his eyes. They glistened above the deep hollows that had suddenly appeared beneath his cheekbones and she knew he was deeply distressed.

"I . . . I do not mean to . . ."

"Pry?" She put up a gentle hand and cupped his cheek. It seemed it was the time for truth and though she wanted nothing more than to keep his love, his respect, the esteem he held her in, the secret she had carried within her, as she had carried the twins, must be made known to him. Before they went further, though where that might be she didn't know, he must be told the truth.

"No, they are not his."

He bowed his head but she put her arms about it and drew him down to her, kissing what she suspected were tears on his cheek, rocking him, thinking how strange it was that a man could accept that the woman he loved had lain with her brutal husband and borne him a child but not another man. Not a lover.

"I was badly mauled about by . . . by my husband when we married. He did things that . . ."

"Don't . . . dear God, don't . . ." His voice was muffled against her breast.

"I must make you understand, Duffy. I had known only abuse, debasing, perverted abuse and cruelty. That is all I knew of men and when I met . . . he was kind, gentle, a friend more than a lover. Indeed he was not my lover but he could see the way I shrank away even from him, the kindest of men so, on one night only, he loved me. He showed me the tenderness a true man shows a woman and . . . it took away the memory of the nights I . . . you will understand. The twins are his."

"Does he know?" His voice had become soft-hued, quiet with tenderness, and, she thought, understanding, acceptance, and his own hand covered hers where it rested on his cheek.

"No. He is happily married. So let us not talk of it again, my darling. It is not important. He is not important, not any more. It was just that I cannot bear there to be secrets between us. There must be truth, trust."

"So, tell me about the way it is at Newton Law and then I will tell you what I want you to do." He spoke with the arrogance of a gentleman. The inborn arrogance of a privileged gentleman of wealth and position who ruled those about him.

"To do? In what way?" Abruptly she sat up in his arms and tried to read the expression on his face but it was almost invisible in the darkness.

"I came as soon as Andrew told me what was happening here. Do you think I could just go back to my home and forget about it? He said he had not seen you for weeks, that you were forbidden the carriage and that only through Rosy had he and Laura heard about you. I got on the first train I could and—"

"To do what, Duffy? Dear God in heaven, I have never been as happy as at the moment Clara said the words "a man from Cheshire", but what can we do, what can we do, my darling? I am still married to . . . to that beast but he leaves me alone and as long as I allow, or at least make no objection to his . . . entertaining the riff-raff he mixes with, he leaves the children alone. He got hold of Robby once, you see, and then . . . if it had not been for Rosy and Jumsie, he would have had me."

He sprang to his feet, almost flinging her on to her back, then strode up and down, up and down, his cloak billowing about him, his breath coming in great angry gasps. For five minutes she watched him, no more than a whirling silhouette against the skyline, then he stopped and came to kneel at her feet.

"He nearly had you! *He nearly had you!* Do you realise what those words do to me? Do you honestly believe I could go back to Ladywood and leave you and the children in such danger?" His voice was like the snarling of an enraged tiger, one defending its own. "You should know by now what you mean to me, you and the children and I swear by all I hold most dear I will never let him get another chance to bloody well *have* you! You are coming back to Ladywood with me. Go now and collect the children and . . . and whatever else you need in the way of clothes. I have a carriage waiting down the lane. There is an overnight train from Newcastle to Carlisle and I intend to be on it. With you!"

28

She had known him for a gentle man, kind and loving, a strong man, an intelligent, well-educated man who had revealed to her many of the countryside's wonders and not just those of the countryside but of the whole world in the stories he told her. His body had thrilled and enraptured hers, his love had lifted her from the pit of hell into which her husband had tried to bury her. A good man then, with more than his share of heroic qualities, and now he showed her a side of him she had never before seen. An unyielding stubbornness that would not be shifted no matter how she pleaded. He would have her and her children on that train to Carlisle or he would accompany her to Newton Law and challenge Sir Robert, not to a duel as a gentleman of older times might, but as a man who loved her and would see her and her children safe. No, he didn't give a damn about the consequences, at least to himself, but he would not allow her to be terrified and humiliated for a moment longer.

She was horrified.

"Duffy, you cannot . . . you *cannot*! He is my husband, the father, or so the world believes, of my children and has the right of the law on his side.

He would have you thrown off his land. He has more than enough so-called gentlemen about him to do it and then . . . don't you see, I and the children would be the ones to suffer. Please, my darling, give me time."

"To do what?" he roared, glaring into her eyes, grasping her roughly by the forearms and shaking her so that her head flopped and her hair streamed over her face. "I love you. I will keep you safe one way or another, by Christ I will. Hell and damnation, I'm a man and would any man who called himself such deliberately leave the woman he loves in known danger? Leave her, and her children, under the same roof as the riff-raff he entertains. Oh, yes, Andrew told me: the street women, men with no morals, and . . . and . . . God almighty, Amy, surely you must see that this . . . this can't go on? He will tire of the constant merrymaking and want something new and who will his eye light on but you. A new diversion, a new pleasure, a new woman, one who is unwilling which will titillate his perversions. I will not allow it, my darling. I love you. I will protect you even against your will. Yes, I mean to do it, so don't glare at me like that."

He dragged her into his arms, rough with her in his desperation to have her safe, to have her where he could see that she was safe and, his manner said, if he had to bind her hand and foot he would have her on that train, if not the overnight then the first one out of Newcastle tomorrow. He strained her to him, one hand at the back of her head pushing her face fiercely into the hollow of his shoulder so that she could hardly breathe, let alone speak.

"Say you will come, my love." He smiled wryly

above her head. "I don't really fancy facing up to that brute of a prizefighter who looks after your husband, nor the troop of performing monkeys he keeps about him. I'm not quite such a fool as to believe I can take the lot of them on single-handed, so if you don't want me to be beaten to a pulp I'm afraid you must obey me."

She struggled to escape him and his arms loosened slightly. Not much, just enough to allow her to look up into his face which was lit by the faint glow of the stars that had sprinkled themselves across the night sky.

"I'm afraid, Duffy," she wailed. "There's nothing I want more than to come with you, though what your family would think of having you trail a woman and her three children, a married woman into the bargain, into their home . . ."

"My darling, my mother would welcome you with open arms." But his voice revealed his uncertainty, for there was nothing more sure in the world than that his mother would be horrified, appalled, enraged, disgraced, she would believe, and would not be able to lift her head in good society again if he was to receive into his home, *her* home, the discarded wife of another man. And that man's children! He could hear her now, the very words she would speak in that cool, well-bred voice of hers and, though it made no difference to his plans to rescue the woman he loved from the depraved man who was her husband, he was aware that it would not be easy.

But first he must persuade Amy.

"Sweetheart, I know it will be difficult but there is no other way. And if you are troubled by the idea of moving into Ladywood there is the dower house which is completely private and quite big enough for you and the children and a couple of servants."

"But that's it, don't you see?" Her voice was urgent. "I can't leave the servants. What would they do with no one to tell them what to do? I have to be constantly vigilant, impressing on them to be the same, otherwise, I'm convinced of it, those . . . those degenerates my husband entertains would . . . well, I leave it to your imagination how the younger women would fare. If I left them Cook would be no match for an employer like . . . like him. Before he became what he is, when he was able to walk, to shoot and hunt and do all the things a man in his position does, Mrs Armitage, the housekeeper, and Holmes, the butler, ran the house and kept the servants out of his way. He was not inhibited in any way and could get about to look for the kind of women he needed but now . . . oh, Duffy, don't you see, they would not last a week with no one to guard them. Without the authority I represent. Please . . ."

She pressed herself against him, trembling violently and he held her close, smoothing back the wild tangle of her hair, murmuring softly in an effort to soothe her fears, but he knew, deep in his wretched heart, that she was right. It needed a strong woman to keep Newton Law safe, if you could call the life they led *safe*. If he was to take her away, leaving the servants to their own devices, no, that was not the word he was looking for, what he meant was how were they to protect themselves, who was to look after and guide, not only them, but the estate itself, for as sure as the sun rose and set every day, Sir Robert Blenkinsopp, in his search for amusement, would let it all go to rack and ruin.

At last he spoke, his mouth against her hair.

"There is only one way, my darling."

She lifted her head, her tear-stained face like a moonflower against the seamed grey rock at her back, her eyes deep, black pools in the darkness.

"Yes?"

"I must take up my job of gamekeeper again. Well, if not gamekeeper then caretaker."

"Gamekeeper? Caretaker." Her voice was filled with horror.

"Yes, or estate manager, steward, whatever you like to call it."

"But . . . but Duffy, he would not employ you again. He believes that you and I were lovers."

"Andrew said something but . . ."

"Platt saw me coming back from your cottage the night before you left and naturally he told his master. He said . . . he said some dreadful . . ." Her voice trailed away in the deepest misery and she hung her head as though in shame.

His heart surged painfully and he wanted to hang his own head in shame for what he had done to her, what he had brought on her, but it would be for the last time, he vowed to himself. She would never go unprotected again no matter what indignities Sir Robert heaped on him. He didn't know how at this precise moment he was to do it but there was a germ of an idea growing in his head. His own estate would be well looked after while he was here, for after his father died he had installed a reliable, honest and experienced manager to look after it, under his supervision, of course, but the man could cope, at least for a while, until he could devise some means of making his beloved and his beloved's children safe from the evil of Sir Robert Blenkinsopp. His mother would be horrified, naturally. There would be no understanding there, no sympathy, no pity for a woman, a female like herself, who had been cruelly mistreated by a husband. Her own, his father, a kindly man, had petted her, cossetted her, lavished his wealth and adoration on her, since she had been twenty years his junior and marvellously pretty when he married her and she would have no knowledge of the brutality of a man like Amy's husband. And if she had she would firmly believe that a marriage, even one such as Sir Robert and Lady Blenkinsopp's, was for life, no matter what the circumstances.

"Dear God, Duffy, what are you to do?" Amy moaned, afraid, he knew, not for herself, but for him.

"Let us go back to the house, my darling. I don't know yet but be assured that you are, and always will be, safe with me."

They were all astounded in the kitchen when their mistress stepped through the door that led from the yard, followed by the figure of the man they had known as Duffy. They were aware, of course, that her ladyship, against the wishes of Jumsie and the other men present, had gone off on a wild-goose chase to meet some gentleman, or so Dicky had described him, and this, apparently, was him. For the last hour and a half the men had been circling the kitchen table, arguing and ready to fight with one another for the honour of going to fetch her, not knowing who it was she had run out of the house to meet. Perhaps one of those rogues who frequented the upstairs rooms with Sir Robert had tricked her. They needed desperately to guard her, for God only knew what dangers lurked out there in the dark. Their master had no guests this evening, which was unusual, but somehow the quiet was as alarming as the rowdy high spirits of most nights and the maids were even more reluctant to venture out of the kitchen in case that beast, meaning Platt, might be lurking round some corner ready to grab them.

"Good evening," Duffy said, smiling his slow, rare smile, bowing politely to Cook who leaped from her chair by the fire as though it had itself become alight. The men froze, not quite sure how to treat this well-dressed gentleman who had once been their equal as far as servant status was concerned, though they had known he was not really one of them. The maidservants sketched a somewhat uncertain curtsey, for though they had known him as a fellow servant he was so obviously not that now they weren't quite sure how to deal with him.

No one spoke.

Amy cleared her throat and moved forward into the room. She smiled brightly. "You all know Duffy, of course," she said nervously.

"Why aye . . ." There was a shuffling of feet and a general bobbing of heads, the men feeling they should be lifting their caps had they worn one.

"Good evening," Duffy said again, pleasantly. "I hope I find you all well."

They exchanged glances, for what was all this about? And suddenly, as though some element of – what was it? – was it hope, something light, something unseen, which they all sensed was good, drifted from him to them and they began to smile.

"Aye, clever the day, thanks, sir," John-Henry said, using the expression which meant in good health in their dialect.

"I'm glad to hear it but please, won't you all sit down."

They looked askance from him to their mistress. Sit down in the presence of gentry, what next? But their mistress smiled and indicated quite firmly that they were to do as they were told.

"Perhaps Tilly might make us a cup of tea, since we are to be here for a little while. Mr Duffy has something he wishes to discuss with us. I'm not even sure what it is myself so if you would . . . please, Cook, do sit," indicating Cook's own chair, seeing that Cook was inclined to argue, for it was the best chair in the kitchen and she meant Amy to have it. "I will sit here," placing herself on the bench at the table and Duffy sat down next to her. Awkwardly the rest of them, John-Henry, Alfred, Jumsie, with Rosy holding his hand in what seemed to be seething excitement, Morna, Tansy, Clara, Cissy and the rest of the kitchen servants crowded together wherever they could find a seat. Rosy's excitement began to transmit itself to the rest and even young Nipper abandoned his boots and crept out of the scullery.

Amy and Duffy and Cook drank their tea from the bone china cups that were reserved for the family, but the rest sipped in the restrained manner they thought appropriate in the presence of their mistress from durable mugs, waiting for what was to be said next.

"First, I would be obliged if one of you men would

just check the door into the hall," Duffy said in a low voice. "I don't want what I have to say to be overheard."

Alfred jumped eagerly to his feet and tiptoed to the door, opening it quietly and peering into the dimly lit hallway. He grinned as he returned, shaking his head. He had never felt so hopeful in all the years since her ladyship had come home. He and the rest of the men did what they could to defend her and her children from the ugly customers who roamed about the place, but after all they were only servants and if the bugger upstairs or indeed any of the buggers who were his guests gave an order they had no option but to obey them. But now, with Mr Duffy back on the scene and with her ladyship hanging on to his every word and if the truth were told, almost hanging on to *him* as well, which was all right with Alfred since Duffy, *Mr* Duffy, had always been decent with them, and was of the same class as his master then he didn't give a rat's arse. He didn't know what the hell Mr Duffy was to do but whatever it was it couldn't be worse than the present arrangements. She needed looking after, did their little mistress and if this chap had it in his mind to do it then good luck to him.

"Do you have your firearms about you?" Mr Duffy began, looking at Alfred, John-Henry and Jumsie, and at once Jumsie sprang to his feet, his hand going to the pocket of his roomy jacket, his young face shining with eagerness to be about the task he had longed to do ever since he had seen his mistress being . . . being molested.

"Why aye, us 'as. Tell us what tha' wants, sir." He

longed for it to be the doing away with Sir Robert and that devil who looked after him.

"Steady on, Jumsie. Don't frighten the ladies." Duffy looked round the excited faces of the maidservants who didn't look in the least frightened. Not now. Not now they had someone in charge with a bit of authority. Not if he was to sort out this dreadful business of going about in pairs, of locking doors, of looking over your shoulder at every turn. They had been terrified for so long they could scarcely remember what it was like to move about the house freely without the prospect of some drunken sod leering at them, and if Mr Duffy was the man to sort it out, then the sooner it was done, with or without firearms, the better.

"Right, then, here's what I want you to do."

Andrew Barrie was astounded and, at first, rather put out to be disturbed so late at night, though as he said to his wife as she helped him on with his coat, it wouldn't be the first time he had been summoned from his comfortable chair and his comfortable fireside just as he was thinking of his bed. Never before by Alfred from Newton Law, of course.

"Do you think I should come with you?" Laura asked him worriedly. "There could be something really serious. Duffy is not a hothead, I know that, but after what you told me and the way he came tearing up here today, and knowing what . . . well, imagining what might have happened, perhaps Amy might have need of me."

"It might be as well, my dear. God knows what has been happening up at that house these last few months. I feel somewhat guilty that we haven't been to call."

"Dearest, you know what Amy said in her note and Rosy was most emphatic that we should stay away. She implied that it would only make it worse for Amy if we called."

"Yes, then perhaps you had better come along. Is my bag there? Good. You'd better tell Jinny we might not be back until morning."

Newton Law was lit up like a Christmas tree with candles on every branch and indeed every lamp in every room had been lit. There was almost an air of festivity about it, a feeling of a party just begun with Morna standing at the door, wide open to the night. She was beaming and bobbing her curtsey for all the world as though the doctor and his wife were the last guests to arrive for the evening's entertainment.

"What is it, Morna?" Doctor Barrie questioned, for it seemed the last person needed in this house of lights was a doctor.

"Oh, sir . . . oh, madam, you wouldn't believe . . . oh, please come in, come in, the mistress is in the kitchen."

"The kitchen?" Doctor and Mrs Barrie exchanged bewildered glances as they stepped into the warm, brightly lit hallway. They handed their hats and coats to Morna who threw them any old way on to the hallstand and led them on dancing feet towards the door that led into the kitchen.

It was then that they became aware of the howling that was coming from above.

Andrew stopped and cocked his head. "What . . . ?"

he began, but Morna took his arm and almost pulled him along the hallway, so exhilarated by whatever was happening she quite forgot all her long training.

"Mr Duffy ses . . ."

"Duffy is here? In this house?" Andrew's mouth fell open and he came to an abrupt standstill so that Laura bumped into him.

"Why aye, sir. 'E's yonder in't kitchen."

The scene in the kitchen was one of unalloyed merriment, not the sort of merriment that is brought on by strong drink but it seemed all the occupants were drunk just the same. Drunk with joy and relief. Drunk with the wonder of being free, of their little mistress being free, and safe at last from danger. Of knowing that those bairns were out of danger and that this house was a home, or would be when Mr Duffy had carried out the plans that he had explained to them.

It seemed – and when they thought about it, was it not staring them in the face? – that there was a simple solution to their dilemma, if you could describe the outrageous things that took place in this house by such a bland name, and that was the removal of Platt!

"Who is it carries out Sir Robert's orders?" was the first thing Mr Duffy had asked them, and for several minutes they had stared blankly at one another.

"Who is it carries messages hither and yon, going to Alnwick to fetch the lawyer and the banker who look after Sir Robert's estate?"

Again they turned to one another, their eyes wide, even their mistress, whose mind had contained but one thought for months and that was how to keep her household safe, in a daze of bewilderment.

"Who is the linchpin who keeps this household running as it does?"

The light that had glowed feebly in Amy's mind suddenly burst into a brightness which was like coming out of a darkened room into brilliant sunshine. She knew what Duffy was going to suggest and she wondered why, for God's sake, it had not occurred to her. Well, it had, of course, but she had discarded it because she was afraid of the repercussions. Afraid of Platt and afraid of what he might whisper about her and Duffy. Now she had Duffy beside her and was no longer afraid. Her mind then had been cluttered with thoughts that had swooped like a flock of birds inside her aching head, confusing her. Now it was clear. She was safe. Her children were safe. Her servants were safe.

Her smile was serene as she turned to look round the circle of bemused, hopeful faces.

They all turned and looked at their mistress but Mr Duffy whipped their heads back again.

"No, not her ladyship, but that devil upstairs," Duffy continued.

Sir Robert?

"The man who is Sir Robert's eyes and ears and legs. His name is Platt. He keeps his master informed of all that happens in this house. I'm sure he hides behind doors and listens to everything that goes on."

The maids looked at one another and nodded. It was true. They were for ever finding him lurking in dark corners and round bends and behind open doors when they entered a room, not only frightening the life out of them with that grotesque face of his but listening to what they might be saying.

"If Sir Robert did not have Platt would it not seem to you that all this terror would stop?" Mr Duffy looked round the circle of astounded faces, smiling pleasantly. He had even, after asking her ladyship's permission, lit a cigar and he puffed at it placidly, blowing the fragrant smoke up to the ceiling which had never known a gentleman's cigar smoke before. Her ladyship stared at him as though hypnotised and it was not lost on the assembled servants, men and women, that she thought the words he spoke might have come from God himself.

"He needs a man to care for him," Mr Duffy went on, "certainly he does, but there are decent men, experienced men, respectable men who can be employed to do it. A man who would not do his damnedest to seduce every woman he can lay his hands on. A man who will take his orders from Lady Blenkinsopp, not from Sir Robert. Your master . . . is not well. A doctor must be summoned to certify that he is . . . not as he should be. A doctor who will recommend a conscientious, reputable man to look after him. A man we can trust to have her ladyship's welfare at heart."

And here was such a man standing in the doorway with his mouth open and a look on his face such as the servants had worn earlier.

"Duffy . . ."

"Aah, Andrew, well timed." Duffy put a gentle hand on her ladyship's arm, looking into her upturned face and the expression on his told them all of his feelings, which mirrored her own. He stood up and moved round the table to the doctor, holding out his hand.

"I'm sorry to get you out of bed at such an hour, old man, but we have something of an emergency here.

You will have heard the . . . noise from upstairs. Yes, you could hardly miss it. I'm afraid Sir Robert is . . . not feeling well and will probably need your attention. We have had to restrain him."

"Restrain him?" Andrew answered dazedly.

"Yes, I'm afraid so. That man of his has been . . . well, there are ladies present" – turning to bow smilingly at the open-mouthed servants – "so I will say no more, but her ladyship has dismissed him and Sir Robert is not at all pleased about it."

"Dismissed him?"

"Dear Lord, Andrew, close your mouth and sit down. Is that a pot of tea I see on the hob, Mrs Fowkes?" The practical, smiling figure of Mrs Doctor Barrie popped her head round her husband's paralysed figure, then she let the rest of herself follow, moving to sit beside Amy where she took her hand and held it tightly.

"How are you, my dear?" she said in a conversational tone of voice as though she and Amy were quite used to sitting down at the kitchen table to drink tea at eleven o'clock at night. "A bit of a rumpus, it seems, but Andrew and Duffy will soon have it under control. And where is that dreadful man? The one you have dismissed."

She could see that Amy was in such a daze, such a happy daze, if her eyes did not deceive her, that she was not awfully sure what was going on. Her eyes followed the figure of Duffy, Lord Alec Murray, who was talking quietly to her own husband, and these servants needed a bit of direction or they would be hanging about all night, rudderless for want of a command from someone. Probably herself.

"Us locked 'im in't tack room," Jumsie told her

proudly, then looked somewhat crestfallen since he and Alfred had wanted to give the bugger a good hiding before he was thrust inside but Mr Duffy wouldn't allow it.

"And the children?"

Amy came to then, her eyes wide with unshed tears and her mouth tremulous. "They've slept through the whole thing so far but unless Andrew gets upstairs and . . . and sees to my husband I'm afraid he might wake them. Morag and Lizzie-Ann are with them, of course, and . . ."

Her voice trailed off again and her eyes went once more to Duffy who turned to smile at her.

So that's it, Laura Barrie thought, her heart saddened, her hand still holding Amy's. So that's the way of it, and what is to happen now? Lord Murray who has an estate of his own to manage down south in Cheshire and will certainly want to marry and make an heir of his own to inherit it, and Lady Blenkinsopp who is married to that monster upstairs who has terrorised her and her children for years and who could never be the wife Lord Murray needs.

29

Though it was hard to understand, indeed Platt was not sure he understood it himself, since he had received nothing but harsh words and many a skelp on't lug from Sir Robert, he felt a distinct sense of outrage on his master's behalf when he was yanked from his room, where he had been putting his master into his nightgown, bundled down the stairs by three or four men, and pushed roughly into the tack room where the key was turned on him.

What the bloody hell was going on? was the first question he asked himself when he had recovered slightly. He had picked himself up, still swearing obscenely at the injustice and astonishment of it, dusted off the wisps of straw that had adhered to his rusty suit as he was thrown to the stone-flagged floor, and staggered to the tiny, barred and cobwebbed window upon which he hammered.

No one came and his aggravation grew. It was quite dark, indeed as black as the hobs of hell, for it was midnight and bloody cold in the tack room where there was no light nor heating. He put his shoulder to the door, crashing against it again and again but it was sturdy and withstood all his attempts to burst it open. Once upon a time he would have had it off its hinges in thirty seconds but years of easy living had slackened his muscles and put fat there instead, though he did not think in such terms, not with his torpid brain.

Judas priest, what for had they put him in here? His slow mind begged to know. And what's more, how had they got the bloody nerve not only to accost him who was his master's right-hand man, but his master who had bellowed like a wounded bull as he was carted down the stairs, past the cowering women in the kitchen, out into the yard and into this bloody place. Just wait until he got out. Not only would he take his revenge but so would the master, for it was he who was in charge now and woe betide her ladyship when it was all sorted out. She must have lost her wits to pull a trick like this and by gow she'd lose more than her wits when his master got at her. And he hoped to Christ he was there when the pawky hoit was given her just desserts. She'd not talk herself out of this one, that was for sure. By gow, it'd be his pleasure to hold her while his master punished her, so it would. His master had been good to him in the two years they had been together. True, he'd been a bugger an' all, but on the whole they had rubbed along right well, and Sir Robert had been generous, not only with the women who came to the house and whom Platt was allowed to use as he wished, but with the silver florins he carelessly flung at him when he had won at cards. Platt had a nice little nest egg tucked in a leather bag which he kept about his person, for you never knew – as now! – when you might need to get your hands on it. If he could get out of this bloody place which stank of horses he could be away and off to Newcastle where, with money in his pocket, he could live like a lord, at least for a while, but what about Sir Robert? The poor old sod would be lost without him and besides, he enjoyed the life they lived together. Where else would he find a job as comfy as this one? He had never eaten as well in his life and if he'd had a mind for it he could have dressed himself up like those dandified popinjays who flounced about the place at his master's beck and call. And the women, of course. Always available and, what's more, willing to perform all sorts of tricks, not just for the master and his friends but for Platt too.

He was considerably startled when there came a faint scratching on the window and someone whispered his name. He was sprawled on a horse blanket which had been draped over a rail, having thrown it to the floor, for he had no idea how long he was to be here and he might as well be comfortable. He was not afraid, for these yokels who served her ladyship were no match for him, or rather for Sir Robert, and so he had settled down, after his initial battering of the door, to bide patiently until one of them came creeping across the yard to let him out. He had absolutely no doubt that his master would get him out and by gow, there would be skin and hair flying then.

"Mr Platt," the voice whispered. "Ista there, man?"

He scrambled to his feet and lumbered across to the barred window where the faint outline of a head could be seen in the murk.

"'Course ah'm bloody 'ere, tha' daft sod. 'Oo's that then?"

"Whisht, oh, whisht, Mr Platt. Dinna mekk a noise or they'll be out 'ere tappy-lappy."

"'Oo the 'ell is it?" Platt's slow brain had been sorely overworked this night as it faltered through its thought processes. It had taken a long while for it to sort out what had happened to him and it had actually hurt his head in his effort to make sense of it. He had decided the best thing was to have forty winks, let morning come and then see what happened, which was all he *could* do really, so who was this blethering on beyond the door?

"Why aye, 'tis me, Mr Platt. Billy. Billy Cummings. Tha' see, I dinna know what ter do . . ."

Billy! Billy Cummings! The lad Sir Robert had employed to wait on the ladies and gentlemen who were guests in his house. A pretty lad who, when Sir Robert had dressed him up in some sort of livery, had proved a great success and not only in the serving of food and drink. God knows where Sir Robert had found him. Through one of his friends, Platt supposed, but he had been a favourite with one or two gentlemen who had a taste for the kind of flesh Billy provided. The lad had slept in a cupboard somewhere and must have been overlooked by those bastards who had burst into his master's bedroom and dragged himself out of it.

"Billy, am I pleased ter 'ear tha' voice the night. Gerrus outer this, there's a bonny lad, and us'll be away tappy-lappy."

"'Ow'm ah ter do that, Mr Platt? Door's locked."

"Ah know that, tha' daft gowk."

"Well . . ."

Platt put his aching head in his hands and did his best to shift his brain into some sort of working mode but it was beginning to ache with a vengeance, and to tell the truth he had been so long without having to make a decision, taking orders from Sir Robert, he couldn't seem to form a coherent thought. He had never been a quick thinker; indeed it was only his great strength when he was a boy that had kept other, more fertile minds from totally overpowering him.

But Billy Cummings, now that he had a protector in sight, someone who would fend for him, since he was a delicately put-together lad, had no such disadvantage. He had used his delicacy, his slenderness, his cherubic face to gain what he needed from life and his own brain was as sharp as a knife. He obliged gentlemen, even Mr Platt on occasion when there were no females available, and he would do it again if needs be. He was a realistic lad and though Platt was gross and careless of Billy's often shrinking flesh he was all Billy had at the moment. He began to cast about along the wall that joined the tack room to the stables, his hands running across the rough brick and then, when he reached the closed door, he opened it and stumbled inside the stable itself where the horses snorted and moved restlessly in their stalls.

At last he found what he was looking for, and with a little sharp intake of breath in triumph he lifted the set of keys from the nail where they hung.

It took several heart-stopping moments as he tried each key in turn in the door to the tack room, then, the door opened, Platt blundered out into the yard.

Despite his certainty that Sir Robert would get him out of this predicament and that all would be returned to normal by morning, Platt's natural cunning and caution warned him that perhaps it might be a good idea to take this opportunity to get away from Newton Law until all this bloody mess was sorted out. He would remain close by, hide up a while and see what happened, and if Sir Robert got the better of her bloody ladyship, which he was bound to do, then he, Platt, would return and share the fun. But for now he'd best put a few miles between him and her ladyship's supporters. It was for the best. He turned and was ready to run like the devil for the gate, but Billy's hand on his arm stopped him.

"What's up, tha' soft sod?" he hissed malevolently, trying to shake the small but surprisingly strong hand off. "Us's ter be as far 'n' fast away as us can."

"Why aye, Mr Platt, but if us were ter lock door again them'd think tha' were still inside." His eyes gleamed with cunning, the cunning he had learned on the streets when he was no more than a toddler.

"Wha' . . . ?"

"Them'll check, Mr Platt. Them stable lads, when they gerrover celebratin', like, an' if they was ter find thi' gone they'd be after thi' tappy-lappy, but we's'd ger a good 'ead start if they think tha's still locked up."

At last Platt got his meaning and a huge, invisible smile split his face.

"Why aye, man, thee 'n' me's gonner gerron a treat."

Billy locked the door and carefully and quietly replaced the keys on the nail were he had found them. Let that teach them, he thought. He had no particular antipathy towards her ladyship, or the men who served her, for none had ever troubled him but he knew where his best interests lay. He always had!

With his hand grasping the coat tails of the man he had freed, he scampered after him, through the yard gate and on to the track that led to Allenbury and the anonymity they hoped to find there. Like the wind he flew at Mr Platt's back, terrified that he might lose him. Billy had been plying his trade on the streets of Newcastle ever since he was eleven years old and though he was still obliging gentlemen in the way he had done for six years he had recently been doing it in the most comfortable, even luxurious circumstances he had ever known in his short life. He didn't want to lose it and it seemed to Billy, bonny Billy as he was known, that the man he followed was the only chance he had of holding on to it.

Sir Robert was safely in the heavily drugged sleep into which Andrew Barrie's sedative had spun him. He had been held down by a couple of the men from the yard who, it seemed to Andrew, took a great deal of pleasure from it, and the potion was poured down his protesting throat.

The servants were still up, milling around in the kitchen, drinking innumerable cups of tea, the maids cheeping and chirping like a flock of sparrows, almost in a party mood it seemed, asking one another glee- fully if they had noticed the look on Platt's face as he was dragged through the kitchen; what did it mean, did they think, Mr Duffy turning up like that after all this time? What was to happen now, with Platt gone, or so it seemed, and who was to see to the master? Not one of them, they cried, their expressions of dismay overlaying, for a moment, the general air of joyous excitement. What a gladness it was to see their little mistress smiling as she had done at Mr Duffy; were Alfred and John-Henry sure that Platt was safely locked up? This from the maids, those who had been intimidated by him in the performance of their duties, and really, they didn't think they would sleep a wink the night, and on and on and on, their voices rising on a tide of excitement. They were so elated by the night's happenings that when Lizzie-Ann was sent down from the nursery by Nanny Morag to find out what was happening, slipping down the back stairs to avoid the master's creature, they all spoke at once, filling the kitchen again with their bird twitterings. Lizzie-Ann couldn't make head nor tail of it, she protested, but if that bugger, and she was sorry, Cook, if that offended her, but if that bugger was gone then she for one would get down on her knees and thank the good Lord for it. In their delirium they chose to forget that they would have to be up at cock-crow the morrow and, with three guests who were to stay overnight, they would be busy indeed. Already fires had been lit in two of the guest bedrooms, the beds made up, fresh towels laid out, hot water taken up and everything made comfy for Doctor and Mrs Barrie and, naturally, for Mr Duffy who was the hero of the hour.

The Misses Blenkinsopp, who had rung their bells all at the same time wanting to be told what all the commotion was about, had been soothed and put back to bed. The master's spinster daughters, though they did not, of course, discuss it with the servants, had been vastly relieved to hear that that awful man, meaning Platt, who had even threatened *them* who had excited no man's attention, was to leave, and that Mr Duffy was once again in charge of the estate.

Coffee had been served in her ladyship's sitting-room, Morna reporting that they, meaning their mistress, Mr Duffy, Doctor Barrie and his sweet-faced wife, were talking ten to the dozen round the fire, and, she whispered this last in Cook's ear, Mr Duffy was holding her ladyship's hand!

"So, Andrew, what is your opinion, your medical opinion of the situation here? We will get to the . . . well, I cannot find a word to describe the . . . the other side of it but you will know what I mean, in a moment."

Laura Barrie sipped her coffee and watched with a keen eye the scene that was being played out before her. Though she would not have said she had known of the relationship between Duffy and Amy before this moment, she admitted to herself now, perhaps in hindsight, that she had been aware, subconsciously, that there had been *something* before Duffy mysteriously disappeared. Their constant companionship as they built the school, the transformation of the lives of the parents and the children who attended that school. The interest that they both took in the welfare of the farm tenants' families and the improvement in the farm buildings, the land, the care of their beasts which Amy had read about in the modern journals, agricultural information which, though not available to them, she had researched and passed on. They had ridden out together across the moorland and farmland checking on her husband's estate which was in the hands of the man who was ostensibly her husband's gamekeeper. They had been seen, the pair of them, with her children on the lower slopes of the moorland, playing some game that the children shrieked over. There had been laughter, so she had heard, though for the life of her she couldn't remember who had told her, for Andrew's patients were not the sort to roam the moors on a sunny day. She supposed there had been talk among the gentry, as they were called, and what the gentry knew so did their servants, who passed it on to other kitchens where the daughters of Andrew's patients often laboured. Though the land was vast and often empty gossip spread as rapidly as wildfire.

So what was to happen now to this woman who had known such cruel treatment at the hands of her husband and yet was glowing with a beauty that she, as a plain woman, recognised but did not envy. She was moved by what she saw now as the female strength of Amy Blenkinsopp, quiet but deep, which had grown in her friend over the years. It was far less spectacular than the armed warrior who was Duffy who, in his arrogant male determination to protect her, looked as though he would kill with his bare hands the first man to lay hands on her, but it was surely more dogged, more patient, longer lasting. She didn't know it herself yet, the exquisite woman who gazed trustingly up into Duffy's eyes, but it was embedded firm as the rocks that scattered the moorland.

"My medical opinion, old chap," Andrew was saying, "is that Sir Robert Blenkinsopp is mentally unhinged and should be restrained, if not here in his own home then in an asylum. He needs constant care and protection, from himself and what he may do to others if left as he has been." He turned hastily to Amy, who, he had noticed, was clinging surprisingly to Duffy's hand like a lost child who has found a parent. No, that wasn't it at all. Her hand was not a child's and Duffy's was not that of a parent but of a lover. He and Laura had exchanged significant glances a while ago at the very tangible tension in which the pair of them were enfolded and if he was right, and he hoped he was, and as they had spent some time together since Duffy had rocketed off in a hired carriage from the railway station, he supposed they might now be more to each other than friends.

"I am casting no aspersions on you, my dear," he declared gently to Amy. "What has been happening here was not something over which you had any control. You were helpless in the face of your husband's . . . er . . . er . . ."

"Debauchery?" Duffy said helpfully.

"I suppose it must be called that, and though the law of this land is firmly on the side of the husband and will admit to no rights for his wife, I believe that a court of law could not fail to be on your side in the face of what has happened here. Your children have been in real danger, not to mention your maidservants. And you, of course. I am prepared therefore to call in a colleague of mine; no, not that old chap who, though very good in his way for a country doctor, has not the qualifications to assess your husband's condition. The man I have in mind is interested in what is being called the science of the mind and will be able to diagnose your husband's condition and tell us, if not how to cure it, then how to contain it. He practises in London."

"In London? But what is to happen to my husband in the meanwhile, Andrew? None of the maids will go near him and I wouldn't allow it in any case. Someone must look after his needs."

Amy turned her trusting face towards Duffy, who sat beside her on the sofa. Her hair still hung in the curling tangle his hands had created, pale tendrils wisping endearingly about her forehead and ears, and Andrew and Laura were held spellbound when his free hand rose to brush it tenderly back behind her ear. She smiled at him and for a moment Doctor and Mrs Barrie were aware that neither of them existed for the couple on the sofa. Was he going to lean towards her and kiss her? Andrew and Laura held their breath, for it seemed he was, then, remembering their presence Duffy drew back.

"Don't worry about it, my love. I shall be here. I'll live in the house if you agree, and the outside men are devoted to you, you know that. You're safe now and I'm sure Andrew will find some suitable chap to look after Sir Robert, won't you, Andrew?"

He turned to frown at Andrew as though to say he better had or Duffy would know the reason why. Good God almighty, Andrew had time to think, his thoughts echoed in Laura's expression, what the devil did he think he was up to, this determined man who, it seemed, was to move into another man's house and, by the look of it, take over as the protector – and God only knew what else – of the man's wife! The news of what had happened here tonight would race like wildfire from estate to estate and those who owned them and considered themselves to be, or at least to have *been*, Sir Robert's friends would be up in arms, and Amy's reputation would be in tatters. Not, by the look of her though, that she would care about that! Talk about a transformation. She was positively radiant. The drooping figure of Sir Robert Blenkinsopp's sad little wife had vanished and in her place was the resolute, hopeful, shining woman who loved the man beside her and was proud to display it quite openly.

"There's not a great deal more we can do at the moment, Duffy. I'll get in touch with John Campbell, the chap I told you about, and arrange for him to come up here and examine Sir Robert. In the meanwhile I'll look about for a reliable fellow to see to Sir Robert, but I'm afraid one of your male servants will have to deal with it for now."

"And I shall be here, don't forget that, Andrew," Duffy said quietly, smiling down at Amy. "I'll keep an eye on things. If you'd be good enough to send on my bag."

"Of course, old chap, but might I ask how long you can remain? Surely your own estate needs your supervision?" Andrew's voice was polite but in it was the question that all of the district would be asking, which was what the devil was going on at Newton Law? At the moment there could be no wondering comments since he and Laura were also guests of Lady Blenkinsopp so it was perfectly proper for Duffy – or Lord Alec Murray as it would soon be revealed he was – to remain under her roof. But not after tonight. He and Laura would go back to Allenbury in the morning and the scandal, for that was what it would be considered, would rock the society in which the Blenkinsopps moved.

"I'm not sure," Duffy began, looking down apologetically at Amy. "I have a good steward looking after things at home but please, don't let's talk about that now. Until I'm absolutely certain that Amy and the children are safe I shall stay, that's if Amy agrees."

"Dar . . . Duffy, how can you say that? You know you are more than welcome to stay here for as long as you can. Not only I but my . . . my step-daughters would be glad of your company."

She smiled brilliantly, triumphantly. God almighty, she was sharp, Andrew thought admiringly. In their concern for her and her household and the possible gossip that might arise should Duffy stay on, they had all, except her, forgotten the three eminently respectable daughters of Sir Robert Blenkinsopp himself. What could be more proper? Three spinsters ladies who were connected to the Church, to the good works they carried out in the community, who were called upon by half the ladies of the district. Three spinster ladies who would be overjoyed to have as their guest a peer of the realm, even though once he had been their father's gamekeeper. They would overlook the curious question of how he came to be here, or why he was taking it upon himself to take over the care of the household. His position, his status, his rank would be enough for them. He was of their class, or better, and they would be only too pleased to introduce him to their friends.

Duffy's smile was ironic, for once it had taken the three sisters all their time to wish him a cold good morning when they came upon him in the grounds, but if it served his purpose, Amy's purpose, he was willing to be as charming and courteous as his pedigreed upbringing had taught him.

"Well, with that settled I suppose we had better get to our beds. Will Sir Robert sleep?"

"Like a baby for twelve hours at least, old man. I gave him a good wallop of that sleeping potion so you can rest assured none of us will be disturbed."

She longed for him to come to her when the house was deep in sleep, longed for the comfort of his arms, but more than that her body desired his with a passion that astonished her. She had known three men in her life, the first her husband who had almost destroyed her with his lust. The second, the kind and gentle man who had fathered her twins and who had done his best to obliterate her memories of her husband's cruelty, and since then there had been no one. She had loved Duffy almost from the first, she admitted that, but they had done no more than kiss one another and that had happened just once. Until today. Today she had been taught the true meaning of love. Her body had totally, utterly and completely surrendered to his, come awake, not just with the tender, emotional love which could at the same time be strong and wilful, but the physical overflowing of need and the satisfying of it. She had gloried in it and she wanted more, more, *more* and she wanted it now. Her body craved for the feel of Duffy's against it. But he would not come, she knew that. Her female need was irritated by it, by the core of decency and honour in him which would not allow him to make love to a man's wife in that man's house. But still she could not help but feel an unworthy petulance that he did not come knocking at her door. And yet, conversely, she loved him all the more for it, loved and respected him while she tossed and turned in the dark waiting for the morning when she would be with Duffy again. When she would see his face with that special expression it assumed for no one but her. She longed for their new life to begin. She had no idea what that life would be, for her son's inheritance was here, her responsibility to her servants was here and Duffy's was far away in the plains of Cheshire. She did not know how she could or if she could, would, keep him by her side, for he was a decent man, a man with the inherited need to pass on his name and title to his son, and how was he to have a son if he stayed here with her, another man's wife, in another man's home, that man still living. She had been so overjoyed to see him, so swept away by the wonder of their lovemaking she had carried no thought in her head beyond *this*, beyond this marvel, this rapture and yet, now that they were apart, her reason, her sense was beginning to ask questions she did not want to answer. Life was teaching her to snatch at whatever joy came along and these past hours had been a treasure that had to be hoarded, but she did not want to hoard them, she wanted to live them, again and again and again, until the end of her life.

Rising from her bed, she stood at her open window, listening to the rustling night sounds, some small creature in the shrubbery, the bark of a dog fox, the cry of the owl that lived in the oak tree, her own body crying out in its great need for the masculine dominance of the man who had, today, become her lover. She shivered, pressing her hot face to the glass of the window and when she heard the commotion from some distant place in the house it filled her with confusion and fear, for it could only be one of the men her husband had about him. But they were gone and her husband was fast in the almost unconscious state Andrew's potion had induced in him so . . . ?

She turned, her back to the window, like a cornered animal for a moment until her mind cleared. Even from so far away she recognised Alfred's voice shouting at the back door for Mr Duffy and then Clara who came shrieking up the stairs, the fear Alfred had transmitted to her making her voice shrill. Platt had escaped, she yelled and Mr Duffy was to come at once, for with that fiend on the loose were they all to be murdered, or worse, in their beds.

Throwing on the first garment to hand she flung the door open and ran on to the landing where she could see the racing figure of Duffy, Clara close behind him, on the staircase. She followed, almost tripping on the floating panels of her negligee, her mind lost in a mist of fear which gradually became a thick fog of terror. Bedlam reigned and before five minutes had gone by they were all there, the maidservants in an assortment of nightwear milling about the room in panic, just as they had done earlier only then they had been overcome with joy. The sight of their mistress in some flimsy wisp of a garment and no shoes on her feet quietened them for a while, especially the grooms who had never seen anything like it in their lives. Mr Duffy, Doctor Barrie and his wife were all fully dressed, at least they had something on, even if they were a trifle less than immaculate.

"Come, my dear," Mrs Barrie said, leading their ashen-faced mistress away from the kitchen and nodding to Cook to do the same with the maids, "let us leave the men to deal with this; after all, there are plenty of them." She indicated to her ladyship's maid that she was to bring up tea while the men scratched their heads and deliberated on how the enormous bulk of a man like Platt could slip through a locked door whose key still hung on its usual place on a nail in the stable.

Not one gave a thought to bonny Billy Cummings!

30

Billy Cummings had begun to realise that far from Platt looking out for him until they returned to the cosy job they had once enjoyed with Sir Robert Blenkinsopp, and would again, they were convinced, the boot was definitely on the other foot. And yet they made a good team. He provided the brains, Platt, or Mr Platt as he still called him, provided the muscle that was needed in the dangerous back alleys and narrow, crowded passages of Allenbury. Lodgings had been easy to find in the close-packed tenements that sheltered the homeless. Thousands of them slept three at a time at two pence a night on a bundle of rags in a bunk, or for a penny were allowed to lie together like sardines in a tin on the cold earth floor itself which was spread, and renewed infrequently, with lice-ridden straw, sharing their quarters with labourers, beggars, vagrants, drunkards, prostitutes and a scampering of rats. Neither Billy nor Platt was unduly concerned, since they had known worse before they fell in with Sir Robert, though it must be admitted that Platt, now and again, through occasional work at the lunatic asylum on the edge of town where his great strength had come in handy, had been employed privately by the various doctors in the district to deal with patients who were a nuisance to their wealthier relatives. He had known better and he had known worse and he was quite prepared to wait patiently until the opportunity arose to insinuate himself, with Billy, of course, who, with his shrewd brain, was a great help to him, back in the comfort of Newton Law.

He couldn't, for the life of him, understand what had happened and he said so a dozen times a day to Billy.

"Wharr ah canna fathom is what medd 'em do what they did, man. Ah mean, there us was, 'appy as bloody pigs in muck wi' maister in charge an' 'er soddin' ladyship under 'is thumb, like, bowin' an' scrapin' an' lerrin' 'im do as 'e pleases, then, canny as tha' like, them buggers coom breakin' in an' drag us down't stairs an' lock us up in't stable. Theer's no bloody sense to it. Wha's goin' on, tha's wharr ah'd like ter know."

"Why aye, 'tis a bloody mystery, man," Billy answered him patiently a dozen times a day until at last, as much for his own sake as for Mr Platt's, he made up his sharp mind to find out, one way or another, how this disaster had come about. There was a multitude of ugly customers who shared their sleeping quarters, ragged gutter-weasels, skinny little half-fed runts, members of the vague and shifting underworld that infested each town where pickings might be found and who, knowing the district and its inhabitants like they knew their own lairs, would, for a few coppers, find out what anyone wanted to know, about anything. It might come in handy one day to know which prominent gentleman frequented which brothel; who had a liking

for virgin females, the younger the better, the sort
Doctor Andrew Barrie patched up when they were
no longer required; men who had secrets that they did
not wish the world to know. They would do anything
if it was made worth their while, these dregs of the
human race, which Billy knew, for had he not been
one of their number until recently.

It was quiet in the cellar, the screams of laughter, the
shouts and swearing voices, the snoring and coughing
stilled as many of the lodgers went about their own furtive business of the day. The drink-befuddled women,
who plied their trade in the narrow, putrid alleys, the
rotten, crumbling warrens that formed the inner circle
of Allenbury, had gone off to earn a farthing or two
in the oldest profession on earth, and those who were
crouched in the dim recesses of the cellar were either
too weak, too drunk or too idle to climb out of their
festering beds.

"Wharr ah canna fathom the day is why . . ."

"Listen, Mr Platt, ah could find out for thi'. Theer's
lads 'ere'd do owt fer tuppence an' they c'n gerrabout
easier than what us could. We's best keepin' under
cover fer a day or so. They might've set polis on
us so best lie low but any o' this lot" – turning
a contemptuous eye on the huddled figures about
them – "'d ask about an' find out what's doin'. That
there doctor might know. Tha' know, the one what
was friendly wi' 'er ladyship."

He and Billy were sitting shoulder to shoulder on the
palliasse they shared, their backs against the foul and
running wall of the cellar in which they had hidden for
the past four days. They were eating a beef pie each,
large and succulent, which Billy had just slipped out

to purchase from the pie woman's stall on the corner of the passage known, incongruously, as Saville Row, both drinking ale from a pint tankard. Twenty-odd pairs of eyes watched avidly from the shadowed, vermin-infested corners, scratching at their flea bites, as Platt and Billy did, with the unconcern of the familiar. Billy on his own would have fared badly, in more ways than one, among the scum who inhabited the dank cellar, but the huge and threatening figure of the brute in whose company the lad sought safety kept them at bay, which was why Billy had realised what a splendid team they made.

Platt scratched at his head, disturbing a scatter of lice which fell to his shoulder. He did not notice or if he had would not have been concerned. It was months since he had taken the trouble to have what he called a "good wash", which meant as far as his neck, his wrists and perhaps a bit of a poke inside his ears. He had been forced, now and again, to shave, whenever his master roared at him to "tidy yourself up" but water, which was hard to come by, and soap, which was non-existent, had not been near him for days. Billy, who had been somewhat more fastidious while he lived at Newton Law, watched him unconcernedly, giving his own person a bit of a scratch here and there.

"Well," said Platt at last, having, it seemed, turned the idea slowly round and round in his head, "it willna do any 'arm, man. Mind, us don't want our business bletherin' about, like," having, at the moment, no idea what their business might be. "We's ter bide 'ere for a while but it'd be 'andy ter ken what's goin' on up at th'ouse. Aye, man, tha' see to it an' when us gets back ah'll let maister know wharra good lad tha's bin."

Heaving himself up on to his feet he lumbered across the room, kicking out at those who got in his way.

"Gerrout o' me road, gowkie," he told one unfortunate who was not quick enough as he made his way to the corner of the room. Unfastening the buttons at his greasy crotch he fished out his penis and relieved himself in a long, stinking stream, indifferent to the drenching he gave to some other man's bit of rags and straw.

The boy – at least he was a boy in years if not in experience – who was given the task of finding out what was happening up at Newton Law – oh aye, he'd soon find it – had the same kind of craftiness, the street cunning that had stood Billy Cummings in such good stead all his life. He was no more than eleven or twelve, his scarecrow shoulders sticking out of the sketch of a jacket he had purloined from somewhere, his thin, rodent face sly, his eyes wise and knowing when Billy told him what he wanted. He'd want paying, mind, and he'd have to grease the palms of a few folk to get the information needed, but aye, he'd do it.

He proved most useful. He had no idea why the big man and the pretty boy wanted the information, nor what they were going to do with it when they had it, and neither did he care with the coins that the pretty boy had given him rattling in his pocket. With ingenuity and cunning, asking here and there, whispering to men, and women, who themselves whispered to others, those who had had recourse to Doctor Barrie's medical attention which he gave free to those who could not pay him, as he had always done; by the simple expedient of getting a few of his marras from the cellar to "knock a bit of sense" into a delivery boy who worked at the provision merchant that supplied Newton Law, and various other "enquiries" he had made, he told Billy cockily, Billy and Platt were at last in full possession of the facts and also of the name of the man who had, with one stroke, cheated them of the good life they had led at Newton Law.

"Duffy . . . Duffy . . . 'oo the bloody 'ell's Duffy?" Platt beseeched Billy to tell him since his own mind was barely capable of remembering what had happened the day before yesterday, never mind earlier.

"Nay, man, 'ow do ah know? There were no talk of a Duffy while ah were there." Billy's voice was irritable and he gave Platt a shake as though to stir him up. It was like a pretty, somewhat unkempt kitten trying to rouse a rhinoceros.

Suddenly, as though a finger had been poked through Platt's thick skull, stirring up whatever it was it contained and making a small peep-hole, a pinprick of light shone in his muddy eyes. It could not be said to light up his face with knowledge but it allowed Billy to see that Platt had at least put a face to the name Billy had disclosed.

"Duffy . . . Duffy . . . why, aye, that were't bloke what used ter be maister's gamekeeper. At least that were what 'e called 'isself. Pokin' an' pryin' 'ere an' bloody there where 'e 'ad no business ter be an', what's more, 'e were doin' er bloody ladyship."

Billy's face was a picture. "Doing" her ladyship!

That slender slip of a creature whom Billy himself had often thought he would like to have in his bed, but he wouldn't, *couldn't* imagine her doing "it" with anyone. She was like an angel with her cloud of pale streaked hair, the shining silvery blue of her eyes, the velvet creamy texture of her skin and her mouth as rosy and full as a child's. Billy had often wondered how in the name of all he held to be holy, which wasn't a lot, she had managed to get three children from the horrible old man who was her husband, how she had endured it, for she gave the appearance of being untouched, innocent, a virgin girl who had known no man's hand. And this Duffy, whoever he was, had been in her drawers! Did Sir Robert know this? Of course he did, for if Platt knew it would not have taken him long to pass it on to his master. Was that why the man had disappeared? And if it was, if he had got the sack – and he couldn't see Sir Robert merely giving the sack to the man who had lain with his wife, a bloody good hiding more like – why had he come back? And how had he got the power to manhandle Platt out of the house and bloody well take over? There had been a great deal of coming and going on the night he and Platt had made a dash for it. Carriages up and down the drive, Sir Robert roaring like a wounded beast, the maids scampering here and there, which had made it very difficult for himself to slip out of the house without being seen. What the bloody hell was going on?

Platt's face was twisted into a snarl of rage, his loose, wet lips lifting to reveal the blackened, rotting stumps of his teeth. He looked like an old lion that is forced to give way to a younger, stronger beast over the carcass of a kill.

"'Tis that sod what's done it. 'E's the one. 'E's got them bloody stable lads on 'is side an' 'e's after runnin' th'ole business. Gerris 'ands on't cash, an' 'er ladyship an' all, 'e reckons, while maister's 'elpless."

"So 'e is, man."

"Aye, but theer's more ways o' killin' cat than chokin' it ter death wi' cream, an' ah know a few, trust me. Us'll need ter be careful, Billy man, tekk us time an' plan summat what'll show that sod 'e'll not gerr away wi' messin' wi' Alfie Platt. By gow thi' an' me 'ad a right good little billet wi' Sir Robert an' no bugger's tekkin' it away. So 'ere's what us'll do."

It was quite amazing, Cook was to say time and time again, the difference in the atmosphere of the house. She was not a fanciful woman, she was also fond of saying to anyone who would listen to her, which was all the maids since they had no option, but really, what a difference in just a few days. Clara and Cissie had even been told off, not by her ladyship, of course, who seemed to walk about in a lovely dream noticing nothing, but by Morna. Singing they were, the pair of them as they did out the downstairs drawing-room, "Cockles and Mussels", if you please, and what if her ladyship had come downstairs and heard them, she declared tartly. The sack at the week's end if they were not careful, but they all knew nothing like that would happen, for their mistress was walking on air, as they all were, and it was all thanks to Mr Duffy.

But to their consternation he was not Mr Duffy after all and when they were told his true identity you could have knocked them all over with a feather. Lord Alec Murray he was and they were to call him Lord Murray, since it seemed he was a baron and if they addressed him verbally, which meant spoke to him, it was as my lord, or your lordship. It took a bit of getting used to seeing as how on occasion he'd sat down with them at the same table, eating what they ate and drinking what they drank, chatting in that cultured voice of his, which, now they knew the truth, they could understand. Mind, if it had not been for the Misses Blenkinsopp, who were overwhelmed by the honour of having him as a guest in their home and at their table, he might have remained as Mr Duffy to them all, since it was obvious from his manner that the fawning adulation of the three sisters did not find favour with him. He was excessively polite, courteous and charming, leading the conversation at the dinner table into subjects that he thought they would find within their capabilities, since none of them was aware of anything that went on outside a five-mile radius of Newton Law. The great distress in Lancashire owing to the partial or even the entire stoppage of innumerable looms which were dependent on American cotton was something that, as Christian ladies, should have concerned them. The circumstances were hardly known to them and if they had been would have made no difference, since, it being so far away, they could do nothing to help. The American Civil War itself in which brother fought against brother was a mystery to them as well, though they were totally against slavery which, like many others, they thought was probably the cause of it. Now, if the conversation turned to their own royal family, then that was a different matter. The dear Prince of Wales had, only six months ago, married the beautiful princess Alexandra of Denmark

and the descriptions of the cortège as it passed along
the route to St George's Chapel in Windsor, and the
ceremony itself, were known to them in every detail
and they could talk about it by the hour, gratified that
Lord Murray took such an interest, as they had done
themselves. They had been taught, as all ladies of good
family were taught, to sew, to speak a few words of
French, to play a simple tune on the piano and to
sing slightly off-key. Every evening after dinner they
entertained him with their arch songs, all three hearts
beating romantically in all three flat breasts, unaware in
their virginal innocence that he and their step-mother
were only awaiting the moment when they said their
fulsome goodnights and went to their virginal beds.

The weather was kind to the lovers that autumn
and Amy was to say she didn't know what they
would have done if it had turned nasty, as it often
did on the Northumberland moorland. The changing
shades of the trees in the woodland and the autumn
colour of the bracken they waded through on the
moor itself, the harvesting of the crops in the lower
fields, the bursting abundance of the fruits of the
hedgerows which they picked for Cook's jams. The
leaves, pink and yellow and gold and russet, that fell
from the branches and the woodland floor where they
wandered became a soft bed on which Duffy and Amy
lay in one another's arms, the scent of the fir trees that
grew on its edge all about them, their love all about
them, their kisses sweet and soft. The dying days held
on tightly to the warmth of June. Days of unmatched
beauty, warm, delicious, calm, a sweet peace which
brooded breathlessly over the mellow sunny days, the
happy stillness broken only by the shrill voices of the

children from across the garden and the soft solitary singing of a robin.

They walked up to the edge of the farmland of Berry Hill, their hands clasped until they came upon Frankie Chambers coming home from the ploughing, his team of oxen red and polished as chestnuts in the sinking sunshine, the chains rattling, Frankie perched on the fore ox.

Hastily, reluctantly, their hands dropped apart as Frankie wished them a cheerful good evening, for it had not taken long for the good news to spread that Sir Robert was once again in close confinement and that Mr Duffy and Lady Blenkinsopp were to call at all the farms as they had done a year ago. Overhead was the vast fleecy sky turning with the light to orange and gold and apricot as they made their way home, the sun floating behind a ribbon of velvet cloud. A tiny sliver of moon hung shyly to the west, and along the return path through the wood the silence was broken only by the occasional pattering of an acorn or a chestnut through the remaining leaves of the trees to the ground.

It was an enchanted time, a time set in a vacuum of magic with no end and no beginning, and yet they both knew it could not last, as it was, for ever. They walked, the days moving slowly, drinking in the simple marvel of just being together, of being given the gift of gazing, with no time limit, into one another's eyes. Eyes that spoke with no need of words of the endless continuity of their love.

"I've loved you since the moment I first saw you climb down from that carriage and march bravely up to your husband, head high, courage written all over you, defying him. You were like a flower, delicate, light, vulnerable. You wore something pale, I can't remember the colour, but you seemed insubstantial, beautiful and I wanted to shout to you to be careful, for even then I knew . . . what he was. It seems so long ago . . . how long?"

"I don't know." She was scarcely listening, bemused by the way his mouth, which did not smile often, curled endearingly up at the corners.

"You have a lovely smile," she told him dreamily.

He laughed then. "Lovely smile! Gentlemen don't have lovely smiles."

"You do, my darling." She stood on tiptoe to place a butterfly kiss on the smile in question.

For hours, up on the privacy and peace of the moors they would consider each other, studying in great detail the soft swell of her breasts which he uncovered, the turn of her neck, the arch of her throat, the slenderness of her ankle and foot, the smooth flatness of her white belly. She was fascinated by the strength and yet fineness of his back, the curve of his buttocks, the scatter of fine blond hair on his chest which darkened and thickened as it reached his penis, the smooth line of muscle from his hip to his knee, his neat ears, the blunt angle of his jaw. They made love high among the standing stones where no one came but the sheep.

"You're beautiful," he told her, his face working with an emotion which had what seemed to be agony in it and inside her something wept, for she knew what it was. Her skin rippled and came alive under his hands, his own needs coming alive in response and when their rapturous voices echoed over the tops the sheep lifted their heads and stared in wonder.

"I love you, Amy," he shouted as his head arched back.

"I love you, Duffy," she echoed, her own body arching to meet his, to melt into his, to get inside his as his was in hers.

It had been remarkably easy to turn Newton Law back to the home Amy had made for herself, her children and the servants during Sir Robert's confinement. Andrew was of the opinion, and he *was* a medical man, and John Campbell, the doctor from London agreed with him, that during his demented tirade against them all when Platt was removed, Sir Robert had suffered another small stroke. His speech was once again no more than a slurred mumble, he could move only his eyes in his suffused face and his one good arm was considerably weakened. Both his legs lay slackly from the chair in which Holden, the man Andrew had found to look after him, had placed him, and though Holden diligently read to him from *The Times*, which was still delivered daily from Allenbury, he took little interest. He ate when Holden fed him, nourishing and ample meals that Cook thought were good for him, and when any of his daughters visited him, which they did now and again he stared listlessly out of the window and seemed not to know they were there. Holden was a clean, respectable, kind-natured man and he had found that if he allowed his charge a glass of whisky of a night before he lifted him into his bed he slept like a baby.

"He had a good night, sir," Holden would say, for what else was there to report to the man who now seemed to be in charge of Sir Robert Blenkinsopp's household and his estate, *and*, it was whispered, though not out loud by her servants, Sir Robert Blenkinsopp's wife.

The school was reopened, to the great relief of Abigail Blamire who had seriously begun to think about looking for another post, taking her anxieties to Lady Blenkinsopp, who was inclined to agree with her. What was she to do? she said, when Sir Robert had ordered the school closed. She was not a maid-servant. The only thing she was capable of was sewing, and sew she did, for hours on end, mending sheets and tablecloths and even the outside men's shirts, those who had no wife to do it for them, darning socks, knitting socks and giving them away to anyone who was needing a pair. She couldn't bear to sit on her hands doing nothing, she told them all, begging for something to do, and now she was back in the schoolroom, eager and delighted to be there, though she knew many of her pupils would not agree with her. Rosy McGovern was hardly more than her assistant now, since she was pregnant with her first child and though she had been married for no more than three months Cook and Morna agreed that she was at least five months gone, the naughty girl! But did it matter? She and Jumsie were cosily married, settled in their little cottage and Rosy, besides helping Miss Blamire out in the schoolroom, was always ready to give a hand in the kitchen.

Not much was seen of her ladyship, nor Lord Murray, since it seemed they were needed up on the farms which surely, in three months, could not have deteriorated to such an extent? But then it was nothing to do with them. If her ladyship, or rather his lordship, deemed it necessary to make further improvements, who were they to argue with him? He had his own estate in Cheshire, or so it was said, so he must know what he was doing, and if they had heard snippets of the gossip that was beginning to creep insidiously about the district they ignored it. She was their little mistress and though they were decent folk, all of them, and would have condemned it in another, she could do no wrong in their eyes.

The children thrived in their regained freedom, running round, getting a bit wild, Cook was inclined to believe, since her ladyship knew how they had suffered from their confinement and how wary they had become of their papa's "friends", who, when they had come across the children had thought it a bit of a lark to befriend them. Now that those friends had gone they were allowed more freedom than they had ever known. You could see, and hear, the three of them racing like the wind across the lawns and into the woodland, flinging themselves headlong towards the lake, trampling on Mr Weston's flowerbeds and into his shrubbery.

It was a lovely time of the year. Pale amber sunshine fell across the reddening October trees, melting the morning mists, and though they knew winter was not far away it seemed those who lived and thrived under the gently sheltering roof of Newton Law were held for a moment in a mellow, unchanging timelessness. Smoke rose from Mr Weston's autumn bonfires, trailing up into an almost windless sky, and the smell of them was heady to the senses. Could it last, this magical time? Amy asked herself every morning when she woke in her empty bed, for Duffy refused absolutely to make love to her under her husband's roof. Could it last? Please, God, let it last. Don't let me think about what is to come, for she knew that their "guest", as her step-daughters fondly called him, could not remain for ever. His mother wrote to him constantly, begging him piteously to come home, or remonstrating with him for staying where he surely shouldn't be, since his own land claimed him. There was wild happiness and yet there was a sadness to it all, for she couldn't deceive herself: soon it would be over. The frost would come. Winter would come and Duffy would be gone and she would be left with nothing but decay . . .

Mr Weston was the first to report the sight of a strange youth wandering down the lane towards the yard gate. A youth who, when challenged, ran like the wind down the lane in the direction of the road to Allenbury. He was seen on several occasions, just a lad really, and though no one knew what he wanted, perhaps looking for work, they were not unduly worried, for he was only a little squirt who could harm no one.

31

The message came from Farmer Will Dawson of Hill Farm, delivered by a scrawny lad who said he was the son of Farmer Dawson's cowman.

"But we were there only a week ago, Duffy, and Farmer Dawson seemed to have no problems then. What on earth can be wrong that he should need to summon you so soon? And why, if he has some difficulty, cannot he get on his horse and ride down here to you?"

"He hasn't a horse, my darling. You know how hard it is for these hill-farmers to make ends meet. If they have any spare cash they buy a cow or an animal that will be useful. If he came it would be on his own two feet and time is at a premium at this time of year. The harvest just in, ewes to be put to the ram, you know how it is."

"You're the best man I've ever known," Amy told him simply. She looked up into his face, her hand on the sleeve of his jacket, on her own face an expression that seemed to say she was filled with the wonder of this love of theirs, but it also said she was uneasy, though she didn't know why. It was just so strange that Will Dawson, a taciturn man with a taciturn way of speaking as though words did not come easily to him, should be so in need of help, or advice, that he had sent his cowman's son for Duffy. Will Dawson was a small man, wiry and lean as a greyhound, but with strength and endurance despite his lack of bulk. He had laboured from cock-crow to nightfall, and beyond, for fifty-five of his fifty-eight years, beginning with the scaring of crows and the gathering of stones from his da's fields. His da's fields were his fields now. But he was fiercely independent, his own master and man, his very manner saying he needed help from no one though his back was bowed and he was bow-legged, for the loads he had carried all his life would have burdened a horse. So what did he want with Duffy?

Duffy bent his head to place a small, tender kiss on the corner of her mouth. "Now then, don't turn me into a saint. I'm far from that, but if the chap wants a bit of help with something, perhaps a loan . . ."

"A loan?"

"I know what you're going to say, he's a proud man, the last to ask for a loan but, well, my darling, I shan't know unless I go up there, shall I? And no, I think it would be better that I went alone. I can go more quickly."

"If you didn't have me holding you back?" She smiled and took his hand in hers, bringing it to her face where she rested her cheek on the back of it. She was happy, blindly, rapturously happy, blissful in the knowledge that when she got up in the morning, when she dressed and went down to the breakfast-room, he would be there, rising from his seat as she entered. The sisters would be there too, chirruping of this and that and of nothing at all, not for a moment believing that this handsome, charming, pedigreed gentleman would choose one of them for a wife, should they want to be married which they weren't awfully sure they did, but gratified that he appeared to be enjoying his stay with them. They did not ask how long that stay might be. They knew it was due to him and the admirable doctors he had brought to the house that their father was once more confined and cared for, this time by a respectable man. That they no longer need fear being molested by the riff-raff their father had gathered about him. That they could once more, without fear of being insulted, invite their friends and acquaintances who shared their interests in the church and the surrounding parish to call at Newton Law.

Since it had grown colder and the rain, the autumn rain that plagued this part of the world, had at last come, she and Duffy had not made love, for it was too cold and wet to brave the moorland. They were content, it seemed, after the wild passion they had shared when he first returned, merely to be together, at least for the moment, to see each other every day, both of them drifting in the sweet harmony that flowed from one to the other. And for now that seemed to be enough. Sometimes, when the rain ceased and a fitful sunshine did its best to escape the fast chasing clouds, they would wrap their winter cloaks about them and walk down to the summerhouse which faced out of the easterly wind that blew across the Norwegian Sea and the North Sea directly from the wastes of Siberia. They would sit together, Duffy leaning against the wooden back of the summerhouse, hers against his chest, his arms about her, his cheek against the windblown tangle of her loosened hair. They talked, she could not remember what about, since it was his beloved voice she listened to, not what he said. She would smile up into his face, his lips would capture hers with a loving patience, soft, gentle, so tender, so . . . so moderate since she knew his need of her body was great. Greater than hers, she was aware. She knew his love was true and selfless and that should she send him away he would go, but she could not bear it, the thought of losing him. But her reason told her that he could not stay here with her for much longer. He had his own estate, his family, responsibilities that a man of property could not shirk and certainly could not direct from a distance, no matter how efficient and conscientious the man who was his manager might be. His mother's letters were becoming more and more urgent, not, it seemed to Amy, because she was anxious about Ladywood but because her woman's instincts told her that there was danger – in the shape of Lady Blenkinsopp – in Northumberland and she wanted her son back home where she could keep her eye on him. Choose a suitable wife for him, one she herself could steer in the direction she thought was desirable: a young, biddable woman of good family, preferably one with a title to match her son's.

"Something like that," he told her now, smiling wryly, lifting his other hand to her hair and smoothing it back.

"I love you so."

"I know. I love you."

"What will we . . ."

"Hush, hush, my dearest love. We will . . . I don't know but we will . . ."

"What?"

"I don't know," he sighed, looking pensively over her head towards the window against which the rain had begun to lash. "I don't know but . . ." Again he sighed and drew her into his arms, and Tansy, who had knocked quietly and then entered, withdrew just as quietly, her own face saddened, for she was to marry Alfred next week and though she was aware that her and Alfred's love was simpler – she would have used the word mundane had she known it – how dreadful it would be if they were to be separated.

He took Oscar, a grey stallion who would be glad of a gallop, John-Henry told his lordship, holding the bridle as he leaped nimbly, gracefully into the saddle. He was a fine horseman, John-Henry knew that, and admired it in him, and though he thought it was a bad day to go dashing off to Hill Farm, the furthest away farm on Sir Robert's estate, it was not his place to say so. He said so to Alfred though when he strode back into the stable, glad to get out of the bloody rain which wet you through to your skin in five minutes. Mind you, his lordship wore an oiled cape over his greatcoat of wool and a wide-brimmed hat known, so John-Henry had heard, as a "wide-awake", though he couldn't think why, and long boots called Napoleons since they were like the ones the Frenchman wore.

His breeches were tucked into his boots, but nevertheless the rain dripped down inside them to soak into his stockings, collected on the brim of his hat and ran in a steady trickle to fall to his cheek where it rested in an icy touch of winter. It came to rest on his collar and cuffs and crept insidiously inside his clothing, and he began to wish Farmer Dawson to the furthest hobs of hell and to curse his own foolishness in coming. What a bloody day to be riding up on the bloody moorland where even the birds were sheltering from the rain. He was glad Amy had been persuaded not to come with him and he supposed, once he got to Hill Farm, Mrs Dawson, who was a hospitable little body, would have him steaming in front of her fire, a cup of her hot, sweet tea in his hand, his boots off and his stockinged feet to the blaze.

They rose from the very ground itself, from under the bedraggled heather and twisted bracken, six of them moving very slowly towards him in a circle, all of them big men with long arms and wide shoulders, most of them with the blank expression of those who enter the prizefighting ring. One of them was the man named Platt.

Oscar, scenting danger, reared up and it was all Duffy could do to keep himself on his back, but it made no difference since they had hold of him by now and had dragged him down the stallion's high flanks to the bare ground. For a moment as he struck out, catching one of them on the side of the head with his gloved fist and kicking another in the belly, he was free and with a twist managed to get himself with his back against a tall pillar of stone.

The outcome was decided from the first. There were just too many of them and though he had done some bare-knuckle fighting in his early youth he was no match for these bully boys. He went down beneath the hammer blows of a dozen fists and when he was down he was trampled into the earth by a dozen booted feet. Six dark, intent figures, five of whom did not even know him or what the fight was about, but since they were being paid for it they might as well make a good job of it as they reduced him to a bundle of bleeding rags. It lasted no longer than ten minutes, then, after depriving him of his fine overcoat and boots which, despite the state of them would fetch a few bob, one of them broke away. The bloodlust had cooled and they all began to shamble off into the sheet of rain, nursing their own abrasions, for the chap had not gone down without a fight. Platt launched a final kick from his steel-studded boot, cursing him obscenely, then followed the others.

It was a mistake, and if Billy had been there it would not have happened. Platt meant to do away with the bugger who had ruined his easy life, do away with him for good, and if he had dragged him off the path he would have succeeded. Billy's sharp mind would have recognised this simple fact but Billy wasn't big enough or strong enough to do the work the bruisers did, so he awaited Platt in the cellar of their – hopefully – temporary home.

The injured man lay on the track where they left him, the rain falling on his unconscious, badly damaged body. Oscar had gone, galloping off in a convulsion of terror. The rain continued to fall and Duffy remained curled like a child in a womb, a position he had adopted to protect the most vital parts of himself against impossible odds, his knees drawn up to his chest, his arms about his head, trying to save his eyes, his teeth and his brain at the sacrifice of his ribs. Slowly, still in the deeply unconscious state they had pounded him into, he began to relax, his muscles softening and letting go, drifting on to his back. Despite his efforts they had managed to kick him in the face and the blood poured from his nose, one cheek gashed to the bone, both eyes blackened and closed, the other cheek embedded with dirt and torn into hanging strips of flesh. But he still, at this moment, breathed, his breath scraping in and out of his tortured lungs.

It continued to rain, falling on his upturned face, washing away the blood, soaking his torn blood-soaked shirt so that the nipples of his breast were dark and visible beneath the sopping material. Rainwater began to gather beneath him so that he lay in a pool of it and in the deep shock of his unconscious state he began to shiver.

It took Oscar three hours to find his way back to his stable. He had in the past two years been ridden only about the immediate environs of Newton Law, exercised by Alfred or John-Henry, and the wide moorland, the criss-cross of tracks and sheep trods with their strange scents, the rearing outcrops of rocky unfamiliar shapes, confused and frightened him. Reins dangling, his eyes wide, his nostrils flaring, he gal-loped madly hither and yon, considerably startling a shepherd or two. At last some instinct led him nearer to his stable and recognising the paths he had ridden with one of the grooms on his back, he flung himself headlong down the track to the gate that led into the yard. He whinnied in great distress, bringing not only John-Henry and Alfred to the stable door, but Jumsie from the paddock where he had gone to fetch in the animals who had earlier been put there in the hope that it might give over raining. It had not. Mr Weston in the potting shed, a sack across his back, looked up from the pot in his hand where he was peacefully setting seedlings for next spring, the commotion causing him and Mr Purvis to step outside in wonder, and Tansy and Morna moved to the kitchen window to peer out into the yard.

"Summat's up," Morna said, her hand to her mouth.

"Why aye, man, 'tis the grey that 'is lordship rode out on this mornin'." Tansy, through her association with Alfred, knew more than the other maidservants about horses. "Oh God . . . Oh God. What'll her ladyship—"

"Come away from that window," Cook ordered, "an' get on wi' what tha' were doin'. 'Tis nowt ter do wi' us."

"But, Cook, that's the beast 'is lordship went out on over three hours ago. Theer's summat wrong. Look at men, tha'r runnin' round in circles."

"'Appen they are but it's nowt ter do wi' thee." Nevertheless Cook left the batter she was mixing and with the dripping spoon still in her hand moved slowly over to the window, the rest of the maids at her back.

It took but a minute or two for Alfred and John-Henry to regain their usual common sense which told them that his lordship had somehow come off his horse and was probably floundering about somewhere between here and Hill Farm. He'd be mad as hell and wet as buggery and the sooner they got out to him the better. Not that he'd abuse them, for he was a gentleman and fair-minded into the bargain, but he would be soaked to the skin and his temper might be severely tried.

"Run to't back door, Jumsie, an' tell mistress me an' Alfred'll saddle up and fetch 'im back." And even as he shouted the instructions to the lad, for the life of him John-Henry didn't know why, some instinct made him take Alfred along. With himself on Jason and leading

Prince for his lordship to ride back to Newton Law it would have been nothing of a job and one certainly within the scope of one man.

The hullabaloo in the yard had brought Amy to the window at the end of the upstairs hallway. She had been up to play with the children, since she knew, with the rain sheeting down, they would be confined to the nursery and with the high spirits that had returned with Duffy, whom Robby had welcomed back with rapture, they would be restless, their active young minds and bodies trying the patience of Nanny Morag and Lizzie-Ann. She had settled them down, the twins somehow squashed on her narrow lap and Robby leaning on her shoulder while she read to them and then, when they became restless again, played a game of lions and tigers. The enormous nursery table with its enveloping red chenille cloth was their tent, though they were not awfully sure what a tent might be, they only knew that it was great fun to hide under it. The chairs against the wall were a forest in which the lions and tigers hid and for half an hour Nanny Morag despaired that she would ever restore her charges to the sort of discipline she liked to see. There had been shrieks and screams and laughter and it was all getting a bit hysterical, she was inclined to think, but her mistress, her good little mistress was also a good mother and with a bit of coaxing and a promise of a walk when the rain stopped she had them dozing in front of the fire, entwined with numerous kittens, before she left.

She felt her heart begin to crash about in her chest as she looked out on the scene in the stable yard. The grey, Oscar, on which Duffy had set off hours ago, was being hauled about by Alfred in an effort to quieten the animal who was rearing and bucking in what seemed to be great distress. John-Henry was shouting instructions of some sort and Jumsie was racing like a madman towards the kitchen door.

So where was Duffy? Dear God, where was Duffy in all this mêlée? She craned her neck to catch a sight of him in some corner of the yard but he wasn't there. Perhaps he had already come into the kitchen but it was not like him to leave an animal in the state Oscar appeared to be in. He loved horses so. What . . . Dear sweet Lord, where . . .

Turning on her heel, the full skirt of her rose-coloured silk skirt dipping about her like a bell in motion, she began to run towards the back stairs which were nearest, going down them two at a time and she had time to think with that part of her brain not totally terrified by Duffy's absence from the scene downstairs, that all it needed was for her to fall and break her damned leg.

They all turned as she crashed into the kitchen, their faces not exactly afraid, but nervous just the same, for somehow John-Henry, who did not even know the source of his own alarm, had alarmed them.

"Where is he?" their mistress shrieked, pushing through the group of maidservants with small regard for their concern, or even their balance.

"Nah then, m'lady," Jumsie, who was still at the back door, began, but she shoved him aside and almost fell into the yard, into the muddly, puddle-strewn, rain-starred yard.

"Nay, m'lady," Tansy protested. "Tha' cloak."

"Where is he?" she shrieked again and the men exchanged embarrassed glances.

"Well, tha' see," John-Henry began, just about to leap on Jason's back but she grabbed the reins, making the hunter jib away and John-Henry almost lose his balance.

"M'lady, if tha' please," he said sternly, for he could see she was going to cause trouble. "Oscar come back no more'n five minutes ago so it looks as though 'is lordship's tekken a tumble. Me an' Alfred'll find 'im."

"I'll come with you." Amy whirled about, beckoning to Tansy to fetch her cloak. She'd not bother changing into . . . she'd bunch her skirts up about her hips. Jumsie could saddle Holly and she'd be off with the men to find . . . Dear God, this rain . . . he'd be wet through . . .

John-Henry's stern voice stopped her. "Beggin' tha' pardon, m'lady, but tha're not ter come."

"Hold your tongue, man, I shall do exactly what I—"

"No, tha'll not. Dost want ter 'old us up? Me an' Alfred'll find 'im a damn sight quicker on us own so stay there wi' women an' do as tha's told."

"How dare you!" Her face was like alabaster and in her eyes was a livid, burning madness and a terror so deep John-Henry wanted to fall back before it, but with a nod to Alfred who leaped nimbly on Prince's back they galloped off at great speed through the gate which Mr Weston held open for them.

She struggled but they held her, Tansy and Rosy, who had come from her cottage to see what all the rumpus was about. They almost had to drag her to the kitchen table and when they had her seated Rosy held her hand and the maids swirled about her in an effort to do anything, anything at all to bring her a bit of comfort. They had known that she and his lordship were . . . well, how could they miss it, for they were women too, and only human, but their devotion to one another was a warm and lovely thing and could hardly be overlooked!

They found him an hour later just where Platt's gang of men had left him on the path between Newton Law and Hill Farm. He had taken his time on his ride up there but the grooms, careless of the horses' legs, had ridden at breakneck speed just as though the basic human instinct that seemed to infiltrate John-Henry's brain knew that time was essential.

In appalled silence, doing their best not to aggravate his already badly injured body, they stripped him of his wet clothes, and, removing their own, wrapped him about as best they could and heaved him, face down, across Jason's back.

Ignoring the rather comical aspect of Alfred in nothing but his long-johns and boots, since there was nothing to laugh about in his lordship's condition, John-Henry told him to ride to Allenbury like the black devil himself was after him and fetch Doctor Barrie while he took his lordship to Newton Law.

The folk who were about the streets of the town at that hour, and there weren't many in such inclement weather, stood open-mouthed and affronted as the man dressed in nothing but his underwear tore through the streets of Allenbury on a ferocious-looking hunter, coming to a dangerous halt outside Doctor Barrie's house. The little maid of all work who answered the door screamed shrilly as he pushed past her and for a minute it looked as though Doctor Barrie, who came to the door of his surgery, was about to engage Alfred in a fist fight.

"Lord Murray . . . please, sir, 'tis Lord Murray," Alfred managed to gasp, bending over, his hands on his almost naked knees, his head hanging, the breath in him hurting his chest.

"What, man? What is it?" Andrew bent to peer into Alfred's face, doing his best to ignore the sight of Alfred's genitals as they tried to escape their flimsy wrapping.

"Accident, sir . . . accident. Come quick."

"What sort of accident, for God's sake?"

"Andrew, can't you see the man is at the end of his tether," a crisp voice from the foot of the stairs said. "Jinny, get Alfred a blanket, if you please, and Andrew, gather your things together and let us be off. Yes, I'm coming with you." For none knew better than Laura Barrie how her friend Amy would be if anything happened to Lord Alec Murray.

Alfred slowly sank to sit on the bottom step of the stairs while the thrilled Jinny, now that her fright was done with, wrapped him about in a warm blanket. What a tale she'd have to tell her mam on her next day off and as she did her puny best to lead him in the direction of the kitchen, wondered cheerfully if any of the old clothes donated by the benevolent and Christian-like members of the parish for the benefit of the poor, and brought to Doctor Barrie's door, would fit this man who had come to liven up her normally tedious day. Well, he could hardly go about dressed as he was, could he?

*   *   *

She screamed, just once, from the kitchen doorway where she had waited, as John-Henry rode carefully into the yard with his unconscious burden, then, throwing off the detaining hands of her servants, who themselves were dithering about in a state of total panic, all except Cook, she began to give crisp orders.

"Jumsie, Mr Weston, Mr Purvis, help John-Henry to lift him down . . . carefully, carefully. I think he is badly hurt, by the look . . . the blood. Thank God he is unconscious. We need a stretcher . . . yes, that's it, good thinking, Mr Wanless," to the carpenter who had produced from the tack room a bit of fencing into which he had been about to hammer a few nails.

"Blankets, Tansy . . . Rosy. Get out of the way, Clara. Those who cannot help keep out of the way. Put him in front of the fire. Dear Lord Jesus, should we . . . I'm afraid to move him again, but should we get him out of those wet things, Cook?"

"Aye, m'lady," the quiet, calming voice of Rosy told her. "Best gerrem off 'im afore 'e catches . . . well, see, sit thi' down next to 'im so 'e can see thi' when 'e wakes. That's right, my lovely."

Gently, doing their best not to move him, which was difficult, they got him out of the garments John-Henry and Alfred had wrapped about him, and when he was naked they just as gently covered him with the warm, light blankets from her ladyship's own bed. He had begun to groan softly and in the background one or two of the maids, the younger ones, began to cry silently, for they had never seen such injuries. His nakedness, though most of them, those without brothers, had never seen a naked man, did not alarm them. Poor soul, who had done this to him? For it was evident, even to the least experienced in such things, that he had taken a terrible beating.

"The doctor'll be 'ere soon, m'lady," Rosy murmured, on her knees beside her mistress who kneeled over the man she loved as though doing her best to put her own warmth, her own living, breathing uninjured flesh and beating heart into his racked body. Her hands fluttered about him, not quite touching him, like butterflies that were not quite sure where to alight, straining her own strength towards him, willing each rasping breath he drew in and then out again, to repeat the next and the next. The blood flowed from him and his skin had taken on a curious waxen colour. The room was quiet, as it was in the yard where every outside man was gathered, for they all respected . . . liked Mr Duffy, and when it was revealed who had done this to him they meant to be there.

With a great crashing of the front door which had been left ajar for the swift entry of the doctor, he was suddenly there, his wife behind him, and everyone in the room let out their collective breaths on a great sigh of relief, unaware, each of them, that they had been holding them in.

32

Holden, Sir Robert Blenkinsopp's manservant, as he liked to call himself, since "minder" sounded a mite disrespectful, was a kindly man. He felt a great deal of sympathy for his master, or patient, depending on how you looked at it. Poor old gentleman, imprisoned in a body that was slowly deteriorating, *despite* the exercises Doctor Barrie had prescribed and which Holden carried out religiously even faced with Sir Robert's total lack of co-operation. Sir Robert just lay there staring at nothing, his eyes blank, only coming alive, if you could describe his state as being alive, when Holden held out the tot of whisky the old man had of an evening. He deliberately kept the tumbler just out of Sir Robert's reach so that he would have to lift his trembling hand, the one that still had function in it, to take the tumbler. He *did* enjoy it, and often, when his rheumy old eyes implored Holden for another, he gave it to him, a good stiff shot which the old gentleman really relished and, an advantage to Holden, he slept the night through without disturbing anyone. He himself was a sound sleeper, thanks to his own sip, or perhaps two, of the same beverage. Sometimes, though he was loath to admit it, he drank more than he should, or at least the level in the whisky bottle went down rather quickly, but then he deserved a bit of cheer, didn't he, since his job was a lonely one, and onerous. He had to change his patient every morning, for he had no control over any of his bodily functions, but that was part of his job, wasn't it, and he was well paid for it.

Yes, the whisky was a blessing and to make sure he didn't run out between one day off and another he kept a small stock in the cupboard that stood to the side of the window. Lady Blenkinsopp, who was kindness itself, and generous too, knew of the whisky he allowed the old gentleman, though not of his own personal supply which, being totally honest, he bought with his own money on his day off in Allenbury. Though he did not say it to her ladyship, for it was obvious she thought nowt a pound to her husband and the rumour was she had reason to dislike him, but surely, Holden thought, the poor old soul was entitled to a bit of comfort.

Holden had formed the habit of talking to his patient, perhaps because it was a change to hear the voice of a human being, even if it was his own, telling him the small happenings of the household, though Sir Robert took scant, if any, interest, and reading aloud from *The Times* which her ladyship allowed him to take when her guest, Lord Alec Murray, had finished with it. Again Sir Robert appeared not to listen, turning his head indifferently towards the window where Holden placed him each morning. His children could very often be seen tumbling about the garden, or heard shouting in the way youngsters did, but Sir Robert might have been deaf or blind or both for all the notice he took of them. He was totally disinterested in the progress of the American Civil War but Holden persevered, for might it not awaken some part of his brain which, in Holden's opinion, seemed to have frozen in his skull.

The commotion, which had the whole house running hither and thither, footsteps running madly up and down the stairs, voices calling one to another, the sound of carriage wheels on the gravel drive and of horses' hooves pounding round to the stables, fetched Holden from his comfortable chair in front of the fire and out on to the landing. It was late October and the night was falling earlier and earlier. It had also been a wet and dismal day, making it necessary to keep lamps lit and the fire built high. Sir Robert had been tucked up in his bed and was ready for his nightcap but for the moment Holden was distracted, and had he looked into his master's face he would have noticed an unusual gleam of what might have been intelligence. An intelligence lit by his indignation that his whisky was not in his hand when it should have been.

"What's ter do, hinny?" Holden called out to the chambermaid who was sprinting along the landing towards the mistress's bedroom, her arms piled high with clean bedding and blankets. Mr Holden was a pleasant chap, repectful, cheerful and not at all like the beast who had reigned before him. They were well shot of *him*, they told one another. The maids, if they had a moment, often stopped to have a bit crack with Mr Holden in the hallway that led from the stairs to Sir Robert's room. They felt sorry that the poor chap was shut up all day with that frightful slobbering monster their little mistress was married to, and so Dulcie, who was the one Holden called out to, halted for a moment, pleased, as those are who have exciting information to impart, conveying to Mr Holden the quite dreadful news that Lord Murray, such a lovely man, had been badly, perhaps even fatally beaten up on the moors and was at this moment lying unconscious before the kitchen fire while Doctor Barrie attended him.

"Dear heaven, 'oo'd do such a thing?" Holden was visibly shocked.

"Why aye, Mr Holden, theer's some bad" – Dulcie nearly said "buggers" but changed her mind on account of Mr Holden's respectability – "lads about the day. A body's not safe but why they picked on 'im is a mystery fer 'is lordship's a fine man 'oo don't deserve it. Mind, they pinched his boots an' overcoat so 'appen it were vagrants 'oo'd tekk owt that weren't tied down. The rips just left 'im in a ghyll an' in all that rain an' all. Practically naked 'e were, poor soul. Anyroad, I'll 'ave ter go, Mr Holden. I'm mekkin' 'im up a bed."

"In God's name, what next," Mr Holden said sadly, turning back into the room where his charge lay. "Theer's always trouble fer someone," he was saying, shaking his head, for he himself had thought his lordship to be a fine gentleman who always had a pleasant word for all the servants.

"Would tha' believe it, sir," he went on, moving slowly across the cosy room to seat himself before the fire once more. "That poor chap 'oo's stoppin' wi't family, tha' know, ah told thi' aboot 'im. Lord Murray. Well, 'e's only gone an' got 'imself a skelpin' up on't moor. Lass ses 'e's badly."

He nearly fell out of his chair when a hoarse voice from the bed rasped across to him, a voice that had never been used these last few weeks. He had begun to believe that Sir Robert had lost the use of his vocal chords, since he himself had barely heard him speak.

"What . . . are . . . you . . . talking . . . about?" A hand rose from its covers and moved in a drifting circle before falling back to its resting place and Holden was so astonished he was unable to speak for a moment. His master was glaring at him from a face that was contorted in its effort to form more words, to convey to Holden Sir Robert's desperate need to know more of what had taken place. Why should he need so urgently, for it *was* urgent, or so it seemed, to hear more of the dastardly attack on Lord Murray? Perhaps this Lord Murray was an old friend of Sir Robert's, before he had his nasty accident, though come to think of it the man had not once been up to see him which was strange. Lord Murray had been a guest at Newton Law for six weeks now. But not just a guest, for the man went about with Lady Blenkinsopp inspecting the newly opened school, approved by Mr Sinclair, the lawyer riding out to the farms, sitting with her ladyship in the estate office and what they did there was a puzzle. He had heard a whisper that Lord Murray had once been gamekeeper here, which was hard to believe, for why would a man as high in the world as he was be working as a gamekeeper? Well, it was nowt to do with him but it seemed Sir Robert thought it was *everything* to do with him.

"Who . . . ?" he began again, his face twisted into a demented mask, his mouth opening and closing, his eyes almost popping out of his head in his effort to convey to Holden what he wanted to say. He lifted his head from the pillow and indicated that he wished to be propped up and Holden scurried across the bedroom to help him.

"Who . . . is . . . ?"

"'Oo's the chap what got skelped?" Holden said helpfully, lifting up his patient with practised ease, plumping up the pillows behind him.

Sir Robert nodded, the sagging flesh of his face wobbling about like a jelly on a plate.

"Ah told thi', sir. Lord Murray. 'Im what's a guest o't ladies."

"What . . . bloody . . . ladies?"

Holden looked slightly shocked, for surely that was no way for a man to speak of his wife and daughters, but he answered patiently.

"The mistress, sir, and . . . well, the Misses Blenkinsopp."

"What's . . . his . . . bloody name?"

"Ah told thi', sir, Lord Murray. Oh, tha' means 'is christian name?"

Sir Robert nodded vigorously and his jowled face shook and his sparse hair fell over his forehead.

"Well, ah did 'ear her ladyship call 'im Duffy but ah'm not . . ."

The effect on Sir Robert was electrifying. He fell back on his pillows and for a moment Holden thought he was gone. His face looked sort of uninhabited, blank, as though the spirit that had kept his master alive for – what was it? – over two years, had finally released him. Flown away and left him in peace, for surely this was no life for a man. Even a man who, or so Holden had heard it whispered, had been a bit of a martinet, and even worse with the ladies, or so it had been hinted. Not a decent man, they said, but

Holden himself, who *was* decent, liked to think the best of people.

"Sir Robert . . . oh, sir, are you not well?" Which was a daft thing to say to a man who had suffered two strokes, was almost paralysed and lived out his life in a state of helpless dependence on others.

Sir Robert opened his eyes and they were suffused with the red colour of either madness, or exultation, Holden was not awfully sure which. They were alive though, luminous with some emotion Holden could not put a name to, a gladness, and yet a fury that, had his patient been mobile, might have spelled trouble for someone.

With the speed of a striking snake he grabbed Holden's forearm, holding it with a strength Holden would not have believed he was capable of, a vicious grip that he could not loosen, dragging him closer until he and Sir Robert were almost nose to nose.

"Find . . . out. Find . . . out," Sir Robert hissed. His spittle sprayed Holden's face and for the first time, since he was not a squeamish man, Holden wanted to flinch away from him.

"What, sir? Find out what?" His expression was bewildered.

"Who . . . he is . . . you . . . bloody . . . mumble . . . fool. What . . . happened . . . how . . . mumble mumble . . . God almighty . . . how badly . . ."

"Tha' wants me ter find out 'oo 'e is, sir, but ah told thi'."

If Sir Robert Blenkinsopp had had his full strength in both arms there is no doubt he would have put both hands round his retainer's throat and throttled the life out of him. Instead he glared madly, hotly into his face, hypnotising him with his malevolence, then shook him off with a sound in his throat like some animal, some ferocious, maddened beast that had better be left strictly alone, one that should not under any circumstances be approached or threatened, or someone might suffer, was *sure* to suffer.

But Holden had, thankfully, though he did not understand, got the message, and backing away from the bed he began to edge round it towards the door.

"Aarrghhhh," Sir Robert mouthed, his hand trembling in the direction of the cupboard where the whisky was kept and with half a tumbler in his hand, put there by the palpitating Holden, he allowed his servant to leave the room to seek out the information that Sir Robert demanded of him.

He was unconscious for several days, or perhaps not quite unconscious, for he seemed to slip in and out of a dark and restful place in which there was no pain and into which he longed to return; to an indistinct hazy agony in which the light was broken up, like a window that has shattered but not fallen out of its frame. There was always a face waiting in the last place, anxious and loving, he could tell that, though he couldn't see it, calling his name but he didn't want to stay there since the pain was too much for him to stand. He couldn't quite decide which part of him hurt the most, for it seemed to him that the whole of his body had been put through a fiery furnace, lying in the red-hot coals, smouldering and taking off his skin layer by agonising layer. In the other place, the quiet place, he found he could endure it and he was not to know that the quiet place was where he went thanks to the laudanum his friend Doctor Barrie administered to him. In what he supposed were lucid moments, though they couldn't exactly be called that, he tried to work out where he was and what had happened to him. He was conscious of the crackling of a fire, the musical tinkling of a clock, the rustle of material as someone bent over him and the lovely fragrance which he knew had given him pleasure at some time. He couldn't see, for his eyelids were, for some reason, glued together, and his mind seemed to have little in it but the memory of a boot being aimed at his head.

Now and again a hand, gentle as the touch of a butterfly, settled on his forehead and the lovely fragrance was stronger. He tried to open his eyes, since he had the feeling the person to whom the hand belonged was dear to him, but when he tried to move his head, becoming agitated, two small hands, infinitely tender, were placed one on either side of his head, holding him steady, and at once he *felt* steady.

"Don't move, beloved," a soft voice told him, "or you might break the stitches," so he did as he was told, slipping peacefully away to the quiet place where he knew no pain. Aye, he knew no pain and yet he felt a sadness, since it seemed to him he would have liked to remain with the hands, the voice, the fragrance of the one who hovered over him.

The first face he saw and recognised through the slits of his eyes was that of his friend Andrew Barrie and beyond Andrew there was someone else, someone trying their damnedest to push Andrew to one side and get to him but Andrew wouldn't allow it.

"Leave him alone, Amy, for God's sake, and go and get some sleep. Laura will sit with him."

"Go to hell, Andrew Barrie," a voice hissed. "I'm staying here until I know he recognises me. Sees me, *really* sees me and knows who am I. Do you think I'm to go off and fall asleep – as if I could – when he . . ." There were tears in the speaker's voice.

"Do . . . as you're . . . told . . . Amy Blenkinsopp." The voice from the bed considerably startled both the doctor who leaned over him and the woman at his back who wrestled to get near him.

"Duffy . . . Duffy, darling," she shrieked and the sound went through his poor mangled head, and though he wanted nothing more than to have her near him, perhaps lying peacefully on the bed beside him, he flinched away from the sound, and the doctor turned savagely.

"Amy Blenkinsopp, if you don't behave yourself and let me tend my patient I shall have you taken from the room. Oh yes, I will and I can, for the men—"

"Will not obey you, Andrew Barrie."

"Yes they will, Amy and you know it so won't you please leave."

Her voice broke painfully. "Andrew, I can't. Please, let me stay. I'll be good."

"Will you promise to go and rest if I say yes?"

"I promise. Please, don't send me away."

"When . . . everyone has . . . finished arguing . . . do you think I might . . . have a sip of . . . water." The voice from the bed was blurred and yet there was a touch in it of the dry, sardonic humour that was an intrinsic part of Alec Murray.

"Dear God, old fellow, what are we thinking about, quarrelling over you as if you were . . . but this woman of yours has been a thorn in my side ever since they brought you home. She simply won't rest."

"How long?"

"Four days now, but see, let me have a look at those stitches. There was dirt in the gashes and I want to check that they are not infected."

"Damage?" Duffy's voice was weak and there was a sliver of fear in it for he might be blind, crippled, who knew what damage that boot – or was it boots, he seemed to remember, had inflicted.

"You've cracked a couple of ribs so I've strapped you up and you've a broken leg, I'm afraid. A fracture of the tibia which is at the front and the inside of the leg."

"So I won't . . . be . . . dancing the polka . . . for a while."

Andrew laughed softly and behind him Amy's tears were silent, since she knew Andrew would make good his promise and send her away, or have her taken away if she disturbed Duffy.

She would never forget the state of him on that appalling day. The blood, the torn flesh that had been scraped raw over half his body, the bruises to his face which had turned the colour of a ripe Victoria plum, the white bone of his cheek where the flesh had been ripped away and the swollen slits in which his eyes rested. Andrew had forced each one open while Duffy was unconscious to check that the actual eye-ball itself was still there, then had gone about the long, and what she recognised as skilful, procedure of putting Duffy together again. Laura helped him, shushing the frightened, pitying servants, giving crisp orders and frowning at Amy whenever she showed signs of getting in the way. She wanted so much to hold him, to weep over him, to kiss him and soothe him, to comfort and give him all the things her deep and endless love needed him to have. To comfort herself by doing it, she realised later, but she was of no use to him then, none of them were except Andrew and Laura and probably Rosy, who was the calmest of the lot of them. Rosy seemed to be everywhere at once. Not only helping Laura and Andrew but keeping an eye on herself, shaking her head and smiling to let her see that all would be well.

And now he was conscious, aware of where he was and who was with him and it took all her resources not to elbow Andrew aside, push him to the floor if necessary to get to the injured man whose injuries, though she couldn't have said why, were her fault. Someone, someone who had a grudge, a deep and hating grudge had done this to Duffy, leaving him, one supposed, for dead, and she supposed again, sadly, for there was no one else with a reason, it could only be Platt. Platt had virtually ruled this house, taking orders from her husband, it was true, but it was he who arranged all the orgies – could she call them anything else? – that had broken the peace and safety of Newton Law. They had all lived in fear, the servants as well as herself, and because Sir Robert had proved to Mr Sinclair and Mr Bewick that he was well again and because of his hold over herself, again through Platt, and the safety of her children, she had been forced to give in to him. One day, when the novelty of the wild parties had begun to wear thin, he would have turned his evil gaze on her again, he and Platt, and because Duffy had come to rescue them Platt had lost

his fine place here, and her husband was back to the
sorry state he had fallen into when she pushed him
down the stairs. Andrew and the doctor he brought
from London had confirmed his inability to manage
his own affairs, to be left in charge of his children,
or *her* children, and somehow, she didn't know how,
especially with Duffy bedfast, she'd get to the bottom
of it. They, she didn't know who she meant by *they*,
had wreaked their revenge on Duffy. They had left him
for dead since dead he would have been if John-Henry
and Alfred had not found him before nightfall. They
obviously imagined, and they were probably right
in that assumption, that with Duffy out of the way,
they, again she was not sure who she meant, Platt,
she supposed, would move back into the house and
resume control, or so they thought.

God, she was tired, bone-weary, exhausted to the
end of herself, as she had not slept, nor even dozed,
since Duffy had been carried up the stairs by the men,
tenderly as a fragile child, and put, to their obvious
amazement, into her bed. A truckle bed, one that
could be pushed under the bed he slept in, was
placed beside it, made up with sheets and blankets so
that her ladyship might be as comfortable as possible.
But it was never used. She sat or kneeled for hours on
end beside his bed, gazing into his pulverised face, her
elbows on the bed, her own face a mask of suffering
no more than an inch or two from his. A room had
been made up for Doctor and Mrs Barrie and she was
to call the doctor the moment the patient moved or if
he showed signs of fever, or indeed if he did anything
at all that the doctor might like to know about.

"I'm trusting you, Amy, to be responsible about this,"

Andrew had whispered sternly. "You cannot nurse him on your own. I'm in the next room and you have only to tap at my door."

"Do you honestly believe I would jeopardise his life in any way, Andrew," she hissed at him venomously. "But I will have Rosy to sit with me then she can run and tap on your door if you are needed."

And so it was. One of the maids sat with her and Duffy, begging her by the hour to change places, to let *them* sit by his bed, to have a little nap in the chair, to lie down – no, she didn't need to take her clothes off – but she wouldn't have it, and now he was with her again. She could actually *see* his eyes through the horrendously puffed lids and he tried to smile at her with his torn mouth. His hands, both bandaged, lay on the turned-back cover of the sheet which was all he could bear to have over him and when his eyes spoke to her she was the only one who read and deciphered the message he sent her.

Andrew had gone down to Allenbury, for he had other patients to see to, he told her, and Laura had gone with him, since she really needed a change of clothing and her Jinny would be wondering where they had got to. Naturally Alfred had taken her a message to say they would be away for a night or two, embarrassed beyond measure by her sly young grin, for the last time he had seen her he had been almost naked, and him to be married next week.

"Rosy, sweetheart, go down to the kitchen and . . . well, go and see that husband of yours. He must be missing you. And you need some rest yourself in your condition."

."Nay, my lass, ah'm as right as a trivet an' as cosy as a kitten on't rug beside this grand fire."

"Rosy, why don't you go and have a cup of tea then?"

"Nay, Tansy fetched me one up not long since."

"Rosy, if you don't go away and leave us alone I swear I'll land you one, and I've a heavy hand when I'm thwarted."

"M'lady," Rosy gasped, for never in a thousand years would her ladyship raise her hand to anyone, but something in the face of the man on the bed who, she could have sworn, was barely conscious, alerted her, and with a start she pulled herself from her chair and scuttled across the room to the door.

"Rightio, then, ah'll go an' get me a cup o' tea. D'yer want one?"

"Rosy . . ." her mistress warned, and Rosy closed the door quietly behind her. She didn't go to the kitchen though, for she knew there would be exclamations of horror that she had left her ladyship and the injured man alone. They would have been running up the stairs, convinced that their mistress was too tired to be left with the care of his lordship and Rosy, who recognised the pangs of love only too well, knew this was not so.

Amy kneeled beside the bed and smiled into his face, which painfully he managed to turn towards her.

"You're not going . . . to seduce me . . . are you, my love? Just at the moment . . . I . . . don't think I could . . . manage more than a twitch here and there and . . . even that . . . might be a bit . . . of an effort."

"May I kiss you?"

"Be gentle with me or I might . . . might scream."

"Don't speak any more, my beloved, my dearest. Lord, how I love you. I cannot stand to think I might have lost you, but . . ."

His slitted eyes shone in enquiry.

"But I am so tired, my love. I need to sleep and so do you, so why don't we sleep together? The bed is wide and I promise not to touch you. Just to lie beside you."

He made a slight movement with his hand which might, in better times, have been the drawing down of the sheet and an invitation to join him.

She took off her dress, the one she had worn the day he was beaten, then, very carefully, lay down beside him, so lightly and so delicately he barely felt the bed move. His heart stirred as though it were melting in his chest and even in the piteous state he found himself in he sensed a warming movement in the pit of his belly, for which he felt a profound gratitude since it meant that that part of him was uninjured. She murmured a time or two, nothing he understood and then, feeling the tranquillity of her beloved presence, he fell asleep beside her.

When Andrew Barrie slipped quietly into the room several hours later, ready to give her the rounds of the kitchen, as his mother's cook used to say, despite her promise not to touch him, she was asleep with her body flush against his. Duffy slept too, a healing sleep without the help of the laudanum Andrew had been giving him.

Quietly he left the room and went downstairs to the drawing-room where his wife was chatting to the Misses Blenkinsopp, who were still in a turmoil over their guest's "accident". It had been felt that they were too delicate to be told the truth.

He nodded at Laura, giving her the look that often passes between husband and wife, understood at once.

"I think I might have a brandy," he said cheerfully, bowing to the three spinster ladies.

33

It was three weeks before he could gingerly heave himself up into a sitting position. Amy had draped a light, crocheted shawl about his shoulders, worked by Cook who was clever with her fingers, delicate as gossamer, the wool she had used fine as cotton, and though he felt an absolute fool in it he was grateful for its lightness.

As he had healed he had become more able to bear a blanket over him, a soft fleecy blanket light as swansdown with a white satin edging which had made him smile that lopsided smile Amy loved so much.

"What luxury. I feel like an infant wrapped in its mama's arms. It certainly isn't like the horse blankets we had at school."

"Well, you're not at school, Alec Murray. You're in my care and I think that a blanket like this, the kind I use myself, is appropriate, so lie still and behave yourself."

"Right, nurse." And since there was no one else in the room he reached up a scarred hand and gently touched first her face then her breast.

She shivered with delight. "Darling, lovely as that is I don't want your temperature to go up."

"I'll chance it if you will." For several moments they engaged in several warm kisses, but as Rosy entered the room, smilingly and diplomatically turning her head away, Amy pretended to be adjusting the blanket.

He was naked beneath it and as Amy said, she didn't care a jot since she had seen him without . . . well, he would know what she meant, but the susceptibilities of the maids, most of them unmarried, were embarrassed by his masculine shape beneath the soft blanket, the breadth of his shoulders and the fine mat of pale brown hair on his chest.

"But they saw me when I was brought back from the moor and, so John-Henry tells me, I was stripped naked as a newborn babe," he had protested, but the shawl was placed about him anyway. John-Henry and Alfred came each day to lift him, wrapping him as tenderly as they might a precious child, in the soft blanket while the maids changed the bed. She and Rosy, since they were both married women and accustomed to a man's nakedness, sponged him down before he was placed, again by the men, back into his clean bed. His body was still a map of weals with torn and bloodied skin on his chest and back and shoulders, and handling him brought back the pain but Doctor Barrie insisted on absolute cleanliness to avoid infection. His bruises were turning from a livid purple and black, to brown and green and yellow and, as he said ruefully, he was not a pretty sight. Andrew had sewed back the triangle of flesh that had hung on his cheek and it was healing nicely, but he still looked as though a steamroller had run over him.

"I think you're pretty," she said, glowing into his

face, spooning into his mouth the good broth in which the best cut of beef and fresh vegetables floated and which Cook sent up regularly. He could feed himself, he told her impatiently, Amy that is, time and time again, but she wouldn't have it, unable to leave him alone, finding it necessary, for her own peace of mind, to be constantly doing something towards his recovery. Her silvery blue eyes were filled, not just with love but with a thankful wonder that he was not only still alive but improving and her soft lips touched his hand and his chin, the corner of his shoulder and wherever there wasn't a bandage. The bandages with which Andrew had strapped his chest and abdomen had been removed, but his leg was still splinted and it would be weeks before he could set foot to the floor.

"We'll see about that," he had answered grimly and if Amy and Andrew had not more or less sat on him, he would have struggled from his bed right then and there. He loved her and he did his best not to be irritated by her constant hovering, anxious presence but he was not a good patient. The swelling of his face was going down and his eyes were almost fully opened, the eyelashes which had been buried in his flesh curling thickly once more about his grey, cat-like eyes, but the forced and frustrating stay in her bed began to tell on his normally even temper.

"Will you lie quiet, man. You need rest. You will do yourself no good fretting on when you're to get up," Andrew told him. "Just lie still and enjoy Amy's ministrations."

Duffy grinned. "Oh, I do, believe me, but good God, Andrew, surely I may be allowed to sit in a bloody chair by the window for an hour?" And so, reluctantly, Andrew let him. He was carried sitting on the crossed arms of John-Henry and Alfred, an arm about each broad shoulder, a pair of soft underdrawers covering his nether regions, the daft shawl clutched about his shoulders, his splinted leg propped on a stool. He could watch the children as they raced about the garden, turning to wave up at him when instructed to do so by Nanny Morag. He could watch the weather edging from autumn to winter, and though it was almost the end of November it was still mild and he took it into his head that if the men, perhaps three of them, for he was no light weight, could sit him in a sturdy chair he might, now that his face was healing and no longer likely to frighten the children, sit in the garden in a bit of sunshine. He longed for some air that did not smell of the sickroom, he told the patient Amy. There was absolutely no need to treat him like a bloody invalid. He longed for so many things and one of them was to get her into his bed, he told her, leering wickedly until she felt inclined to blush, but his bloody leg kept him captive and when, dear God, when would that bloody doctor, meaning Andrew, allow him the support of crutches instead of keeping him here absolutely helpless and at the mercy of everyone in the house.

"Soon, my darling, soon," she soothed him, sighing as though in the deepest dejection.

"You see, even you're tired of it," he told her furiously, "and you profess to love me." He was sorry as soon as it was out but it was too late. She leaped to her feet, her face a scarlet mask of outrage.

"Profess. *Profess!* What the hell d'you think I'm

doing sitting here day after day and night after night if all I feel is some kind of pity? I have put up with your impatience, your irritability, your constant whining to be out of bed and quite honestly I have a mind to hand you over to some nurse or other. I have better things to do than tiptoe lightly round your temper, my lad."

"Then why the hell don't you go and do them?" he snarled, and at once, a look of horror spread over both their faces and she fell to her knees at the bedside, clutching at him. His arms, though it caused him some pain, lifted to hold her close to his chest and for a moment he believed they were both going to weep. The anxiety, the frustration, not only of his injuries and his inability to get over them quickly was not really, and they both knew it, the cause of this outburst but what was to happen *afterwards*. When he was mended and able to walk, to walk to the carriage which would take him to the train that would carry him out of her life.

"Darling, my darling."

"I know, I'm sorry."

"You know I love you, you're my life."

"I know. I know, my heart."

"What will we do?"

"I don't know but there must be something . . ."

"I can't bear it."

"Do you honestly think I would let you out of my life now? Now that we have . . ."

He buried his poor face in her soft hair and they held one another with an almost frantic need, for the idea that soon they must part, and for ever, was not to be borne.

*   *   *

There was another occupant of the house who was saying it was not to be borne, to himself, and to the man who day after day did his best to soothe the patient in his care.

"In . . . her . . . mumble . . . bed . . . the whore . . . *my* bed . . . where she and I . . . Good Christ . . . if I . . . could get . . . this bed I'd . . . take a whip . . . mumble blood ran . . . both of them . . . drive her out . . . with her . . . mumble bastards."

It was the first Holden had heard of any bastards and he wondered who Sir Robert was talking about. Three children up in the nursery, two boys and a girl, and though one of them, the elder boy, was certainly dark like his master the other two were fair. But then so was she, so what the dickens was the poor, deluded fellow talking about? He wished to God he hadn't told the old gentleman of the nursing arrangements that had been set in place in the house. He had himself thought it strange that her ladyship had put her guest in her own bed, *and* that she seemed to be nursing him herself, but he had made it his business to find out that there was always another woman there, one of the maidservants, and he had told his master this, but still Sir Robert continued to rave and foam at the mouth, his eyes slitted gleams of hatred. If it wasn't for the whisky which, he must admit, for a bit of peace from Sir Robert's ranting voice, he gave to him in larger and larger doses, and more often, he thought he might hand in his notice. There was always work for men like him, and Doctor Barrie, who looked in now and again on Sir Robert, would soon find him another place.

"Want to see . . . mumble bloody lawyer . . . a bloody . . . disgrace . . . that . . . swine . . . the . . .

whore . . . in . . . my . . . mumble . . . throttle her . . . and cut off that bastard's balls . . ."

And on and on he rambled, for that was what Holden believed it to be, the ramblings of a man who was not right in the head, almost a lunatic and certainly if there had not been money that was where he would be: in the lunatic asylum on the outskirts of Allenbury, probably chained to the wall to prevent him from hurting himself and others. Still, he might as well be chained to a wall for all the good it did him, fastened like a felled log to his bed, carried by Holden to the window, though he often wondered why he bothered, for the man never took the slightest interest in what went on beyond it. He really did think he might change his job for something a bit more . . . well, he was going to say cheerful, which looking after bedfast folk never could be, but perhaps a man with a bit more liveliness in him, or at least in his mind. He was getting quite depressed, he told himself, sitting here hour after hour listening to the old man, and he had it in him to wish the chap hadn't regained, or at least decided it was time to regain, his power of speech. Sir Robert had had his tot and was fast asleep, and really he felt the need himself for a stiff one, perhaps two, or even three, since no one took the slightest interest in him.

He sighed heavily and with a last look at his sleeping patient, for he was nothing if not conscientious, he took a full bottle of whisky from the cabinet, going to his own room where he closed the door. He lay on his bed and filled his glass and began to drink, but when the glass fell to the floor he seemed unable to reach it so he thought he might as well drink from the bottle, which he did, until it was empty, when he fell into a deep, drunken sleep, the first time he had ever done so while he was on duty.

Sir Robert Blenkinsopp waited what he thought was probably about an hour before he began on the doughty task ahead of him, one that he had been planning since he had heard that his gamekeeper was sleeping in his wife's, and not only his wife's, but *his* bed, since he was the master of this house and the husband of the whore who ran it.

His brain raced and raced, on fire with his need to be stealthy, to do everything in the proper order as he had planned, and to do it while that bugger in the next room was asleep, when they were *all* asleep. It would take a great deal of . . . he had been about to say cunning but it was not really cunning, though that came into it, but sheer bloody strength that was needed; and though he had seemed to be unconcerned with Holden's manipulations with his damned arms and legs, he knew they had been beneficial. He had had a bit of a practice a time or two when the man was asleep and he had been able to slither from the bed and crawl in some snail-like way to the whisky cabinet where he had helped himself to the fool's supply. Not too much or he would have become suspicious but enough to satisfy his craving for it, for the only bit of pleasure he was able to obtain in this bloody miserable world. He didn't really care whether he lived or died, now that the fun Platt had provided was denied him, but if he was to go, by God, that bitch, at least, was to go with him. And her lover if he could manage it, but certainly her. And if it all worked out as he hoped he might be able to get Platt back again by some means or other.

Her two bastards would be sent off somewhere and he would have the bringing up of his son, the next in line for the baronetcy. Jesus, it was almost more than he could encompass, anticipating the joy of it, but first he must get himself along the landing and into *her* room. He had a walking-stick with a curved handle, one that had been provided when it had been believed he might walk again, and it would be needed to lift the latch of the door, since he knew he couldn't stand. And even, he tittered to himself, already a little drunk on the whisky Holden had given him, the stick, which was heavy, might come in handy to split her bloody skull with!

But first he must have another little drink. A heartener, a bit of a lift to get him from this room to the one where she was. The stick was just by the bed where some optimistic fool had left it, and reaching out his hand for it he was furious when he could not find it. Where the bloody hell was it? He couldn't even get out of the bloody room without it, never mind down the hallway. Bugger it, why hadn't Holden left a candle or a lamp lit? The curtains were drawn across the window and even the meagre light of the stars could not penetrate their thick folds. But he knew a candle stood on the low table in the bay of the window, with matches beside it. He knew in which direction to go so it was just a matter of going there and then he could look round him for the walking-stick. It had probably fallen down beside, or under the bed.

Painfully he shifted his crippled legs until they were dangling over the edge of the bed, hesitating for a moment as he listened to the deep silence that lay over the house. Quiet as the bloody grave, he chuckled to himself, the chuckle revealing how close he was to the edge of total madness. His head was spinning and his arms were trembling with weakness as he lowered himself to the floor but he ignored it and began his slow crawl towards the table where the candle lay and the cabinet where the whisky was. His heart was pounding and he was trembling violently when his good hand encountered the table and on it the candle. It took him a long time to light the thing, for he had to lean his back against the chair, holding the candle on the floor between his legs. At last the match was lit and a small flame spurted, and with a great effort and by dint of holding one trembling hand with the other, he held the match to the candle, put the candle back on the table and there was his goal, lit up by the flickering flame. The cabinet, the whisky, the walking-stick lying beside the bed, all of which would get him along the hallway to where *she* was. The woman who had put him where he was, thrown him down the stairs, cheated him with another man and by all that was holy tonight she was to pay for it.

Tipping up the whisky bottle with his good hand he slobbered several great gulps down his throat. It splashed on to his nightgown and trickled into his hair and hardly before he realised it the bottle was empty. Bloody hell, where was Holden's supply? There should be more than one bottle, for hadn't he seen the sod put two there only the other day. Reaching unsteadily inside the cabinet he lost his balance, falling flat on the carpet and as he fell his shoulder hit the table. It wobbled dangerously, then righted itself but the candle did not. It hit the floor beside him and rolled into the folds of the curtains.

*   *   *

Amy, turning restlessly on the truckle bed, was still asleep but even in her sleep some sense that is given to all creatures, whether they be human or animal, told her there was something wrong. Some danger, but her sleeping mind, which was starved of the rest it needed, held her fast. For over three weeks she had barely had an unbroken night; the first few nights after Duffy's beating she had not slept at all and her body was badly in need of proper rest. Over the last three weeks if Duffy so much as moved an inch in the night she was awake but this was not Duffy who called out to her but some other nagging unease which she did her best to ignore. She was dreaming of a train coming into a station, a huge roaring monster with a red glare pouring from its innards. She could even smell the smoke from its funnel and when the hand on her arm shook at her frantically she cowered back in terror until her eyes, in the dark, picked out the crouched figure of Duffy.

"What are you doing out of bed?" she asked him, incensed by his foolishness after all she and Andrew had told him, but he continued to shake her with a violence that startled her.

"Wake up . . . for God's sake, wake up, woman. Can't you smell it, and hear it? Something's on fire. Get up, Amy, get up. Get something on."

"What?" She was confused, her nightmare of a train thundering towards her down a long dark tunnel still with her, holding her fast in her bed. She felt she wanted to hide beneath the covers, but there was a faint roaring coming from somewhere and though she was still furious with Duffy for getting out of his bed since he was far from healed, she put her feet to the carpet and stood up.

"Darling, wake up, we've got to get out."

"Out?"

"Jesus Christ, Amy," Duffy was snarling at her as though she had done some awful thing, "must I hit you to get you on the move."

"Duffy . . ."

"*Your children are in danger,* Amy," he screeched into her ear, making her jerk backwards but he had her attention now. She could smell the danger, a dry, cindery smell that took away her breath; in fact she was finding it difficult to breathe but Duffy's words had become understandable and she listened to them. Obeyed them. He had thrown the crochet shawl about his shoulders, since it was the first thing that came to hand and, standing on one leg, ignoring the agony of the one that was broken, he draped her about with the blanket from the bed and, hopping beside her, one arm about her shoulders to balance himself, he led her to the door. The smoke was worse on the landing, acrid, making them both cough violently, but there was no sign of fire, only the roaring from further along the hallway.

"The children, Amy, the nursery. Get Morag and Lizzie-Ann . . . go down the back stairs." And even as he spoke a line of flame crept across the carpet from the main stairway. She began to scream, but with a savage twist he forced her to turn and look at him.

"Go, Amy, your children need you."

"But Duffy, you . . ."

"I'll get the servants up."

"The stairs . . . how will you manage the stairs?"

Tears streamed down her face as the flame crept towards them.

"I'll crawl."

"Duffy . . ."

"Go. Down to the garden. Get well away from the house."

She could hear the sound of voices, shouted voices from somewhere far off, a scream, she thought, which might have been Rosy, but he had her focused now. Her children . . . down the back stairs . . . the garden where he would bring the women who, she supposed, would still be sleeping peacefully on the top floor.

The children were asleep and fretful when she wakened them and from the adjoining room where Nanny Morag and Lizzie-Ann slept there came the sound of movement and sleepy voices asking what was to do. The children never woke in the night unless they were unwell and when they had been put to bed they were lively as crickets so what . . .

The pair of them, pulling on the warm and sensible dressing-gowns that are a part of the wardrobe of women who sometimes have to get up in the night to children, were astonished to find their mistress roughly pulling at Robby who didn't want to get up, he whinged, and shouting her head off to anyone who would listen. The twins sat up in their little beds and began to cry, afraid of this noisy mother who rarely raised her voice to them.

"Robby, get up." She lifted him forcibly, screeching in his ear so that he flinched away from her and yelled at Nanny Morag and Lizzie-Ann to carry the babies.

"But, your ladyship, what's up?" Lizzie-Ann did as she was told, picking up the yelling Cat, turning in perplexity to Nanny Morag who did the same with Davey, and though they hadn't the faintest idea what was happening, they obeyed her orders as they had always obeyed the voice of authority.

"Fire, you idiots . . . fire. Down the back stairs . . . follow . . ."

On the landing they met the first of the terrified maidservants, all clutched about with the first garment that came to hand, Cook with her pinafore, the one she wore for cooking, over her voluminous nightgown. She had her arm around Phyllis and, coming down the stairs on his bottom, the last in the ragged group, his splinted leg stuck out before him, was Duffy.

There was some congestion on the back stairs that led into the side garden, for the men from the stables, John-Henry and Alfred among them, were on their way up, since the main staircase was ablaze and impassable, but within minutes, after some confusion, they were all out into the cold of the night. Rosy was there, sobbing dementedly, clutching at anyone she could get her arms about, taking Robby who was glad to go, Jumsie with a bucket of water in his hand, Mr Weston and his plump little wife in her old coat, the one she wore to feed her chickens, all ready, even the men, to weep with relief at the sight of her and her children. Someone even fetched a chair for Duffy to sit in as they watched the lovely old house which, for so many years, they had called home, burn brightly against the dark winter sky.

She was to ask Rosy later if she remembered where everyone finally rested their heads that night, for really the whole thing was a hazy blur in her mind. Once she had made certain that every member of the household was safe, not even a burn among them, she seemed to slip into a dream world in which she went where she was led, drank whatever was put in her hand, sat where she was put and finally, though she was scarcely aware of it, slept in some bed which she was told later was the one in which Mr and Mrs Weston had started their married life. Her children, safe with Rosy and Nanny Morag and Lizzie-Ann, were taken to Rosy's cottage and, in a truckle bed in the Westons' kitchen, Duffy was tucked up after being examined by Andrew who, somehow, appeared on the scene. She remembered Laura, her face drawn and pale, and Cook holding her own hand while she told her that poor Mr Holden, who seemed to Cook the more worthy of her sadness, and Sir Robert, had not survived.

For several weeks over Christmas she and Duffy, the children and Nanny Morag with Lizzie-Ann were the guests of Laura and Andrew, much to the delight of Jinny who was thrilled with the excitement of it all. She and Duffy spent their days making arrangements for the future of her servants, since she was adamant that not one of them would suffer because of what had happened. Jobs must be found for them with *good* people, though naturally she would be taking one or two with her when she went to live at Ladywood.

"You must take who you want, my darling, for you will be mistress."

"Your mother . . ." she murmured hesitantly.

"Will love you as I do and Gussy will be enchanted to have someone of her own age to do . . . well, whatever women of your age do. Besides, they will naturally move to the dower house." And if Amy had doubts about this, since Andrew had warned her of her ladyship's disposition and Duffy had read her letters out loud, she kept them to herself. There would be storms ahead, but then hadn't she braved worse storms than the prospect of a jealous and possessive mother-in-law!

The house had not been completely destroyed. The wing in which Sir Robert and Holden had died was almost gutted but it was as though the fire had become subdued, as though it knew the evil was destroyed, turning back on itself when it had taken that part of the house. They would rebuild, Duffy said, for this was Robby's – the new Sir Robert Blenkinsopp's – home, his inheritance, and must be kept in good heart for him. That was where Rosy and Jumsie came in, and Tansy who had married Alfred, Morna and Cook, John-Henry and Alfred himself, Mr and Mrs Weston, who were all to be regarded as a skeleton staff with the task of looking after the place until Robby brought *his* bride and new life to Newton Law. Until then it would need caring for and who better than those who had cared for not only the house, but the family who had sheltered beneath it.

If the parson and his wife, who liked a nice wedding, particularly of the gentry which these two were, were astonished to see the couple who were to be married limping down the aisle arm in arm, they did their best to conceal it. She was beautiful, the bride, dressed simply but, the parson's wife who knew about such things since she visited many in the same state in her duties, was visibly pregnant, five months she would have thought, and the groom stumbled along on a stick.

It was February, a lovely time of the year when the spears of daffodils, the shy crocus and wild hyacinth were pushing eagerly through the greening grass under the trees in the churchyard, towards spring, towards that new beginning when promises of hope and peace and joy lifted hearts and heads.

They smiled at one another, the bride and groom, a smile so filled with sweetness and love, the parson's wife couldn't help but smile too, though strictly speaking, in her position, she should have been shocked by the bride's condition.

When the ceremony was over they turned to one another and kissed with such intensity she felt she should look away.

"Well, my love, my wife," she heard the groom say, "it's been a long journey."

"Yes, my dearest, but we've reached the end at last. A place called hope."